DOCTOR WHO

THE ADVENTURESS OF HENRIETTA STREET

LAWRENCE MILES

Published by BBC Worldwide Ltd
Woodlands, 80 Wood Lane
London W12 0TT

First published 2001
Copyright © Lawrence Miles 2001
The moral right of the author has been asserted

Original series broadcast on the BBC
Format © BBC 1963
Doctor Who and TARDIS are trademarks of the BBC

ISBN 0 563 53842 2
Imaging by Black Sheep, copyright © BBC 2001

Printed and bound in Great Britain by Mackays of Chatham
Cover printed by Belmont Press Ltd, Northampton

FICTION

'The secret springs of events are seldom known. But when they are, they become particularly instructive and entertaining... the greatest actions have often proceeded from the intrigues of a handsome woman or a fashionable man, and of course whilst the memoires of those events are instructive by opening the secret workings of the human mind, they likewise attract by the interest and events of a novel... [I intend to be a] faithful historian of the secret history of the times.'

– Georgiana, Duchess of Devonshire, 1782.

'Our Revolution has made me feel the full force of the maxim that history is fiction.'

– Citizen Robespierre, ten years later.

The Prologue

This is true:

Halfway along the Strand, half an hour and a dozen streets from the dead heart of London, there used to be a zoo. This in itself might have been something of a surprise – for a zoo to exist so far from any park, so close to the polite decadence of Covent Garden and the daily business of Holborn or Fleet Street – but the truly notable thing about the London menagerie was that it was located inside a building. A perfectly ordinary building, as well, which (if you could overlook the gaudy pictures on its outer walls, of the roaring great cats and the Barbary apes with their dangerous red eyes) could have passed for any other house or shop in the shadow of Charing Cross. Not only that, but the animals themselves were housed on the *first and second floors up*, prowling in cages little more than three times the size of their own bodies, some of them stacked on top of each other like cargo-crates in a tea warehouse. An elephant – an *elephant* – had been winched into the building by some miracle of metropolitan engineering, and had spent many years staring forlornly out from behind the bars a whole storey above street level.

It was fashionable, in its day. The well-dressed gentlemen of London would parade before the cages in the room of animals, with equally well-dressed women on their arms, examining the beasts as if they'd somehow caged their own animal natures and could now look the wilderness in the eye with impunity. Some claimed that you could hear the apes screaming as far away as St James's, while others held that the hall was a wilderness in smell rather than sound, and that most of the screaming was drowned out by the hackney cabs on the cobbles outside. Nonetheless, those who lived in the streets near the Strand still believed they could hear the growling and the scratching at night, ringing through the wooden beams of the zoo and into the ground, the streets themselves purring with the dreams of the jungle.

Of course, by 1782 the zoo had lost something of its appeal. Animals weren't the fashion any more, said the *haut ton*, not in an age when de Vaucanson could fascinate the masses with his clockwork defecating duck and the grand masters of Europe could play chess against a machine which (allegedly) had the mind of a man. It was even rumoured that Mr Pidcock – the owner of the establishment – had deliberately set some of the animals free on the streets of the city, to once again pique the capital's interest, although less gullible Londoners pointed out that the worst thing Pidcock had ever done was spread those kind of rumours himself. Nonetheless, every now and then 'beast' stories would circulate in high society, usually regarding the more dubious members of the aristocracy. The Duke of Such-and-Such once murdered his servant and disposed of the body by feeding it to a panther; Catherine of Russia had given King George himself a mammoth, a *live* mammoth, as an arcane gift; and so on. But the age of the animal, said the men in the coffee-houses and the women of the *bagnios*, had ended at the same time that the infamous Hellfire Club had disbanded. The Club had owned some great vicious ape, it was said, and when they'd held their blasphemous rituals in the caverns of their Abbey this hairy, slavering creature had presided over the ceremony as a representative of Satan himself.

Lisa-Beth Lachlan had her lodgings in one of the streets off the Strand, a good half-dozen doors away from the menagerie. And yet she'd still occasionally hear the screeching in the rafters, although she suspected that she *could* have been imagining it: the woman in the rooms immediately below Lisa-Beth's had a smoking-jar permanently stationed in a room near the bottom of the wooden stairway, so late at night the opium fumes would frequently make their way up to the landing. It wasn't hard to work out that under that kind of stimulus *any* creaking of the floorboards could sound like an entire bestiary on heat.

But then, to begin with, Lisa-Beth never heard the apes. That only happened one night in March 1782, while she was occupied with what her associates might have called a 'gentleman of the Westminster persuasion'.

The man was, without doubt, a Member of Parliament. Lisa-Beth knew this, because he seemed to expect everybody to know it, but even though she was more or less sober there was enough alcohol in the atmosphere of the Shakespeare's Head to convince her that one politician was much like another. He'd sat with her in the Tavern – along with two other women from Covent Garden, although they'd left when it had become clear that His Lordship was only interested in paying for *one* of them (and Lisa-Beth was, the others had known, the best at putting up a good fight) – where he'd made a great show of hiding his face, pretending to be terrified that the other patrons of the Head would recognise him.

Wants to be a libertine and a gentleman-around-town, Lisa-Beth had thought, the kind of man who could stand up in the little cramped hall of the House of Commons and speak to his peers as a man of great appetites as well as great wisdom. She sometimes wondered why the Opposition didn't just wop out their manhoods and lumber around with the things dragging along the floor of Parliament. So His Lordship and Lisa-Beth had sat there in the Head for an hour or more, watching the posture-girls strike obscene poses on a patch of the floor where none of the regular customers had either spilled their drinks or urinated. Even so, he could barely keep his eyes off the centre of Lisa-Beth's forehead. Which meant, as Lisa-Beth had known right from the moment she'd picked him up, that he wanted *black coffee*.

In herself, Lisa-Beth was not in any way an *exotic*. She was blonde, and she was petite: she made a habit of keeping her dress on for as long as possible, to stop people realising that despite her size most of her body was made up of muscle. Not enough to win an arm-wrestling contest at the Head, perhaps, but enough to give another *demi-rep* a good punch in the face if there was a territory dispute. More importantly, her skin was pale, the hair pulled back behind her head to turn her face into a pretty white oval. She'd been told, more than once, that if her eyebrows weren't formed into such a permanent scowl then her eyes would have been big and blue enough to make her look like a child, or at worst like a child prostitute. So: the last kind of person one would expect to indulge in *black coffee*, not like one of the popular negresses of London, not like one of the tanned women who inhabited the seraglios of Covent Garden and had spent the last summer dressing up in the style of the *Arabian Nights*.

But Lisa-Beth had an advantage. Lisa-Beth really *had* lived in the lands where the East India Company was King, and more importantly that was where she'd been trained, in the house of Mother Dutt herself. Men would see the little red diamond she'd painted in the middle of her forehead and be, as the French might say, *Mesmerised*. That diamond promised things. A little window into lands of unknown pleasures. A promise of temptations and techniques never before practised on the shores of England, the *tantra* and the *Wheel of Kali*. Everyone had heard of the mysterious *Kama Sutra*, for God's sake, even if almost nobody had actually seen the text (let alone an illustrated version).

Ironically, Lisa-Beth *had* read the *Kama Sutra*, or at least browsed through it. But contrary to popular belief a lot of it had seemed to be about women teaching animals how to speak, and in Lisa-Beth's line of work that wasn't a great way to make a living.

By midnight the politician was lying prone on Lisa-Beth's bed, with his pantaloons unbraced and an expectant look on his ruddy red face. Lisa-Beth felt confident that the scene was exotic enough for his tastes. The bitch downstairs had obviously been using the jar again, filling up Lisa-Beth's space with the opium fumes, but that was all for the best: once Lisa-Beth had the lamps lit, the smoke gave the air a blurry, greasy feel that made your head swim and coloured everything yellow. If you squinted it was almost like being in an Indian *ashram*, the thick, sticky atmosphere turning the shadows into pools of velvet and making the brass bedpan gleam like gold. The room was small, but here and now it felt like an eastern boudoir rather than a London hovel. The mixture of oil and old wood made the house smell of exotic flowers burning on a funeral pyre, and all of a sudden the drapes around the bed – satin, but so worn at the edges that at times they reminded Lisa-Beth of an old bat whose wings had been shredded – looked dark and secretive, like cobwebs spun around a holy shrine.

The more practical part of Lisa-Beth's mind, which was undoubtedly the *larger* part, deduced that the woman downstairs must have been filling the house with fumes for bloody hours.

'Well,' said the politician, as Lisa-Beth climbed on to the bed and straddled his waist. 'Well. Well now. Where shall we begin, hmm?'

He doesn't know, thought Lisa-Beth. He's never had the nerve to pay for *black coffee* before.

Which means I can pretend *anything's* a mystical experience. And if he thinks I'm holding something back he'll just come back for more.

'Let's begin with something simple,' she said. 'The Rite of the Mare Ascendant.'

The man nodded gratefully, evidently glad she'd taken the lead. Lisa-Beth finished the job of unbuttoning him, and tried not to smirk when his big pink gut wobbled its way out into the open. She herself decided to keep her corset on, although by this time her chemise was already folded over the chair by her dressing-table. She briefly wondered how long she could keep the man happy before he worked out that the Rite of the Mare Ascendant was just another way of saying that he'd be flat on his back and she wouldn't. No doubt the *Kama Sutra* had an even more impressive name for it.

When the 'Rite' itself began, it was, as Lisa-Beth had expected, staggeringly dull. His Lordship was one of those annoying men who went 'oh!' whenever she so much as breathed on him, the noise suggesting such ecstasy that frankly she couldn't even be bothered trying. She just kept herself moving back and forth, working the man and the bed up into a single rhythm of creaking and mumbling. She tried to keep a smile on her face, but he hardly could have noticed, seeing as his attention was still focused on the red diamond.

Running like a machine, thought Lisa-Beth. Once, not long after she'd come home from India, she'd seen the insides of a factory in Manchester where a huge, fat, belching device had been constructed. The device could work cotton, the foreman had said, and he'd been certain that soon all the work would be done on machines like this even though it hadn't worked properly half the time. An infernal machine with a hundred arms, hands bent into claws, stretching raw matter into thread with its innards hissing like gas. The *kadaka-kadaka-kadak*, going on and on and on without ever stopping, in exactly the same rhythm as the *ga-bonk-'oh!'-ga-bonk-'oh!'-ga-bonk* of the bizarre animal/bed construction which Lisa-Beth now found herself operating.

In the future, thought Lisa-Beth, will there be machines to do this job? Will the de Vaucansons and the factory-men set their mechanical courtesans on the hapless men of Westminster, a race of clockwork dolls to pound the living daylights out of any politician who crosses their path? *Kadak-'oh!'-kadak-'oh!'-kadak.* Perhaps that hag downstairs is one of them already, thumping away at all hours God sends and blowing infernal opium fumes out of her backside.

It was only when Lisa-Beth found herself actually trying to look into this strange new world that she realised she'd gone into *Shaktyanda*.

That was understandable, as Mother Dutt had taught her. Up in the jute-stinking room at the back of the House of Dutt – because *everything* stank of jute on the Bay of Bengal, or at least, that was Lisa-Beth's memory of it – the Mother had taught her about the secret muscles of a woman's body, those contours and areas which the scientific minds of the age had spent many, many hours avoiding. Lisa-Beth remembered sitting on a bed covered with animal-hair, alongside the other English girl who'd been brought to the house, the one Mother Dutt called 'the Little Rose'. They'd learned about the hidden rhythms, the tappings and the drummings that lay concealed inside the body: the little rhythms of the pulse and the lungs, and the grander, slower, twenty-eight-day rhythm of what the *haut ton* now amusingly called 'the Prince'.

'Time is the key,' Mother Dutt had explained. Little Rose had looked alert and attentive, while Lisa-Beth had also taken note of the lesson, knowing even then that this was exactly the kind of talk which kept a man interested. If you knew how to play the part.

5

It was like being drunk, the Mother had said. Wine changed the rhythms of the body, made the blood go to your head, caused tiny little chemical outbursts inside you that all the physicians in Europe couldn't begin to explain. When you were drunk, your body took on a rhythm all to itself, one that no clock could measure.

'Think about the last time you drank,' the Mother had said, and Lisa-Beth had known that the look on Little Rose's face was due to the fact that the girl had never drunk more than a thimbleful in her life. 'You were content, were you not? And yet, despite your joy, when you next looked at a clock… if there was such a thing at hand… you found that you had lost far more of your life than you believed. Or perhaps the reverse. Perhaps, in your drunkenness, you experienced a daydream which seemed to last a lifetime. Yet to those outside of your world, only a minute had passed.'

This had been true enough. When she drank, Lisa-Beth lost her sense of daylight even faster than her sense of balance.

'There,' the Mother had concluded. 'When these changes are in your blood, you are no longer one with the common rhythm of things. We live to the world's sense of time, and become one with it until we never even notice its power over us. To break that rhythm… to stand aside from time… much needs to be changed within your body. Wine alone could never bring you to *Shaktyanda*.'

And then she'd started explaining the muscle techniques.

Kadak-'oh!'-kadak-'oh!'-kadak, went the machine under Lisa-Beth. Perfect timing: without thinking, she'd started working the man/bed in time with her own private rhythms. It was like a meditation, like the chanting of monks, like the words repeated over and over by the *Mesmerists* in Paris until their victims' minds were taken miles out of their own bodies. The rhythm of the noise, of Lisa-Beth's muscles as they clenched and unclenched inside her, lazily performing the techniques of Mother Dutt. The timbers of the house kept squealing in tempo, making Lisa-Beth wonder how long it'd be before the fumes made her start thinking it was the apes from the zoo she could hear. Not just the apes that were there now, but *all* the apes who'd ever lived and died in the building, all the generations laid on top of each other, all their screeching and shrieking brought together in a single chorus. Entirely by accident, then, she'd entered the no-time of *Shaktyanda*.

Kadak-'oh!'-kadak-'oh!'-kadak went the man, the bed, the machine, and the apes that haunted the walls. The question was, how long had she been doing this? How long had she been sitting on top of her bed-beast?

Seconds or hours? No: she doubted the man could have stood it for hours. Still, she couldn't help hoping that she was speeding up her own body-time rather than slowing it down. Back in the House, a month into the teaching, Mother Dutt had talked Lisa-Beth through a procedure – the gentleman hadn't objected – in which time seemed to be suspended indefinitely, in which Lisa-Beth's body stopped altogether and whole new worlds unfolded from a single moment. For that one moment, endless as it seemed, time had no longer been just a question of numbers on a clock face. Time had been a *thing*.

Whenever Lisa-Beth had tried to explain that to anybody afterwards, it had sounded like madness. Besides, there was no money in that kind of talk. Unless you were French.

It was, the Mother had said, all about control over one's own body, about the time inside oneself, so only during the 'rites' could the rhythms best be synchronised. That was why the Houses run by men had no understanding of the *tantra*, she'd said. Then again, the Mother had once claimed that she'd been able to actually *roll time backwards* during the vital act. Lisa-Beth had always wondered what it might feel like, to deal with a client in reverse. As disappointing as it felt the right way round, she supposed.

'But one must be careful,' the Mother had warned her and Little Rose one day. 'Everyone who understands these things understands that there are difficulties. Because there *must* be difficulties.'

'The pox?' Lisa-Beth had ventured.

'Demons,' the Mother had explained.

'Oh,' Lisa-Beth had said, trying not to sound too bored.

The *kadak-'oh!'-kadak-'oh!'-kadak* was still going on, somewhere in another world. Lisa-Beth was reaching that point in the *tantra* where memory folded in on itself, where the old sensations buried deep down in the body came back to haunt the skin, woken up by the rhythm. Her body was moving on its own by now, pumping and flexing in her own personal kind of time, and now she came to think of it... now she came to think of it, wasn't *kadak* the noise the machine in the factory had made? Wasn't the bed in her room supposed to go *ga-bonk* instead? And wasn't the old, soggy, rotting mattress supposed to smell of ground-in poppy seeds rather than the oil that kept the machinery running?

And couldn't she hear the apes in the zoo, screaming in their cages?

Her rhythm was growing faster. Yes, thought Lisa-Beth, the world's definitely speeding up for me. Which was a mercy, anyway. The man's cries of *'oh!'* were speeding up too, so either he was close to satisfaction or she was accelerating into her own future too fast. There: catch that thought. *The future*. The idea that the future is a real thing, not just a place that's invisible. All time's like that. *Tantra*: the Sanskrit word for 'warping'.

And now she was there, lying spread-eagled on a bed somewhere in India, looking up at a faded (and mildly erotic) picture of Hanuman that somebody had painted on the ceiling. She could feel Little Rose next to her, and Little Rose was screaming, and ten minutes later Mother Dutt was shouting and swearing at them because Little Rose had tried to do something stupid with her own 'private time' and come face-to-face with the demons. Lisa-Beth hadn't seen any demons, of course. She was fairly sure that Little Rose was just imagining things, as eleven-year-olds had a tendency to do.

Hard to stay in one place and time. *Kadak-'oh!'-kadak-'oh!'*. Lisa-Beth found herself back in the Shakespeare's Head, as the half-drunken politician began to explain how King George was actually mad and still thought the British could win the war against America: and Lisa-Beth was biting her lip so as not to point out that *all* the ruling classes were mad. She thought of the Hellfire Club, in their sweaty cavern underneath Medmenham Abbey, with their nun-prostitutes and their Satanic ape and their rich, bored, lust-crazed inner circle. The machines in the cotton factory were speeding up, matching her own rhythms, more *kadak* than *'oh!'* now. Lisa-Beth moved forward and backward through her own private time, not actually peeling it back the way Mother Dutt had allegedly done, just feeling the memories prickle under the surface of her skin and break out in beads of sweat and experience. And the apes in the zoo? Perhaps she'd woken them up as well, woken up the old memories of the house while the rafters creaked and groaned.

'*Babewyn*,' she heard Mother Dutt shout, two years ago when Lisa-Beth was barely seventeen. Because the Mother always spoke in French, never in English, and that was the word she used when she meant *demon*. 'Babewyn'. Like one of the brutal, leering, sexually-excited gargoyle-animals that lurked on the roof of Notre Dame. For a moment, Lisa-Beth was so lost in the Mother's words that she nearly convinced herself she'd achieved the impossible, and rolled time backwards until she was right there in the Indian bedroom.

'Time will move for you,' said the Mother, looking seriously from Lisa-Beth to Little Rose. 'But there is only so far you can go. There is only so much of time that one can understand. There is... *what's the word*... there is a horizon, which you will never reach. It is too far to go. At that horizon is the realm of *babewyns*. In places of understanding no man or woman will ever be able to look. If you should become lost... lost in your own past, as you deal with your client... then look towards that horizon. You will see it, and find your way by it. Your memories will drop away, and once more your old rhythms will return to you. But do not move towards the horizon. You will not reach it, and *babewyns* may discover you.'

Yes, thought Lisa-Beth. I'm getting lost. She remembered the Hellfire Club again, watched the ape-creature that squatted in the corner of their cave, and only then realised that this was something which had happened before she'd been born. She considered the possibility that she'd looked so far back through time that she'd seen things she'd never actually witnessed, but when she remembered that this was impossible (even the Mother had said so, and was saying so now, in India) she guessed it was pure imagination. The gargoyles of Notre Dame, monkey-faced and smelling of stone dung, leaned in closer. *Kadak-'oh!'-kadak-'oh!'-kadak*, went the man-bed-cotton-machine. Little Rose began to cry, shamed in front of the Mother, but it was still better than the screaming. The apes of the menagerie? They were all around her now, cackling and shrieking, clawing at the architecture and making the house creak itself apart. The live ones and the dead.

Time to end this, she decided. Time to look up at the horizon and find my way home, to go back to time the way the rest of the world knows it. Time to get back to His Lordship. Lisa-Beth sucked in a deep breath, not sure whether she was really sucking it in or just remembering a time at some point in her past when she'd done such a thing. Through the opium she tried to find the horizon, focusing on the sound of the bed (*not* the cotton machine) and the smell of sweat from the wobbly pink politician.

But the screeching of the apes stayed with her, as if the room didn't want to let it go, and she could still see the cavern of the Hellfire Club around her. The ape in the corner slowly raised its head, even though she'd never been there and it couldn't have seen her. She concentrated with the senses of her body, looked for that all-important horizon, that one lifeline which could restore her balance and her rhythm and her city and her bedroom.

All of a sudden, the horizon found *her*.

Lisa-Beth gasped. She gasped as she lay on the bed in India, she gasped as she looked up at the stone gargoyles of Notre Dame, she gasped at the age of seven as someone pulled her out of the shallower waters of the

Thames with a mouthful of black water. All these little gasps came back to her at once, formed one immense gulp for air which swept over her entire body, and in one moment she knew that every gasp she'd ever taken was just a tiny fraction of this, a small rehearsal for the surprise she felt now.

Because the horizon was *there*. Not in the distance, not further than any woman could reach. It loomed over her. Advanced on her. Reached out for her.

A band of black around the world, around *her* world, the limits of all human knowledge. Lisa-Beth realised that she couldn't slow down, couldn't stop, couldn't pull herself away from either the man on her bed or the edge of the universe hovering in front of her eyes.

'Oh, dear God,' she said, at some point in her life. 'Have I really come that far?'

It was made up of things no human being could ever know, that no person on Earth could ever understand. It was ignorance, it was darkness, it was time in which nobody could live. It *squirmed*, like a zoo, unknown animals exploring unknown pleasures and climbing over themselves to reach out for the woman who now approached them. *Kadak-'oh!'-kadak-'oh!'-kadak* went the ape-machine, but Lisa-Beth opened her mouth a hundred times at various points throughout her memory, and tried to scream at His Lordship to stop.

That was when something came out of the wall at her. Lisa-Beth was vaguely aware that she hadn't gone too far at all – that the horizon had come to *her*, that the limits of a human's knowledge had simply rolled across time to swallow her up – but it hardly seemed the issue as she looked into the eyes of the creature which detached itself from the darkness and leaned towards her.

'*Babewyn*,' said Mother Dutt, and Lisa-Beth realised that there was something important about the word '*babewyn*' she'd forgotten.

The ape looked up at her from the darkness. Not from the darkness of the Hellfire cave, where Lisa-Beth had never been. It was squatting in the darkness of the horizon. That was the form the creature took: an ape, its fur dark grey and matted with blood, its hide covered in scratches where it had clawed its way over its fellow apes to reach her. She couldn't see its eyes, as if they'd been poked out, or as if they were simply reflecting the darkness around them. She watched the muscles ripple in its face, following the line of its long, blood-wet snout, watching as its jaw fell open. Saliva in strands between its teeth, the stink of cannibalised meat in Lisa-Beth's face.

It was the Satan of the Hellfire Club. It was the monkey-faced thing that ruled Notre Dame. It was *the animal*, the beast, the leering, biting, unthinking demon that lay in wait for all unwary witches who tried to go too far into *Shaktyanda*. This slavering, idiotic guardian of the threshold, this stinking, blood-soaked little god at the edge of time

That's it, thought the practical part of Lisa-Beth's mind, the part which was, undoubtedly, no longer in control. That's what I was forgetting about the word *babewyn*. The fact that the English turned it into the word *baboon*. She'd heard Scarlette say it, once. Not that you could trust a word the mad witch said, but… but in front of her, the mindless bastard ape-god raised its arm, bloody fur stretching across muscles that flowed like time itself. Lisa-Beth looked up, with eyes that she rationally knew wouldn't be looking at anything other than the ceiling of her room, as the ape swung its arm with appalling speed and its claws came down to rip through her chest.

Fortunately, there was just enough self-control left in Lisa-Beth's body for *some* part of her to move. She pushed herself back, away from the claw, and felt gravity tug her balance away from her body.

She fell from the bed, tumbling off the edge, not knowing which world she was about to land in. The rhythm stopped, the machine stopped, and in the walls the screaming of the animals was replaced by the ordinary creaking of the house. There was a moment of peace, a moment when Lisa-Beth saw the blackness at the edges of her vision and realised, with some satisfaction, that she was about to pass out. Even now the practical part of her mind was telling her that if she lost consciousness then anybody could just walk into her house and take everything she had, but the rest of her no longer cared.

At that point Lisa-Beth hit the floor, her head cracking against the chair by the dressing-table. In the moments before she passed out her eyes flicked to the bed, and even from the floor she could see the politician's face. It was ruddy and bloated, and the big sweaty bald patch on his head exactly resembled the big sweaty pink gut that still protruded from under his shirt. Oddly, though, the man wasn't watching Lisa-Beth. His eyes were wide and shiny, like balls of glass, and they were staring up as if something far more important were hovering at the end of the bed.

Lisa-Beth didn't have time to move her eyes again, to take in whatever it was the man was staring at. The last thing she saw was a shadow falling over his fat belly, cast in the purest black thanks to the oil lamp at the end of the bed. But to be honest, it could just have been the concussion.

* * *

11

While she was asleep, Lisa-Beth didn't dream. She wouldn't have let herself. More importantly, while she was asleep she didn't *die* either. She woke up blinking, staring up at the ceiling, with her back to the Indian rug on the floor. The fumes fading away in the air, the oil lamp flickering down into half-light somewhere outside her vision.

Someone moved in her room. Someone turned over a bedsheet.

Lisa-Beth was up on her backside in seconds. She thought of the things she might find moving around in her bedchamber, of the sweaty politician rifling through her belongings. Of the woman downstairs and the apes in the walls. But when she sat up, the figure she saw standing at the end of her bed – stretching a sheet over the mattress, as if making the bed were a perfectly normal thing to do in the circumstances – came as a surprise.

At first, Lisa-Beth thought it was a man. It took her a moment to see past the clothes, the oversized black greatcoat that the visitor had bundled herself up in. Pulled tight across a dress that needed laundering. Like Lisa-Beth, the woman was blonde and she was skinny. Unlike Lisa-Beth, she was tall, and spindly rather than muscular. Her long hair was bunched at her neck, her lips were a tight little 'w'-shape, and resting on her (depressingly small) nose was a pair of spectacles. The fact that an obvious *demi-rep* might be wearing spectacles was surprising enough in itself, but the frames around the glass looked as light and as fine as cheese-wire. They rested halfway down the bridge of the nose, giving the woman a slightly upper class look that she obviously didn't deserve. She turned to look at Lisa-Beth in a fairly unconcerned fashion, and that was when Lisa-Beth recognised her.

Her name's Rebecca. She works at Scarlette's House. The spectacles, something of a selling-point in the *bagnio* culture of Covent Garden, were said to be Italian: but then, everything fine and delicate and fragile-looking was said to be Italian.

Lisa-Beth narrowed her eyes.

'What are you doing in my house?' she asked.

Rebecca shrugged, and wrinkled her nose in a way that the majority of London's gentlemen would have paid extra for. This irritated Lisa-Beth, not least because the gesture was so completely natural.

'I think you should come and see Scarlette,' said Rebecca. 'Before you summon anything else.'

That was when the woman glanced at the bed. Which, in turn, was when Lisa-Beth realised what she'd been covering up with the sheet.

HISTORY

'In its rites, representation of a deity in union with his consort was used to express this religious realisation... taken literally, it could lead to rejection of celibacy and ascetic morals.'

– *Collier's Encyclopaedia*, on the subject of *tantra*.

1
The House

It was, of course, in 1782 that the infamous Duchess of Devonshire made her comment about the 'secret springs of events', almost a whole year before she herself was to prevent the fall of the entire British administration simply by knowing how to flirt with the Prince of Wales properly. Had London society known the 'causes little imagined' behind the events of that year, then the Great Fireball of 1783 might have seemed like an even greater omen of doom. To understand the *real* history of the events leading up to the Siege of Henrietta Street, it's probably best to start with the ball that was held there on March 20, 1782, long before the Siege itself: a ball which, incidentally, would see the society debut of a young lady who stood on the verge of a truly remarkable transformation.

Scarlette can't have chosen the date of the ball by accident. It was effectively the day the British government fell, the day the old Prime Minister, wounded and shuffling after the defeat of the British army in Virginia, finally faced the House of Commons and announced that he had no option but to step down while he still had his sanity (unlike the King, some would have said, who'd done everything possible to keep the American War going even when it was clearly suicidal to do so... nonetheless, it'd be another six years before George III would lose his mind completely and attempt to throttle his own son over the dinner table). It snowed that March evening: spring was a colder time then. True, the ball must have been arranged well before Prime Minister North's announcement, but predicting the end of British civilisation as the world knew it – because that final, crushing acknowledgement that the American colonists had *won* proved once and for all that the King's power was no longer as absolute as history had believed – can't have been hard. Particularly for a woman who claimed to have at least one visionary, one *prophetess*, under her roof.

So it seems likely that Scarlette planned the ball as a kind of funeral. The North administration had overseen the tea fiasco in Boston; the defeat of the British at the hands of General Washington; the banishment of all Scarlette's 'tribe' from the Americas; and the death of the courtesan-cum-sorceress colloquially known as 'the Queen of New York State'. Scarlette must have intended the ball to bury all the memories of the previous twelve months. Though none of the invitations survive in any archive (it's possible that guests were invited through word of mouth, via the bagnios and brothels of Covent Garden), it's said Scarlette herself gave strict instructions that only red and black were to be worn to the event. One of those present later described the scene:

> The hall of the house was in red and black, and red and black only. Drapes of the finest satin decked every wall, giving the ceremony something of the flavour of an Arabian House. There were roses and dark orchids… strung from the walls on ribbons of silk, though the flowers looked not so much like blooms as velvet themselves [folded] together in the most delicate manner… and it appeared that all was lit by the glow of the red and the black candles in the chandeliers. The men wore black and as a rule did not seem wont to impress, the ladies present wore crimson and vermillion yet the mood was not a sombre one. Lord _____ wore buttons on his jacket in the most macabre European style, fashioned to give the appearance of skulls… [t]hough it was not a masquerade, there were those that came masked out of discretion. At the foot of the stairway I encountered a gentleman whose face was concealed by a hood of red velvet, with no expression and nought of his face [showing] but two of the darkest eyes. Stitched into the forehead of that hood was a sigil in the shape of a triangle [almost certainly a Masonic symbol], while the neck was tied by fine red satin. Yet he had the bearing of a perfectly charming gentleman, with one hand folded behind his back and the other carrying a flute glass of wine… as if one might wear such a hood at any polite gathering. One hostess, a pretty little red-head, was made uneasy by this and neglected her duty greatly in not engaging him in conversation.

Hardly a typical ball, then. But Scarlette had been selective in inviting her guests. Moreover, the ball was remarkable for starting at *midnight*, well after acceptable social hours… and to hold a ball in a house known to be a *seraglio*, a 'house of leisure', was itself hardly in line with protocol. Twenty years earlier, when a fashionable gentleman of the *haut ton* wouldn't have been seen dead in town without a Covent Garden courtesan on his arm, such a thing might have seemed daring and the height of taste. But the age of the fashionable *demi-rep* had ended when the notorious Fanny Bradshaw had moved out of Covent Garden and brought the era of the 'Great Harlots' to an end. To have assembled *any* members of society at the House on Henrietta Street, let alone so many, must have been an achievement in itself.

It's safe to assume that the 'hostesses' mentioned in the letter were the women of the House, those who conducted their business in the employ of Scarlette: at any gathering, Scarlette herself wasn't prone to make an appearance – and therefore make an impression – until later on in the evening. Many of these women's names have been lost to history, but a few are notable. There was Rebecca Macardle, who'd been among the last of the 'Deerfield witches' to evacuate America in 1781. There was the plump, dark-haired Russian girl Katya, whose ample seventeen-year-old bust concealed a pendant ostensibly given to her by the personal coven of the Empress Catherine (naturally, she was thought to be a spy as well as a ritualist). Later on there was Lisa-Beth Lachlan, whose bad-tempered practicality did much to keep the House alive before the horror of early 1783. But the 'pretty little red-head' was almost certainly the girl referred to by friends and visitors as Juliette.

Many of Juliette's letters survive, not to mention a curious dream-journal from the summer of 1782. From these it's fair to say that she was remarkably acute and intelligent, especially given her age. However, visitors to the House described her as quiet, polite, and apparently subservient to Scarlette herself. It's not difficult to imagine this. Though much of Juliette's past remains a mystery, it's known that Scarlette was the one who found her, brought her to the House, and made the decision to tutor her in the ways of Scarlette's own tradition. Perhaps it's best to think of Juliette as Scarlette's 'apprentice', and her quietness was possibly just a sign of her willingness to listen. Juliette seems to have felt not only a great deal of affection for Scarlette in her early years – arguably, even a crush – but also a passionate sense of duty. It may be true that the hood-headed Mason disturbed her that night at the ball (hardly surprising, given the overwhelming nature of some of the attendees), but despite the letter most accounts agree that Juliette did her best to conduct herself with the utmost deportment in what must have been trying circumstances. It's notable that Juliette wore a black rather than a red dress that evening, as if in deference to her mentor.

'Only someone who knew her well,' Scarlette wrote of the night, with typical verve, 'could have looked into the green fields of her eyes and known the apprehension.'

But there are other factors that might explain Juliette's unease, which Scarlette would never have let herself acknowledge. There were, quite clearly, ill murmurings in the House on that evening. Though many of the guests moved in the same circles as Scarlette – the Freemasons, the witch-cults, even a representative of the Roman Catholic Church if Scarlette's own journals are to be believed – and though Scarlette had persuaded them all to at least attend the ball, there was a general feeling that the whole thing was a waste of time. Scarlette had only come into possession of the House in January, and the ball was in many ways her housewarming party. In the days of high fashion the local watch might have turned a blind eye to such a blatant bordello being opened in the shadow of the Drury Lane Theatre, but to open such an establishment now… and in *Henrietta Street*, of all places…

The feeling was that Scarlette had become out of touch with the times, despite being barely into her twenties. She'd been poisoned, said the whispers, by stories of the good old days: the days of the Hellfire Club, the days when Casanova could take a rich old aristocrat for all she was worth by pretending to be able to transfer her mind into somebody else's body just through a kiss. The *haut ton* was terribly bored by that sort of thing now, at least in England, although word had it the French were still gullible enough to make the two-thousand-year-old Count Cagliostro the talk of Paris. Did Scarlette really believe that by dressing the House up in her old-fashioned Hellfire mysticism, by presenting her women as half-sorceress and half-prostitute, she could *impress* anyone?

It was over, the rumours said, and Juliette must have been troubled by that. A 'stray' with nobody to turn to outside the House, she must have secretly wondered whether she had any more future now than she'd had when she'd first arrived in London as a twelve-year-old. Katya, the alleged Russian spy, was so involved with various members of the foreign office that it seemed unlikely she'd stay at the House for long: always one for self-expansion, in *every* sense, she was seen leading the 'Marquis of H_____' to an upstairs room at the ball even though Scarlette had instructed that no business was to be conducted that night. One of the guests, the Countess of Jersey – nicknamed 'the Infernal' in society circles, partly because of her occult pedigree, partly because she was regarded by many as an infernal nuisance – was loudly scornful of both the House and its crimson-and-black decor that evening, although observers noticed that she quietened down considerably when Scarlette herself finally made an entrance. Did Juliette hear the Countess's loud, vulgar criticisms? Did she begin to wonder, even as she held up her chin and did her duty as hostess, whether she'd be in the gutters before long?

In fact, the only woman in the House who seems to have remained loyal to Scarlette was Rebecca. And this is odd, because – to begin with, at least – Scarlette didn't trust her in return. A handsome, literate, bespectacled *demi-rep*, Rebecca had been with the Queen of New York State herself on the day that the British army had surrendered at Virginia and the United States, under General Washington, had been declared a 'no-go' area for those of Scarlette's tradition. The Queen had died that day, and since then the *tantrists* of London had begun to whisper that the very ground of the Americas was poison to all of their kind, that any English witch or ritualist who set foot on independent American soil would instantly burst into flames... although whenever Rebecca was asked what had *really* happened in New York, she'd simply shrug and turn her attention back to her deck of cards.

There was a kind of stain on Rebecca's honour, then. Rebecca had been in America when terrible things had happened there – when Matthew Crane, Hidden Master of the Grand Lodge Temple of St Andrew's Trust, had ordered the covert exile of all foreign mystics and courtesans from every colony, New York to Virginia – and even if Rebecca herself hadn't in any way been to blame (she was, after all, still only nineteen) she was considered by many in London to be something of a curse. Typical of the era, when she received a visit from 'the Prince' her blood was said to turn to poison. Perhaps this is why Rebecca often seemed so detached from those around her: or perhaps it was her habit of matter-of-factly making predictions about the future ('oh yes, there are going to be men flying in balloons... there will be whole wars fought in the sky') and then changing the subject completely.

So, all things considered, there must have been a great deal of unease in the air on that night in March when the red-and-black people met, drank, milled and speculated inside the House on Henrietta Street. The world was changing, society was unsettled, and Scarlette's decision to hold the ball in the first place seemed somehow fundamentally *wrong*.

Then, on top of all that, there were the rumours about the Doctor.

MASTER OF THIS HOUSE

Lisa-Beth moved into the House on Henrietta Street some time in late March. She was definitely living there by April, when her journals describe the peculiar experiments being performed in the House's cellar, but if Scarlette's diaries are to be believed then her first visit was on the night of the ball. According to Scarlette, Lisa-Beth had summoned up something which 'the witch couldn't put down'; Rebecca had been sent to help her, probably some time around half eleven; and Lisa-Beth had arrived at the House around midnight, when the ball was in full swing but Scarlette had yet to show herself in front of the guests. (How Scarlette *knew* that Lisa-Beth had summoned such a 'creature' isn't made clear. There's a suggestion that this may have had something to do with Rebecca's alleged preternatural knowledge, but there was at least one other individual living at the House who might have been able to sense such a disturbance.)

Lisa-Beth distrusted Scarlette and felt, like so many others, that this 'mystical adventuress' had been milking the legacy of the Hellfire Club for far too long. So why did this most cynical of *demi-reps* make the decision to move all her things, from her Indian wall-hangings to her surprisingly large collection of books – including the hilariously pornographic *History of Marie-Antoinette* and Wessel's futuristic *Anno 7603* – from her lodgings off the Strand? Lisa-Beth's own 'experience' on that night had something to do with it, of course. But the *babewyn* Lisa-Beth ostensibly summoned was only part of the picture.

Two weeks earlier, a prostitute named Anne-Belle Paley had been picked up by the watch near Marylebone, to the western side of London. The Roundhouse had been unusually full that night, and as a result the watch had decided to take Paley to a different place of imprisonment just outside the city. The rest of the story reads like some horrible gothic fantasy. The woman had been bundled into a cab, and at first she'd put up no resistance, even flirting with the arresting sergeant (not uncommon in Covent Garden). But as the cab had approached the city limits, the woman – alone in the back of the cab, the watchman being on the roof – had begun to scream. Assuming that she was simply either drunk or hysterical, the sergeant had ignored her, until at last the woman had begun to thrash so violently in the cab that the driver had been forced to stop on the north-western boundary of the city.

It seems almost unnecessary to complete the story, or to describe what the cabman and sergeant claimed to have found when they'd looked into the back of the cab. As Lisa-Beth would have well known, the story of the *mystery beast* had been popular throughout the era of the rakes and their blasphemous rituals. The endings of these urban folk tales were predictable. Man found trampled to death in the fields near the Edgware Road; scraps of flesh and clothing discovered in a back street of Holborn, suggesting that someone had been eaten alive; street-walker clawed to death by unseen animal. Indeed, a critical mind might have asked whether Anne-Belle Paley had ever really existed at all.

But this particular story had been given an interesting incidental detail. According to the sergeant, the thing the woman had been screaming as the cab had moved out of London was: *'We mustn't go through the wall.'*

This is so suggestive of the *horizon*, the 'wall around the world' described by the *tantrists*, that Lisa-Beth must surely have pricked up her ears. The *babewyns* had, at least in rumour, drawn first blood. While high society was fretting over the imminent fall of the government, the women of the streets and seraglios were finding their own reasons for concern. In such an age of suspicion and rumour, it's possible Lisa-Beth began to feel that even if Scarlette's tradition was an outdated one, it was at least something. The protection of a House was always an asset, even if the House seemed to be built on shaky ground.

According to Lisa-Beth's own version of events, she was 'unimpressed' by those assembled at the ball. She refers to various masked entities gathered in the hall, including a man wearing the face of a mandrill, who danced in an exuberant manner with a lady Lisa-Beth didn't recognise. This seems to suggest that the masks were worn by the men not as disguises (this was hardly an era of discretion), but as indicators of the orders and lodges they represented. Lisa-Beth also noticed the red-headed Juliette at the ball, and later noted:

> Scarlette's got this one well-trained. I wonder what she's going to do with it [i.e. Juliette]? The girl was wearing a ring, I couldn't get close enough to see the seal. The symbol of Scarlette and her kin? The bitch-mother, I think, is trying to start her own coven here in London. I doubt London will even notice.

It was shortly after this that Rebecca led Lisa-Beth into one of the backrooms of the House, presumably the one in which Scarlette is known to have kept her office, complete with a wooden desk, wooden bookshelves, and all the paraphernalia of bureaucracy (quills and ink, largely). It was here that Lisa-Beth and Scarlette finally met.

Oddly, when Lisa-Beth entered the room she found herself witnessing a swordfight. There were two individuals in the office, both of whom were wearing what Lisa-Beth called 'masks of crossed metal' (fencing masks?). They failed to pay any attention to Lisa-Beth as she entered, but carried on with their duel, repeatedly thrusting and parrying at each other's blows. This isn't hard to believe, given Scarlette's character. While those in the main hall of the House were waiting for the Great Hostess to show herself, Scarlette was at the rear of the building, 'relaxing' with this physical exercise before making her *grande entrance*.

Scarlette was very much a woman of her time, even if there was a feeling in society that the time in question was ending. During the American revolution, US publications were full of stories about the 'amazons' who fought like hardened soldiers for their country: women who dressed as men to fight as men, or in some cases hid flintlocks and gutting-knives beneath their petticoats. Illustrations depicted such adventuresses as classical heroines, hands on their waists, booted feet resting on the fallen bodies of the British enemy, the rolling plains of the New World in the background. Patriots to the Americans, harridans to the English. Scarlette herself was English, naturally, but contemporary descriptions of her make use of the same imagery. She would always wear dresses in red, but apart from (rather dandyish) ruffles at her collar there would be few concessions to femininity. The dress would end at least two inches above the floor, and those who dared look at her feet couldn't help noticing that under the dress, and the white underskirts just visible beneath, she seemed to permanently wear a pair of riding-boots. Whether this was a fashion statement, or the mark of a woman of action, is hard to say. Her bearing was such that even those who knew her well felt as if she could, at a moment's notice, pull a pair of muskets from her belt and fire them both simultaneously. A noted swordswoman, from the descriptions one could believe that if her figure weren't quite so athletic she would have kept her sabre in her *decolletage*.

Despite the mask, Lisa-Beth would have recognised Scarlette immediately, not just from the clothes but from the dark and all-too-long hair which had been tied into a single strand behind her head. On the other hand, her masked opponent was a man Lisa-Beth couldn't possibly have known, though she describes his clothes as 'overly simple… none of the expected vanities and appendages, not even a hem on his jacket or ankle-socks to keep his trousers to his legs.'

This man was to become vitally important to the history of the House – indeed, the axis around which it revolved – but Lisa-Beth couldn't have guessed his significance at the time. By March he'd been residing at the House for nearly a month, in which time he'd absorbed more of the local custom and lore than could have been expected of anyone: he was the one, for example, to whom Rebecca gave what's thought to be her only account of her last days in the Americas (now sadly lost), and he was the one who convinced Scarlette to take Lisa-Beth into her 'inner circle' despite Scarlette's reservations.

Lisa-Beth seems to have been fascinated by the swordplay despite herself. Though she clearly had no knowledge of the art of swordsman/womanship, in her account she vividly describes how Scarlette bested the man with the tip of her blade, penetrating his defences and wilfully making a bloody cut on his right hand (to make a point, one supposes, and no doubt the man would have done the same to her). Then – using a move Lisa-Beth seems unable to properly describe – the man somehow let his blade fly, sending it through the air with such unexpected verve that Scarlette had no option but to drop her own weapon, leaving both of them disarmed. It's interesting to note that Lisa-Beth describes the sword as 'hanging in the air', suggesting a frozen 'private time' much like that described by *tantrists* in the state sometimes called *Shaktyanda*. Once both combatants had considered the fallen blades, and it had become clear that neither was prepared to dive to the floor to re-arm themselves, a conversation passed between them which Lisa-Beth records in detail. It's worth quoting it in full, not only because it says something about the teasing relationship between Scarlette and the man but also because it demonstrates the somewhat startling wit for which Scarlette was famous among *demi-reps*:

SCARLETTE: Predictable. You really *must* be sick.
THE MAN [evidently with some surprise]: You expected me to do that?
SCARLETTE: I expected you to do *something* remarkable. You really couldn't have done anything else. That's why you're so predictable.
THE MAN: Ah. Yes, you may have a point.
SCARLETTE: Now. As we've lost our weapons, I suggest we continue this practice unarmed. We'll try wrestling on the floor next. And as this is supposed to be a precise simulation of genuine combat, I suggest we do it naked.

The man's response to this isn't recorded. But it was only now that Lisa-Beth's presence in the room was noticed.

It's safe to assume that while all this was occurring at the back of the House, Rebecca had returned to the main hall, because several gentlemen in attendance at the ball reported seeing her at the cardtable at around half past midnight. At *any* society function, a card table was *de rigeur*. Game of choice for most gamblers of the upper class was *faro*, and it's a testament to the nature of the era that a game such as this, in which

23

chance was the only element and nothing the gambler did or said made the slightest difference to the outcome, should be the height of fashion. As a hostess, Rebecca often did her duty by manning the cardtable at the House of Scarlette, a popular dealer with the gentlemen thanks to her unusual visionary claims.

At this point in time there still wasn't a distinction between *playing* cards and *tarot* cards, and it's not hard to see how this might have worked. If tarot cards and playing cards are treated as the same kind of game, then predictions become self-fulfilling prophecies. According to the old system, the Three of Spades suggested *Loss*, and indeed a Three of Spades drawn at the faro table had such a low value that by and large its appearance would signify quite a loss for the gambler. But Rebecca's predictions were known for being remarkably long term. It was said that several young aristocrats had drowned themselves after receiving portents of life-long doom from Rebecca, although this is provably untrue and no doubt another result of her unfortunate reputation. It doesn't seem to have bothered her.

It's said that when the man known as the Doctor first arrived at the House of Scarlette, Rebecca spent some time watching him draw random cards out of her pack: whereas most people could have their fortunes read with just a single card, an entire *quarter* of the deck was used up in the Doctor's case. But the card in the dead centre of all those drawn, the one to which Rebecca is said to have ascribed the most significance, was the Ace of Hearts. (There are many interpretations of this. The story in the 'Sabbath Book' to the effect that the single red heart on the card turned *black* the second it was revealed by the Doctor is unquestionably apocryphal.)

Although there were no formal invitations to the ball, Scarlette *did* produce a number of envelopes, which she distributed amongst the guests at the House that night. Each was unusual, in that it had a sheen on it like the shine of an oil lamp, although each was a bright red in colour (an expensive little folly, for the time). Thirteen of the envelopes were created, one for each of the major factions, both those who'd sent representatives to the ball and those who either wouldn't or couldn't attend. The names on the envelopes were written in a dark, spidery handwriting, undoubtedly the Doctor's. Scarlette must surely have warned him that it was impractical to deliver them to those 'cults' in America and the West Indies, and certainly she would have told him that the *Mayakai* wouldn't come to the ball. Or wouldn't be *seen*, anyway.

Perhaps the envelopes were still on Scarlette's desk when Scarlette and the Doctor removed their masks to speak with Lisa-Beth. Lisa-Beth gives some account of all the questions she asked Scarlette, though without all the answers. She no doubt stood with her arms folded, scowling and unimpressed, while she asked why Rebecca had brought her here. Curiously, in Lisa-Beth's account there's no reference to what surely must have been the *big* question playing on her mind.

When Lisa-Beth had regained consciousness in her rooms, she'd pulled back the sheet and discovered what Rebecca had been trying to hide from her: a large bloodstain, where her Westminster client had been lying. It's hard to guess at the significance of this. Did Rebecca's supposed *babewyn* slaughter the politician, and if so then did Rebecca dispose of the body before Lisa-Beth awakened, putting Lisa-Beth in her debt? Or did Rebecca arrive at the rooms in time to break Lisa-Beth's 'summoning', again putting her in credit (in which case, one supposes, the unfortunate man would just have run off in a panic)? No answer to this is even hinted at in the accounts. Perhaps it's understandable that Lisa-Beth didn't dwell on it. She wasn't the kind to be in anyone's debt. All that can be said for certain is that there's no Parliamentary record of a politician disappearing that night.

Either way, Scarlette must surely have reminded Lisa-Beth about the story of the dead prostitute found in the back of the cab, heart (or lungs, depending on the version) torn out. And when Scarlette explained that something *truly* terrible was about to happen to the capital? When she suggested that from Covent Garden to St John's Wood, those trained in such things had seen the *babewyns* trying to scratch their way into the world? What did Lisa-Beth, straightforward to a fault, make of that?

It's easy to be wise in retrospect. By the end of the year, it was obvious what had been moving in on London and how close to the edge the city truly was. But at the time, with only vague rumours and one *possible* manifestation to go on, Lisa-Beth must have been sceptical. It was probably the Doctor who finally made up her mind.

The word Lisa-Beth might have used to describe the Doctor might have been 'Byronesque', if it weren't for the fact that the future Lord Byron hadn't yet been born. She found him not displeasing in appearance, and she took him at once to be the aristocrat-poet type, some weeks later saying that he looked like the kind of well-bred individual who'd 'end his days as an outcast either for unnatural acts or crimes of religion'. She noticed, almost immediately, that he was wearing a ring exactly like Juliette's: this must have convinced her that he was a follower, rather than a friend, of Scarlette's. She had no way of knowing, yet, that it was the Doctor who'd provided both of the rings. In her initial account Lisa-Beth also makes note of the Doctor's beard, the moustache and neat triangle of hair on his chin, which to her looked slightly darker and more forbidding than the curly brown hair on his head.

The Doctor immediately tried to convince Lisa-Beth that something had gone very, very wrong with the world, which was remarkably in keeping with the mood of the country as a whole. In fact, Rebecca recorded his address to her in detail, but although it's an important source it has to be remembered that it was written later, and from memory: it may have been influenced by the stories about the Doctor that circulated *after* the March ball. Furthermore, Lisa-Beth had her own prejudices about the man's intentions as a cohort of Scarlette. In the following text, the section in italics is particularly suspect. Also, some of Lisa-Beth's more archaic English has been neatened into a slightly more modern version.

> 'Think of it as a kind of story. Once upon a time, there must have been a race of what I suppose you'd call... elementals. A race who pinned down time like tacks in a seamstress's shop. Who made sure that time didn't tear, or shred, or pull away at the edges. Except that the elementals don't exist any more, Lisa-Beth. And they never did.'

(Note: it's unclear whether the word 'seamstress' has a deliberate double-meaning here, given that it's often used as a synonym for 'prostitute'. Note also that to a *tantrist* like Lisa-Beth, this 'objectifying' of time can't have been as anachronistic as it might seem.)

> 'So. With the elementals gone, nothing's holding time together. Except, of course, that you can't remove their kind of power from the universe and expect it to vanish completely. Too many consequences. Too much history. Which is why there are so many people now trying to do the job the elementals used to do. Which is why the old knowledge of time seems to have worked its way into your culture, admittedly in a particularly arcane form.' [At this point, Lisa-Beth asked whether he was referring to the Hellfire Club.] 'The Hellfire Club. The Grand Lodge Freemasons. The witch-cults in Russia. Some of the newer religious orders in the West Indies. People like you. All holding fragments of the truth. The last line of defence against the beasts. You see? It's up to us, Lisa-Beth. *We have to make a stand against them. Us and our coven. That's why you have to join us.*'

This isn't all that Lisa-Beth records about her first meeting with the 'elemental' known as the Doctor. But it's the first time, in any written form, that the philosophy of Scarlette's House becomes obvious. Not only did Scarlette believe herself to be upholding an ancient tradition – not only did she see herself, like the original Hellfire set, to be using her grasp of *tantra* and arcane law to defend certain principles – she saw the Doctor as a kind of sign. An omen, much like the later Great Fireball, a messenger sent to help her run the Henrietta Street seraglio as the last refuge when the *babewyns* came to rip apart all those women who saw, knew and did too much.

When Lisa-Beth heard all this, two things seem to have struck her particularly. The first was the thought that the Doctor didn't look anything like any other brothel-keeper she'd ever met. The second was the Doctor's response when she asked him exactly what the *babewyns* were, and why they were suddenly capable of being summoned into the world.

'I don't know,' this apparently all-wise magus admitted. 'I think it's actually going to be quite important.'

As far as can be gathered from any of the surviving accounts, the Doctor himself never made a public appearance at the ball, though his presence was discussed by (among others) Lady Jersey. But it was shortly after the meeting with Lisa-Beth that Scarlette made her own, typically dramatic, entrance. The Doctor probably remained in the office while she handed out the envelopes, which made Scarlette's plans for the future quite clear, to those who knew how to read between the lines. Or perhaps he retired to the House's cellar, where most of his work was done during his time on Henrietta Street, at least before he fell sick and became bed-bound in October.

It's unquestionably true, though, that he was alone for most of that evening. Which is why, when one of the 'guests' made a devastating assault on him, nobody else was there to witness the attack.

BLOOD, FIRE AND TIME
'He walked here.' That was all Scarlette would ever say, when anybody asked her how the Doctor had come to be staying at Henrietta Street.

Only one portrait of Scarlette exists, and even this was painted much earlier in her life, when she herself was an 'apprentice'. Even given that eighteenth-century portraits tended to flatter the subject – witness the traditional image of a *sober* Prince of Wales – the woman it depicts is unquestionably striking. It's not so much that she appears beautiful, although with her almond-shaped eyes, her fashionably pale skin and her vaguely aristocratic looks she certainly must have been far more appealing than most *demi-reps*. The most notable thing is that she clearly has the face of an actress. In the portrait, her hair is a mane of black pulled back to the nape of her neck, almost a halo of mystery and intrigue (but then, Romney was always a romantic when painting society portraits). There's the trace of a smile on her lips, a suggestion that the smile is the only *real* part of her face on display, the look of someone who knows nobody's ever going to penetrate the mask. Some of the great actresses-cum-mistresses of Drury Lane have similar expressions in their portraits, and it's hard to believe that Scarlette can't have been more than seventeen when the picture was painted.

But then, her age was always something of an enigma. Like any good actress, she hid the truth well, although – remarkably – it was generally believed that during the crisis of 1782, she was still only in her early twenties (it has to be remembered that women grew up faster then, that there was no such word in the English language as 'teenager' and that many girls began working in seraglios at the age of twelve). All Scarlette herself would ever say was that she'd been born in the same year in which Mary Culver, the last of the great London 'witch-mistresses' and a cornerstone of the original Hellfire Club, had ritually slit her own throat with a jagged piece of glass in order to perform one of the most remarkable rituals in history. But even Scarlette stopped short of suggesting that there was a direct link between Mistress Culver's sacrifice and her own arrival into the world.

What was known by everyone, however, was that Scarlette had truly 'come of age' two years before the arrival of the Doctor, in the year when London had burned and the sky had turned to blood.

It's perhaps surprising that the great Gordon Riots of 1780 aren't a better-known part of English history. Possibly it's a kind of embarrassment: the English don't need to be reminded how easy it is for the nation, or at least its heart and capital, to slip over the edge of reason and into mass murder. The events of June 1780 are too complex, bloody and vicious to fully explain here, but it's enough to say that it began when Lord George Gordon – a flame-haired, wild-eyed peer of the realm quite clearly on the edge of a complete nervous collapse – led a mob of fifty thousand Catholic-hating citizens, plus various opportunistic criminals and prostitutes, in a march on Parliament itself. The crowd held the honourable members hostage for a whole day, while Gordon burst into the House of Commons to threaten, cajole and harangue the nation's leading politicians, who could do little but shrink back in fear.

In itself, the notion that a man could do such a thing to the throne of democratic power is surprising. But so began nearly a week of carnage, in which rioters burned down entire neighbourhoods at the dead heart of the city. Innocent bystanders were burned alive or hacked to pieces; every prison in the city was razed to the ground, and every prisoner released; streets were flooded with blood, alcohol and vomit; the watch stood by and did nothing, or in some cases urged the rioters on; extortion gangs began to divide up the whole of urban London between them; and for the best part of a week the night sky was lit up in bright red as the entire horizon caught light. By day, all was quiet. By night, the people of London became beasts. Stories circulated that the King had been butchered, in circumstances not unlike the later Revolution in France, while there were several tales of animals being released from zoos and slaughtering passers-by in the urban jungle. There was, as there often is in such circumstances, at least one report of human cannibalism.

Until the sixth day of the riots, many genuinely believed that English civilisation had fallen for ever. Some said the carnage had been masterminded by the French, or even by American manipulators like that sinister Freemason and lightning-god, Benjamin Franklin. Those with more arcane minds held that something had been awoken under the city, that tunnels full of satanic monks were performing foul rituals beneath the capital, spilling English blood in the name of pagan gods. It's certainly true that John Wilkes, former Mayor of London and fallen member of the Hellfire Club, seemed determined to stop this vicious and chaotic kind of black magic.

Newgate Prison was burned to the ground on June 6, 1780. While those prisoners who couldn't get out in time screamed in the debris, released mental patients stood on the windowsills and urinated into the flames under a sky full of black, fat-filled smoke. Scarlette was there: this much is certain. If there really *was* something ritualistic in the bloodshed, then Scarlette was undoubtedly involved in it. The Gordon Riots were her baptism of fire, her first good look into the face of the horror which her kind were, traditionally, sworn to hold back.

Though her exact role at Newgate in 1780 is unclear, it was often suggested that a man had been involved. Scarlette is known to have studied ritualism under one of the *Mayakai*, and such instructresses tended to frown on the male ability to 'perform' in a ritual sense, but it seems that an effort was made to seduce the young Scarlette by a gentleman of another tradition. This isn't surprising. In that era, occultism

29

and libertinage went hand-in-hand, and wherever there was black magic there were prostitutes: great libertines were often regarded as great miracle-workers (Casanova, Francis Dashwood, etcetera). It may be true that part of Scarlette's 'initiation' under the sky of burning London was a confrontation with her would-be lover. It's tempting to think that perhaps the man who attempted to seduce her was one of the *opposition*, in league with the unholy monks supposedly at work in the tunnels... that his purpose was to corrupt her and bend her to his own will... but this could be sheer fantasy.

It's even more tempting to think that, after such a distressing affair, the Doctor was Scarlette's attempt at finding the *right* kind of man.

From her journals, it's easy to see how Scarlette remembered the Gordon Riots. That was the time when she first saw the world the way the *tantrists* saw it, in patterns of blood, fire and time. Those who entered the *Shaktyanda* state, like Lisa-Beth, often spoke of seeing the world around them as a spectrum of time and space, in which the traumas of the past could make their way up through the skin of the world and be 'physically remembered'. This is in effect what happened to London in 1780. Every burning, hateful impulse the city had ever pushed down beneath its surface had been summoned out into the moonlight. As far as Scarlette was concerned, when the creatures Lisa-Beth called *babewyns* began to appear in 1782 it was just an extension of the process that had started two years earlier. Though the details are maddeningly vague, Scarlette speaks of the way the Doctor 'walked' through *Shaktyanda* (through the 'wall', or time itself?) to arrive in her company. *Tantrist* lore holds that *Shaktyanda* was occupied by godlike, elemental creatures called *Vidyeshwaras* – best translated as 'Lords of Wisdom' – so perhaps Scarlette saw the Doctor as such a being.

She also records his first words to her, when they met on a street in Marylebone: 'Hello. Are you a magician, by any chance?'

Within days the Doctor had settled into the House, where he soon set up his own study (Lisa-Beth uses the word 'laboratory') in the cellar and where he took an immediate interest in the other women of the House, though for reasons that seem to have been entirely at odds with what one would normally expect. He took a particular interest in Juliette and Rebecca, it seems, but no apparent interest in Katya at all despite her numerous attempts to bed him. Rebecca's supposed ability to predict future events was obviously of interest, though what fascinated him about Juliette is harder to define. Much later, Juliette would write (in personal correspondence with a typical absence of punctuation):

30

He perceived in me something which despite all my learning since I find difficult to properly describe... it was as if some fragment of himself or of his own heritage had become caught up in my blood. I felt they [the Doctor and Scarlette] wished me to *become* something and I felt they were in some accord as to what.

(Note the mention of blood, a theme that reoccurs throughout the surviving documents: it's significant that traditions like Scarlette's often place great importance on the menstrual cycle and describe a female's first true sexual act as a 'blooding'. Although Juliette sadly kept no journal of her own, from what's known of her it's fair to say that she'd already begun to develop something of a *talent*, one which she can hardly have understood in depth. The Doctor and Scarlette may both have wanted to develop – or exploit? – this.)

What were the Doctor's intentions in the House, then? All accounts agree that the work of the women disturbed him a little, possibly a result of his reported travels through more restrained lands, but he always made an effort to judge people by their own standards and never interfered in the primary business of the House. It was Scarlette who looked after the practical day-to-day concerns of the seraglio. The Doctor repeatedly stated that his mission was simply to solve the mystery of the *babewyns*, a mystery in which he felt he had a personal stake, but how did he intend to make the House the 'last bastion against the Beast' described by Scarlette?

To answer this, we should consider the thirteen envelopes distributed by Scarlette from the night of the ball onwards. Though it's not possible to give the personal names of those who received them, it *is* possible to list the 'orders' to which they were sent. The following inventory is taken directly from Scarlette's documents. In some places the handwriting is illegible, which is unsurprising. Given that it was a rule of society that educating girls was a waste of time, and that only a clerk would be vulgar enough to need good handwriting anyway, it's something of a miracle she was literate at all (and in at least two languages, too).

- *The Order of Saint Francis of Medmenham* [i.e. the Hellfire Club, still technically in existence but quiet since 1770].
- *The Grand Lodge of British Freemasonry, 33rd Degree or Higher.*
- *The Church* [some disdain here, possibly].
- *The Ereticy* [Russian witch-cult, ostensibly patronised by the Empress Catherine herself].

31

- *The Personal Attention of Cardinal de Rohan* [French nobleman, known for both his gullibility and his interest in the occult].
- *Family* [this item written in the Doctor's hand].
- *The Grand Lodge Temple of St Andrew's Trust* [the American movement: curious, as the Lodge should have been Scarlette's worst enemy].
- *The Mayakai.*
- *Mrs Gallacher's House of Flagellation* [another London establishment, opened in 1778 to much acclaim].
- ??? [this item represented by a Chinese pictogram].
- *The Followers or Family of Mr Mackandal of Saint-Domingue* [religious/political guerrilla movement in the French West Indies].
- ??? [the handwriting on this item is unreadable].
- *The Attention of the Service* [more on this later].

Not exactly a 'Who's Who' of high society, then. But if Lisa-Beth's account is accurate, with the Doctor describing pieces of an ancient lore scattered throughout humanity, then possibly the list represents a directory of those groups whom he believed had kept part of that lore… though the reference to Mrs Gallacher is admittedly puzzling. So was it true, as Lisa-Beth suspected, that the Doctor and Scarlette wished to unite all these factions? Pooling the 'ancient wisdom', in order to revive the traditions of the Doctor's people and therefore defend London (or Britain, or even the world) against the *babewyns*, whatever they might have been?

If so, then it would have been quite a task. Even apart from the differences between these groups – it's difficult to imagine, for example, the followers of Mackandal fighting alongside the French slavemasters responsible for culling so many of their people – it mustn't be forgotten that the House of Scarlette was largely considered an oddity. Even with Lisa-Beth on board, girls like Katya were beginning to grow restless with Scarlette's running of the establishment, and Katya was presumably the envoy by which the Doctor hoped to convey a red envelope to the Russian *Eretics* and thereby to Catherine the Great.

Two other points should be considered in understanding the plans of the House. First, the time the Doctor had spent with Rebecca on his arrival in London. It's already been explained that Rebecca spent some time preparing a card-reading for the Doctor, but in the same amused section of the 'Sabbath Book' it's also claimed that once, the women of the House found the Doctor and Rebecca surrounded by several entire *decks* of cards, as if attempting to inspect the fate of an entire world.

'A very very bad place,' the Doctor says, in the story, as he grimly examines the future. 'The question is, is it where we've got to go, or where we are *now* after things go wrong?'

Secondly, there's the visit the Doctor received on the night of the ball. For the most part the Doctor never kept a journal either, which means that the exact events are lost to time; but the basics are clear enough. While Scarlette was making her big entrance in the hall, the Doctor was physically attacked, by a guest who can only have entered the House through the rear (pantry) door. If the Doctor was indeed planning a war, with the House as his base of operations, then this was where it began.

A CERTAIN KIND OF WARFARE

The name *Mayakai* should be explained at this point. It was the name of a race which ceased to exist in the late eighteenth-century, any genetic survivors of the *Mayakai* people having been subject to such inter-breeding that none can be truly said to have been alive even by the middle of the nineteenth century. Like the Samoans or the inhabitants of Easter Island, the *Mayakai* were Polynesian, occupants of one of the minor Pacific island-groups. But unlike the people of Rapa Nui they left behind no impressive stone heads, no major monuments, no evidence of their remarkable interests. Yet their legacy is perhaps more important, as one of the 'secret springs of events little known', than any number of prehistoric artefacts.

There was something of an obsession with Polynesians in eighteenth-century England. The first South Sea Islander to set foot on British soil did so in 1760, and it's impossible to imagine the impact this must have had. The people of London had seen Africans, and Turks, and Chinese: but this newcomer to the city, this big, powerful-looking man who wasn't *quite* black, who wasn't *quite* an Arab, who wasn't even *quite* Oriental… he must have seemed genuinely alien, a living olive-skinned idol dressed up in society clothes. It must have endeared him to the nation, too, when on meeting King George III himself – and this, remember, in an age where protocol was so tight that the King refused to let Pitt the Elder *sit* in his presence, even though one of Pitt's legs was practically dropping off from gout – the visitor addressed his majesty with the immortal words: 'How do, King Tosh.'

The obsession with the Polynesians lasted as long as to 1779, in fact, when Commander Cook had his skull smashed in on the shores of Hawaii and obscure tribes suddenly seemed a lot less amusing. But the contribution of the *Mayakai* was special. The *Mayakai*, for cultural reasons almost impossible to imagine, felt they had a certain special relationship with time. The first westerners to meet them failed to understand a great deal of their vocabulary, simply because many of their nouns related to things they couldn't simply point at. Just as the Eskimos specialise in words for 'snow', the *Mayakai* specialised in words that described the shape of time, the size of time, the *direction* of time: or at least, that was the conclusion etymologists would reach over two hundred years later, when the old accounts would be re-evaluated. Much of the *Mayakai* vocabulary is subject to guesswork, but the one inescapable conclusion is that they saw the world much as the *tantrists* saw it. They didn't need muscular techniques, and they didn't need rituals. For the *Mayakai*, it was a part of the culture.

The idea that one of these strange and incomprehensible people should have attended Scarlette's ball seems peculiar enough in itself, even if Scarlette had indeed been partly tutored by one of the *Mayakai* brought to Britain in the 1770s (as stories suggest). But the notion that a *Mayakai* could have crept into the House unseen... it seems to beggar belief, and only later events can really explain it.

It was towards the end of the ball, when the guests were summoning hackney cabs and discreetly disappearing into the snow outside, that the Doctor's prone body was found: either in the rear office, or (less likely) in the cellar study. It was Juliette who found him. Having discharged her duty admirably at the ball, Juliette was instantly 'shocked and concerned' by her discovery, as the ring on her left hand bound her to the Doctor as much as it bound her the House. She responded to the crisis by (typically) calling Scarlette away from the remaining guests, careful to disguise her panic. By the time Scarlette reached the bruised, prostrate Doctor, he was beginning to regain consciousness.

It immediately became obvious that he'd been attacked. Someone had entered the House by the pantry entrance, assaulted him, and departed. The obvious questions were *who* and *why*. The assailant had vanished without trace, leaving the Doctor battered and helpless, so the attack couldn't have been an attempted assassination even if there'd been a reason for such a thing. Was it a warning, then? And as for the *who*... this is where accounts become muddied. Scarlette herself fails to go into detail in her journal, and though Lisa-Beth records a few theories there are important pieces of information missing.

In retrospect, the reason for Scarlette's silence begins to make sense. The Doctor knew, right from the start, who his attacker had been and why the assault had occurred, although all he'd say at the time was that he'd evidently 'attracted the attention' of hostile forces. Following his recovery, a conversation took place between him and Scarlette, a comparing of notes which Scarlette didn't wish to record. Partially, this may have been because the Doctor had recognised the attacker as one of the *Mayakai*, whom Scarlette had previously considered to be friends and allies. But there was another reason. Recording the rumours in the House, Lisa-Beth states that Scarlette asked Juliette to leave the room during her conversation with the Doctor, which Juliette dutifully did. Yet one word Juliette heard the Doctor say, the word which had caused Scarlette to ask for privacy, was: 'Sabbath'.

This word had a particularly bad resonance for Scarlette. The reason will become obvious soon enough.

It's best to pause here and look over the facts. We will assume the Doctor's intention at the House was to marry together those secretive factions which had somehow retained a 'lost knowledge', but one of them seems to have sent a representative whose mission was to physically intimidate him, as if to warn him off. Add to this the fact that a name from Scarlette's own past was in some way involved, and the word 'politics' hardly seems big enough. 'Intrigues' might be more accurate.

But there's something here that's easy to miss. The fact is that *the attacker was easily capable of overpowering the Doctor and rendering him unconscious*. The Doctor was no helpless, foppish aristocrat. Apart from his obvious ability at swordplay, he was (to varying degrees) an adventurer, an escapologist, an athlete, a pugilist and an amateur inventor. It's hard not to think of Lisa-Beth's claim, that during the fencing practice with Scarlette the Doctor's blade 'hung in the air' as if suspended by its own private kind of time. From all reports, the Doctor seems to have been able to face down the greatest dangers by this remarkable awareness of the space and time around him. Yet his assailant apparently had no difficulty in rendering him helpless, the marks on his face (according to Lisa-Beth) 'like little lumps of red tar'.

Of course, the Doctor was known to be sick when he arrived in London, an unexplained distemper which he claimed he'd been suffering for some years and which had recently been worsening. But he was by no means incapable. Was it the *Mayakai*'s special awareness of time, an awareness perhaps much like the Doctor's, that allowed the attacker to do such damage with so little effort?

The question would become more important later on, when it would be revealed that the assailant had indeed been a *Mayakai* warrior (one of few to survive the great plague devastation of 1773), who'd entered the House robed in pure black and quickly been spirited away again, by persons unseen. It was this warrior who'd mentioned the word 'Sabbath' to the Doctor, and who'd caused him such damage.

But for now, that information was only known to the Doctor and Scarlette. It was hidden from the other women of the House, for obvious reasons. Already anxious about Scarlette's over-ambitious plans, how would they have felt if they'd been told that the Polynesian warrior who'd defeated their 'elemental' had been a sixteen-year-old girl?

2
London

On March 20, 1782, the government fell and a new era of history began: an era not marked simply by a new administration, but by a struggle just as fundamental as the one grinding to a bloody halt in America. Within days a new government stood in Parliament, with the increasingly distressed King insisting that the Opposition (already making bets on how long the old fool would last) and his own supporters should form the ministry together. It was an uneasy alliance, and nobody expected it to work. Many were of the opinion that soon things would fall horribly apart again, and that the chaos of 1780 would return to the capital.

Naturally, exactly the same description applied within the walls of the House on Henrietta Street. As above, so below.

In addition to those notable 'Votaries of Venus' who lived in the House – Juliette, Rebecca, Lisa-Beth, Katya – there was one more young lady who deserves to be mentioned here. Her name was Emily Hart, and although she wasn't a permanent member of the household she certainly visited the House on occasion: from what's known about her, it's unlikely that she was a true proponent of the *black coffee* arts in the way that, for example, Lisa-Beth was. Emily was an attractive, skittish, auburn-haired sixteen-year-old, pretty but possibly a little on the childish side. Her letters suggest a young woman with an overenthusiastic love for drama and passion, inclined to sweep her arm across her forehead and cry out 'o, woe is me!' at the slightest tragedy. Probably not an actual *demi-rep*, she was kept as a mistress by a politician named Greville – one of the many who lost his position with the fall of the old Prime Minister – and by April 1782 she'd been moved by him into an address on Oxford Street (being a rough, undeveloped road in London surrounded by fields).

A flighty girl with a habit of becoming affectionate with everyone she met, she's worth mentioning because it's thanks to her that some of the most detailed descriptions of the House have been preserved. It's in one of her letters, for example, that the first description of the Doctor's study/laboratory can be found (in her usual messy, over-excited scrawl):

O! It is a strange and alkemical place. All around there are vats and such in glass, full of things I know not what that swim in water. There are devises that crackel with lightening, that even Mr. Franklin in America [sic: Franklin was in Paris at the time] I am sure would not touch. All is lit by oil and the sparks from the devises...

There is a girl, who helps Doctor _____ with his experimants. Her name is Juliette and she is quiet, but has been never less than plesant to me. She stands by with the gratest patience while the Doctor perfects his devises or even cuts into flesh... but never does she complain and once she smiled at me in a most anxious manner when it was the Doctor's buisness to perform an examination of an animal... the Doctor too is most polite and funy, but he will not spare the feelings of a lady when about his work. He is I think too absent minded to be delicat.

Yesterday there was the body of a beast on the table in the middle of his study. It was an ape, which he tyed to the table though it was quite dead. When I came down into the study he was slicing into the chest of the animal making a grate deal of fuss over it, and Juliette thought I should look away though I confes I could not help myself but look.

There can be no doubt at all that the 'beast' on the Doctor's table was one of the *babewyn*-creatures. As Emily's letter was written in April, it's possible that Lisa-Beth's aid was enlisted to summon the beast directly to the House, though one can only wonder who might have assisted her in such a 'ritual'. Some of the Doctor's notes from these autopsies survive. His handwriting is almost unreadable, but the rough sketches show what's clearly meant to be the internal physiognomy of the animals. What's puzzling is that, if the pictures are to be believed, the animals had *very little* physiognomy at all. Beneath the skin, the drawings suggest enormous blank spaces, and in some pictures the Doctor has filled in the blanks with large question-marks. Yet Emily's letters record that the Doctor removed several 'large and distresing parts', i.e. organs, from the beast.

What are we to make of this? Or of the Doctor's claim, again recorded by Emily, that 'the animals possessed none [organs] other than those that were expected'? The belief the Doctor seems to have reached, unscientific as it sounds, is that in some way the *babewyns* weren't actual animals as such: as if they stayed alive by sheer will, and their physiognomy was designed just to satisfy the investigator. This kind of mystical biology was quite common in the eighteenth century (q.v. the commonly-held belief that entire toads could thrive inside the human intestinal tract), and it's not surprising that an eccentric like the Doctor should have subscribed to it.

Emily didn't just record the study. Her letters also record her opinions of many of Scarlette's acquaintances and 'employees', and her opinion of Lisa-Beth wasn't high. According to Emily, during her first month at the House Lisa-Beth loudly sneered at Scarlette's running of things, considering the Mistress of the House to be poor at handling money (probably a fair point, given Scarlette's other interests). Lisa-Beth was known to have unfortunate connections in high society, clients whom even Scarlette's women wouldn't have deigned to do business with.

Indeed, it's likely that it was only through the Doctor's insistence that Lisa-Beth's presence was tolerated in the House at all. Although he wasn't as close to her as he was to Juliette, he must have seen something in Lisa-Beth he recognised.

Once again, it's wise to consider the books which Lisa-Beth brought to the House. Her most recent acquisition was Johan Wessel's *Anno 7603*, first published in 1781, a story in which a faerie transports a pair of lovers (the hero and heroine) to a society nearly six thousand years in the future, where men are cast in the roles of women and vice versa. To the modern reader, this might seem a twee fairy tale, but its significance can't be underestimated. Quite simply, *Anno 7603* was *the first work ever published in the western world which related directly to travel through time*. In the past, there'd been numerous myths and legends about characters falling asleep for a hundred years, or finding themselves stuck in a world where time froze and eternal day or night fell upon the world: but here, for the first time, was a fable in which time was something one could move *through*.

Is it really coincidence that such a book should have been owned by someone like Lisa-Beth? However ruthless she might have liked to be, she must surely have been fascinated by such an overt suggestion of her own practices. The Doctor must have felt they had something in common.

In fact, he had more reason to be wary of Lisa-Beth than he knew at the time.

In March and April, Lisa-Beth was still frequenting the Shakespeare's Head in Covent Garden. The tavern was a known centre for prostitutes and libertines of all classes and descriptions. Those who could avoid the frequent and vicious drunken brawls were encouraged (for a certain price) to ogle the bare-breasted women who danced on the tables or squirmed half-naked on the floor. More importantly, though, it was a major stalking-ground for agents from the British secret service.

The Service had no real name in this era, and in its covert practices there was a streak of darkness that's hard to accurately describe. The occult interests of the British spymasters were well-known, even at the time. After all, the Service had been founded in the Elizabethan era by John Dee, who was not only a master of espionage but also a man who used bizarre cryptographic codes to communicate with what he believed to be angels and demons (and this great spy-magician's own personal code-number was 007, such a ludicrous historical fact that modern researchers often assume it has to be some kind of latter-day joke). When the Service was expanded and restructured at the start of George II's reign – so that, by the time of the American war, it was swallowing up most of the country's intelligence budget – many of those in the King's court were either practising occultists or at the very least Freemasons. The assassins of the Service weren't simply hired thugs, but philosophers as well as killers, keepers of secrets in every respect. *The Service* was, of course, one of the thirteen names on Scarlette's list.

Lisa-Beth's journal tells the story best. On the first day of April, Lisa-Beth met with an agent of the Service at the Shakespeare's Head. Posing as a libertine with an interest in *black coffee*, the agent paid Lisa-Beth in hard cash for information regarding operations at Scarlette's House. The Service had read the contents of its red envelope, and had been suspicious. The Doctor and Juliette, rather than Scarlette, were the most important subjects of discussion. Lisa-Beth informed the agent (whom she simply called 'R_____') that some magical/symbolic ceremony was certainly being prepared, in which Juliette's heritage and virtue – for 'virtue' read 'virginity' – were both important considerations. Lisa-Beth then suggested to R_____ that if he had a personal interest in *black coffee*, she could show him a thing or two that would make more sense of events at the House. She also suggested that she knew things about Juliette which neither the Doctor nor Scarlette had discovered.

The term *black coffee* is an interesting one. 'Coffee-house' was an established euphemism for 'brothel', especially in Covent Garden, but only those of Scarlette's tradition seemed to have used the word 'coffee' as a codeword in itself. *White coffee* was their name for the standard form of business practised across the city. *Black coffee*, on the other hand, was the name given to those somewhat arcane special services in which both Lisa-Beth and Scarlette were so well trained. What's most interesting is that the term *black coffee* hadn't yet entered the common parlance as meaning 'coffee without milk', so it's possible that like so many other things – the song 'Here We Go Round the Mulberry Bush', for example – the phrase originated amongst the prostitutes of London and then spread to the rest of society.

But the fact remains that within weeks of arriving at the House, Lisa-Beth was already selling information on Scarlette's activities to those parties whom the Doctor hoped to recruit. Her reasons for doing this were far more acute than anyone might at first assume.

POLITICAL ANIMALS

Whenever there was a change in the government, it was customary for Members of Parliament to re-offer themselves for election. The old administration had fallen, the King had felt the rug being pulled out from under him, and the men of the Opposition were moving in for the kill: but many saw the Opposition as untrustworthy, as libertines and gamblers and revolutionaries, so it was important in those first few weeks for the new blood to make a good impression. They did this by staging rallies in London which, in retrospect, come across as the first truly modern political campaigns. (It's difficult defining eighteenth-century party politics, mainly because, by today's standards, both sides were right-wing. It's enough to say that the Opposition was made up of Whigs, those who opposed the divine right of the King and advocated strength through free trade, while the King's followers were known – disparagingly – as Tories. Odd as it may seem, the blasphemous, depraved, church-baiting occultists of the Hellfire set were all Tories... even the Earl of Bute, the hero and mentor of the King as a child, was a covert member of the Hellfire Club. But then, you'd hardly expect a group of wenching black magicians to be *democratic*.)

The first rally was held in London at the start of April, in support of the infamous Whig and Westminster MP Charles Fox: a fat, gargoyle-faced man with bushy eyebrows, much-loved by opponents of the government despite his habits of playing cards for twenty-four hours straight and spitting on the carpet in polite company. It was almost as if a grand society ball had been somehow poured out on to the streets of the city. Huge crowds gathered to cheer, jeer, or just see what everyone else was doing. The roads were lined with banners of blue-and-white, the colours of Whig society, while 'FOX' ribbons were colourfully scattered throughout the crowds. The glamorous women of the Whig party moved through the mob, fox-tails in their hats, suggesting that some American-style revolution was on its way to London to personally dispatch the

41

King (or 'Satan', as Fox so charmingly called him). Leading the women's delegation was the Duchess of Devonshire herself, that most celebrated of political celebrities, finding herself at the forefront of English history and not for the last time.

The Doctor was there, in the crowd. So was Juliette. So was Rebecca. Scarlette wasn't, and it's not hard to see why. The Whigs chose blue-and-buff as their colours because they'd been the colours of General Washington's army in America, and for Scarlette that would only have brought back memories of the curse of Matthew Crane. Also, the shops had started selling fashionable fans painted with the Duchess of Devonshire's likeness – sex appeal brought to politics for the first time – and Scarlette, who later admitted that her kind's need for secrecy was a major irritation, would only have been jealous that another great would-be adventuress was getting all the attention. She may not have been a royalist, but Scarlette wore the red and black of the Hellfire set. On April 3, she would have found herself chronically out of fashion.

There were many women of the streets at work in that crowd, either looking for custom (even in broad daylight) or picking pockets. And there was the Doctor, with his own little coterie of *demi-reps*, albeit with a very different purpose. The Doctor was anxious that day, as he later confided to Scarlette. Rebecca was, as ever, distracted and unconcerned, content to watch as the dumpy little form of Fox himself appeared on the podium above the cheering heads of the crowd. Juliette was typically quiet, taking in the scene around her whenever she took her eyes off the Doctor. It's easy to imagine the Doctor himself urgently scanning the crowd, looking for the disturbance which he knew was inevitable.

At around four o'clock in the afternoon, Rebecca nudged the Doctor's arm and nodded through the crowd, towards a woman – her name never recorded – leading a well-dressed gentlemen out of the throng and in the direction of a well-known Coffee-Shop. The Doctor agreed that the three of them should follow, and Juliette's initiation into his 'war' truly began.

It was a good month for political initiations. Some time later, on April 20, the King held court at St James's Palace to meet with the Whigs who'd pushed their way into the government. It was supposed to be a 'Drawing Room', one of those events at which the King and Queen would regularly meet with the lords and ladies of society, but the King was so thoroughly dejected at the thought of handing over power to ugly little men like Fox that instead of holding the usual ceremony he just sat grumpily in his chair while the Whigs filed into the hall looking smug. Tradition held that *any* lady or gentleman was welcome at such a meeting, and somehow both Scarlette and Lisa-Beth were there to witness the new political age being clumsily born. Perhaps the sorcerors of the Service gave them leave to enter.

The reason for the visit was clear, however. Scarlette, already in the process of uniting the more *dubious* elements of high society, wanted to show Lisa-Beth the battlefield on which they were now playing. Like the Doctor, Scarlette knew how important it was for all the 'soldiers' of the House to be of one mind. There was a tradition, in seraglios run by women, that after a while the biological cycles of all the women in the House would synchronise: that when 'the Prince' came every lunar month, it was as if the House *itself* were bleeding. This was what occurred on Henrietta Street that April. The House was getting into the rhythm of a new and terrible world order. The question is, was the rhythm set by Scarlette or by the Doctor?

Mere yards from the body of the King himself, the two courtesans stood in the select crowd of spectators and respectfully bowed as the King grudgingly passed the symbolic garter to the senior Whigs. Scarlette noted that Lisa-Beth acted with great decorum, not scowling, swearing or even shuffling her feet. It's reasonable to say that Lisa-Beth knew at least as much as Scarlette did about how to behave around the upper classes. In fact, Scarlette must have been far more uncomfortable than Lisa-Beth was. To see the friends of America given such power… it can hardly have helped that the Whigs were handed a *garter*, the traditional symbol of witchcraft recognised for over a hundred years.

But earlier, on April 3, the 'synchronisation' of Juliette was to be far more disturbing than a simple attendance at a society function. After Rebecca pointed out the nameless prostitute in the crowd, she and her associates followed the woman and her client into the Coffee-Shop, only to see them vanish through a rear door and into a small backstreet nearby. What's most notable about all this is that, to the Doctor, the idea of chasing after a prostitute and her client was a perfectly straightforward task. The streets behind the shop were narrow, spaces between the rear walls of buildings rather than actual thoroughfares. Given the nature of the time, then, it's entirely believable that a streetwalker might have taken her client there even in the afternoon. Few people would have passed by, and those that did would have been wont to turn a blind eye, especially if the gentleman were a *gentleman*.

It's impossible to say exactly how many *babewyns* were sighted in London during the first two months of the Doctor's war. Accounts are many, but as with the story of Anne-Belle Paley many of them are almost certainly folklore, older tales of escaped wild animals given a sexy new dimension by the rumours of what was happening on Henrietta Street. And the newspapers were hardly likely to report drunken tales of cannibal apes told by the ladies of Covent Garden, even if such tales were all the rage in coffee-houses. But the manifestation behind the Coffee-Shop, in which Juliette came face to face with the horror ahead for the first time, can't have been the only such incident since the night of the ball. The only real description of the event comes from young Emily, and though she doesn't name her source it's easy to see that the story was related to her by Juliette:

> Such horror! It was a *thing*, I am told, such as in any zoological garden, but if it had bin fed on raw meat or even (dare I say) human flesh. The ape had a bloody snout and jaws that mite have dripped the blood of its victims. There was spit around its mouth and it had claws that swung like blades. O my dear Lady, the face of the thing describ'd to me was enough to make me feel quite ill. It could have bitten a man in two, I'm told, but the worst thing was its *family*, for just as sure as it stood there in the alley there were a hundred others of its kine only waiting for there opportunity to make themselves known.

This may well all be exaggerated, but it makes a point. When Lisa-Beth had reported her own experience at her rooms, there had only been one *babewyn*, and it had been summoned (real or imagined) by the practice of *black coffee*. But two weeks later, things had worsened. As the prostitute behind the Coffee-Shop isn't even named, she probably wasn't known to anybody at the House and therefore would have most likely been a *white coffee* girl. Assuming the Doctor and friends had followed the woman and her client at speed, the encounter in the back-street can hardly have begun by the time the creature appeared: Emily's account suggests that it launched itself at 'my friend' (Juliette?) as soon as it had materialised, with the unfortunate prostitute and her client vanishing amidst a fury of screaming, 'still unbraced'. It hadn't been some obscure ritual that had called this beast forth, but a perfectly normal, if sordid, backstreet transaction. If the woman had used any form of *tantra*, then it could only have been a mild version, perhaps picked up from one of London's many foreign prostitutes. No doubt it was only the special 'sensitivity' shared by Rebecca and the Doctor which had led them to the scene in time.

There's a sense here that the *babewyn* attacks were becoming more random, less predictable. And not all of them involved prostitutes. In the months that followed, there'd be similar 'savage animal' stories as far afield as Ostend and the French West Indies. Like cautionary tales, there was to be an underlying theme in these folk stories that the victims had been attacked because they'd *done* certain things which were best left alone. It's notable, too, that the Coffee-Shop incident occurred in a dirty alley. In the old days, no real gentleman would have considered such a tryst outside a House, and it was the lure of these female-run Houses that had made many women in London rich enough to own vast tracts of Covent Garden... far more than a supposedly *respectable* woman would have been allowed to achieve. A Puritan might have argued that with the arrival of the apes, the professional women of London were paying the price for their success.

Evidently the Doctor felt that he was capable of holding off the beasts, at least in small numbers. Scarlette calls his method for dispelling the apes a 'banishing', and it's possible he may have taught the technique to Rebecca soon after his arrival on Henrietta Street. It's also possible that he was attempting to teach Juliette the same thing, which might be why, despite his great regard for her, he brought her to attend the Coffee-Shop manifestation. In Lisa-Beth's notes, there's the implication that the ring he gave to Juliette was in some way a weapon, or at least a protection against the monsters, despite the fact that by April Lisa-Beth knew full well what the real significance of the item was.

Emily states that Juliette 'was ask'd once more by Doctor _____ after that whether she wished to *assist* him further' (notice the emphasis on *assist*, implying something much greater), and Juliette did her duty, as usual, by telling him that she did. Perhaps significantly, Emily also records that 'my friend came away from the terrible thing with her dress splashed by its beastly blood, from jaws where it had bit its kine to be first into the lite'. Again, the image of blood and blooding, the hint that from this point on Juliette was *marked* and that there was no way back for her now.

Perhaps the Doctor wished there had been. There was certainly a lot on his mind. By April he'd been at the House for six weeks, but he understood that it wasn't his real place of power. Scarlette's journal relates that one evening, she found him staring into the looking glass on her dressing-table. She watched him for a while, before realising that his attention seemed fixed on his beard and moustache. From time to time he'd raise his hand to stroke it, as if he couldn't quite believe the reflection was his own. It's worth repeating their conversation in full.

SCARLETTE: Do you feel well?

DOCTOR [after some hesitation]: It's all right. I think I've just worked something out.

SCARLETTE: Oh yes?

DOCTOR: I think I know how to change myself into pure energy. Which means, I suppose, that I could move as fast as light.

SCARLETTE [playfully]: Impressive. How would you do it?

DOCTOR: Well, it wouldn't be easy. It'd need a lot of concentration. I'd have to slowly self-adapt my biology. The tricky part's forcing my body to convert the cell formations without disturbing the overall balance. It'd take a lot of practice and meditation.

SCARLETTE: Oh? How *much* meditation?

DOCTOR: I'd say it should take me about… ohhh… three thousand years. Less, if I could find a way of stopping myself getting distracted.

SCARLETTE: Three thousand years. To become a creature of pure light.

DOCTOR: I'm trying to decide whether it'd be worth the bother.

Odd as it might sound, there *is* a connection between this conversation and the Doctor's beard. It's hard to escape the impression that the Doctor was unsure of his role in the struggle of Henrietta Street; that his new position, as House elemental and co-owner of a seraglio, was outside his usual frame of experience; that he was starting to feel unsure of the limits of his person. Scarlette states that he had no beard when he arrived in February, and it's easy to feel that he grew it as a deliberate change, just to see whether he *could*. Described by many as a man of habit, the Doctor was starting to see some great and terrible change in the universe around him, just as the whole of London society was. He must have wondered whether he himself should be engulfed by that change, and being who he was he saw little difference between growing a beard and metamorphosising himself into energy.

And there were other matters playing on his mind, other 'changes' he knew had to be made.

On the same day as her society outing at St James's, Lisa-Beth met once again with the mysterious R＿＿＿＿ at the Shakespeare's Head. This time she was evidently more direct with him, and as she didn't return to the House until the early hours in the morning it's even possible she may have been paid to perform some *black coffee* act. There are many contemporary reports of peculiar rites in the 'offices' of the Service, in which a single woman would be hired to act as a priestess in a symbolic sacrificial ceremony, standing naked in a star-shaped chamber during a ridiculous-sounding rite designed to 'bring vitality to the soil of Great Britain'. But at first she supplied R_____ with more information about the activities of the Doctor and Scarlette. Lisa-Beth told the agent that Juliette had been prepared for the ceremony to come, not just by her 'blooding' but in a more elaborate ceremony in which she was dressed and instructed by Scarlette herself. Lisa-Beth also revealed that the Doctor was making desperate moves to contact the more awkward names on the 'red list' of thirteen, something that apparently required the presence of what he called a 'Tardis'. And behind Scarlette's back – perhaps more to spare her feelings than anything – the Doctor had asked the other women to gather any information they could about an individual called 'Sabbath' who'd been present at the Gordon Riots in 1780, or about the dying Polynesian tribe called the *Mayakai*.

So it was that all this information ended up in the files of the Service. But the information wasn't all one-way. Lisa-Beth discovered much from agent R_____, including the fact that the five highest councillors of the Service had met to discuss the situation (no doubt in their star-shaped chamber), and that some of them were considering putting pressure on the watch to shut the House of Scarlette down. The King was in a precarious position, said the mandarins. His Majesty might not have known the first thing about demons, but the last thing he needed was some mad tart of a witch reminding people of the Hellfire Club and the excesses of the King's old court. Certainly, nobody in the Service was paying the slightest bit of notice to the red envelope their agent had received at the ball. The invitation inside, said R_____, was clearly an irrelevant fancy on the part of either Scarlette or her pet elemental.

Naturally, by this time Rebecca knew all about the contents of the red envelopes. The message inside each one took the form of an invitation, and one copy still survives. The card on which the invitation is printed is black, the calligraphy a sombre red in colour. The only thing that immediately needs explaining about the invite is the name given to the Doctor: 'Jack-of-the-Moon' or 'Flighty Jack' was a term used at the time to denote someone who dwelt on high-minded things at the expense of the everyday world, and there's no reason to think that this was supposed to represent a real name (or even a nickname) for the Doctor. It's also worth mentioning that the name 'Vierge' is also likely to be a false title used for the sake of convenience.

The card reads:

Your representative is cordially invited, on the first day of December, seventeen-hundred and eighty-two, to the wedding of DOCTOR 'MIGHT JACK-OF-THE-MOON' and MISTRESS JULIETTE VIERGE. The ceremony is to be held according to the strictest traditions at the Church of Saint Simon, St Belique; and in the Vault thereof. House colours will be observed throughout. Political colours will *not* be acceptable for ladies or gentlemen, except with the express permission of the House of Mistress Scarlette. All protocol will be considered while in Church by the parties involved.

A response would be appreciated at some time prior to December.

ACTS OF MAGIC

A city which might have been built for human beings, but with the rooftops collapsing into rubble and the bleak, endless weather wearing down the walls; buildings that once might have looked as fine as those of the Grand Tour cities, of Florence or Venice, faded to grey and reduced to drab, endless ruins; ditches full of bones where there should be canals; a dry, never-ending wind; the scent of animal dung and blood-matted fur on every corner; a hundred thousand idiotic apes, scratching and mating and chewing at each others' pelts in the debris; bloody, rheumy-eyed baboon-creatures lazily spreading themselves over the streets of bone; the all-pervading sound of grunting and howling, as the residents feed and sweat in the wreckage of a dead civilisation…

This was what lay ahead, according to the Doctor. Juliette is known to have dreamed of it on more than one occasion, as is Rebecca, and Lisa-Beth, and possibly even Scarlette herself. Perhaps the biological rhythms of the House's women had already started falling in line by April, synchronising their dreams as well as their bodies. Or perhaps the influence of the Doctor had pressed the importance of their mission on them so greatly that they couldn't help but dream the same dreams.

Or perhaps it was a kind of prophecy. At various times between March and May, the Doctor apparently changed his mind about whether the destroyed city was the fate that would befall the world if the House failed in its task, or simply the place from which the *babewyns* had come. But what's inarguable is that the vision disturbed Juliette greatly.

Right from the time when Scarlette obtained the House, Juliette had been given the room at the top and the front of the four-storey House, a cosy boudoir with a large window overlooking the narrow, cobbled byway of Henrietta Street. As the only woman in the House who *wasn't* available for hire by the gentlemen of the city, Juliette must have spent many an evening watching the men get out of the hackney cabs outside and nervously stroll up to the front door, wondering whether she'd eventually be asked to take up the same occupation as the other girls (although, as she must have known, she was expected to remain a virgin at least until the marriage ceremony). Dutiful as she might have been, it's not surprising that Juliette felt anxious and restless. She knew she was to be an important part of something, but she had no immediate role to play and nothing to do but assist the Doctor in his cellar. Did the dreams start to play on her mind?

Thanks to Emily, it's possible to say that the answer was a definite *yes*. Because from March onwards, Juliette was performing her own form of ritual in the privacy of her upstairs room. The Doctor was unaware of this, and at least once Scarlette had explicitly warned her not to attempt any kind of ritual without the guidance of the Master or the Mistress of the House. But like Scarlette herself, Juliette was inquisitive, and literate in both English and French. Alchemical texts were her favourite form of reading matter. She consulted several of the works in Scarlette's office, books in which Scarlette herself had only a passing interest. When she was sure that nobody in the House was likely to disturb her, she'd often sneak materials out of the Doctor's cellar and perform her own small experiments behind closed doors. Again, it's important to note that this wasn't out of any kind of ambition or personal desire. Juliette felt herself to be part of something she couldn't quite grasp, and most probably only wanted to understand it better. More than that, she perhaps felt she had a duty to something she couldn't quite define. Her exact words:

> 'I do love them [the Doctor and Scarlette] as much as I can. But I feel a great undertaking has been put before me… in which the world has never given me option. I would never wish to disappoint them.'

Her only confidante in these little 'dabblings' was Emily, who witnessed several of Juliette's experiments in the top-floor room. Emily records that on two occasions, Juliette mixed a variety of esoteric materials in one of the Doctor's glass beakers and surrounded it 'with such a variety of strange devises' (meaning occult charms rather than actual machines). The mixture of substances might sound scientific, in an amateur sense, but in fact Juliette's aims were ritualistic. The experiments were always accompanied by a large amount of ceremony and incantation, and once Juliette even managed to get hold of Scarlette's own personal totem – a piece of old, jagged glass, which Scarlette usually wore on a chain around her neck and to which she attributed great power (about which, more later) – to some effect. When the fumes from the combined chemicals filled Juliette's room, both she and Emily seem to have been overcome by the noxious vapours. In Emily's words:

> There was such an air [i.e. gas] in the room that I feard I mite choke. But when my eyes started to water I heard a crack and I saw the glass jug from the cellar had broken open. But, o! The peeces did not fly at all directions or fall. I saw them hang in the air for a moment after the jug broke. I thought this mite be the water in my eyes, but my friend was staring at the glass in an intens manner and saying her charms under her breath, so I knew that it was she who held them in place. It lasted a second or little more before the peeces flew out.

Some might argue that this was a demonstration of the 'potential' which the Doctor saw in Juliette. However, it seems more likely that (as Emily herself considered) it was an effect of the fumes: noxious gases can indeed make time seem to slow down, under certain conditions. This doesn't mean that Juliette's experiment was worthless, though. She'd been told to maintain her virtue, and so had set about entering a state much like the *Shaktyanda* of the *tantrists* through chemical/alchemical means. She was trying to alter time, or at least her perception of time, and with remarkable success. It's indeed lucky that this didn't lead to an infestation of the 'demons' so feared by the Doctor.

(Incidentally, it shouldn't be thought that Emily was just a giddy-headed, witless observer. When the artist Romney used the young Emily as a model for his painting of the mythical sorceress *Circe*, he portrayed her as a vivid, dark-eyed, secretive beauty. Perhaps there was more of a witch inside Emily than many of her friends suspected.)

Juliette's restlessness was echoed not just amongst the other women of the House, but in London in general. Beginning in the spring of 1782, there was an increasing hostility in the public and the press towards the city's prostitutes, an ill-feeling that seems hard to explain or justify. It's as though London's inhabitants *noticed* that something was wrong, even if they couldn't say exactly what and were hardly likely to attach any credence to stories of ape-faced monsters. More and more, the women of the seraglios were blamed for bringing some terrible moral catastrophe down on the heads of the English. The subtext of the many editorials in the press was that some terrible darkness was waiting to engulf the city, a darkness that the houses of leisure could only worsen.

The women of the House were cursed, then. Rebecca might have blamed herself for this, as if her impure blood had somehow brought shame to Covent Garden. Scarlette might have seen it in more ritualistic terms. After all, the March ball had been designed as a kind of ritual, to bring together the women and make their resistance known: the decor of the ball itself, the black-and-red drapes and blossoms, was almost a reflection of the blue-and-white balls held for the Whigs at Devonshire House. Scarlette might have said that *her* art was all about changing the mass-mind of the people, and she must have perceived society as a battleground where the forces of black/red magic and white/blue magic would meet. And ready to strike from the shadows, the real enemy: the apes, and anyone who might have been controlling them.

Lisa-Beth, on the other hand, already knew that the Service was turning against the seraglios. She doubtless would have understood that the mood of the press was largely controlled by such cliques: in the single year from 1782-83, around £2,000 (a massive amount in eighteenth-century terms) was spent by agents of the government on bribes and payoffs to newspaper editors. If the mood was changing, then it was with the consent, if not the actual backing, of the Service. Lisa-Beth's solution to this was presented to the House on the night of April 10, the very same evening that Juliette and Emily observed time slow down in the upstairs boudoir.

Lisa-Beth had been given a room on the ground floor of the House, into which she'd moved most of the furnishings and effects from her old residence near the menagerie. On that night she'd been seen taking a client into her room, definitely *not*, records Scarlette, one of the House's regulars. Apart from Katya, none of the other women were occupied on that evening. While Lisa-Beth attended to her gentleman, Scarlette, the Doctor, and some of the other women were in the main salon of the House, reclining on the red velvet *chaise longues* and engaging in the normal evening pursuits of cards and town gossip. The Doctor was apparently engrossed in a copy of the *Gentleman's Magazine*, most particularly the science pages.

At around half past nine, Lisa-Beth walked out of her room and addressed all those gathered in the salon, telling them that there was something she thought they ought to see. Curious, the others followed her back to her room, the Doctor and Scarlette at the front of the party.

The gentleman client lay on Lisa-Beth's bed, stripped to the pantaloons, his wrists and ankles tied to the bed's four posts (bondage was as great a part of eighteenth-century prostitution as it would be in later centuries). There was a gag in the man's mouth, and from the sweat on his face the gentleman in question was scared out of his wits. But most importantly, several words had been painted on to his chest in a thick red ink, words in an alphabet Scarlette didn't recognise but which she later described as 'almost Egyptian'.

All this was Lisa-Beth's work. When Scarlette asked, reasonably, *what on Earth she thought she was doing* – and while the Doctor simply looked curious – Lisa-Beth moved to the end of the bed, extended a finger in the man's direction, and spoke five simple words.

No record reveals these words. Whatever Lisa-Beth might have said, the effect on the man was immediate. His 'eyes widened like billiard-balls', and he immediately began to struggle (if one believes Lisa-Beth) or cry (if one believes Scarlette).

Even if the words themselves have been erased from history, their import is obvious. They were the five secret names of the Points of the Star, as represented by the Service's star-shaped room. The five names were the most secret of secrets in government circles, and by using them in this context Lisa-Beth was demonstrating a very real power. In retrospect it's clear what she'd been doing, since the beginning of the month. She'd been consorting with agents of the Service, indulging in *black coffee* with them, possibly even acting as a 'priestess' in their ceremonies. While the Service had believed her to be a mere woman of leisure, Lisa-Beth had carefully been digging out the Service's secrets, either by unravelling the ceremonies or by using her extraordinary musculature to seduce the answers out of the five gentlemen of the Star Chamber. True, she'd passed on the secrets of the House, but while they'd gloated over this information she'd quietly and efficiently prized far more powerful knowledge from her supposed paymasters.

The man on the bed was an agent of the Service, and Lisa-Beth had made the threat plain. If the Service continued to harass the House of Scarlette, then the sacred names would be distributed throughout Covent Garden and within a week every brothel-goer in central London would have these most secret words either written or tattooed on their chests. To the Service, symbols were power, none more so than the five Names of the Star which had been passed down by Dr Dee ten generations earlier. When written on the body, the words were intended to lend a great and holy strength to the Service's men. And if such power – real or simply imagined – were to be given to all and sundry… as Scarlette said, they now had the Service '*aux les couilles*'.

Shortly afterwards the man was untied, and left to go on his way, picking up his clothes and (as Scarlette records, with her usual rude humour) 'leaving the House with his tail between his legs'. Scarlette had always considered Lisa-Beth to be a mercenary, but Lisa-Beth knew which way the wind was blowing and by now had become convinced that the Doctor was their only hope of holding back the *babewyns*. Not only would this performance hopefully stay the Service's hand, it might also be used as leverage, to ensure the Service's attendance at the December wedding. The Doctor was said to be 'delighted' by this, although he confessed that Lisa-Beth's methods left him rather puzzled.

Lisa-Beth had proved without doubt which side she was on. More importantly, she'd shown that in spite of insurmountable odds, in spite of public hostility, aristocratic apathy, and the distrust of the thirteen groups on the 'red list', the plans of Scarlette and the Doctor could be put into operation. The Service had been cowed, if not exactly brought to heel, and the House still had another seven months in which to bring the other groups around. By this one ritualistic, magical, *symbolic* act, Lisa-Beth – unlikeliest of soldiers – had proved the war to be worth fighting.

But at roughly the same time, several factors were continuing to complicate matters. Just two floors above, Juliette was showing a kind of initiative that might have both disturbed and appealed to the Doctor. And meanwhile, at Westminster, other events had been set in motion.

The Countess and the Lord

When it came to ritualists, there was no solid line between one lodge and another. The Masons had links with the Service, the Service had links with the Ministers, and the Ministers slept with the *black coffee* artistes in the bagnios. Sooner or later, it was inevitable that factions would overlap and supposed enemies would find themselves on the same side. Such is politics.

For example, on April 16 the watchmen in charge of the territory just north of the Thames found something suspicious in the inner grounds of Westminster Abbey. It happened in the shadows of the western towers, and the watch had to bring in lamps before they could make sense of the scene, but at the centre of it all was a well-dressed middle-aged man who seemed to be engaged in some form of satanic practice. A circle had been scratched into the stone path around the side of the Abbey building, and inside that circle – the reason the watch had been alerted in the first place – was some species of bloody-snouted ape. The ape was in a fury, tearing and clawing at the air, as if the circle were in some way keeping it confined. Its heavy forelimbs were bleeding, as though it had torn its fingers to shreds ripping at a wall that wasn't there. The man, meanwhile, looked terrified when the watch appeared and began to blubber that none of this was his fault.

The watch knew when they were out of their depth, and via the 'gentleman's network' of Westminster called in people more qualified. Masonic archives reveal that the first two 'experts' called in to attend the scene were Lord _____ and the Countess of Jersey (neither of them are named in the archives, but the Countess at least is easy to identify from her description), who promptly dismissed the watch and attended to the matter themselves. After the Battle of the Saints and the ruination of the French fleet in the West Indies, things actually seemed to be going right for the new Britain, so the last thing these two establishment arcanists wanted was for somebody to rock the boat now.

These occult troubleshooters have already been described, in part. It's tempting to think that Lord _____ would have arrived at the Abbey in the same blood-red hood he'd worn to Scarlette's ball; and that the Countess, another attendee, would have arrived carrying her pipe. An ambitious, manipulative, somewhat vulgar but unquestionably seductive noblewoman, the Countess was known in society for her affiliations with both the more shadowy *demi-reps* and members of the royal family itself: in the future, she was to have a long-lasting affair with the Prince of Wales. Though she never smoked it at respectable society balls – God forbid – when attending the more sinister functions she was usually seen with a pipe, filled with a noxious weed which certainly *wasn't* tobacco. It was unladylike, but it was rumoured to induce celestial visions of some form. She despised Scarlette, despite receiving an invitation to the March ball, where many remarked that the blue smoke-rings from the pipe quite wilfully clashed with the colours of the House. (Aptly enough, the Countess was indeed one of the blue-and-white Whig brigade.)

The 'lost' Masonic archive at Musselburgh, Scotland, claims that this seemingly ill-matched pair – who'd apparently worked together before – wasted no time in getting to the bottom of things. The terrified man at the Abbey was a member of the House of Lords, described only as the Marquis of M_____. Both the Lord's Masonic lodge and the Countess's inner circle would have known about the *babewyn* threat, but even they must have been surprised to learn that this Marquis had summoned the ape intentionally. The ritual of summoning is described by the Masons in detail, but it's incredibly tedious and self-important, involving a variety of pseudo-mystical pentagrams and Greek incantations.

The reason for the Marquis's attempt to call and bind the ape? Because, he said, he'd been told to. He was in the employ of a higher power. While Lord _____ 'dispatched' the *babewyn*, the Countess demanded to know who or what this power might have been, and with some reluctance the Marquis told her that he believed his employer to be working for the Service.

Wheels within wheels, then. The Countess was convinced that no agent of the Service would do something so risky, particularly not in the occult 'hot zone' of Westminster Abbey, whose western towers had after all been designed by the architect Hawksmoor as a monstrous satanic joke. Yet the ritual used to call the beast did seem to have the Service's po-faced air about it. Both the Countess and the Lord must have realised the implication of this: that a Service ritualist, evidently a powerful and influential one at that, had acted alone for unknown reasons.

There were few things more dreaded then a rogue Serviceman. After all, master-agents were trained not just to be assassins but survivors of almost superhuman talent. Though the minor agents might have been little more than information-gatherers, the top men of the department were trained in all the arts of combat, subterfuge, psychology and mysticism. As disguise was an important element in fieldwork, it was a nigh-impossible task to even find a gifted Serviceman, let alone bring him down. Indeed, there's some evidence that the great mystique of the Service was really just a control mechanism, a way of balancing the agents, convincing them that they were part of a greater daemonic whole and that to break away from the organisation was to invite the wrath of hell itself, or at least the wrath of True Government. Similar practices had been employed ever since Dee's experiments with the Enochian language in Elizabethan times, a process best described in modern terms as 'brainwashing by angels'. So unsettling was the idea of a rogue ritualist that the Service even set up its own sub-clique in 1760, euphemistically known as the *rat-catchers*, to enforce the conditioning of the department. By 1782, only one renegade had ever escaped the rat-catchers' zealous eye.

Was a rogue Service agent responsible for this affair, then? The Countess and the Lord must have suspected as much, even before they managed to extract from the unfortunate Marquis the name by which his employer was known. The information didn't come easily, as the Marquis was under the impression that if he said too much then other agents of his employer would hunt him down to the ends of the Earth.

But surely, both Jersey and the Lord would have understood the significance of the name 'Sabbath'.

Back at the House, the Doctor was certainly beginning to. In the wake of Lisa-Beth's triumph over the Service, the Doctor spoke privately to many of the women in the House, giving each of them instructions and advice (but never actually *orders*) as to how they might prepare themselves for the challenge ahead. Now that she'd demonstrated her loyalty to Scarlette's faction, the Doctor seems to have opened up a little more to Lisa-Beth. It was only now, for example, that she started to understand the true significance of the marriage ceremony planned between the Doctor and Juliette. It had always been quite clear to her that it wasn't a bond of true love, although there's no doubt that the Doctor had the greatest affection for Juliette and that Juliette had the greatest respect for him. The Doctor spoke in hints, apparently always distracted by other matters, but gradually Lisa-Beth began to understand the symbolic significance of the wedding. She did, however, insist on referring to it as 'the virgin sacrifice'.

The dreams of the House's women also began to intensify. There were further visions of the realm of the beasts, particularly (no surprises here) during that time of the month when the House *en masse* was visited by the Prince. Sometimes human beings would be seen in the dreams, rendered limb from limb by the claws of hungry, demented apes. A throne was glimpsed, obviously made out of the stacked skulls of feeding-victims, and on it was perched a figure so dark and bloated that it became impossible to properly envisage. On one occasion the sky over the doomed city grew quite black, as if something dark and truly monstrous were gazing down on it. There was the general feeling that the apes were watching them, judging them, ready to impose their own bestial law on the House and its occupants.

Many of the women, Juliette especially, came to think of the Doctor as a tragic figure: an elemental cast out of his own world, trapped at the House perhaps as a kind of penance. It was as though he'd been removed from his place of power, and had the uncomfortable sense that he was interfering in things which were now none of his business. It's probably true to say that he often wondered whether Scarlette, with her fragments of ancient lore and her determination to pull the House together, could have done the same job without him. But Scarlette obviously felt she needed him around, perhaps because he was the best justification she had, the best proof that her tradition still had power.

Yet ironically, he still had to move behind Scarlette's back on occasion. The morning after Lisa-Beth's victory, the Doctor went to the top of the House to speak to Juliette in private. The exact conversation is lost to time, but they must have discussed many things, including their forthcoming marriage. Later, Juliette would tell Emily of the conclusion.

There was, said my friend, a certan *man* who was wanted by Doctor _____. Scarlette knew of the appearance and history of this *man*, but her hart was sore from it and it would do her no good to speak of it. It was the Doctor's thinking that this *man* had a certan knowlege of the terrible apes, but how or why he could not say. It was the task of my friend to use all her talents to find this *man*, who had many agents that mite have left trails behind them… the Doctor felt there was something in my friend which made her fit for this [but] perhaps this was to be an intation [initiation?] of a kind. The Doctor I'm told was most grave when he said this and did not know for sure whether it was rite to involv her in such danger. He told her she would have help, in that other elementals would be called to do her bidding.

The reference to 'other elementals' is the first indication that the Doctor had friends outside of the House who could be 'summoned' to give him aid. These unearthly friends, he told Juliette, would soon arrive at the House. He couldn't say when, as before he could call them he had to complete certain scientific work in his laboratory-study.

It's true that the Doctor was spending longer and longer periods downstairs. This could partly be explained by his work on the process of summoning, but there's another possible explanation. On the last day of the month, Scarlette knocked on the door and received no reply: there was no sound from within, not even the crackling of his electrical devices. Being the only one in the House who ever risked disturbing him, she opened the door and descended the stone steps into the cellar.

There she found the Doctor, a nearly burned-out lamp by his side, slumped over the big wooden table in the middle of the room. She took him to be asleep, but later realised that his state was closer to what might in modern terms be called nervous exhaustion. She thought it best not to awaken him, although in her journal she does pause to wonder how many hours he spent asleep or unconscious behind that door.

He'd been sick when he'd arrived in London, for reasons Scarlette couldn't deduce, but which she felt may have been related to the absence of his *Tardis*. Now he was obviously getting worse. And, ritualistic as she was, she couldn't help connecting his malady to the malady of the House itself. Lisa-Beth's victory wasn't enough to permanently lift the House's spirits, especially not when, on April 24, Katya was attacked in Maiden Lane: not by an ape, but by a crowd of drunks who tore off her dress and nearly left her scarred with a broken bottle before she managed to make her escape.

And there was one final ill omen. During the Whig campaign in Westminster, Charles Fox had asked several notable political figures to help him drum up support. One was an individual whom many still saw as a spokesman for liberty despite his reputation, an individual who'd been responsible for a great deal of damage in the past – who'd once even been thought of as insane – but who'd now repented and was eager to prove himself a force to be reckoned with in the new era.

His name was Lord George Gordon, instigator of the Gordon Riots of 1780. The skin of London continued to prickle.

3
England

A NIGHT OUT

In the first week of May, 1782, a box at the Drury Lane Theatre was reserved at the request of Miss Scarlette of Henrietta Street. This is remarkable in itself, given her reputation: boxes at the Theatre were generally the preserve of the particularly fashionable or royal. The names attributed to her party include 'Doctor J', also of Henrietta Street; Miss Juliette Vierge, to whom he was said to be engaged; Mr Fitzgerald Kreiner (a German, apparently, rumoured to be a distant relative of the royal Hanoverians); and Miss Anji Kapoor. When the party entered the box there was hissing from the crowds below, but this was nothing unusual. The Theatre was a noisy place, and the *bon ton* liked to judge their standing in society by the reaction they were given from the cheap seats. Scarlette would have been easy to recognise as one of the 'suspect' *demi-reps*, though she, of course, didn't even acknowledge the sound. She was reported to have had a satisfied smile on her face as she took her seat.

Because so many of the accounts of Scarlette come from Lisa-Beth, it's easy to see this Procuress of Henrietta Street as a woman living in a world of her own. But even apart from the great impact she obviously made on those around her, tales of her exploits are legion. She was said to have bested the famous dandy highwayman and wencher 'Sixteen-String Jack' in a drinking contest shortly before his public execution, and to have disarmed him of his weapon one-handed after he took the defeat badly. And she was just as formidable on the night of the Theatre visit. Arriving by hackney cab outside, her party had been met by a group of prostitutes from south of the river who abused her friends and threatened her with violence, stating that she was bringing disrepute even to *their* kind. According to one popular story, Scarlette responded to this by casually drawing a musket and pointing it at the leader of the women, saying: 'If it's blood you wish to see, then let it be on my hands.'

In fact, this story is apocryphal. The truth about the encounter was stranger yet, as later events would show.

Scarlette's demeanour was one of perpetual calm, and she appeared amused by events around her no matter what the threat. In this respect, she must have got on with the Doctor remarkably well. She spent more time in his company than any other individual at the House, leading to (entirely untrue) rumours that they were having an affair; that his marriage to Juliette was part of some dastardly plot masterminded by Scarlette herself; even that the Doctor was some demonic reincarnation of Francis Dashwood, a rumour given weight by the fact that the founder of the Hellfire Club had died (in suspicious circumstances, naturally) just weeks before the Doctor had arrived.

One night the Doctor and Scarlette spent the entire evening, alone, drinking wine in the salon of the House. Scarlette claims that they lay together on the floor, staring up at the rafters in the ceiling, trying to see through the wood and into *time itself*. This was punctuated by some giggling – even from the Doctor, it would appear – and the pair attempted to outdo each other with tales of their adventures, the Doctor claiming that he'd once been invited into the boudoir of Marie-Antoinette, Scarlette claiming that she'd once ridden a woolly mammoth (still not believed entirely extinct) which had been a gift to George III from Catherine of Russia. It was probably now that the Doctor made his notorious 'two hearts' claim, exactly the kind of story which would have been told by charlatans like Cagliostro in France. When either the alcohol or the meditation caused them to be successful in their efforts to see through the ceiling, Scarlette fashioned a pair of crowns for them to wear out of dyed paper and declared them to be 'the King and Queen of All Time'. The Doctor ostensibly stated that he was reluctant to become *any* kind of king, so Scarlette instead crowned herself the Queen and declared him to be her Physician in Ordinary. (She jokingly said that she was still waiting for somebody *truly* special to be her Physician in Extraordinary.)

At the Theatre, many members of the party were evidently nervous at the crowd's reaction, particularly Mr Kreiner and Miss Kapoor. They must have been taken aback by the audience, and probably put out by London society's habit of loudly talking through the performance about the latest scandals amongst the *bon ton*. Drury Lane was a place in which one was seen, not a place for seeing. Scarlette had chosen the performance believing it to be a fantastical story of 'unlikely adventures on the newly-discovered star, Georgium Sidius', but the information was inaccurate and she spent much of the evening using her discretion-glass to observe the other boxes.

There were more women waiting outside for them when they left. This time they spat at Scarlette and her friends. The Doctor urged Scarlette to ignore the distraction and move on, but Scarlette insisted on stopping right in front of the delegation of prostitutes. This is where the story of the drawn musket probably originates. Scarlette reached into the top of her dress, but the item she drew from her corset, dangling on a piece of cord, was no firearm.

It was a piece of jagged glass: the greatest surviving relic of the bloody, gothic events of 1762, when Mary Culver slit her own throat in the name of ceremony. Did the women outside the Theatre understand the importance of this totem, or was it simply Scarlette's determination that had an effect on them? Either way, all accounts agree that the leader of the women visibly flinched. There was no more jeering as Scarlette's party climbed into the cab and told the driver to head home.

It's worth stopping here to consider the nature of the two newcomers, Mr Kreiner and Miss Kapoor. They'd arrived at the House on the first day of May, one of the most important dates in the calendar of ritual, coming as it does straight after the mass wenching-and-exorcism ceremonies of Beltane. And it's true that according to Scarlette the newcomers had been 'summoned', though by her own admission the charms and totems used to call them had been the curious devices in the Doctor's study. Even so, May 1 was one of the House's 'bleeding days', and it was due to this (said Scarlette) that the Doctor's more mechanical experiments had succeeded.

The stories of the summoning are varied and contradictory. It's clear that *something* happened, and the one recurring theme is that of a 'great light', like 'an indoor comet' or even 'the great opening of a door'. There must surely have been much electrical crackling from the Doctor's study before the Doctor himself ran out of the door at the top of the stairs and excitedly warned everyone in the salon to take cover behind the furnishings. A lot of the women later described the experience in surprisingly biological terms, as if the energy came from within their own bodies. Juliette was one of those who saw 'blood before her eyes… and a series of visions'. She later claimed she'd seen the future, not just the world of the *Shaktyanda* but an *actual* future, in which she'd glimpsed a great metallic war-machine and realised that such things were inescapable. Scarlette herself could only comment that 'the horizon had opened' for a moment.

The end result was agreed on by everyone. Two human figures emerged from the doorway to the study, both of them stark naked and somewhat bewildered, the woman more put out by this than the man. Born out of the blood, fire and time so recurrent in the accounts, the

House immediately identified them as elementals. Their nudity was described by the Doctor as a 'teething problem'. (There is, of course, the possibility of some chicanery here. If the Doctor did indeed have something of Cagliostro's showmanship in him, then it's only fair to mention that Cagliostro himself used elaborate pyrotechnic trickery and weird alchemical fumes to work his 'miracles'.)

It's hardly surprising that Scarlette and her kin should so readily have accepted Fitz and Anji as elementals, or at least people from elsewhere. The previous year, Herschel had discovered a seventh planet orbiting the sun, which he'd named *Georgium Sidius* (George's Star) in honour of the King: Herschel was never one to let politics temper his judgement, or he might have called it *Washington's Star* instead. Herschel had made it quite clear that he expected the new world to be inhabited, but then, he expected *all* worlds to be inhabited, and this most famed of Royal Astronomers believed he was just a step away from categorically proving the existence of people on the lush and verdant grasslands of the moon. He also made a point that the sun was almost certainly occupied, under the hot surface ('we need not hesitate to say that the Sun is richly stored with inhabitants,' quoth he). The people of the new Seventh Planet were a recurring theme in theatre and literature, though mostly these aliens were of the man-in-the-moon variety. Next to the speculations of Herschel, the arrival of the Doctor's associates from some other realm of being would have seemed almost mundane.

The summoning of the elementals on May 1 must have been a welcome omen, because the mood was worsening by the day. Although the Service had ceased its press campaign, Scarlette was starting to become aware that the women under her were being tempted away from the House. One of the girls (her name isn't known) had already left by early May, and at least one other was considering a move upmarket to Marylebone. It was almost as if money was being supplied to other houses of leisure by some unknown source, giving them the resources to 'poach' the staff. This left Scarlette with a problem. In order for the Doctor's plans to succeed, the House had to operate as a seraglio, but with Scarlette's grim reputation finding new staff was almost impossible.

Her task was made harder still by the fact that she had ethics. In this respect, Lisa-Beth was right: Scarlette was a relic of the old days, when women of surprising virtue had kept orderly disorderly Houses and thus become some of the wealthiest landowners in England. But the age of the pimp was coming. Organised men would 'rescue' poor young girls from the gutters, giving them food and clothing until the only way the girls could pay them back was by selling themselves, quite legally, into the men's service. Scarlette would never have resorted to these methods, and as the women began to vanish around her she realised the extent of the difficulty.

Shortly after the arrival of Fitz and Anji, a meeting was held in the salon of the House with everyone in attendance. Fitz (dressed in ill-fitting knee-length socks and a waistcoat that was ten years out of fashion already) and Anji (in an old dress of Rebecca's) looked thoroughly uncomfortable while Scarlette asked the women whether there was anything they wanted to say to her face. Nobody spoke, but a few stared down at their shoes. Even Juliette looked uncertain, perhaps still shaken by the visions she'd had on May Day. Lisa-Beth notes that Scarlette gave Juliette an awkward glance during the long silence, apparently knowing what was waking up inside the girl's mind.

What was it that had caused the women to be drawn away from House and home? To understand that, it's necessary to move outside the confines of London and focus on events unfolding in Cambridge, where those two ill-matched investigators – the Countess and the Lord – were continuing to follow up the trail of the Westminster affair.

WAYS TO AVOID DROWNING

Cambridge had always had a morbid reputation, especially the ancient University. In the 1740s the notorious 'Appalling Club' had become extinct when its seven founder members had all been slain, one by one, the last few members apparently murdered in a sealed room by the ghosts of the earlier victims. Though all this had been smartly glossed over by the relevant authorities, and the alleged haunted area of the University had been hidden behind a hurriedly-constructed brick wall, Magdalene College was still something of a magnet for those with Masonic connections. If it happened once, went the argument, then how much else could we get away with there?

It was in a set of rooms at Magdalene that the unfortunate Marquis of M_____ was kept, following his discovery at Westminster. Though he wasn't in prison under the *law*, as such, the Grand Lodge of Freemasonry had made it clear to him that he wasn't expected to leave his rooms for fear that the Eye of the Great Architect would be on him. The Masonic sign of the Eye was even posted on his door. He was, in short, deliberately kept in a state of terror while the relevant authorities – as personified by Lord _____, who must surely have kept the red hood on throughout the interrogation – bled him for further information.

The Service also contributed to the interrogation, partly because it wanted to know everything that happened, partly because its archons must have felt shamed that one of their number had slipped through the grasp of the *rat-catchers* and caused this trouble. It's from a combination of the Marquis's statement and the Service's files, then, that a picture of the frightened man's mysterious employer emerges.

The agent in question had been indoctrinated into the Service in 1762, during the chaos of the Seven Years' War, significantly the same year as the apogee of the Hellfire Club. The initiate had shown a keen mind, specialising in engineering (possibly meaning the occult geometry of the Masonic movements, rather than actual physical engineering) and with a seemingly impossible talent for escaping tight corners. A talent which was to come in very handy indeed.

It had been a Saturday when this talented young man had received his final induction into the Service, which, given the Jewish cabbalistic trend in the Service, might explain the Confirmation Name he later chose for himself. Every initiation was different, in order to stop new recruits exchanging notes, but the basic principles were always the same. When testing a new ritualist, the Service would put the young man (because a ritualist was *always* male, while spies could be of any gender) in a situation of extreme peril and tell him that he had to survive by himself. If the initiate succeeded in escaping the trap, he would become part of the organisation. If not, he would very rarely survive and the integrity of the Service would remain intact.

The initiation of this particular agent had been especially spectacular, but the oracles of the Service had calculated that it best suited his own talents. That Saturday morning the initiate had been taken to a building on the banks of the Thames, in the shadow of St Paul's Cathedral; escorted on to an elongated platform, specially erected on the roof; bound with 'thirteen chains, thirteen locks and thirteen garters [?]'; covered by a hood of black sackcloth, which had covered his head and shoulders but left the eyes uncovered; hung with measures of lead weighing at least three hundred pounds; and – after the appropriate amount of ceremony – pushed off, into the river below.

At least, this is what the files claim. But this is all anyone really knows about the early career of the man who would later call himself Sabbath. Agents of the Service had their past identities removed with some precision, so apart from some inkling of his time as a student there's no way of saying who he'd been or where he'd come from, but his entrance into the world of espionage had been made at the age of twenty-one when he'd sunk to the bottom of the Thames and somehow, *somehow*, survived. There was no 'correct' way out of any Service initiation, so whatever Sabbath had done had been improvisational. Perhaps he'd used the *siddhis*, the alleged supernatural skills stolen by the Service from the Eastern *tantrists*: or perhaps it was elaborate muscular techniques that had allowed him to shake his bonds, like those later popularised by escapologists (though this is unlikely, as in this case the chains would have been real and no trickery would have been involved). A romantic might suggest that he'd found a way to stop time before he'd drowned. All the records state is that Sabbath *never came up from the river*, and his initiators had assumed him to be lost until he'd casually appeared at Cambridge, bone-dry and unharmed, the following morning.

His survival might have seemed impressive at the time, but now the Service had reason to regret it. According to the testimony of the Marquis of M_____, Sabbath had become, if anything, more alarming than the intense young initiate of the 1760s. When a Service agent left the fold he generally used his secret knowledge to blackmail, swindle or otherwise get rich quick, and the *rat-catchers* were frequently called upon to storm some expensive well-defended fortress out in the African colonies or up in the Scottish highlands. Yet the Marquis stated that Sabbath wasn't *rich*, as such. He simply knew how to use resources. He knew what levers to pull in order to get what he needed, and if money were required then it was no object. But the terrifying thing, said the Marquis, the terrifying thing wasn't Sabbath's great power or influence. The terrifying thing was the company he kept.

Thus began a story of inhuman creatures so bizarre that the Countess of Jersey later declared it to be the rantings of a terrified, hallucinating idiot. The Marquis depicts Sabbath as some huge, all-pervading shadow, like one of the ogreish master-villains in the later works of the Marquis de Sade. A man whose face was rarely seen, but who lurked in dark places, as if hiding in the belly of some monstrous leviathan which moved unseen below the surface of human affairs.

Meanwhile, the Doctor was discovering much of this information from his own sources, mainly Scarlette. She had, after all, been party to the events that had first seen Sabbath break away from the Service in 1780. The Doctor made plans accordingly.

One afternoon in early May he took a trip by carriage to Tyburn, not exactly the teeming centre of the metropolis and quiet enough on most days, but famous for being the site of the country's most noted public gallows. Travelling with him were Fitz and Lisa-Beth. Lisa-Beth describes

Fitz (with sarcasm, we feel) as 'likeable enough, though you would expect a more alert countenance from an elemental'. Fitz was in his early thirties, and in the House it was considered that he'd have been something of a rake if he'd been better bred. He had a habit of grinning inanely at the women who lived in the House with him, as if he weren't sure what the protocol was supposed to be. He'd frequently look away nervously when he saw Lisa-Beth in a state of undress, though Lisa-Beth was utterly unconcerned.

The purpose of the Tyburn trip was odd, to say the least. There was no execution scheduled for that day, and even if there had been it's unlikely that the Doctor would have wanted to spectate. The previous night, the Doctor had enlisted the services of Rebecca, Juliette, Lisa-Beth and two of the other women in what had appeared to be an elaborate seance. The Doctor had placed a red envelope in the middle of the floor – one of those wedding invitations which hadn't yet been delivered – and instructed the women to focus on it, all the time asking curious questions, apparently to whomsoever the envelope was addressed. Rebecca had used various items, including her deck of cards, to supply answers. When Anji had impatiently asked the Doctor what he was doing, the Doctor had replied: 'Navigating.' Indeed, he did seem to have been trying to ascertain a certain *place* through this ceremony, although Lisa-Beth's suggestion was that he was actually navigating through *time*.

The Doctor ordered the cab to stop when it reached the end of the long dirt road that led from central London into Tyburn. He walked around the area for some time on arrival, inspecting the gallows and the empty spectator grandstands, searching for an exact spot (the spot indicated by the 'seance'?) while Fitz and Lisa-Beth looked on. Finally he settled on the huge gallows structure itself, which he claimed was 'probably' the correct site. He carefully removed one of the supporting beams of the structure, then placed the red envelope inside the framework before replacing the beam, sealing the invitation away out of sight.

He evidently believed that from the hangman's platform the invitation would somehow make its way to its proper destination. Lisa-Beth records that she saw the writing on the envelope, in the Doctor's hand, and that it simply read 'Family'. How he expected anyone to find it in Tyburn she didn't know, but she admits that several months later she went back to the site to see if the envelope was still there. It was, even though the Doctor was by then claiming that the invitation had been received.

But there was another reason for this day out on the city's outskirts. It was on the way back home that the Doctor gave certain instructions to Fitz, instructions he didn't want to speak of in the presence of Scarlette. While Lisa-Beth listened, he said that it'd be Fitz's task to find Sabbath, and that he already knew where the hunt should begin. The Doctor must have perceived this shadowy, unseen agent as some kind of monster – a brooding presence, throwing his considerable bulk up against all the old orders and factions – and if there was one thing the Doctor couldn't ignore, it was a monster.

So if Scarlette's relationship with the Doctor was starting to suffer at this point, then it was hardly a surprise. The Doctor was summoning up old ghosts, and he wasn't the only one.

Throughout this period Scarlette spent several afternoons at the site of Newgate prison. Scarlette had been there, in 1780, when the most notorious and dungeon-like prison in London had been razed to the ground. In 1782 the authorities began rebuilding Newgate, and Scarlette would stand there for hours, watching as the ghost of the building was summoned up out of the city's dead flesh. Another portent. The once-mad Lord Gordon himself was publicly stating that the King was risking revolution here just as in America, while blood and fire were expected in Ireland in the not-too-distant future.

Once, the Doctor found Scarlette there at the Newgate construction. He stood with her a while and talked, though what they talked about is anybody's guess. Maybe Juliette was discussed: Scarlette was beginning to worry, that much is known, starting to wonder if what they were doing was only a step away from pimping and/or child slavery.

Juliette was definitely disturbed throughout the month, and it's a pity she didn't record her own thoughts. It was around this time that she started wearing red, Scarlette having presented her with a gift of a new dress on the same day as the Great Companion Summoning. According to Scarlette, it was a way of affirming her synchronisation with the House, if not with the Earth itself. The biological rhythms so important to the *tantrists* were being applied on a massive scale, almost as if Juliette were being primed to become one with the world around her.

Naturally, the red dress (matching her hair) drew attention to her in the House, not all of it good. In mid-May she overheard Katya making a loud criticism of Scarlette and her 'elemental lothario', and leapt to Scarlette's defence, insisting that the Doctor's plans were vital for the well-being of all the world. At this point Katya turned on Juliette, screaming at her for refusing to face the facts and 'doing everything that *vyedma* tells you'. She also repeated certain rumours about Juliette which she'd allegedly heard from Lisa-Beth. Juliette must have been shocked when it seemed that Katya was about to assault her physically, but the fight was prevented by the other women. (In fairness to Katya, she herself had been attacked on the street by this time. Furthermore, Katya herself had been given an offer of money to leave Scarlette and head into Marylebone: to Katya's credit she stayed at the House, at one point even asking her 'friends' at the Russian embassy whether this would inconvenience their own plans for her.)

It must have come as something of a relief when the time came for Juliette to leave the House with Fitz. They were to work together in their search for Sabbath. On the night before their departure from London, Scarlette blessed Juliette in a manner which was described as 'unusually solemn, for her'. Scarlette made a particularly big show of taking the glass totem from around her own neck and hanging it over Juliette's. If she'd known that Juliette had already used the glass in the bedroom experiments, of course, she might have been less willing to part with it. But clearly she felt that Juliette would need luck, even if the Doctor had given Fitz instructions just to *find* Sabbath, not to engage him in battle. The Doctor's own goodbye was wordless but touching, nodding to Fitz in a manner that suggested they'd gone through this sort of thing before, and kissing Juliette affectionately on the nose.

The next morning, most of the women from the House were on the pavement of Henrietta Street to wave the hackney cab off, a cab that was to take Fitz and Juliette on the first leg of a journey north. By this time Fitz and Juliette were already well-acquainted, but it's interesting to speculate on what they might have talked about on the trip. It seems to be at this time that Juliette first learned something of the Doctor's *Tardis* – which Fitz, a few days before, had told Lisa-Beth should be written TARDIS (it must have seemed like mere effect to Lisa-Beth, as acronyms weren't commonly used at the time) – and understood that this strange, as-yet unseen box was the closest thing the Doctor had to a centre of power. In return, Fitz must have picked up something about the customs of the *demi-reps* and the seraglios. Lisa-Beth notes that he was shocked when he discovered Juliette had only been born in 1769. If he and Juliette compared notes on their journey, then they would have reached the same conclusion Scarlette had already reached... that something about the change in the 'horizon' was disturbing *Shaktyanda*, or disturbing time itself, around London; and that it was this disturbance which had forced the Doctor to 'walk' here. Certainly, many of his experiments in the study were directed towards finding a way of bringing his TARDIS to the House undamaged.

Their destination was Cambridge, the start of the great hunt for Sabbath. If the Doctor had known all of the facts – that Juliette's progress had been monitored for some months by spies within the House itself, and that by the time Fitz's mission began the Marquis of M____ had been ripped to pieces and partially eaten by a wild ape in the apparent safety of Cambridge – he might have insisted on going along himself.

VISITS

It wasn't without good reason that the Doctor sent Fitz in search of Sabbath. The Service had been after Sabbath for the last two years, but had eventually 'decided' to let him do as he pleased, provided he didn't disrupt the nation in general. The Doctor evidently felt that his companions had a better chance of getting a lead on him. Or, in short: it was going to take an elemental to do the job. And as tracking Sabbath would involve *thinking* like Sabbath, Fitz must have seemed the obvious choice. According to Juliette's later testimony, Fitz did everything he could to adopt the mind-set of a secret service agent. She reported that once, at Cambridge, he bluffed his way into a private archive by claiming to be a Serviceman himself. He even changed his voice when playing this part, although Juliette admitted that his new voice made him sound nothing at all like the Servicemen she'd met at the March ball. On this occasion, Fitz even identified himself with the infamous code-number used by Dr Dee in the Elizabethan era, which must have startled the keepers of the archive. The trip to Cambridge is well documented, as during the weeks he spent there Fitz sent several detailed reports back to Henrietta Street, and the trail began at the University where Sabbath himself was said to have studied.

Sabbath's rooms at the University still exist. Notably, they're located in an area remarkably close to the walled-off rooms where the 'Appalling Club' met its end, and it's unlikely that this is a coincidence. Cambridge was a prime recruiting-ground for the British secret service in the eighteenth century, as it would continue to be for the next two hundred years. The Service must have realised something of his potential, either by examining his past records or by Dee's occult 'scrying' process. No doubt some spy in the University arranged for Sabbath to be quartered so close to the 'secret' section, in the hope that some of its influence might rub off on him. (It was a common belief in such circles that any ritualist required a 'place of power' where he could root himself. Whether this is because such sites were supposed to be outlets for some kind of secret energy, or whether it was just a case of preparing the initiate with the correct kind of ambience, is unclear.)

Fitz and Juliette seem to have had no trouble accessing Sabbath's old rooms, which were apparently unoccupied during 1782. Although nothing of Sabbath's remained in the old, musty, wood-lined quarters, there must have been something in the atmosphere which the Doctor's agents believed they could pick up on. Showing them around the College, in the mistaken belief that Fitz worked for the authorities, was an edgy and balding old member of the University staff: in his letters, Fitz described this Professor as having 'eyebrows like hedgehogs' and eyes that seemed determined not to make contact with anything or anyone else. He also had a big nose, which apparently looked 'like it was going to start dripping any second'. The Professor can't have felt comfortable showing these two peculiar visitors around, given the amount of attention the University had been receiving recently.

He must have become less comfortable still when Fitz and Juliette first inspected Sabbath's rooms. Although they found nothing of their prey, Fitz did notice traces of chalk on the floorboards, evidently recent and not properly erased. When he questioned the Professor on this, the Professor 'shuffled his feet' and claimed that errant students were always taking over unoccupied rooms for their own illicit social functions. Fitz was suspicious, and speculated that the rooms were still being used for some form of foul practice. He told the Doctor that if they could find out what was being done at the University *now*, they might have some clue as to what Sabbath had done there.

Scarlette's journal doesn't record the Doctor's reaction to Fitz's letters, because throughout the later half of May Scarlette was spending time in Windsor. So was Lisa-Beth.

It seems odd that Scarlette would spend so much time away from the House in the company of someone she'd only just come to trust, but it has to be remembered that Scarlette was a master (mistress?) when it came to manipulating personal circumstances. For example, two nights before Fitz and Juliette left for London most of the Doctor's 'coven' were assembled in the salon of the House. Young Emily was present, and describes 'the room ful of fumes, from some devise put by Scarlette in the room for the enjoyment of all'. She describes the fumes in much the same terms as those from Juliette's secret experiments, and notes that many members of the House present – probably not including the Doctor – slowly entered a merry, intoxicated state. Only Juliette remained stony-faced, as alert as ever, while Scarlette lightly flirted with Fitz (Emily writes as if Scarlette were older than Fitz and toying with him like a teenager, though in fact he was her senior by far). Emily writes:

> …Mr. K [Fitz] became glass eyed and philosophickal in the fumes. It was as though he felt he could see further than most in this euphoria and the Doctor appeard conserned though he said nothing… Mr. K said that he now understood how fragile was the world, and more that beloe it he could see the way the horison had changed. Scarlette teased him at this before asking him a question. 'Tell me Mr. K,' said she. 'Did you ever feel that the world was but a dream, and should someone pinch you you would wake to another world all together?'. Mr. K appeard serious and said that he did. To which Scarlette said: 'Perhaps someone should pinch us, Mr. K, so that we should know for sure.' At this Mr. K whose propriety was lessened by the fumes, reached out and pinched Mistress Scarlette on the top of the leg… there was a look of shock on Scarlette's face, but then in a blink Scarlette vanished before our eyes! We were amazed and none more than Mr. K (though the Doctor thout it most funy).

It's best not to take this story at face value. Scarlette may have 'disappeared', but as Emily points out the room was both 'hidden and intoxicated' by the fumes, and Scarlette spent some time before her disappearance building up the correct atmosphere for those assembled to believe in her seemingly magical transportation. It was, by her own admission, a kind of trick: and only the Doctor seems to have spotted how it was done. But it must have made an impression on Fitz, who regarded Scarlette as a powerful presence from that point on.

Now that Juliette had left London, Scarlette knew there were certain issues she had to address with Lisa-Beth, and felt it was best for the two of them to get out into the fresher, greener atmosphere of Windsor. She and Lisa-Beth would regularly display themselves in the Park during their visit, wearing their best clothes (Scarlette in red, Lisa-Beth in black), letting the rich young gentlemen of the town buy them coffee and chocolate. On one occasion they even saw the King himself, taking his stroll through the grounds of the Park surrounded by family members and rod-wielding guardsmen. Scarlette and Lisa-Beth both bowed when the procession went past, but Lisa-Beth noted that Scarlette was uttering a curse under her breath that the King-father would have to 'bleed like a woman': Scarlette still blamed George III for what had happened in America, and though it's doubtful that this 'lunar curse' actually contributed to the King's eventual madness Lisa-Beth did point out that from 1782 the King did look curiously haunted. Then again, that was probably just politics.

The two women also visited the bookshop in Windsor, itself often frequented by the King. Literacy was probably the strongest bond between them. It was during such a visit, while browsing through the latest publications, that Scarlette first brought up the topic she'd brought Lisa-Beth here to discuss.

In their journals, neither Scarlette nor Lisa-Beth overtly state what this matter was. But it's not hard to guess. As early as April, there were certain *rumours* circulating in the House, rumours about Juliette's past and pedigree. After all, Juliette had been brought to London – some might have said 'summoned' – by Scarlette, who'd never given any indication of where this girl had come from or why she was important. Lisa-Beth's own notes suggest that when Lisa-Beth first visited the House, she recognised Juliette at once. Was Lisa-Beth the source of these rumours, then? And if so, then what were they?

And in Cambridge, Fitz was already forming his own opinion of Juliette. When the Professor left them alone to investigate Sabbath's rooms, Juliette suggested to him that they should hold some form of ritual to look towards the *horizon* and divine the answers they needed. Fitz quite rightly felt that such a ritual wouldn't be practical (and besides, having seen Scarlette's idea of a 'ritual' he must have been worried about what they'd actually have to *do* in the room). But he was struck by the matter-of-fact way in which Juliette suggested the idea, a trait which, he wrote to the Doctor, 'reminds me of you'.

In retrospect, he might have been closer to the truth than he thought. Throughout his stay at the House the Doctor had been starting to change his usual routine, as if he felt that the limits of his old life needed re-definition, although it's ironic that this wish to expand himself should result in the wedding (an act that would permanently 'root' him to the House). Though he might not have consciously realised it, there was a sense that Juliette, Scarlette and their kind were taking on the mantle of his own people, the mantle of the Doctor himself. In short, he was beginning to think of Juliette as the next generation of elemental, the inheritor of a legacy with which he no longer felt comfortable.

It's no surprise, then, that when Fitz and Anji had arrived at the House the Doctor had decided that Anji – another elemental influence – should share Juliette's room. Juliette had accepted this, even though the co-habitation doesn't seem to have been very successful. Juliette found the

Doctor's companion to be snappish, overbearing and impatient, but in fairness this was probably only because the two of them came from such different lifestyles that Juliette interpreted Anji's somewhat sarcastic wit as actual aggression. Certainly, Anji would shake her head disbelievingly whenever a 'client' visited the House, a kind of contempt that Juliette hadn't seen even in Lisa-Beth.

Also, although Anji's history was uncertain, she was obviously of Indian descent. Juliette seems to have had difficulty with this, although the reasons hadn't become apparent and Anji must have (wrongly) believed it was down to blind prejudice. The other women in the House still tended to think of Anji as a force of nature, and on more than one occasion Katya sat at the feet of Anji to ask her worried questions about the future, as if Anji were a kind of prophet. (The women must have seen Fitz as an oracle, too, but they had a tendency to giggle every time he walked past, so they weren't likely to share their intimate problems with him in quite the same fashion.)

Part of the Doctor's rationale for sending Juliette with Fitz was that it could hardly have hurt her to spend more time with other human beings, or at least very *minor* elementals, before being permanently bound to him in December. Also, it gave him the opportunity to complete some tasks of his own. He'd already sent the invitation out to his 'Family', and now he was busy trying to find a priest who'd agree to the wedding ceremony – it was quite vital that the marriage should be legally binding, as well as symbolic – not to mention having to decide who was going to be his best man. If he saw any problems in Juliette spending so much time with Fitz, then he obviously didn't let it bother him.

THE MASONIC ACCOUNT

The chalk circle on the floor of the Cambridge rooms was drawn there mere days before Fitz's visit. Those responsible were the Countess and the Lord.

On their last day of interrogating the Marquis of M_____, the two arcanists had finally cut through enough of the Marquis's babble to uncover the *reason* he'd summoned an ape at Westminster. The ape wasn't simply to have been *called*, it was to have been *bound*: the implication was that the Marquis had been attempting to gain control of the beast rather than just setting it free to cause havoc. When the Lord asked his contacts in the Grand Lodge to examine the ceremony, the Masons concluded that it had been phrased in Greek simply because the Marquis happened to be familiar with that language. In fact the 'workings' of the ritual were quite original and in no way ancient, the summoning designed for maximum efficiency... *engineered*, one might say.

Until recently, those *tantrists* who'd noticed the presence of the apes had concluded that some form of 'natural' phenomenon was the cause. No individual, as Scarlette herself pointed out, could possibly move the horizon and cause demons to appear in the world: even the summoning at Westminster would have seemed impractical, even *silly*, a few years earlier. Now the Countess and the Lord were faced with the possibility that the ape manifestations were an attack. Those who'd read the *Kama Sutra* in its Sanskrit form knew that the book was a manual of spells as much as it was a list of sexual tactics, and knew that (unlike the early English translation produced at Medmenham) the original continually hinted at the 'demons' which could be brought forth by malice or carelessness. Though Sabbath wasn't believed to be vengeful – he was thought to have his own agenda, and to regard the Service as a trivial distraction rather than a sworn enemy – it must have worried many to think that the rogue agent might want to get his own back on those parties who had, on at least two occasions, tried to assassinate him.

As they moved through the halls of Cambridge, one with a crimson hood over his face and the other with her pipe still in her mouth, the Lord and the Countess must have asked themselves why apes, rather than any other kind of beast, should be anyone's weapon of choice. But the details weren't as important as the implications. Because if Sabbath was now capable of summoning and binding the demons, then *anybody* was.

There were protocols of the highest importance, amongst the Servicemen, amongst the Masons and amongst the various British witch-cults, forbidding any of their number to deliberately upset the balance of the ritualist community. Most of these protocols were utterly ignored when, in the middle of May, the Countess and the Lord transferred the Marquis of M_____ to the rooms which had once been occupied by Sabbath. It was a place of power, and if the two investigators wanted to see the beast tamed then this was the best place for it. The Service may have joined forces with the Lodge in this. The agents of the King had very little else to do, now that all British military operations in America had been officially suspended.

The Marquis was led into the old rooms, quite terrified, at the stroke of three o'clock. The Lord had sent word to London regarding this potentially dangerous affair, and the Service had responded by sending three of its *rat-catchers* to attend the event, all of them dressed in the finest black and all of them hidden under the black-and-gold hoods of

74

their order. They stood silently at the back of the room while the Marquis was given his instructions, hands folded politely behind their backs, and their presence can only have further intimidated the man. In front of all those present, the Marquis was requested – *requested* – to etch the circle in chalk in the middle of the wooden floor.

What happened next is difficult to ascertain, as although the Masonic archive records events in detail it does so in an annoyingly obscure code which insists on describing everything in alchemical terms ('scrying-bone' for chalk, 'red dragon' for sulphur, etcetera). What can be said with *some* certainty is that the ape appeared, and began tearing at the walls of its invisible prison. Traditionally any summoned thing is incapable of crossing a chalk line, and in the Westminster account the animal tore its fingers to shreds trying to rip its way out of the circle. There was a lot of blood ('fire vitae') on the floor, and the screaming of the ape was so great that students as far away as Pembroke College were said to have complained that a murder was being committed. When the Marquis began the binding process, the ape didn't calm down, and by the time the ritual was finished the saliva from its jaws was so thick that it looked as if it had become rabid.

It was at this point that the Grand Lodge's representatives told the Marquis to step into the circle.

According to the principles of the ritual, this was perfectly safe. The only way to complete the binding was to step over the chalk line, leaving oneself at the mercy of the animal: only when the ritualist made this 'sacrifice' could the beast come under his will. It goes without saying that the Marquis was horrified at the suggestion, but he doesn't seem to have had much choice. It wasn't just that the traditional penalty for those who disobeyed the Grand Lodge was to be hanged below a bridge with their intestines cut out. It was that the Marquis needed the Lodge's protection. He was betraying Sabbath even by revealing the ceremony, and that must have scared him even more than the *rat-catchers* did.

So the Marquis, it seems, stepped into the circle with the ape. The Masonic account becomes increasingly obscure at this point, but the 'fire vitae' is mentioned quite a lot.

Evidently, Sabbath's ritual wasn't exactly foolproof. Indeed, in the weeks that followed there was some speculation that the binding process didn't work at all, and that Sabbath had concocted the entire thing as some monstrous practical joke. Days later Fitz and Juliette found the scrubbed remains of the chalk circle on the floorboards, but there's a contradiction here, of course. In his letter to the Doctor, Fitz doesn't describe any blood: it's difficult to remove bloodstains from wood at the best of times, but the idea that a floor could have been washed clean of blood *yet still have chalk marks remaining* is nothing less than ridiculous. Possibly Fitz's account is incomplete, or possibly the Masonic archive is, not unusually, exaggerating. Scarlette would no doubt have claimed that he ghost of the chalk circle had worked its way up through the ground, just like the ghost of Newgate Prison. Whatever the reason, Fitz believed the marks to be significant, and (rightly) found the behaviour of the Professor/guide suspicious. When he finally asked the Professor for access to one of the University's more esoteric archives, in the hope of finding material written by Sabbath that hadn't been destroyed by the Service, the Professor filibustered for some time (waffling about 'bureaucratic process') before granting Fitz admittance.

As expected, nothing of importance was found in the archive. But documents relating to Sabbath were already in Fitz's possession. Scarlette had known Sabbath before his fall from grace with the Service, and (through routes she never cared to explain) some of the documents earmarked for collection by the Servicemen had fallen into her possession two years earlier. Fitz had been given copies of these manuscripts before leaving London. In its original form, the writing is in Sabbath's own hand, and it's a first-hand account of his initiation. Sadly, it doesn't reveal how Sabbath escaped the deathtrap of the Thames, though it does record his thoughts on sinking below the surface:

I knew, then, that there are certain boundaries mankind should make every effort to cross. I also knew that the majority of human beings are in no way prepared for this crossing. It is often said that a drowning man will sense a great calm and clarity as he dies, and this was certainly my experience. There was a moment, I recall, when the inevitability of my own death became tangible. The understanding this brings a man cannot immediately be described… it was then that I saw the bed of the river below me, and then that the shadow fell over the sand and the silt before my eyes. I knew at this moment that *Leviathan* had come to find me, although on reflection the blackness may have merely been the blackness of unconsciousness. I thought of Jonah and his whale; I thought of the island-fish of the Arabian Nights. *Leviathan* was there, a power and a darkness that swam at the bottom of the river and waited to consume the dead. It was only then that I remembered my purpose here was not to die, but to avoid dying.

(The biblical references here are typical of a Serviceman. Religious imagery was common in Service lore – note that many agents chose Biblical confirmation names, including 'Hiram of Tyre', 'Meshelemiah', even 'Sabbath' himself – even though the majority of recruits were free-thinkers. It should be remembered that although the Service was dedicated to a form of mystic logic, the organisation was technically sworn to protect the King and the Protestant Church.)

However useless the archives might have been, Fitz and Juliette do seem to have been inspired by the atmosphere of Cambridge. It was on the first night of their investigation, for instance, that Juliette related to Fitz the vision she'd had back at the House, when Fitz and Anji had first stepped out of the light. And so it was that, in a hired room over a public house in Cambridge, Juliette first told Fitz about the apparitions she'd seen: about the shadow which had filled up the sky, and the engines of war so well-documented by Lisa-Beth, cold and dark and metallic.

Fitz reached the conclusion that the darkness in the sky was some form of god, something powerful and elemental, which almost certainly controlled the apes. And Sabbath? Perhaps he too was now an agent of the shadow, given the odd reference to *Leviathan* in his writings. The theory must have found favour with the Doctor, who for some time even before coming to London had been nursing the suspicion that *something* was affecting the 'horizon' and therefore time as a whole.

But a week after his arrival in Cambridge, Fitz found an entirely different kind of lead.

On May 20, Fitz and Juliette visited the University archives for the last time. Their session in the reading-room was cut short when the Professor arrived, flanked by three tall and serious-looking men who never spoke a word throughout the entire encounter. The Professor hurriedly explained that 'circumstances had changed', and that for a variety of reasons Mr Kreiner would no longer be allowed to consult University records. Fitz responded by flouting his (forged) Service credentials, but this time the Professor was unmoved.

Three large men. Were they the three *rat-catchers*, still in Cambridge after the Marquis incident, but this time unmasked? In any case, Fitz took the whole thing quite lightly, curiously giving the startled Professor a large and unmanly hug on the way out of the University grounds.

That evening, the Professor left his rooms at the University and, keeping his face down under his coat, made his way towards the banks of the nearby river Cam. Fitz's last letter from Cambridge records this in some detail, because Fitz was following the man at a suitably discreet distance. The letter suggests that Fitz employed some kind of device to keep track of the Professor's location, possibly one of the many peculiar electrical gadgets created in the Doctor's cellar laboratory. By half past nine there were few people by the part of the Cam closest to the University grounds, so when the Professor covertly met with an acquaintance behind the Harbourman's Tavern nobody was around to witness it... except for Fitz, naturally.

Fitz was forced to keep his distance in order to remain unseen, but he still saw enough of the Professor's contact to send a good description back to the Doctor. The Professor was meeting with a female, probably below the age of twenty, who wore a black winter cloak despite the mild weather. The woman's head was largely obscured by the hood of the cloak, which Fitz suspected was designed to hide her hair rather than her face. The cut of the hair seemed unusual, certainly for that period. Fitz had never seen her before, yet described her as 'sort of oriental... with this smooth-looking skin'. In a word, Polynesian.

The Doctor would have wasted no time in making the connection. The Professor reporting to the *Mayakai*; the *Mayakai* reporting to Sabbath; Sabbath working towards... what? Fitz tried to follow the girl, but he had no way of keeping track of her as he did with the Professor, and as a result all he could report was that she vanished along the path by the side of the river.

It was during the following days, while Fitz and Juliette saw the sights in Cambridge and considered their next move, that Fitz slowly developed his new theory. At some point he began to make a connection which nobody else had made, and which even the *rat-catchers* (with a less impressive knowledge of the historical process than even a minor elemental, one assumes) hadn't spotted. *Leviathan*, Fitz must have thought. Sabbath, initiated in the Thames. Sabbath the occult engineer. Juliette's vision, of metallic, futuristic war machines...

The next few weeks in Cambridge would be a flurry of letter-writing, as Fitz communicated with the Doctor and via the House sent missives of enquiry to all manner of officials, artisans and tradesmen across Britain (Juliette must have helped him, surely). By the end of May, Fitz had learned enough not only to decide that his guess was correct, but actually to make a good guess as to where Sabbath's current 'place of power' might have been.

By then, Scarlette had returned to Henrietta Street from Windsor. She arrived to find that business had dropped radically in her absence, as the Doctor, never one for practicalities, had neglected the housekeeping in favour of his own studies. To her surprise, though, no more of the women had left while she'd been gone. Perhaps they were wary of turning their backs on the elemental and his Indian oracle. No sooner had she stepped through the front door than Scarlette discovered that, with little regard for the cost, *all* the remaining women of the House had been dressed in new clothes: dresses of black velvet, but decorated with red muslin, the colours of the House turned into something approaching a uniform. Even Anji wore such a dress, though she looked distinctly awkward in it and insisted on adjusting it so as to make it appear less glamorous. Only the Doctor remained in his own colours.

When Scarlette asked the Doctor why he'd done this, and while Lisa-Beth wondered how much the couturier's bill had come to, the Doctor replied with some enthusiasm that events were moving on apace. Fitz and Juliette had discovered something of importance, he said. The great struggle that had been anticipated ever since the *babewyns* began to appear was beginning. With that, he cheerily announced that 'a grand outing' was planned for the whole House. All the loose ends in London had been sorted out, the Doctor claiming to have worked out who he wanted as best man. For now, though, Scarlette's extended family – described by the Countess of Jersey as 'an army of the pox', led by two elementals and the last great Hellfire Mistress – had certain tasks to perform, and to begin with all of them had to go straight to the heart of Sabbath's power. Northwards, to Manchester.

Scarlette simply asked who was going to pay for all of this. It must have occurred to her that if Fitz and Juliette really *had* found a lead to Sabbath then Sabbath would know they were coming.

4
The Kingdom and its Environs

BEES

There was another ape attack in June. This time it took place on board a mercantile ship *en route* from Dover to Ostend, curiously in the same part of the ocean where, a year later, the Great Fireball would explode into sparks and vanish beneath the waves. The Service tried to maintain the nation's dignity, as ever, by claiming that the 'cannibal ape' story was just an exaggerated folk tale put about by sailors. And true enough, the only evidence that an attack occurred on the ship at all comes from the friend-of-a-friend anecdotes of the seamen. The crewman who allegedly had his heart torn out inside a closed and bolted officer's cabin was never named, so it's impossible to say what he might have done to attract the ape-gods' attention, although there were the usual whispers that the ship had been carrying 'unholy relics' in a secret smuggler's compartment below decks.

By the summer, the authorities had more than enough to think about already. The King had reportedly stated that he wished he were 'eighty, or ninety, or dead'. He looked haunted, and he wasn't the only one. Some gentlemen of the civil service even began to whisper that a conspiracy was afoot, that the tales of monstrous beasts were part of an elaborate conspiracy to weaken the resolve of the state. One of the busiest centres of business, they might have argued, was Manchester... and a new group of women, with more than a whiff of the occult about them, had in recent weeks been noticed frequenting the Manchester docks. There was a feeling in some circles that these women were the ones spreading the horror stories amongst the merchant seamen.

This 'cult' was, of course, the Doctor's army. The women of Henrietta Street arrived in Manchester in early June, and in the weeks that followed they were often seen stalking the streets near the shipyards after dark, patronising the taverns where the dock-workers hung out. The intrigued gentlemen of Manchester couldn't fail to notice these curious females, all of whom wore the same colours as if they were in uniform. But not all the attention was welcome.

Manchester already had more than enough prostitutes of its own, although, unlike the Covent Garden breed, they'd never been objects of

80

fashion and were coldly, aggressively practical about their work. After all, Manchester was about to become the most industrialised city in Europe, even the world. Within a few years, the machines would be moving into the factories by the thousand; the skyline would be choking with great black towers and devious machines; families would begin to live underground, in dark, damp, crowded spaces without ventilation or highly-taxed windows; the canals would become the black, pulsing arteries of the industrial age; and as a result, Manchester would be the cradle of some of the greatest technological progress in history. By 1782, even the prostitutes were becoming part of the machine.

The first fight occurred two days after the arrival of Scarlette's party, and predictably it was Katya who was the cause of it. In a tavern Scarlette calls 'The White Hart' (ironic, in such a pitch-black city), one of the local women turned her back on a potential gentleman customer for two minutes in order to relieve herself in a back-alley. When she returned, she found Katya sitting on the man's knee making what Scarlette calls 'a great show of her fat chest' and using the red tassels on her dress in a most improper fashion. Needless to say, the local woman wasn't happy. There was ill-feeling towards the London set anyway, the Mancunians referring to them as 'the bloody bees' (because of their uniforms?) and sarcastically calling them 'courtesans'.

The distinction between 'whore' and 'courtesan' was always a fine one – generally it depended on how rich your clientele was – so although it might have been a compliment to Scarlette's crew in London, here it was a reminder that Manchester was built on sweat and cotton, *not* on class. Even in the north of England, people had heard of *Harris's List of Covent Garden Ladies*, that most fashionable guide to the bordellos of London, and the women of Manchester would have known by reputation the kind of threat Scarlette's crowd presented to business. In the end, it was actually a fairly muted Doctor who ended the squabble in the tavern.

There was actually another reason for the women's animosity, and that was soon to become clear.

So why had the Doctor insisted on coming here? The answer lies with Fitz. Fitz was also spending time at the docks, although (thankfully) for very different reasons. On June 15, after some weeks of chasing leads, he and Juliette finally found a location at the docks which, he was convinced, was the next step on the trail to Sabbath. The site was a building which no longer exists, but which was later described as:

Enormos… it was part of the shipyards, tho while most of the

81

grand vesels of Manchester were built at dock this place of construction had been covered by a truly giant ceiling of canvas and struts of what I took to be iron. There was a reserve [i.e. reservoir] of water at the hart of the bilding with wooden platforms all around for the workers, so I took it that the waterways themselves had been bent in there course to fill the place. There were workman on every platform that worked in metal with fiery tools, and there were small boats tied to posts for perhaps rowing out to the rest of the river. The whole of the construction smelt of burning things, [but] I did not see any ship in the water there tho there was sertainly room for one.

This 'indoor shipyard', then, was more reminiscent of one of the new factories than a normal dockyard. To Fitz, who seems to have had no difficulty infiltrating the building and observing the workmen cutting steel and hammering metal plate, it was confirmation that his theory had been correct. Sabbath was an engineer; Sabbath seemed to stick to water, whenever possible (perhaps a compulsion left over from his initiation); Sabbath had seen, or believed he'd seen, a *Leviathan* in the Thames; and one of the key images in Juliette's visions was of *metallic* war machines. Fitz's conclusion was simple. Sabbath would be found on a ship. Indeed, given the man's propensity for finding resources, Sabbath would almost certainly have his *own* ship.

Of course the Service had never reached this conclusion: they, unlike Fitz, were victims of their own age. In the 1780s, the majority of ships were still uneasy, wooden things, lethal in naval war but hardly a place in which anyone would choose to reside. Nobody in the eighteenth century would ever have considered a ship as a *headquarters*. But things were different, Fitz would no doubt have claimed, in the world of elementals. To him, a ship could be something as solid as pig-iron. And you couldn't build your own battleship without someone noticing. In their last weeks at Cambridge, Fitz and Juliette had dispatched subtle missives to exactly the kind of suppliers, administrators and engineers Sabbath would have needed to create his own metal Leviathan. The trail had led here.

In modern times, in an age when metal battleships are exclusively owned by governments, the idea of one man building his own ship might seem odd. But in this era, it wasn't unusual for ships to be built by public subscription. Indeed, in 1782 the Duchess of Devonshire herself – a recurring name in this story – announced that she wished to start a subscription to construct her own battleship, just as the fashionable adventuress-women of France had done during the American war. Curiously, nothing officially came of these plans... as the Duchess was certainly one of those high-society 'resources' being tapped by Sabbath, perhaps the proceeds of this subscription helped fund his own project. But when Fitz and Juliette arrived at the yard on June 14, there was no sign of any ship. Most of the workers there had retired for the evening by then, and Fitz avoided the rest for long enough to deduce that as there were smaller rowing-boats around the covered yard, the warship he was looking for was somewhere out of dock.

By this time Fitz no longer had to make written reports to the Doctor, so accounts are maddeningly short on detail. What's certain is that as Fitz and Juliette left the dockyards to report back to the Doctor, they were waylaid and surrounded in the darkened streets near the banks of the canal.

This time their attackers weren't *babewyns*, Polynesians, or agents of Sabbath. They were all women. Juliette must have immediately identified them as the working women of Manchester, and realised that they'd waited in ambush outside the covered yard, recognising her and Fitz as 'bloody bees'. It's not known what Fitz's reaction was, when surrounded by a mob of prostitutes.

Meanwhile the Doctor was with Scarlette, and, as on most nights, they were at the White Hart. By now Scarlette and her family had established themselves as regulars at the tavern. The Doctor was uneasy with this state of affairs – he seems to have been particularly disturbed to see Rebecca attaching herself to the drunken riverworkers who frequented the place – but Scarlette insisted that if you took a coterie of *demi-reps* on this kind of adventure, you had to expect them to employ themselves. The Doctor and company would sit in the downstairs rooms of the tavern most evenings, while Anji and Lisa-Beth often sat together glumly at the back of the room. Partners in aloof cynicism, Anji had taken to covering up her uniform in order to avoid approaches from the men of Manchester, and even Lisa-Beth was starting to give her potential clients short shrift. Whatever she and Scarlette had discussed in Windsor, it was still playing on her mind.

It was just before nine when Juliette entered the tavern, out of breath and with the black velvet ripped to shreds across the front of her dress. She aroused much attention amongst the crowd, but made her way straight to the Doctor, who – says Scarlette – 'jumped straight to his face with a look of the gravest concern on his feet' (either an error or an obscure joke).

Juliette hurriedly explained what had happened at the docks. Although Juliette had been 'manhandled' by the attackers, it was, strangely, Fitz on whom the local women had focused. They'd descended on him like a pack of animals, said Juliette, for some reason calling him a 'killer'. Juliette had thought it was odd that they should have attacked with such precision and determination. They'd eventually dispersed, leaving Fitz a bruised and bloodied wreck.

What Juliette didn't explain, and what only became clear after Fitz made his own report to the Doctor, was the *reason* the prostitutes had dispersed. Exact events are unclear, as Fitz was half-unconscious at the time, but it seems that the women backed off only after Juliette *said* something to them. Yet if Juliette had succeeded in facing off an entire mob of attackers, despite her age and size, then why didn't she mention it herself? Modesty? It should be noted that the encounter wasn't unlike the occasion when Scarlette had intimidated a crowd of London women outside the theatre… and of course, at this time Juliette still wore Scarlette's glass totem around her neck.

The Doctor instructed Juliette (somewhat unnecessarily) to sit down and recover herself, while he headed off to find the semi-conscious Fitz. It's interesting to note that both Scarlette and his fellow elemental Anji stayed at the tavern: although the Doctor did take a companion with him to the docks, it was *Rebecca* he chose for the job. As Juliette had already told him about the covered shipyard, it's possible that the Doctor felt Rebecca's talents might have been useful there. Whatever the reason, Rebecca accepted this mission 'with a shrug'.

Juliette was right in thinking that the actions of the prostitutes were unusually determined. When the Doctor arrived at the shipyards he found Fitz – coughing up bile and with his face covered in bruises – propped up in a darkened side street , with his back against the wall and, fortunately, nobody else in sight. The Doctor apparently made a great show of checking Fitz's health, but he was probably even more concerned about the tale Fitz had to tell.

According to Fitz, after Juliette had left him the prostitutes had vanished into the night: but once he'd crawled into the side street , he'd seen other figures heading towards the great reservoir building. Fitz estimated that there'd been six of the men, all sticking to the shadows of the old buildings by the side of the canal, converging on the shipyard.

The Doctor put together the pieces at once. Service records confirm that throughout the 'Sabbath affair', the Service's spies in Manchester were using the local streetwalkers as surveillance agents. The women had been following Fitz and Juliette not just out of spite, but because they'd been paid to. Had they also been hired to rough up Fitz, to distract the Doctor's people while they made their own plans? If the women did indeed refer to Fitz as a 'killer', then perhaps somebody told them he worked for the dangerous courtesans of Covent Garden, whose exploits had already caused several prostitutes to suffer grisly deaths.

As in Cambridge, the Service's watchers were everywhere, letting the Doctor's party lead them to Sabbath. Now they evidently felt their prey to be close, as the six hooded *rat-catchers* were moving in to raid Sabbath's ship-building operation. The Service intended to get to their rogue agent before anybody else, and the Doctor clearly felt he couldn't allow that. So it was that Fitz ended up being left in the side street, declaring himself to be well enough, if battered, while the Doctor and Rebecca made their way into the covered dockyard.

If either of them were perturbed by the idea of following half a dozen highly-trained government-funded assassins into unknown territory, then neither of them mentioned it when they came to tell the story later on.

IT AWAKENS

What exactly did the Doctor and Rebecca find in Sabbath's shipyard? Although getting a straight answer out of Rebecca was always difficult, she later related that there was definitely *something* under the dock's canvas roof. When asked why Fitz hadn't noticed it, all she'd say was: 'He couldn't see properly.'

There were no Servicemen to be seen, though. Those few workmen who remained at the site aren't mentioned in Rebecca's stories, so either the Service had chased them out or in some way neutralised them. As has already been recorded, there were a number of smaller boats tied to posts around the dock, and when the Doctor arrived several of them were missing, presumably taken by the *rat-catchers*. The Doctor himself wasted no time in climbing into one, gracefully holding out a hand to help Rebecca before taking to the oars.

And that, says Rebecca, was when 'the Leviathan woke up'.

Back at the White Hart, trouble was brewing once again. The tavern apparently saw the Doctor as Scarlette's male protector – ironically enough, even her pimp – just as Scarlette saw him as her *elemental* champion. Not half an hour after his departure, a group of local women entered, all of them wearing blue and white. It was as if it were a deliberately rehearsed statement, the locals developing a uniform (and in Whig colours, no less) to challenge Scarlette's. They may well have been from the House of Mother Shaw, a well-known procuress in the area of the docks. For the first few minutes, the blue-and-white brigade merely stayed on the opposite side of the tavern, eyeing up the competition but saying nothing. Anji and Lisa-Beth buried themselves in their ales and tried to look inconspicuous. Scarlette couldn't fail to notice Juliette fingering the glass totem, 'as though the thing were her own'.

At around half past nine, someone threw the first beer glass. Accounts differ as to who started it, but Katya was upstairs with a local magistrate so for once she can be absolved of the blame.

And meanwhile, Rebecca and the Doctor were busy boarding Sabbath's battleship. If this seems like a big jump in the narrative, it's only because of the distracted, non-linear nature of Rebecca's stories (although the sudden appearance of the ship is something that will be dealt with shortly). Suffice to say that Rebecca soon found herself staring up at a great 'wall of metal', as the little rowing boat drifted up alongside the vessel in shallow waters. The Doctor obviously had some difficulty boarding the vessel, as the deck was a good five yards above him, and he noted at the time that the *rat-catchers* had obviously come prepared for this with boarding-ropes. The ship was eventually accessed by a method that seems as remarkable as everything else in Rebecca's unpredictable tale. The Doctor pulled a device from his pockets, she says – a certain glass-tipped item fashioned in his basement workshop – and, with a smell 'like the burning of a forge', set about attacking one of the metal plates at the side of the ship. Or perhaps it's more accurate to say that he attacked the material which held the plates together.

The space below the decks of the metal ship was dark, but what Rebecca found most notable was the noise of it all. There was a kind of *humming* in the walls, something she'd never heard of in any of the wooden ships of the day. As she headed through the darkened spaces inside, right on the Doctor's coat-tails, she admits to having been greatly disorientated: as if the noise, the vibration and the all-pervading smell of gunpowder had been designed deliberately to throw her off-balance. When they got closer to the heart of the ship, it grew lighter, revealing dirty steel walls held together by 'big bolts and lines of purest black'.

The warship can't have been more than twelve yards across, so it couldn't have taken as long as Rebecca suggests to find the first of the Servicemen. He was dead by the time the Doctor stumbled across him.

When it came to death, Rebecca tended to swing between disturbing casualness and utter silence, and on this occasion she inclined towards the former. There was blood, more of the 'fire vitae' described at the

Cambridge slaughter. The Doctor knelt over the corpse with some concern, although he can hardly have been feeling for a pulse: the man had been virtually disembowelled. Rebecca described his face, or rather the absence of it, a hood pulled over his head in the manner of an executioner with a golden triangle sewn into the forehead, clearly modelled on the Masonic hood. The Doctor didn't uncover the man's face. He believed the wounds to have been caused by an animal, which had presumably come at the man out of the humming darkness and torn into him with its fingers. There was a blood trail nearby, suggesting that either the animal or another *rat-catcher* had gone away wounded.

Regardless, they carried on into the bowels of the ship. Given what they later found, it's almost certain they would have *heard* something of what they were about to walk into.

It's best at this point to take a step back and consider the whole picture. Despite the best efforts of the Service, the *rat-catchers*' attack on the ship clearly wasn't unexpected. Indeed, by the time the Doctor found the first body another of the small rowing-boats had already been lowered out of the warship, carrying one of Sabbath's envoys – the young *Mayakai* – in response to the Servicemen's assault. Had the Doctor known this, he might have reflected that the survival of himself and Rebecca depended on the discretion of the ship's owner.

At some point during the exploration, Rebecca saw the Doctor stop dead in the gloom ahead of her. They'd reached a larger area, a full-sized chamber rather than the narrow iron passages they'd seen so far. The Doctor, Rebecca later recalled, stood for a few moments observing the scene in front of him. At more or less the same time that Rebecca stepped forward to see for herself, the chamber became suddenly well-lit, as the Doctor calmly took 'one of Mr Franklin's lanterns' from his pocket and began casting the light around him.

Even Rebecca must surely have been unnerved by what she saw in the flickering light. When she told the tale to Scarlette she was as non-committal as ever, but when Scarlette wrote it down there was a certain black romance to it:

> It was not unlike being in the heart of a throbbing, black machine. The chamber was iron as [was] the rest of the vessel, high as it was wide, the walls being laid with pipes or passages through which the oily life-blood of the device ran... there were levers and wheels smeared with grease so that pressures and differences could be measured. But though it was these things that caught the

attention of Jack [her name for the Doctor], Rebecca's interest lay elsewhere. For they were not alone in this dark and brooding hall of metal. There were galleries and platforms set round the walls of the chamber, so from these Jack and Rebecca found themselves watched by burning and sunken eyes. The machine was a ship of apes... the creatures leered from above like the gargoyles that gave them their names. They hooted and cackled, with black lips drawn back in hisses of venom. The smell from them was great enough to overcome the [smell of] oil. Their pelts were dark and matted, in some cases their snouts wet with blood, not without reason. Rebecca recalls that there were at the least three bodies there, all in blackened hoods. They had been *éventré* [French for 'eviscerated'] by the Beasts. Their bodies had been torn open by terrible, animal hands. In one case an ape had torn from a cadaver the bone of a thigh, still red though stripped of flesh by its teeth, which it shook at Jack. They shrieked their lust at my associates, yet from all Rebecca says Jack appeared unshaken. 'This,' he said, 'must be the crew.'

While all this was happening, Scarlette was still at the White Hart, where a major brawl had begun. Lisa-Beth, in concert with Anji and two of the other London women, had been drawn into a fight in which they'd enticed two of the rowdier gentlemen to battle for their honour. Juliette was trying to calm down some of the other locals, probably not using the glass totem in such an indiscreet place. But Scarlette simply sat at her table, contemplating her cup of cheap, watery chocolate, by her own admission hardly taking an interest in the events around her. It's odd to think that none of the combatants bothered her.

According to Scarlette's journal – though not Lisa-Beth's – during the fight one of the male denizens of the tavern edged his way through the violent crowds and quietly seated himself at Scarlette's table. Though no name is given for the man, Scarlette says that he was 'a gentleman of distinguished nature', clean-shaven and dark-haired, and at first she thought he might have been in the market for business. She does note, however, that on the lapel of his black clothing he wore a rosette in blue-and-white. It would have marked him out as a member of the Opposition, but nonetheless he was quite gracious and civil.

The man was as untroubled by the violence as Scarlette herself, evidently having seen much of it before. Despite their obvious differences, the two of them began to talk. They spoke of current events;

about America; about the rumours from London which stated that the Prince of Wales had become obsessed with the Countess of Jersey, who'd in some way bewitched him (although the Countess denied everything, claiming that if 'the Prince has fallen in love with me then it's not my fault'). The society affairs of London, the stories of illicit couplings in theatre boxes and sedan chairs, were notorious even in Manchester. At one point a bottle was thrown across the room, and Scarlette ducked her head to avoid it. At this point the man is said to have simply glanced at the brawl, tutted, and said: 'Politics.'

Perhaps because the man was a complete stranger, the two of them ended up speaking of things which Scarlette had never even confided to the Doctor. She explained her fears for both Juliette and the House, and seems to have talked of them as being very nearly one and the same. She also feared that 'summoning Juliette had been an error', though as Juliette was clearly a normal girl and not any kind of elemental this says interesting things about the way Scarlette perceived her.

'So many changes,' mused the man with the blue-and-white rosette, in the end. 'So many unforeseen circumstances.' They both drank to that, while the violence went on around them.

It was an oddly tranquil scene, but then, it may not really have happened. It's not that Scarlette lied in her journal: it's that she used a language just as obscure as the irritating alchemical code of the Masons. Even the name of the tavern is suspicious. No 'White Hart' is known to have existed in that part of Manchester described by Scarlette, so either she got the name wrong or simply changed it to something she felt more fitting. 'Hunting the White Hart' is a familiar mythic ritual in folklore, and may have an alchemical significance. (Certainly, later in the year one of Sabbath's agents would write of his 'need for the Black Hart', suggesting a more sinister version of the same ceremony... opposites were common in alchemical thinking, so, for example, it was said that when the Duc de Richelieu performed *his* dark ceremonies his 'evil monks' would sacrifice one white goat and one black.) Was Scarlette, in this story of unexpected friendship in the White Hart, saying something in code? And if so, then what?

The meeting seems especially odd given the events unfolding at the docks. The next account that should be related comes from Fitz, but the stories he later told the House make even less sense than those told by Rebecca. Unwilling to be left out of the action, Fitz left the side street as soon as he felt himself able to, and instead of returning to his lodgings cautiously headed back towards the shipyard.

He found nobody there, although he spent a few moments calling out for the Doctor. He was on the verge of leaving, or so the story goes, when he heard the noise. It's described as being much like the noise Rebecca noticed on the ship, a dirty, heavy, mechanical rumbling, which 'shook the very boards under Mr. K's feet'. It was at this point that his attention was drawn to the large expanse of water in the middle of the covered area, which presumably led out to the canal. Fitz later described the way the water began *sinking*, but only in the middle, as if some great force were pushing on it from above and (bizarrely) making a dent in the water itself. As the rumbling grew louder, Fitz considered leaving, but before he could act...

...and this is where accounts don't merely differ, but become so horribly jumbled as to render them meaningless. Based on Fitz's claims, Scarlette writes that at this point '*it* flickered into being, its grand and ugly body guttering like the light from a newly-lit oil lamp'. Other claims are wilder still, and involve the stopping of time; a blazing, electrical light; even a multitude of visions and hallucinations. Lisa-Beth puts things in purely tantric terms when she describes the arrival of the ship as 'a rendering [of *Shaktyanda*?] like none ever seen... I can only think that so much wanton lust had been built up in the world that even something on this scale could manifest itself'.

So what, precisely, happened? One moment there was nothing: the next, the ship seemingly appeared out of nowhere. Fitz believed that the ship had been magically transported to the dock, but this is scarcely feasible even by the tortured logic of elementals. Bearing in mind Rebecca's comment that the Doctor could *see* something in the dock that Fitz couldn't – bearing in mind, also, that the Doctor deliberately brought Rebecca with him, *a woman known for her unusual states of perception* – it's easier to believe that the ship had been there all the time, but that something had prevented Fitz from noticing it. That would certainly explain the gap in Rebecca's narrative, between arriving at the dock and boarding the ship. In fact, the whole episode closely resembles the 'trick' Scarlette performed back at the House, when she herself had become temporarily invisible.

The methods Sabbath used to pull off his own mammoth 'trick' may be arguable, but the Service must have been familiar enough with them for the *rat-catchers* to board the vessel. What's less vague is the nature of the ship itself. There are many accounts of the warcraft, but the thing every single description agrees on is that the ship was a *monstrosity*.

For a battleship, it wasn't large, a device of metal twenty yards long and no more than a dozen across. But its form, to the eighteenth-century mind, was unthinkable. Ships were things of grace and romance, yet Sabbath's vessel was a testament to efficiency, to brooding, blunt-nosed *need*. To build an all-metal ship would have been an uncanny enough idea in itself, but it was as if the designer had deliberately set out to demonstrate that the showiness of His Majesty's navy was of no importance whatsoever. The metal was grey, although in the water it looked black, the overlapping plates making the body appear sharp and jagged. A black rail ran around the smooth iron deck, the struts 'as fine as razors' (Scarlette), giving the impression of 'a machine trapped by piano-wire' (Lisa-Beth: 'trapped' meaning 'booby-trapped' rather than 'stuck'). There were no sails. There were four metal domes welded to the surface of the deck, laid out in a square, each one seven feet tall and housing stairways that led down into the machine's guts. Cannons were mounted along each side, giving the 'appearance of teeth'. It was, in short, a ship like no other on the face of the Earth.

Overall it seems to have struck those who saw it as being a *darkness*, the kind of jagged silhouette one might see at an eastern shadow-puppet show. Small for a battleship, perhaps, but so unthinkable in its nature – so like a creation of a gothic fantasy, like one of the death-machines of Sade – that many who saw it felt themselves to be overwhelmed, or even '*absorbed*' (Lisa-Beth again), by its metallic mass. At this point even Robert Fulton himself (the man who would, in the following decades, offer Napoleon the designs for the first submarine) was still years away from creating his early steamships, having failed to find the funding for anything larger than a model.

Then again, funding wouldn't have been much of a problem for the owner of this particular vessel.

SABBATH

It reads almost like a fairy tale. The Doctor, facing a horde of hostile beasts with no weapons other than his wits and only Rebecca at his side; the apes, like storybook monsters, hissing from the balconies; the doorway on the other side of the chamber, the only way to reach the heart of the warship. Faced with such a situation, most people would probably have turned back and run.

But the Doctor's response was quite different. What he did, according to Rebecca, was step forward into the room as if there were no threat whatsoever. And instead of heading for the doorway into the next chamber, he calmly moved towards the nearest of the bodies.

One of the apes was perched over the corpse as the Doctor approached, and it was from that particular cadaver that the animal had ripped the bloody thigh-bone which it was now wielding as a weapon. Perhaps the Doctor felt that the death of the *rat-catcher* needed to be acknowledged, but his move towards the body wasn't just a case of saying last rites. Later, the Doctor would make disturbing, brooding sketches of that corpse: they survive, in a creased and yellowed form, among the papers left at Henrietta Street. The drawings are anatomical in nature, but the face of the man on the page is blurred rather than masked. The pictures are the work of someone with a lot playing on his mind. There are detailed illustrations of the wounds, and next to them are scrawled, almost illegible notes comparing the scars to those which might be caused by the known ape species. And it's in these notes that the Doctor records what must have only become obvious later on, the fact that the dead man hadn't been killed by the animals at all. His neck had been cleanly snapped across. It was the *Mayakai* that had killed the man, on her way out of the warship. The apes had dragged the corpse back into the bowels of the vessel, to dismember at will.

Also, there seems to have been an important issue bothering the Doctor for some time. His notes are covered in question marks, and if he'd put the question into words he might well have put it like this:

These apes, these babewyns, are an elemental force. They appear to be everywhere and to exist in their millions. Then why have I, with all my experience of such matters, never seen anything like them before?

Doubt, uncertainty… and sickness. Everyone agreed that the Doctor's mood had been, to say the least, *unstable* in the weeks leading up to his first meeting with Sabbath. There had been many more occasions on which he'd been spotted mulling over his beard (and at least one squabble with Anji, after she'd suggested that it didn't suit him). Prone to rapid mood swings, at the start of his stay he'd been a dynamo of action at best, merely a little haunted at worst. But increasingly, those around him noted less and less humour in his character. Once, shortly before the House had de-camped to Manchester, Rebecca had disturbed him in his study and asked him whether she could borrow some of his writing materials. The Doctor had responded by suddenly snapping at her, with some anger, and even throwing one of his curious devices across the room in her direction. When the machine had shattered against the wall, it had apparently shaken the Doctor to his senses and he'd immediately apologised: Rebecca had simply shrugged. But on her way out of the basement, Rebecca later said, she'd heard the Doctor gasping for breath. More than once, he'd been seen clutching his chest as if in pain.

He'd improved a little when Fitz and Anji had been brought to the House – perhaps, when he'd 'opened up time' for them, he'd felt briefly in touch with his TARDIS again – but the relief hadn't lasted long. Unfortunately, he was constantly evasive when anyone asked him what the matter was. Fitz's opinion was that the Doctor simply didn't know himself, although there's some evidence that he perceived a link between the ape attacks and his own sickness, the typical magician's belief that his own well-being is connected to that of the whole world.

What nobody knew, not until much later, was that the Doctor wasn't just sick. His body was actually dying.

Yet despite all this, he felt no fear on board Sabbath's warship. He confided to Rebecca that it was only a matter of logic. The apes hadn't attacked as soon as he'd entered their lair, despite their vicious nature, so therefore something was *stopping* them. He concluded from this that whoever had 'trained' the beasts was quite prepared to let himself and Rebecca pass, and in this he turned out to be correct. Once the Doctor had finished examining (blessing?) the body, he had no compunction about entering the chamber beyond, and Rebecca seems to have had no compunction about following.

The chamber turned out to be the closest thing the warship had to a bridge. With no crew other than the apes, there can hardly have been a need for the usual structure of a military vessel. The heart of the craft was a command centre, cabin and war room all in one, and waiting there was Sabbath himself.

The bridge-room is worth describing, as so much is known about it. Apart from several accounts, there's even a sketch, though not in the Doctor's hand. The room was the largest on board the warship, over twenty feet wide and thirty long, by the ship's standards a great vaulted steel hall which ran halfway along the length of the vessel. But although it was wrought out of metal, with archways of welded steel and walls of riveted black iron plate, there was something of the feel of a classical temple to it. ('Classical' was a recurring motif in the architecture of the period, and had been ever since Pompeii had been excavated, when the British had become obsessed with ancient, majestic things preserved for all eternity. But Sabbath's ship comes across as a kind of deliberate parody, a Temple of Oracles built by industrial methods.) There was a 'gentle throbbing' in the room, according to Rebecca's story, a sound she could only liken to the beating of a monumental heart. And when anyone moved across the steel floor, their footsteps would ring out in a manner that made walking itself seem almost disrespectful.

But perhaps the most notable features of the room were the alcoves. Set into the two side walls were rows of arches, in the style of classical cloisters, again wrought out of black metal. Each one was lit by a lamp, modern gas rather than oil, and although the sketch deliberately avoids depicting the alcoves' contents the accounts describe them in detail. Each alcove contained an idol, set on a metal plinth. From the middle of the vast, humming room, the faces of more than a dozen gods looked out at the observer.

Did Sabbath worship these totems? Or was it all an obscure, blasphemous joke? Without knowing the exact nature of the idols it's hard to say, though one witness records that 'some had faces so monstrus I could not bear but look' (bad writing, or did she mean it that way?). As Rebecca mentioned at least one in the Polynesian style and one following the fashion of the West Indian witch-cults, perhaps Sabbath saw the icons as an inventory of all the world's major systems of ritual. There was even a crucifix, complete with a sculpture of Christ, described with maddening vagueness as 'obscene'. Possibly Sabbath believed that by keeping this inventory, he could (symbolically?) keep an eye on all those who moved in the same circles as himself. In which case, the bridge-room was almost a three-dimensional rendering of Scarlette's own Red List.

The other noteworthy feature of the room was the map. One entire wall, the far wall from the entrance, had been covered by an enormous map of the world almost twice as tall as a man. This was common in the 'war rooms' of the late eighteenth and early nineteenth centuries. Napoleon himself had a map that took up a wall of his study, as did the British Prime Minister during the Napoleonic wars. On Sabbath's map, dark red (almost blood-coloured) continents floated on metallic grey seas, spidery letters marking out settlements as far apart as Paris and Botany Bay. Interestingly – because it was a practice which didn't become common for another century – small 'flags' were always pinned to the map, markers of red and black and white and blue. There were so many of these on the map that they seem to have formed patterns, like contour-lines, although as these lines swept across whole oceans they couldn't have indicated military units.

(However, there's mention in the Doctor's yellowed notes of 'time walls', the language he uses suggesting the isobars or 'pressure lines' used on modern weather-maps. The Doctor believed that it was the erratic movements of these strange contours which had prevented his TARDIS entering the eighteenth century, and that if he could navigate a path through the contours then he could finally summon the device. If this is what Sabbath's chart represented, then the Doctor must surely have been interested that Sabbath's research was ahead of his own.)

Rebecca's story is most specific about what happened in the room, though it sounds so dramatic that it may all be part of the Henrietta Street folklore. Sabbath himself was standing before the great map when the Doctor entered. His back was turned, and his two plump hands were folded behind his waist. He was staring up at the chart, regardless of his visitors, even though he can hardly have been unaware of their presence. It's an image straight out of melodrama. The casual, confident villain waiting patiently in his lair, finally turning around only after the Doctor greeted him ('hello, I'm the Doctor, but I suppose you knew that').

What can the Doctor have expected from Sabbath, this mastermind who'd amassed such a powerbase without ever being seen? An adventurer? An assassin? Certainly, it would have surprised many to find that Sabbath appeared quite the way he did. But descriptions of Sabbath in this period are common, and all of them are in agreement.

Sabbath was overweight, though not grossly so: he'd chosen to become the spider in the centre of the web, and by 1782 simply didn't regard his physical appearance as an issue. His figure is described, in several accounts, as 'powerful' (or, as one acquaintance put it, 'he casts a grate shadoe wherever he walks'). His bulky body was built of muscle as well as fat, though since his youth the balance had shifted towards the plump side. He had, by all accounts, fists like great hams, and it was impossible to imagine him hurrying anywhere. Though he doesn't seem to have been overly tall, his presence was such that he struck those few people he met as being as big as the room around him. When he spoke it was in a low rumble, the words rolling around in his stomach before finally arriving at his mouth, something which led many people to follow his commands without stopping to think about them.

Yet he was also, without doubt, a man of great wit. Despite the menace in his voice and in his presence, there was a distinctly dry irony in his words. There was said to be a sense of amusement in everything he said, as if there were subtle layers of meaning in every sentence and he found himself entertained by the fact that nobody understood it all. His features reflected this, although it's unfortunate that no actual portrait of him was ever painted. His face was pale and fleshy, but not at all unattractive as he entered early middle age. In his youth he was, allegedly, a master of seduction as well as the other arts in which the Service trained their agents. The famous Covent Garden celebrity Fanny Murray was rumoured to have fallen for his charms as early as 1762, and his history with Scarlette has already been mentioned. The amusement he displayed at those around him was most evident in his mouth, which was often fixed in a slight half-smile on the left side of his lips. Most importantly, there were his eyes. Universally described as 'dark' and 'deep-set' (Rebecca says brown, Lisa-Beth says dark green, the only discrepancy in the accounts), they were said to perpetually 'twinkle with intelligence', though whether this was literally true or just eighteenth-century romantic folly is hard to say.

Rebecca describes his appearance on the warship as remarkable. It must have struck her as notable that his head had been shaved. Though not bald there was only a thin layer of dark hair on his scalp, perhaps what in modern terms might be called a 'skinhead', but which at the time was unknown outside of any monastery. It's possible that Sabbath had just decided that hair was a waste of time and effort. His clothes, too, were notable. His portly figure was covered with a loose grey overcoat, of the kind famously worn by military men like (again) Napoleon. Once more, there's a sense of irony here. Sabbath is known to have considered the military – with its insistence on protocol and uniform – as absurd, so the greatcoat was almost certainly intended as a form of joke. Sabbath was the captain of this ship, but it was a ship of idiotic, drooling animals, and the idea of any form of *decorum* being observed must have amused him greatly.

So it was that the two men faced each other for the first time, the Doctor on one side of the room, a casual, intelligent Napoleon on the other, and it's worth noting how often descriptions of the two overlapped. Both of them having something of the charlatan in them, both of them realising it was all part of a greater game in which symbols were their most effective weapons. Just as the Doctor had Juliette as a form of apprentice, Sabbath had Tula Lui, the *Mayakai* amazon, whose importance had yet to become clear.

And Sabbath's first words to the Doctor were reported to be: 'I'd be more impressed, Doctor, if most of the people who use that title weren't either third-rate quacks or pedlars in pornographic literature.'

Hardly surprising that there are so many legends about the confrontation. In Masonic circles, for example, it was said that at the very moment the Doctor and Sabbath came face to face, Scarlette – still back at the tavern – became aware of the meeting. The story goes that she stood from her table, and in front of her assembled women announced,

96

'the White Hart has met the Black, and I pity the world for the consequences!'.

But this is provably rubbish. At the moment Sabbath and the Doctor met, the fight at the tavern was just winding down and Scarlette was simply brooding. The mysterious (and possibly mythical) man with the rosette had evidently departed, because as the last of the rowdier men were escorted off the premises Lisa-Beth scowled her way across the room and sat in the seat across the table from her employer. She found Scarlette still hunched over her cup of chocolate, 'reading the stains at the bottom of the cup as if she thought herself an augur'.

Chocolate and the *tantra* were inexorably linked, in the eighteenth century. Houses of ill repute were often referred to as 'chocolate-houses', as the refreshments they provided included hot chocolate (still regarded as a little exotic) as well as more carnal pleasures. Also, it's worth pointing out that much of the *tantra*, at least from a woman's point of view, was connected to blood and the lunar month: and that chocolate had a reputation for both calming and 'synchronising' the body's menstrual cycle. It's a well-known fact that chocolate does indeed cause distinct chemical changes in the female biology (largely due to the forced production of seratonin), and it's therefore logical that cocoa was seen as an almost mystical substance. Many would perhaps be surprised that, far from hemlock or newt's-eye, in some circles chocolate is regarded as the definitive ingredient of witchcraft.

It was possibly the effects of the chocolate which caused Scarlette to open up to Lisa-Beth in a most unexpected way. Lisa-Beth records that Scarlette said nothing for a moment or two, but continued to look down into her emptied cup. Then, at last, she looked up and made eye contact. All she said was:

'It doesn't matter about Juliette.'

Lisa-Beth merely nodded. It was an acknowledgement, more than anything. Scarlette was making it clear that she knew the secrets Lisa-Beth had been keeping – relating to Juliette's own background, many suspected – but that she was now prepared to forget the past. Both Scarlette and Lisa-Beth knew that things weren't going well for their kind, and that things would get even worse before the end. Both of them now accepted that they had to face the future together.

If she'd known how close Sabbath was, Scarlette may have been less confident. Indeed, only moments later Fitz dragged himself into the tavern to report what he'd seen at the docks.

* * *

QUESTIONS OF IMPORTANCE

Magical theory states that a person is inseparable from his or her place of power. Scarlette *was* her House, or at least connected to it; the Doctor obviously believed he *was* his TARDIS (though later events would prove him slightly mistaken); perhaps Sabbath was his warship. It thus follows that King George III *was* Britain, and an elementalist might have argued that his later descent into tortured, frothing madness was initiated by the events of that summer.

The King was spending much of his time at Windsor, where he'd often take walks around the farms and shops of the community, thoroughly confusing everybody he met. He'd frequently talk with local farmers or tradesmen, about agriculture and local affairs and even religion, but between May and July many of those he spoke to later admitted that he seemed... *unwell*. He'd switch rapidly from topic to topic, punctuating every sentence with cries of 'eh?' and 'what?', as if something were following him and only by changing direction could he throw it off his scent. It's surely significant that when he finally lapsed into permanent madness, in 1811, one of his recurring delusions was that his country was sinking and that he was a beast on board Noah's Ark.

The Service became concerned. Still believing Sabbath to have been the root cause of all the trouble, they started speculating that the whole thing was an attack on King and Country. They hardly would have been reassured if they'd known that Sabbath considered King and Country to be gloriously irrelevant

No reliable account of the Doctor's first conversation with Sabbath exists, but what follows is an approximation. It's been assembled from Rebecca's tales, from the Doctor's own recollections (as they're recorded), and from things known about Sabbath. Rebecca related that during the encounter, the Doctor constantly paced the hall, making the decks ring out as he examined the icons and the alcoves and Sabbath regarded him with cool interest. Rebecca herself remained silent.

> DOCTOR: I can't say I think much of your crew, by the way. It must be hard finding the staff.
> SABBATH: Finding staff isn't difficult. Finding staff who are capable of discretion, however...
> DOCTOR: Hmm. You trained them yourself?
> SABBATH: By proxy. The process isn't reliable.
> DOCTOR: Yes. But you're not the one responsible, are you?
> SABBATH: 'Responsible'?

DOCTOR: You're not the one causing the attacks. Scarlette thinks you are, but she's, ah… not unbiased.

SABBATH: I should imagine. Might I ask how she is?

DOCTOR: She sends her love.

SABBATH: I'm sure. Well now. You seem convinced of my innocence. I'm gratified.

DOCTOR: You're riding the wave. For some reason, the ape-elementals are being summoned to Earth. Or at least, they're just bubbling under the surface. You think you can control them. You've been calling them deliberately, then binding them. But you're not really in control at all. You're just trying to turn the situation to your advantage.

SABBATH: That's something of a narrow perspective. But I'm the host here, it'd be bad manners for me to argue.

DOCTOR: You can't control *all* of them. There must be thousands waiting out there.

SABBATH: Millions, I should think.

DOCTOR [some of the conversation may have been lost here]: But it strikes me we've got very similar aims. I don't want to see the *babewyns* overrun the Earth. I don't know what your agenda is, but I'm fairly sure you don't either.

SABBATH: I see. Why do I feel, Doctor, that you're about to suggest an alliance?

DOCTOR: There are more important things to think about than your private army. If we're going to achieve anything, we're going to have to find out the truth. We need to work out who's really responsible for all this. Who's letting the apes come into the world.

SABBATH: Really? I would have thought that was perfectly obvious.

DOCTOR [presumably surprised]: You know?

SABBATH: Of course I know. It's not difficult to work out.

DOCTOR: Who, then? Who's behind all this?

SABBATH: *You* are. Why do you think I invited you here?

What happened next is obscure. The Doctor apparently reacted badly to this, and began arguing with Sabbath in a flustered manner, but all Rebecca could later remember was that the two men spent some time discussing (or arguing about) technical matters. They may have talked about the contours on the peculiar map, though whether Sabbath fully explained his strange accusation against the Doctor is unknown. What's

99

known is that after a while the Doctor fell into an uneasy silence, and ceased pacing the bridge-room.

This is when he reached into his jacket pocket, took out a bright red envelope, and handed it to Sabbath.

That the Doctor invited Sabbath to the wedding ceremony is remarkable in itself. It was the envelope marked out for the *Mayakai*: with the race almost extinct, the Doctor may have seen Sabbath as the last guardian of the *Mayakai*'s heritage. Or maybe he felt that as one of only two *Mayakai* known to survive was in Sabbath's employ, the invitation might as well have gone to Sabbath as to anyone. By this time Tula Lui had already embarked on her mission of revenge against the Service, and if the Doctor had known of its bloody consequences he might not have been so willing to hand over the envelope.

Sabbath knew all about the Doctor's proposed marriage. In a fragment of conversation which occurred towards the end of the encounter, the men even discussed the matter:

> SABBATH: I see. And you believe, I presume, that this *ritual* can help you?
> DOCTOR: It might not help *me*. But it'll help.
> SABBATH: And does the young lady understand the consequences of what she's doing?
> DOCTOR: I'm trying to teach her. Do you really care?
> SABBATH: Oh, I have a certain casual interest in these things. Of course, you realise… this isn't going to change my opinion of you.
> DOCTOR: Mmm. You're the one trying to shut our House down, then?
> SABBATH: The machinery's already in operation. What happens next is hardly my concern.

Unsurprisingly, Rebecca understood little of this exchange. She might have been expecting a battle, not a polite (if vaguely menacing) conversation. She was certainly surprised when the Doctor, after asking one more simple question, wished Sabbath a good day and turned to leave the room. Sabbath's response was simply to nod back.

So it was that the two of them left the warship, not in a fury of action but with a mere goodbye. The apes continued to spit at them on their way out, but this time they left by a steel stairway, arriving on the ship's deck rather than crawling back out through the side of the vessel.

When they emerged into the dim light of the covered shipyard, they found they weren't alone. On the jetty by the warship, Scarlette was waiting for them, along with Fitz, Juliette, Anji, Lisa-Beth and the rest. Dressed in their clothes of red and black, they must have looked something like a guard of honour, but their faces were grim. They were carrying lanterns, as if the affair were a vigil. The Doctor had made contact with the enemy: even the Doctor himself must have been expecting some kind of conflict, which was presumably why his army had accompanied him here. Legend has it that Scarlette's face, lit by the dull yellow glow of her lantern, was so fixed and calm that she hardly seemed human at all. As if she knew how close she was to her old enemy-cum-suitor, and knew she couldn't allow herself to even acknowledge it. This time, legend is probably correct.

It wasn't until the long journey home to London that Scarlette discovered the truth, and found out exactly what the Doctor had said to Sabbath. One can only guess how she must have felt, when she learned that the Doctor had asked Sabbath to be his best man.

5
Europe

NIGHTMARES AND GHOST STORIES

It was a year of great literary note. Or at least, it was a year of literary note: whether the literature qualified as 'great' is a matter of taste.

It was in summer that a French nobleman, incarcerated in the dungeons of Vincennes (second only in reputation to the Bastille), began work on the rough notes of what later generations would regard as his masterpiece. For political reasons, the governor of the prison insisted that the nobleman's real name should never be spoken: in another of those quirks which modern readers often believe to be some kind of obscure joke, the prisoner was known only as 'monsieur le 6'. His book, *The 120 Days of Sodom*, would come to be reviled by many as the most blasphemous, bloodthirsty work of pornography ever written... its true significance would only become clear centuries later, when historians would realise that 'Number Six' had written – in his own, admittedly vitriolic, style – the first work of clinical psychosexuality. 'Six' had set out to record every imaginable perversion that might be enjoyed by the corrupt ruling powers of France, in a style that bordered on the horrific.

On the other hand, the second important work to be started that year was written by the Doctor.

What inspired the Doctor to sit down and write a book remains unclear. It could have been that he wanted to further expand his horizons, or that the conversation with Sabbath had been playing on his mind and he needed a way to exorcise his doubts. It could have been that he simply felt like it. The unwieldy title was *The Ruminations of a Foreign Traveller in His Element*, and it has more in common with the work of 'Number Six' than one might expect. Although sex is never discussed by the Doctor, much of his *Ruminations* takes the form of a catalogue, an assemblage of demons fought, people encountered and dream-worlds visited, in no order that makes much sense. But as *tantrists* such as Lisa-Beth made a strong connection between the body and the world of 'private time' (indeed, violent or unpleasant perversions such as those listed in *Sodom* are referred to in many texts as 'demons'), modern psychologists might find peculiar parallels between the two works. It's interesting to think what might have happened if the Doctor and Number Six had compared notes.

The Doctor was no author. He saw himself as an adventurer, a gentleman-traveller, and as a result his *Ruminations* is an awkward and often deliberately obtuse work. His thoughts fill the pages as though the memories of several lifetimes have been painfully scrambled and forced into words. Then again, the book was most probably written for a readership familiar with coded alchemical texts. Although the *Ruminations* was eventually published in 1783, it had a tiny circulation. A copy is known to have been held in the Windsor bookshop for several years afterwards. Yet however tangled it might be, the book contains several insights into the Doctor's thoughts at this stage. Here, for example, are some telling notes on the topic of mortality:

The purpose of all alchemy is to find the Philosopher's Stone, the key to immortality. But let us suppose there was a coven, or a whole race of people, which had discovered such a Stone. Let us suppose that if a member of this race died, his body could heal itself and allow the man to live again. There is a problem, naturally. Death means change; ergo, without death there would be no change. The society of such a people would be a dreary and stagnant one... [but] let us not imagine they would be fools. They would realise this. The Philosopher's Stone has the ability to re-make a man as he was before he suffered his unfortunate death, but in an effort to allow at least *some* development in their society these immortal folk might mix the Stone with other compounds... to ensure that when a man of their number was re-born, he would become a *new* man. Therefore change among these people would be a case of sudden and jarring steps rather than a constant spectrum of development. In this race, each man would be his own coven...

The difficulty with such stability is that it goes against the grain of all other life in the universe. Even if such a race were not *entirely* unchanging, their lack of motion might cause them to become as a solid rock in the middle of a river. All other life would flow around them, until the universe itself accepted their presence as part of its function. Terrible to imagine the consequences of such a race being suddenly removed from that universe.

All this is speculation, though, because I can truthfully say that no such race exists in this universe...

* * *

And this is in a section of the book that's supposed to be about the habits of pigeons.

Later in the book, he returns to the subject of these 'immortals' and suggests that if they existed, they could use the 'Philosopher's Stone' to re-birth themselves in any number of new forms, 'from great three-headed things to bodies made of pure heat'. Again, we get the impression of a man who's been pushing his limits ever since his arrival (Scarlette records that although Fitz and Anji accepted the Doctor's marriage without question, they did so 'in a manner which told me they were merely so shocked as not to dwell on it'). It was as if the Doctor had suddenly realised that the Philosopher's Stone was his, and that there were no others of his kind to limit the way in which it was used. What's most striking of all is the tone of *surprise* that runs through the book, the sense that the Doctor hadn't even considered these ideas until he'd put pen to paper and let his subconscious pour itself out on to the page.

His new interests didn't stop at literature. More than once he visited the Royal Academy – he seems to have had no difficulty charming the Academians, nor in gaining their immediate trust – where he was particularly taken by a painting that had recently arrived there, Fuseli's *The Nightmare*.

It's hard to explain the impact of *The Nightmare* on the world of art. A haunting, murderous vision of a painting, even the conservative Sir Joshua Reynolds acknowledged it as like nothing he'd seen before. A woman lies on a bed, prone and sprawling. Velvet drapes hang like shadows around her; a creature, part goblin and part simian, squats on her chest like a predator while eyeing up the audience in search of further victims. It had a massive influence on the fantasy literature of later centuries, and like Wessel's *Anno 7603* opened up whole new realms of artistic thought. Significantly, it also became the first known painting to inspire a cartoon parody: in 1784, the *Covent Garden Nightmare* would be published in the popular press, depicting the Duchess of Devonshire as the prone woman with Charles Fox as the bloated demon on her chest. Appropriate, then, that it should have been painted in the same year as the Doctor's arrival.

From the Doctor's point of view, it was a portrait of an intrusion from another world. He's known to have stood for over an hour in front of the *Nightmare*, and at one stage he even conversed with a gentleman of the Academy (it may have been Joshua Reynolds himself, Reynolds being a notorious patron and painter of courtesans) without taking his eyes off the canvas. The Doctor, it's said, asked if he could have a print of the painting for the House. When told that this would be impossible, the Doctor noted that this would be a piece much sought after by the public. History proved him right: *The Nightmare* became one of the first prints to be mass-produced, starting in 1783.

There was one other thing the Doctor is thought to have said, as he stood next to his fellow Academician before the Fuseli. His words are recorded to have been: 'Painting. Yes. That's where I should go next.'

Evidently, he was well aware of his limitations as a writer. But then, the Doctor's new hobbies could have been a result of him having little else to do. Because in the weeks following the meeting with Sabbath, the House began to split apart. By the second week of the month, both Scarlette and Lisa-Beth were in Paris, staying in a bright and sunlit room overlooking the open streets near the Place de Grève.

At the end of June another of the women left, heading for a more successful bordello to the north of London. Business dropped still further, to the Doctor's quiet relief but at the expense of the House. Gentlemen were avoiding Henrietta Street, seeing the House (ironically, given its link to the lunar cycle) as 'cursed'. The watchmen who patrolled Covent Garden were starting to circle like sharks. They could frequently be seen, lamps in their hands, eyeing up the windows as if wondering how long it'd be until they felt safe enough to pounce.

During his meeting with Sabbath, the Doctor had learned the truth of it. Sabbath, like the Service itself, had indeed been using his resources to make things hard for Scarlette's operation. He'd supplied small amounts of money to Scarlette's rivals, spread stories among the watch and the Bow Street Runners, encouraged his contacts in high society to think that these 'witches' carried diseases spawned by the Devil himself. He'd explained his reasons, but only in vague terms:

SABBATH: It's a question of control, I think.
DOCTOR: You mean, you want more of it?
SABBATH: Not at all. I mean, you don't possess *any* of it. Do you know the consequences of what you're doing, Doctor? Does Scarlette?
DOCTOR: Oh, don't worry about me. I'm a professional. So's Scarlette, I suppose.
SABBATH: You *were* a professional. Your company has… so to speak… gone bankrupt.

Sabbath had admitted that he'd tried to shut the House down, as he'd felt it to be an 'unacceptable risk'. Following his meeting with the Doctor, it's obvious that Sabbath changed tack, and allowed the Doctor to think the two of them could work together. But the wheels had already been set in motion. Funds had been paid, rumours spread: and when the Doctor had asked Sabbath to use his influence to *undo* the damage to the House, Sabbath had refused. It was, Sabbath had explained, a maxim of his always to see something through to its conclusion.

'Think of it as an initiation,' Sabbath had said, probably with that famous half-smile. 'If you don't have the power to put your own House in order, then you can hardly have the power to save the whole of the world.'

So Scarlette's departure to France came at a bad time. Worse, she left immediately before a 'bloody weekend'. As has already been recorded, the women within the House had all become part of the same lunar cycle, including Anji and Juliette. There was a long weekend in every month in which 'the House would bleed', business would be suspended, and much chocolate would be drunk. Fires would be lit in every room after nightfall , the raw flames visible in the windows and making it clear to all passers-by that the building's blood was up. The occupants of the House tended to shut themselves in their rooms during bloody weekends. The pianoforte in the salon seemed ill-fitting, somehow. Frequently, in the red-lined room on the second floor up, Juliette, Rebecca, Fitz and (sometimes) Anji would sit together around a fire in an incense-bowl that was the only source of light. Rebecca would tell ghost-stories about America, because, by definition, *any* story told about America was a ghost-story. Often Juliette would fall perfectly silent and stare either into the fire or just at the floorboards, leading Fitz (correctly, or not?) to conclude that she was becoming as sad as the House itself. On one occasion Juliette picked a card at random from a deck of cards, the first time she'd ever let Rebecca make an attempt at reading her fortune. Her future was the Knave of Hearts. Rebecca's interpretation of this isn't known.

What Fitz can't have guessed, at least not in the summer, was that Juliette's 'rooting' to the House was only the first step in a process by which she was to become linked to the *planet*.

There may have been an element of escape in Scarlette's decision to go to Paris, but she had good reasons for being there. It had started the week after the Doctor had met Sabbath. A most notable body was found in London: a second turned up fifteen days later. The first body had been found dangling beneath Blackfriar's Bridge, within sight of the spot where Sabbath's initiation had taken place, the deceased's intestines ripped from his body and hung around his neck. It was the traditional method of Masonic execution, for those who betrayed the Brotherhood. The second was found in the river itself, but two miles away from central London. Stones were found in his pockets, though some of the stones had come loose and allowed him to be caught up in the mooring-rope of a boat by the riverbank. The magistrate called to the scene noted the blackly comical detail that 'a family of small shelled fish had made their home in the space of one nostril, and none who found the unfortunate had the stomach to evict them before burial'.

Both victims were members of the Service, and both belonged to the five-strong Council of the Star Chamber. These were big targets indeed. Although the Council was known in underworld circles to be the nominal leadership of the Service, the truth was that the *real* heads of the organisation were safely tucked away in obscure offices at Westminster. The five Councillors were purely symbolic figureheads, who carried the vestments of the Service's occult heritage for all to see. Nonetheless, anybody who attacked the Council was making a bold gesture. When the still-new Prime Minister Rockingham dropped dead on the first day of July, leaving the American peace negotiations at an uncertain point, some immediately assumed that it was part of a ruthless attack on the very foundations of the country (though it soon became clear that the death was due to nothing more sinister than influenza).

But there was definitely a threat. When the *rat-catchers* had tried to assassinate Sabbath, Sabbath had sent his agent on an errand to assassinate the Council in return. It was a message to Westminster: 'I'm *not* going to be intimidated, so please stop bothering me.' And this must have troubled the Doctor. He was still intent on bringing together all factions, using the wedding as a focus, so for his best man to be murdering the other guests was impolite to say the least. He knew that Sabbath would have left Manchester by now, and decided that the best way to stop the slaughter was to stop Tula Lui herself. Which meant finding the other three members of the Council.

But after the first two killings, the three survivors had gone to ground. Rumour had it that they'd fled abroad. The only one whose exact whereabouts could be traced had gone to stay at his continental residence in Paris. There he'd formally asked for the protection of the Royal Lodge of Commanders of the Temple West of Carcassonne, a group whose secrets no historian has *ever* unravelled, and which in 1782 had just initiated the American ambassador-cum-scientist Benjamin Franklin into its ranks. The Temple was still considering its reply.

The Doctor knew that Sabbath himself wouldn't be in France. This could be why Scarlette so readily volunteered to cross the channel, taking only Lisa-Beth as a companion.

Besides which, Scarlette had her own interests in the *Mayakai*.

THE CITY OF LOVE

The Polynesian race known as the *Mayakai* essentially ceased to exist around 1773, when a South American survey of their native island found 'a blasted and appalling land... bodies lie wasted on the shore, and no man has reason to give them decent burial'. As the *Mayakai*'s first contact with Europeans had occurred less than a decade earlier, many believed that it was European disease which had decimated the population, as with so many Polynesian peoples.

A scant handful of the race survived, and by 1776 were taking refuge in Europe or the Americas. Though no first-hand writings exist, it's worth examining the few stories told by these refugees. Although western disease is mentioned (it's described, not entirely accurately, as a 'pox'), the *Mayakai* had their own beliefs as to what had caused their destruction. It was, they said, all about the *Moak*: often translated as 'gods', but in fact closer to 'giants', albeit giants of a spectral rather than physical nature. The *Mayakai* essentially believed themselves to be the chosen ones of these giants. The giants had suffered a great battle – the *Mayakai* lived on too small an island for them to have created a word for 'war' – which had lasted for generations, in which many of the greatest gods had been smitten by the *Na Koporaya*, a word notoriously difficult to translate. The greatest of the giants had passed on to the Polynesians the duty of guarding the ancient wisdom, ready for the day when they would walk again in this world to reclaim what had been lost in the battle.

Although the stories speak of the battle as a physical thing, it may well have been a metaphor for the disease which ravaged the island and virtually destroyed the pure *Mayakai* bloodlines. One of the few who survived was Tula Lui, and she can't have been more than seven when she left for the western world. From Sabbath's own recollections, it's known that he first encountered Tula Lui as a child of ten in 1776. He immediately took an interest in the girl, possibly seeing the great similarities between the ways of the *tantra* and the time-oriented beliefs of the survivors. But the *Mayakai* were warriors too, and Sabbath the strategist must have seen the appeal of taking on one of the few survivors as an 'apprentice'.

108

By 1780, the year in which all ties between Sabbath and the Service were finally broken, Tula Lui was under his wing. Perhaps as an entertainment, he took the girl to several society functions shortly before his fall from grace, where he dressed her in sombre black clothing but made no attempt to cover up her hairstyle (*Mayakai* women shaved off all hair on the scalp but for a small patch, and let that patch grow indefinitely, letting the seemingly endless strands fall loosely over their faces). Those members of society who deigned to approach this curious girl found that she had 'an ill disposition' and was 'unable or unwilling to speak English', though she did apparently understand Sabbath. She was described as being very nearly feral, not unattractive though with a flattened nose and 'skin near luminous'. She snarled at anyone who attempted conversation, no doubt to Sabbath's amusement.

Of course, 1780 was also the year in which Sabbath had tried to seduce Scarlette, and very nearly succeeded. So, as she sought out Tula Lui, how did Scarlette see this sixteen-year-old assassin? Did she see the girl as having taken the place Sabbath had marked out for Scarlette herself, and if so, was there a secret element of jealousy present?

It was on July 17, 1782, that Scarlette came the closest she ever came to meeting her 'replacement' face-to-face. She and Lisa-Beth had taken an upstairs room in the region of the Place de Grève, the expense of which had caused some concern to Lisa-Beth. But Scarlette was determined to enjoy the sojourn. Paris, at the time, was a far less industrial city than any of those Scarlette knew: though the French winters were often murderously cold, in summer the skies were a pure and liquid blue that no resident of Covent Garden could have anticipated. Scarlette would spend great lengths of time by the (glassless) window, the shutters open, the sunlight streaming into the soft-wood interior of the building. Scarlette would take deep lungfuls of fresh air while Lisa-Beth would lie on the bed in the background, shaking her head and working on her journals.

In fact, Scarlette's deep lungfuls of air can't have been all that pleasant. A non-industrial city is, after all, a city of excrement rather than smog. But Scarlette had practical reasons for standing at the window as well, as she'd already located the third member of the Star Chamber, known in both women's journals as 'Johnny Lucifer-in-Britches'. The room overlooked a thoroughfare between the man's Parisian home and the wider street to the north, home to the region's more tasteful *boutiques*. In the afternoons the man would often be seen strolling along the thoroughfare beneath the window, enjoying the sunshine and regularly being propositioned by the local harlots. Scarlette described them as 'not at all up to scratch, when you think that this is supposed to be the *ville d'amour*'.

Whenever he passed by, Lisa-Beth would ask Scarlette whether they shouldn't follow, in case Tula Lui was close. Scarlette would generally say no, claiming that she'd know, at a glance, when the man would be in danger. Lisa-Beth notes that Scarlette would often fiddle with the seams at the front of her red dress when she said it, as if reaching for the shard of glass that no longer hung there.

On July 17, things were different. On that day, records Scarlette, she 'saw Johnny Lucifer-in-Britches passing by and knew his life was in peril'. Exactly what this instinct might have been, Scarlette doesn't say – no doubt she would have claimed that she could sense the closeness of a *Mayakai* – but Lisa-Beth was obviously convinced.

Scarlette's instincts apparently weren't good enough, though, because five minutes later 'Johnny' was as dead as his two comrades in London.

At the junction of the street to the north there was a butcher's shop, owned by a notorious slaughterman named Brillot. Brillot had achieved some fame in the 1770s for his claim that he could prepare *any* animal for the table, no matter how small or paltry: the only meat he'd refuse to touch was horse, as he felt it was too 'common' and beneath his capabilities. This pride in his work would later rebound on Brillot and bring him close to a lynching when, during the French Revolution, the streets of Paris would fill up with human cadavers and the patently false rumour would be spread that the infamous butcher was serving his customers with delicacies of human flesh.

By the time Scarlette and Lisa-Beth arrived on the fetid street, their quarry was some way ahead of them, turning into the gaudily-painted door of M. Brillot's establishment. Shortly thereafter, Brillot himself – a plump, bald man who constantly carried a cleaver in one hand as if it were a sign of his masculinity – came running out on to the street, somewhat damaging his macho reputation by shouting that most French of exclamations, '*à l'assassine!*'. It took the London women some moments to squeeze through the gathering crowd, and some moments more for them to slip past Brillot, who was convinced that they were ghouls intent on pillaging at the crime scene.

Scarlette was first into the *boucherie*, but only by moments, so it's hard to explain the discrepancies between her account and Lisa-Beth's. According to Lisa-Beth, when they entered the shop it was clear that they were too late. The shop was dimly-lit and stank of blood, hung with the hides of butchered animals, but there were no human beings to be seen. No live human beings, at least. For the man they'd come to save, still in his English waistcoat and breeches, was already dead on a cutting-board. His head had been removed, by the cleaver which now lay at the side of his body. As Lisa-Beth describes the scene, the victim's expression was one of quiet bewilderment, as if the head had been severed so quickly that he'd had no idea what to make of it.

But Scarlette tells a different tale. Though she too relates that the body was on the board, she claims that as they entered *the man's assailant was still standing over the corpse*. Her story puts great store in the fact that the murderess whirled around to face her, and that just for a moment Scarlette looked into the angry, wrinkle-nosed face of a young Polynesian woman, whose strands of hair were plaited and who wore some form of monastic cloak which covered most of her body.

The end of the story is typical of Scarlette's effective-but-theatrical style. The *assassine* turned away from Scarlette, and Scarlette believed the girl was about to run. But then…

…I heard her growl a single world [sic] beneath her breath. She ran, yet I did not and could not see the direction in which she ran, save to say that there was no exit from the shop in that direction.

There *does* seem to have been an exit at the rear of M. Brillot's shop, through which the girl could have made her escape. Yet Scarlette's account makes it sound as though the killer simply vanished into thin air, or through a solid wall. Doubly curious, then, that Lisa-Beth mentions seeing no such assailant. Then again, perhaps due to the pleading of the British ambassador, there's little record of the death at all.

It might sound like a terrible joke on Tula Lui's part, to have slaughtered a man in the style of an animal. But the *Mayakai* were always a deeply ritualised people. Those of the Masonic tradition expected to be executed by hanging below a bridge, and on the Thames that was how it had been. Perhaps Tula Lui simply killed according to what seemed most *correct* at the place of execution. Perhaps she saw the remains of the animal carcasses around her in the *boucherie*, and believed that this was how any killing should be done when in France.

Things and people vanishing off the face of the Earth or mysteriously appearing are common themes in the narrative. The assassin in the *boucherie*; Sabbath's warship (later to be named, with the usual irony, the *Jonah*); Fitz and Anji on May Day. The Doctor was definitely convinced that he could force solid objects to appear at will. From mid-June, new diagrams begin to appear in his yellowed, arcane notes. Until June there are a few anatomical drawings, but mostly mechanical designs, machines that seem to have no practical value at all. After June there are illustrations that look suspiciously like maps, with contours in coloured inks, just like the great chart on board Sabbath's warship.

The Doctor wished to bring his TARDIS to the House, and on the warship he'd seen a new way of approaching the problem. If the first chart the Doctor drew was based on Sabbath's, then his memory must have been truly remarkable, as the detail is astonishing. Precise whorls, referred to as 'walls of time' (the *tantrists'* 'horizon'?), sweep across rough representations of the then-known world. In certain areas – primarily London, Hispaniola and the Americas – the contours are so dense that they seem impenetrable, as if those cities were being slowly surrounded by the strange, invisible forces of time. Later charts are variations, the Doctor's predictions as to how the patterns might move, and alarmingly many of them show London and Paris completely cut off from the rest of the world. 'Islands of time,' perhaps.

While Fitz and Juliette reassured each other by firelight in the upstairs room, the Doctor set about his task of navigating a safe path through the storm. The House had already seen him open a way into the world of elementals, though admittedly he'd only succeeded in bringing Fitz and Anji through naked and without possessions (when the Doctor had 'walked' to London, he'd done so fully-clothed, which perhaps suggests that he saw his clothing as being as much a part of his identity as his flesh). Now he seemed sure that he could achieve something more ambitious. On the same day that Tula Lui murdered Johnny Lucifer-in-Britches, the Doctor decided to test his new methodology.

GETTING SOMEWHERE, GOING NOWHERE

It was in July that the House announced its wedding list for the marriage of Juliette and the Doctor. As the thirteen guest-parties at the wedding were all *organisations* rather than people, it would have seemed churlish to ask them for expensive gifts, and as a result the items on the list had a somewhat fetishistic flavour. They were tokens more than anything else, like ingredients for some unthinkable magic potion, and this suggests a change of emphasis. In the past, the Doctor had only required mechanical parts for his studies. But suddenly there was a markedly ritualistic feel to his requirements. (Then again, it's feasible that he only wanted 'the egg of a tartan bird, bred by the Lodges of the

112

Highlands' because he liked the sound of it... it's even feasible that it may have been *Juliette's* request.) At best, some of the items on the list were crossbreeds of alchemical ingredients and scientific components: for example, what's anyone supposed to make of 'six glass phials containing liquid mercury, of the type which might be used to forge the link between the worlds'?

On July 17, Juliette was alone with Fitz in her boudoir. The room was technically Anji's as well as Juliette's, but Anji spent as little time at the House as possible and generally used her days to feel her way around the streets of London. Fitz and Juliette were talking at length on that afternoon, though it's not known what the subject matter was. However, the conversation was interrupted when Juliette abruptly clutched her stomach, complaining of 'sudden cramps'. At first Fitz was merely concerned, but then he too became aware that something was very wrong.

The two of them stepped out of the room, to find that Katya was also at the door to her quarters. Scarlette (not even in the country, of course) would claim in her journal that 'every woman in the House bled at once', but this clearly isn't supposed to be taken literally. Smoke was rising up the stairs from the ground floor, and all those present in the House began to move towards the salon, fearing the worst. Just before he himself reached the ground floor, Fitz heard a voice cry out and recognised it as the Doctor's.

'Magic words' are important in ritual, as any form of ceremony is about the power of symbols more than anything else. Even hard-nosed Service lore held that Sabbath had learned a certain word which had allowed him to escape his initiation, but if Fitz was to be believed then the noise the Doctor made was a cry of alarm rather than an incantation. As Scarlette so vaguely puts it, 'the Doctor needs no words: his words are in his hearts'.

When Fitz and Juliette arrived in the salon, they found it full of a thin, sickly smoke. This may have affected Fitz's perceptions, because although there was no sign of the Doctor he claimed to have briefly seen a 'Doctor-shaped hole' in the smoky air.

A search of the room revealed a note, in the Doctor's hand. It read: GONE TO FRANCE. BACK FOR TEA.

Where did the Doctor actually go? His failure to keep a diary of his own means there's no first-hand account of what really happened that day. But one description *does* exist, in the fragments left behind by Sabbath himself. Sabbath later extracted the entire story from the Doctor and friends, and one of his agents (somewhat clumsily) recorded the details. The thrust of it is as follows.

The Doctor stepped out of time, with the same skill ascribed to the giants of *Mayakai* folklore. His ability to do this was due to his elemental nature, at least according to Sabbath, who also felt that only the unstable nature of the 'walls of time' had allowed the Doctor to do this: the same weakness in time which allowed the apes to manifest presumably granted elementals a fraction of the same power. How much of this account is to be believed is up to the individual to decide. The story goes that the Doctor didn't arrive in France, as he'd planned (possibly he chose the destination only because Scarlette was already there). Instead he found himself in 'a stranj and terrible place, under the site of the great black eye'.

This mysterious place isn't described in full... at least not in the Sabbath account. But here the Doctor made *himself* clear, as the realm of the 'great black eye' is described in his *Ruminations*. Quite patently this is the same location which Juliette had seen in her vision. The Doctor's description is written in the style of a warning to other travellers.

It's a terrible place, although it's probably not like any terrible place you might have seen in art galleries. There's no hellfire or pits of agony. It's a city, the greyest, bleakest city you could imagine. There are buildings, beautiful buildings, but every wall and every brick has been bleached of its colour, worn down by the wind, pulled into ruins, scratched into rubble. There are statues there, like the statues you might see on the Grand Tour of Europe, but they too have been reduced to pale, bleached things with their arms snapped off and their faces scraped clean. The wind never stops making you itch... and everywhere is the smell of animals. Apes, so that the smell isn't quite far enough from that of the traveller's own body to make it seem truly alien. Yet the sky is a bright and beautiful blue, which is a cruelty in itself, because under that sky the earth and the city seem more horrific still. Occasionally, parts of the ruined architecture will be familiar. The buildings behind you might remind you of your own place of residence. A distance away you might see places which make you think of the boulevards of, say, Paris. It's almost as though the traveller brings some of his own city to this graveyard-of-cities, only to see it reduced to a grey husk.

But it's the sun that strikes you most. At least, the traveller will at first assume it's a sun. When you see the pure blackness of it, surrounded by a halo of light against the blue, you might think there's a simple eclipse. Then the sun will turn in the sky, like an eyeball turning in its socket. The sun will look at you, and when you find yourself staring into its terrible dark centre you'll be forgiven if you feel like crying out. Be warned, though, that if you make a sound then your cry will sound like an animal's cry. It may even summon some of the creatures who live in this horrible place, and bring them bounding out of the ruins with their knuckles on the ground.

If you find yourself in this place, then turn back. You have put a foot wrong somewhere. This is the *horizon*, but the horizon made of flesh and plaster.

These 'turn back!'-style warnings are common in the mystical texts of the period, though usually if there's a reference to demons it's code for the creatures of the reader's own psyche, terrible things one can see if exposing oneself to too many poisonous vapours. In fact, there's a sense in which the Doctor's journey reads like a hallucinatory experience, at least partly brought on by the smoke. And it's an indication of the Doctor's somewhat erratic style that this warning to travellers is placed in the *Ruminations* between a series of predictions on the subject of America, and a passage which at first sight seems to be a description of a terrible multi-eyed many-limbed monster but which on closer inspection is revealed to be an elaborate recipe for bread-and-butter pudding. (Interestingly, given that the Doctor was said to have a special interest in *history*, the predictions of America's future are all utterly wrong. By contrast, the American predictions of the Marquis de Sade – the legendary 'Monsieur le 6' – are all accurate. Believers in the Doctor's powers might like to think that this was all a complicated joke.)

The other thing to note is that this passage sees the first mention of the 'black eyeball', observing the realm of the *babewyns* like some form of primitive god. This would be a recurring feature in later accounts.

Although the Doctor describes the dangers posed by the apes, it seems that he himself wasn't immediately attacked by them. It's perhaps significant that in the *Ruminations* the Doctor makes mention of buildings like 'the boulevards of, say, Paris', because the account that comes via of Sabbath holds that as soon as the Doctor arrived – or as soon as he accustomed himself to this bleak, black-sunned nightmare-place – he realised he wasn't alone.

Tula Lui was also in the place of beasts. Cutting through the romanticisation in the account, it nonetheless seems to be the case that a confrontation followed. Tula Lui was also off-balance, even bewildered, on her arrival. It may have taken her a while to find her bearings. When she did, she 'posed herself like a coiled animal about to strike and growl'd like a panther'. The Doctor merely raised his hands, in an attempt to placate this amazonian warrior.

If this encounter truly took place, then the Doctor must have been wary of the girl, who had already attacked and defeated him once before. Then, as now, she'd been dressed in the prim dark robes which Sabbath used to hide what must have been a highly-trained body. The Doctor did his best to reason with her, to speak to her in English, then in sign language. He even tried to indicate the world around them, in the hope that she'd understand he wasn't the threat. But he must have known that Tula Lui would suspect him of diverting her into this nightmare. Worse, there was a 'most loud scratching' nearby, the sound of claws scraping across cracked, grey pavements. Perhaps it was this noise which broke the tension of the moment, and which spurred the young warrior to finally lash out at him.

The story of the encounter ends in a typically melodramatic fashion. The Doctor falls, a pained look on his face. In the distance, the apes begin to howl. The last thing the Doctor sees as he hits the ground and loses consciousness (and there's no way the author could possibly have known this for sure) is Tula Lui, turning her back, shedding her cloak and bounding away across the rubble of the city like a wild deer. The story also makes much drama out of the fact that even as the Doctor was collapsing on to his back, with the black eye of the sun staring down at him from on high, the apes were picking their way through the devastated streets. Eyes shining, claws dragging, drool spilling from their lips. It's all terribly gothic.

A DEATH IN THE FAMILY

The French judicial system was regarded as barbaric even by the most loyal of the King's subjects. Before the Revolution, *all* justice was a matter of personal satisfaction between the monarch and the common man: he who broke the law broke Louis XVI's law, and had to be punished in a manner fit for the entertainment of a King, even if the King himself didn't have the stomach to watch it and rarely observed executions. Torture was all part of the spectacle. Torture was still an important tool of the Inquisition in the southern Europe states, and the French court saw no reason to give up methods which were officially endorsed by the Church.

Given this zealotry, it's notable that Scarlette managed to extricate herself and Lisa-Beth from the scene of the butcher's-shop murder so easily. Even without her glass totem, Scarlette had the power to charm the socks off the local watchmen (France, like Britain, still distrusted the idea of a fully professional police force). A doubly impressive feat, when one considers that French wasn't even her first language. She walked proudly away from the *boucherie*, commanding admiring glances from the men as she passed them by, Lisa-Beth skulking behind her with somewhat less enthusiasm.

The two women still had vastly different styles. Lisa-Beth was as blunt as ever, while Scarlette understood that charm and persuasion were the *real* weapons of choice for those of her tradition. To make the Tower of London vanish, she once said, all one had to do was talk everybody in the city into *seeing* it vanish, and she put great store in the fact that the word 'glamour' – which had once only described a kind of magical enchantment – was now beginning to have a far more fashionable meaning. But the women worked well together nonetheless, particularly now that all Lisa-Beth's secrets were out in the open.

It's a fact, judging by Lisa-Beth's journals, that she recognised Juliette at once on the night of the March ball. So where had they met before, and why was their relationship spoken of in such hushed tones and vague rumours?

The simple answer is: it's impossible to say for certain. Lisa-Beth gives teasing hints in her journals, but never comes out and says it. The best clue we have is in the nicknames Lisa-Beth gives her colleagues. Time and again, Juliette is referred to as 'the Flower'. This might seem a harmless enough appellation, perhaps a slightly mocking reference to Juliette's somewhat vulnerable nature. But other sources lend a more ominous significance to it. Nonetheless, whatever had passed between them in Manchester, by the time of the Paris murder Scarlette and Lisa-Beth were comfortable enough with each other's company to return to their room at the guesthouse and openly discuss their next move.

It's around this point that the Doctor's narrative can be resumed. From hereon his story becomes slightly less *fantastic*, as the scene was reported by a witness who was, within limits, reasonably reliable. Because when the Doctor awoke from unconsciousness, he was to find himself on board Sabbath's warship.

The Doctor had been placed in one of the ship's cabins. Sabbath had few guests, although when he did they were given every amenity they could need (including access to Sabbath's impressive library). But the Doctor had been picked up at short notice, so the cabin would have been largely bare, a grey metal box lit by the latest in gas technology. It's interesting to speculate on what the Doctor's first sight would have been, when opening his eyes. He may well have recovered to find an ape, one of Sabbath's trained minions, looming over him with blood on its breath. If so, the manner of the ape's dress can hardly have done anything but puzzle him. By July, Sabbath had begun to dress his 'crew' in grotesque parodies of the British naval uniform, without shirt or breeches but with navy blue jackets and (on formal occasions) black admirals' hats. It must have looked revolting, to see these matted, black-furred creatures squeeze into the clothes, and it's safe to assume that it was another of Sabbath's jokes at the expense of authority.

There were certainly two uniformed apes in the room when the Doctor recovered, no doubt hissing with frustration at their inability to tear him apart. If Sabbath wasn't there to see the Doctor come round, then he entered the cabin shortly afterwards. The two men greeted each other in formal, civil terms, before Sabbath engaged his 'captive' with the usual laconic wit. Sabbath remarked that he was amused by the Doctor's efforts to travel along the 'contours': amused because, as an elemental of the old order, he wouldn't have expected the Doctor to have trouble with anything so primitive. According to Sabbath, the Doctor had been *neither one place nor another* when he'd been picked up by the ship. If he had indeed journeyed to some strange beast-realm, then he'd left it again when he'd lost consciousness, to enter what Sabbath described as a form of limbo. And the *Jonah* was a ship of limbo. Perhaps the Doctor had drifted through the same strange, arcane spaces to which Sabbath's vessel retreated when it wasn't visible to the world. Significantly, there's no suggestion of where the ship might have been moored while Sabbath and the Doctor had this conversation.

What they spoke of next, both men equally guarded, was 'shop talk'. The general gist seems to have been this. Sabbath had some time ago plotted out the 'contours' on his charts of time, and worked out (with the help of his 'magic words'?) how to navigate his ship through the currents. In fairness, the Doctor's ability to do this all by himself – and with so little research – is a testament to his abilities, though his exact methods remain vague. It may be important, though, that the House had recently 'bled'. In the same way that a *tantrist* could use hormonal techniques to enter states beyond normal time, there's the implication that the Doctor had turned the House on Henrietta Street into what might be described as an enormous resonator, an idea suggestive of the bio-electrical experiments being performed by Mesmer in the salons of Paris.

Though he was unsure of the details, Sabbath believed that the damage to local time – the crisis which had summoned the *babewyns* – was in some way a result of *tantrists* like Lisa-Beth and 'dabblers' like Scarlette, though he was only too ready to ascribe a lot of the blame to elemental meddlers like the Doctor. As Sabbath once wrote himself, 'time is too precious an artefact to be pawned off by prostitutes'. He allowed Scarlette and the Doctor to continue with their work only as long as he could watch them from a discreet distance.

When the Doctor told him that the experiment had only been a partial success, Sabbath at first believed that it was a result of the Doctor's inexperience, more 'dabbling'. But as the conversation went on, and the trained apes began to scratch at their parasites in the corner, Sabbath apparently became unsettled. The Doctor described the ape-world, including the black eye-sun, something which didn't surprise Sabbath in the least. But when the Doctor mentioned that he'd been trying to get to *Paris*, even Sabbath's amused, chubby face must have turned grave. And when the Doctor explained that he'd seen Tula Lui in the ruins…

Sabbath began pacing, it's said, tucking his big hands behind his back and letting his heavy frame roll backwards and forwards along the length of the cabin. He'd believed that the 'magic word' technique of fast-transit, as used by Tula Lui, was 'safe'. He shook his head while the Doctor talked, rumbling 'no, no,' on occasion. Then he turned to head for the bridge-room, to consult his chart, and despite the screeching of the crew-apes the Doctor followed.

In front of the great chart, Sabbath indicated the coloured flags across the continent of Europe. The account isn't detailed enough to identify which flags meant what, but evidently Sabbath had managed to plot out the position of the 'horizon', that far-away place which no *tantrist* was supposed to be able to reach but which had been slowly closing in on the western continent. From the Doctor's notes, it's plain to see that the horizon (and therefore the threshold of the world of beasts) did indeed brush the northern edge of London, before curving through the continent, across the northern part of Africa and towards the West Indies. Yet on Sabbath's chart, it was nowhere near central France. Probably still shaking his head, Sabbath announced that even given the horizon's habit of moving, there couldn't possibly be any risk of running into the ape-

119

creatures on the way from London to Paris.

That was when the Doctor stepped forward and began rearranging the map, 'with some cleverness of mathematicks'. Looking at his notes it's clear that the Doctor believed the horizon's movement was quickening, that the 'storm in time' was worsening at an exponential rate. Calculating the movement of the contours based on this theory, he proceeded to move several dozen of the flags on the chart... forming a line which swept right through London, through Paris, through Hispaniola and all the way to Virginia, USA.

This was the first time in the relationship between Sabbath and the Doctor that Sabbath became disturbed. 'Taking a grate breath,' says the second-hand account, 'he turned to his evil crew, and ordered the ship to set sail.' Not, of course, that the warship had sails.

So much is made of Sabbath's monstrous qualities, of his ruthless determination and his ability to dispose of his enemies as nothing more than an irritation, that his human aspect is often forgotten. His first priority was doubtless to protect Tula Lui. True, he'd adopted the girl with the purpose of turning her into a kind of right-hand-woman, but for the most part she was the only real human company he must have had between 1780 and 1782. It's fair to say that there was some deep level of communication between them, despite Tula Lui's reluctance to use English. It's fair to say that there was a great deal of affection between them, too. Perhaps most of all, Sabbath was *driven*, though it wasn't until the following weeks that the Doctor would understand his agenda. To an extent she was Sabbath's heir, a ward if not exactly a daughter.

At some point Sabbath led the Doctor up on to the deck of the ship, though what kind of view the Doctor would have had from there is open to question. The warship must have been something to behold. When in motion four of the uniformed apes would 'man' the deck, one of them acting as a lookout, screeching and cackling to those below even though Sabbath could hardly have cared what lay ahead. As the Doctor and Sabbath took positions at the bow, the *Jonah* was already approaching the dock. Sabbath is said to have stood with his big ham-fists clutching the railing, staring dead ahead, a grim look on his face. He must have felt some degree of guilt. It was he who'd shown Tula Lui how to use the 'magic words', and he who'd failed to assess the threat of the horizon. When he'd set her on her mission of vengeance, this hadn't been what he'd expected. It's the first recorded instance of Sabbath making a mistake, with the possible exception of his 'attempt' on Scarlette in 1780.

At this point events become vague again, probably because it once more deals with the dream-world of the realm of beasts. The legend holds that the ship found itself sailing on an ocean of grey, and that dead ahead lay the harbour, its crumbling buildings leaning against the larger ruins further inland. From the ship, those on deck could see the skyline of the city of apes, bleached landmarks in the style of London, Paris, Rome and Vienna, falling into decay and into each other. The sky still perfect blue overhead.

If it seems odd – or convenient – that the city should have had a harbour, then bear in mind the Doctor's suggestion that 'the traveller takes part of his own place of residence with him'. Sabbath had brought the ocean as well as the ship: getting into the realm was never as hard as surviving it. As the warship ploughed through the grey murk towards dock, the Doctor is said to have looked up, to see the blazing black ball of the sun swivel in his direction, 'an eye made out of pupils'.

'Don't look at it,' Sabbath told him, while keeping his eyes fixed on the harbour. 'Don't give it the satisfaction.'

Strange, how so many descriptions speak of the eye-sun as if it were some form of god. There's certainly a suggestion that the apes feared it. This, the texts seem to imply, is the great dark power under whose gaze everything in the place of apes comes to pass. Sabbath certainly spoke of it as though it were the *true* enemy, often referring to it as 'the Opposition', but maybe that's not surprising. He'd been trained by the Service, and to a covert intelligence operation like the Service an all-seeing eye was the worst kind of enemy there could be. John Dee, when he'd founded the British intelligence community in the Elizabethan era, had written of a mythical arch-nemesis known as 'Choronzon': a demon often depicted in occult lore as a gigantic eye. Although the sun-god of the ape world certainly wasn't Choronzon, its appearance must at least have had resonances for Sabbath.

By the time the ship finally came to a halt at the harbour, the Doctor and Sabbath had already gathered something of the events taking place inland. At this point it's best to repeat the account word-for-word (which should give some indication as to who eventually wrote the story down):

There was a grate skreeking from the city, like as the aipes were performing the most indelicate acts or were angry. My friend Mr. S [Sabbath] had been conserned for some time approching the dock but now he was more conserned still. When they went to disembark from the ship they saw movement in some of the streets ahead and the Doctor said there were two aipes he had

121

spyed bounding throu the ruins towards a place not far away. The Doctor also said he recognised bildings nearby as being in the French style and knew he was not far from where he had been before…

Mr. S wished to go towarsd the sound and the smell of the aipes with his own crew squawking at his back, but the Doctor said they were to be careful. Mr. S was quite determind. Though they did not go far into the city they soon turned into a street that (says Mr. S) was 'a street of London with the excrement of aipes in every doorway'. At the end of the street they could see a crowd of the stinking animals, and the animals were clawing and biting at each other and trying to climb over themselves. Mr. S and the Doctor could only watch and hope the aipes would not see them wile more joined the crowd from the streets around.

That was when *with a grate cry* another figure was there in the midst of the filthy apes. It was the girl, whose name I cannot spell in English, and as my friends watched this girl pulled herself up out of the screeching hurrah of the aipes. Mr. S does not want to speak of her injuries, but there were red clawings on her face and yet she still looked angry. There were as many as a dozen of the creetures on top of her before her face was lost amongst all there hair and teeth. I am told that she killed two of the animals with her hands as they tore at her (for she could snap bones). But when the dead beasts would fall away the others would only drag away the bodies to be eaten while others jumped on top of that poor girl's back to drag her down the more.

It must have been a terrible site for Mr. S. I see him with that look he has when he is determind, when his face becomes so serious that you would think a storm was coming up from inside him. But the Doctor rested a hand on him, even thou I would never dare. When the poor girl vanished beneath bodies and claws Mr. S clenched his fists as hard as rocks, and said 'we must act'.

I do not think anybody could survive such an attack as was described to me being done upon that poor foreign girl.

If anything, this is the one occasion when the account isn't quite dramatic enough. Perhaps the author was being tasteful, but the full horror of these events – and their effect upon Sabbath – is difficult to overstate. Tula Lui wasn't simply a warrior, a pawn in the game. She was a sixteen-year-old girl. And as for the Doctor… the *Mayakai* was to

122

Sabbath what Juliette was to him. The Doctor had long experienced guilty feelings about Juliette, about the things he knew he had to put her through before the end of the battle. This was a reminder of exactly how dangerous it could be, to be an apprentice to a ritualist or an elemental.

There, in a hallucinatory world somewhere between London and Paris, the Doctor and Sabbath watched as a girl was torn limb from limb by some of the most savage, brutal beasts the world had ever seen. The consequences of this would be vast, as would the change it was to have on the relationship between Sabbath and the Doctor.

The Doctor didn't see Scarlette again for another week, when they finally met at Calais, the port from which England could most easily be reached from the French coast. By that stage the Doctor had made an agreement with Sabbath which he knew Scarlette would find uncomfortable, yet which he believed was necessary if he were to recover his TARDIS. But perhaps it's for the best that he had something to confess to Scarlette, because Scarlette also had something to confess to him.

123

6
The Colonies

In 1758, on the West Indian island of Hispaniola, a man named Mackandal was tied to a stake and publicly burned by the authority of France and the colony's governors. Negro slaves had been escaping into Hispaniola's jungle interior ever since the 1730s, and the French slavemasters expected to have to burn the occasional popular figurehead, but Mackandal was a special case. Because Mackandal had been establishing *schools* for the rebel leaders – much to the surprise of both the French authorities and the pro-slavery Catholic Church, who'd assumed that 'schooling' was impossible even for the majority of their own kind, let alone the Negroes – and out of this organised campaign had emerged an intelligence-cum-terrorist network which had spread across the whole of the island. It must have particularly galled the Church that Mackandal had stolen much of their mythology, and that his followers had made dedications to all manner of Saints as they'd poisoned the French wells and ceremonially disembowelled their old overlords.

Mackandal always claimed that no European authority could hold him, of course, so when the French finally caught up with him it was widely believed that he'd find a way to escape. As it happened he *was* burned, although when the stake broke halfway through the execution many of those present took it as a sign that Mackandal had somehow escaped his own skin at the point of his death. Really, the French should have known better than create that kind of martyr. Perhaps they felt the slaves were too *primitive* to understand the power of symbols. Which is one of the reasons that, by the 1780s, the Hispaniolan colony of Saint-Domingue was entering a phase of bloody guerrilla warfare which would see the dark, sweaty jungle interior run with the blood of a thousand ritually-severed limbs, both white and black.

It was in 1782, as summer began to roll into autumn, that the 'silver ship' was sighted off the shore of the island. If any of the rebels saw it, they must have taken it as a sign.

What must Sabbath have been thinking, after the brutal death of Tula Lui? Events must have shaken him, as much as events ever did. Yet even if his infamous half-smile had vanished from his face, he certainly hadn't been diverted from his self-appointed mission. And the Doctor, with his almost childlike optimism and his insistence on making friends with everybody while holding grudges against nobody... easy to see how the Doctor could start to work his way into Sabbath's confidence. What's ironic is that by this time, thanks to Sabbath's meddling, the House back in London was on the verge of closing its doors for good.

Between July and September, several members of the House spent time abroad. But Juliette remained back at Henrietta Street, where business had almost run dry. With Scarlette concerned with other matters, the House had lost both its star attraction and its infamous protector. Those 'gentlemen' who called to see Katya and company were generally drunkards, stumbling into the nearest seraglio they could find. At one point Katya is known to have argued with Juliette again – implying, perhaps, that she felt Juliette should 'help out' in the most physical way – until Fitz stepped in to separate them (Katya seems to have been easily swayed by Fitz, for some reason).

And much is known about Juliette's state of mind in this period, because although she never kept a proper journal, at this stage there *was* a record of her internal world. Juliette had begun to keep a 'dream diary'. This means that although her *thoughts* may not be known, her *subconscious* is there for all to see.

Why, though, had she begun to make this record? Perhaps the best way to understand her reasoning is by reading the early entries in the log, a harder task than one might imagine as for much of it she used her own rather obscure form of shorthand. It began, it seems, on the third day of August. That night, Juliette woke up in the middle of the night to smell 'a peculiar scent in the air, like the burning of grease'. Her room was lit only by the moon outside, and Anji, in the bed on the opposite side of the room, was still asleep. Juliette climbed out of bed, and 'driven by some impulse not identified' crept downstairs, later noting that she couldn't even hear the sound of her own footsteps.

It has to be remembered that this was recorded in her *dream* diary, so it shouldn't be taken on face value. Certainly, what happened next has the feel of a vision. Juliette arrived in the salon, to find that the walls had been curiously redecorated. There were banners and rosettes across the walls, covering every surface: they're described as being just like the decorations which had adorned the March ball, but this time in pure black instead of red. Juliette spent some time trying to get her bearings, wondering what had happened here, before she noticed the black-clad figure standing before her in the middle of the floor.

> It was a woman but she was dressed darkly and the black of her dress was no diff'rent from the black of the wall. She stood in high boots and I think valvet [sic] gloves but she wore over her head a [Juliette's symbol here is unclear] so her face could not be seen. I started at seeing her for I had seen nothing of her because of her dark aspect. She was watching me but in such a way that I thought she might at any time draw a weapon for she had that look of a soldier about her.

Without over-analysing this, it's important to note that 'the look of a soldier about her' suggests the way Juliette often described Scarlette.

> The woman spoke to me although I could not afterwards remember her voice. She told me that I must pay particular attention to my visions for I had reached the point where they would be an education. I was informed that this House was both *red* and *black* in its colours and I had passed through its red nature by the bleeding that had begun for me in January. It was now time for me to understand its black nature and this is why my visions were of importance.
>
> I did not understand this and said so but the woman told me to return to bed. I did this and found I fell asleep again as soon as I returned.

Needless to say, when Juliette awoke the next morning there was no sign downstairs of the previous night's black decorations.

A woman all in black: the dark side to Scarlette's red, perhaps? A modern psychologist might interpret the strange figure as Juliette's subconscious reaction to the Mistress of the House. She seems to have confided the dream to at least one friend, who recommended that she write down all her dreams from that point on.

Before this narrative becomes bogged down in dream-imagery, it's best to consider one detail. By August 3, Scarlette had returned to the House from France. It's worth mentioning this for one reason: despite its striking imagery, over the following weeks Juliette failed to dream of the black woman again (in fact, the black woman wouldn't reappear until the very end of the month). *Almost as if the 'dream' of the black room wasn't part of her usual dreaming at all.* And note that curious detail, the fact that Juliette was awoken by the smell of *smoke*.

In many forms of witchcraft, it's traditional for a young member of the coven to enter a darkened place and undergo initiation at the hands of a mysterious black-clad figure, often just the head of the coven in disguise. It was certainly Mackandal's technique in Hispaniola. With nothing more than some burned herbs (to dull the senses) and some black decorations, it would have been easy to fake this supposed dream-journey... to psychologically prepare Juliette for what came later.

Before moving on, it might be a good idea to consider one other entry from the dream diary of early August. Although this is by no means the most detailed or explicit entry, it does sum up Juliette's night-time experiences best. Not only that, there are also overtones of events in Saint-Domingue and the other West Indian colonies:

> I was paralyzed as if I were rooted in the Earth like a tree although I knew I had been there longer than any tree. I could feel myself bleeding but when I bled it was as the whole of the ground had split open... I was in the jungle that was burning and I could feel my skin prickling when they tore at me. The animals were watching from the darkness and I knew they were apes though I could not explain how I knew it. The apes were clawing over my flesh and tearing at me as they ran over my body to pull at the dead men who had fallen in the fighting.

This description is confusing, until one realises what Juliette doesn't seem to have been able to express in words. The underlying theme here is that in some way Juliette *is* the Earth. The apes, as they spread over the planet, are described as swarming over Juliette's skin.

This shouldn't be misconstrued. The decades that followed would see the birth in the human psyche of the 'Gaia myth', the idea – which evolved from the 'natural whole' theories of eighteenth-century writers like Rousseau – that the Earth is a single evolving organism, and that all forms of life are merely extensions of its body. Of course, the Gaia myth is simply a kind of latter-day folk story, a mythical oversimplification of the concept of evolving ecosystems. But consider the nature of the Henrietta Street House. The women had been brought in tune with a single biological cycle, just as the women in older witch-cults attempted to put themselves in tune with the moon itself. So there's a suggestion, in Juliette's dreams, that Juliette was being deliberately exposed to influences which could somehow bring her in line with the whole planet... scientifically ridiculous, of course, but rituals like the wedding were *symbolic* rather than scientific.

(The Doctor told many stories of his travels, most of them involving fabulous creatures and bordering on the inexplicable. Notably, the Doctor had told Scarlette that two of his most recent adventures had taken place in 'two most remarkable worlds… one called Ceresalpha, where the children were as ghosts, and another where faerie-tales came true'. And the Doctor had described *both* these worlds as being in some way 'alive'. Whether to believe these unlikely tales of the Doctor's exploits is for the individual to decide, but if taken literally it could be argued that the Doctor had travelled to both of these peculiar realms, subconsciously or otherwise, in order to get himself into the right frame of mind for the ritual he was to perform at Henrietta Street.)

One final point is worth mentioning. The more Juliette dwelt on her dreams the more intense they became, and – not surprisingly for someone of her age – there's an increasing amount of sexual imagery as the diary goes on. On the night of August 15, she records:

> I was once again rooted to the ground and unable to move but this time there was cold Earth on all sides of me. I was not afraid. It was as if I had been put in the grave and I was dressed all in black. This time there was no scratching from the animals but when I looked up I saw _____ standing over me. [She uses a proper name here, but her symbol is impossible to decipher.] _____ nodded at me and told me that I had done well to be so calm in my tomb. It was then that he lowered himself into the ground with me and so we lay together for a while… not touching though his expressions to me were most intimate. I found that the ring had gone from my finger but now _____ had it and it lay there on his chest above his heart. I could not feel but that the grave had teeth around its edge.

There are more explicit dreams, but this sums up the mood of them.

If the woman in black was indeed just a part of Juliette's initiation, then it's likely that the Doctor knew nothing of it. Although Scarlette was back at the House by August, the Doctor wasn't. The Doctor had last met Scarlette in Calais, where Scarlette was awaiting the packet-boat that would take her back to England. In one of the journals, Lisa-Beth records that the three of them met 'as if by chance' at the docks, where the Doctor was found sitting with his legs dangling over the edge of the harbour on a breezy summer's afternoon, feeding the gulls while watching the sailors load their ships for the West Indies. Even Scarlette was surprised by the Doctor's appearance, with his trousers rolled up and his bare feet over the side. It hardly matches the slightly sinister aspect the Doctor had taken on, with his villainous beard and his increasingly sombre clothing.

The three travellers spent the afternoon at the harbour, and it didn't take long for their conversation to get round to topics more serious than paddling. Once again, the subject of Lisa-Beth's secret rears its head. This was the conversation in which the Doctor finally admitted how important Sabbath was going to be to their cause, and confronted Scarlette with the fact that she'd have to meet her old nemesis-cum-lover face-to-face before this was over. Perhaps because of this, Scarlette felt it was time to tell the Doctor what *she'd* been withholding.

So what could this mysterious secret have been, which somehow linked Lisa-Beth to Juliette and which was of such concern to the House? What significance was there in the fact that Lisa-Beth constantly referred to Juliette as 'the Flower'? What was all this really about?

Of course, it's impossible to say for certain. But many of Lisa-Beth's journals refer not only to her time at Scarlette's House, but to her younger days as well, specifically the years she spent in India from the mid-1770s until 1781. Lisa-Beth had been trained by Mother Dutt, a notorious eastern procuress known for both her great wisdom and her utter ruthlessness. So it may be of note that the girl who slept in the bed next to Lisa-Beth at Mother Dutt's brothel, under a blasphemous painted ceiling depicting the god Hanuman in a lewd posture, was an eleven-year-old English girl; a girl who had the *tantra* training forced on her, and who would struggle and cry out as the Mother enforced the discipline of the House; a girl generally referred to as 'Little Rose'.

If these details were of any relevance, then perhaps that day in Calais the Doctor had to face the fact that Juliette wasn't quite the girl he'd intended to marry.

LOVE

Scarlette left Calais for England on August 4, Lisa-Beth following her two days later. It was on her last day in France that Scarlette saw the 'shining ship' again, though as yet she'd still managed to avoid meeting Sabbath face-to-face.

Scarlette's own description of the event is typically romantic. She describes standing alone at the Calais harbour, but this time at sunset, the orange light burning the walls of the harbour buildings and turning the ships into shadows on the water. She describes the Doctor, rowing himself out to sea in one of the little boats that Sabbath used for transporting his agents to and from the *Jonah*. She relates that he was forty yards from the dock, little more than a blot in the distance, when he stopped to look up at her and wave. She waved back, and it was at that exact moment that the ship appeared as if from nowhere, a silver gleam on the horizon which made her wince and look away. The Doctor had promised her that on board the ship he'd have everything he needed to complete his work, a host of miraculous scientific paraphernalia which would restore him to his place of power. But as Scarlette describes it, the ship was more a deathtrap than a scientists' paradise.

Then, she claims, she realised there was someone standing next to her. A figure 'garbed for the most part in black' had appeared with the same suddenness as the ship itself, and like Scarlette he watched the Doctor's boat shrink into a tiny black speck.

Scarlette doesn't name the man at the docks, but her description exactly matches the curious clean-shaven, Saturnine individual with the blue-and-white rosette from the Manchester tavern. Once again, the man with the Whig colours on his lapel was pleasant and witty, and Scarlette seems to have enjoyed his company… if, indeed, he wasn't simply part of Scarlette's invention. On watching the *Jonah* vanish, the man told Scarlette that 'he's taken up the position rather nicely', although whether he was referring to the Doctor or Sabbath is unclear. And this time, there was physical evidence of his existence. He gave Scarlette a gift, 'to take back to your House… whoever might need it'.

The gift was a pair of rings, each one crafted in fine polished silver. Scarlette would later present them to the Doctor, so it's feasible that she only made up the story of meeting the man at the harbour to cover up a more dubious provenance for the jewellery.

The Doctor spent much of this period on Sabbath's ship. What the two of them talked about is anybody's guess, but it's doubtful the Doctor spent much time consoling Sabbath on his bereavement (the death of Tula Lui apparently upset Scarlette more than the Doctor, and on her return to England Scarlette insisted on visiting the last known *Mayakai* in Europe – now an old woman, residing in St James's and considered by many in society a great curiosity – to 'bury' the girl in the manner of her own people). What's certain is that two days later, the warship departed for Hispaniola.

On the night before Lisa-Beth was to follow Scarlette back to London, she and the Doctor spent the evening together in Paris, watching the magic-lantern shows and strolling players at an open-air establishment owned by the Duc de Chartres. The Doctor was 'excited', Lisa-Beth later recorded, although she noted that he was still looking pale. The Doctor's enthusiasm was perhaps fuelled by the very atmosphere of France at the time. Even apart from suspected cranks like Mesmer, science was the order of the day. The Montgolfier brothers were on the cusp of sending the first prototype hot air balloon soaring into the sky over the Champs de Mars, and it was commonly believed that men would take to the air within the year. While the intellectuals of France debated the possibility of airborne warfare (much in the 'we can drop things on the heads of the English, and we won't *need* their damn treaty' mould), the Doctor was planning similar excursions in another dimension altogether.

From his garbled words, Lisa-Beth established that Sabbath was engaged in the feat of actually leaving Earth's entire demesne, using to his advantage the same weakness of space which had let the *babewyns* in... but that Scarlette's old flame had, as yet, not found a way of doing this without himself and his passengers losing their 'integrity'. When Lisa-Beth asked what Sabbath was lacking, the Doctor cheerfully tapped himself on the chest and replied: 'Me.'

But Lisa-Beth, like Scarlette, was wary of Sabbath even now that he'd supposedly been cowed.

So much had been said about Sabbath in the House that the main threat, the threat of the apes, had been somewhat neglected. Yet in her dream diary, Juliette repeatedly makes mention of the black-eyed sun, that mysterious dark god of the ape-world. There's a definite sense that she felt it was watching her. Although the eye she saw in her dreams was nothing but a nightmare, her paranoia wasn't unique. Rebecca, like Juliette, would frequently suffer bad dreams. Though she only spoke of them occasionally, it's known that she suffered nightmares about her experiences in America. She more than once dreamed of Mistress Deerfield, the 'Queen of New York State' and the last true American *tantrist* before Crane and Washington's Revolution, hanging from a crucifix in the middle of the blue-skied cornfields of Virginia. By August 1782 the dream had expanded to include the detail of the black-eyed sun, boiling in the sky directly above the cross, watching Rebecca as she turned her back on the crucifix and ran for her life through the corn.

Juliette's dream diary is equally disturbing in places, but often just downright odd. For example, on the night of August 12 Juliette claims she was awoken from her sleep by the same smell of smoke that had awoken her once before. Again she crept downstairs, but this time the salon seemed normal, if dark and empty, and she was on the cusp of believing that she was actually awake when she noticed a piece of paper which had been left on top of the House's pianoforte (if this was a dream, perhaps it was inspired by the memory of the Doctor's GONE TO FRANCE note, which had also been left on the piano… the Doctor was certainly nowhere near London on August 12). On unfolding the note:

> I found that the paper was plain but for a single word and that word was _____ [symbol incomprehensible]. At this I felt a great flush over me such as I had not felt except in the dream of myself being in the cold grave. I felt some excitement as I read the word out loud. I did not know what it meant but as I said it there was a burning in my blood and the smell of salt water. For a moment I believed I was drowning and then there was a sudden rush and I was gone.

This is curious, particularly given what Anji experienced on that same night, an experience she later shared with others at the House. Anji claimed that she was woken in her bed by a sound from the salon, which she *thought* sounded like somebody shouting but which at the same time made her feel 'uneasy'. She also noticed that Juliette's bed was empty. Anji apparently didn't think enough of this to go downstairs and see what was happening, but it later transpired that one of the other women in the House felt the same thing and *did* take a look into the salon. Nothing was happening; nobody was there.

Given his usual concern for Juliette, one might expect that when the Doctor returned to the House (in late August) he'd be worried about these stories. But it seems not, and by that stage he'd already been told a thing or two about Juliette's past. He may have realised that his and Scarlette's control over her had become too tight, that he was expecting unrealistic things from her, that his plans for her were too close to the kind of ruthless manipulation practised by Sabbath. He may have believed that if Juliette was becoming restless, if her thoughts were becoming intense and her interests increasingly esoteric, then it was part of puberty and he should leave her well alone.

If the speculation about the connection between 'the Flower' and 'Little Rose' has any weight, then one can only wonder whether the Doctor ever questioned Juliette about her own *integrity*. Scarlette states repeatedly that the Doctor was a perfect gentlemen, but then again he was a man who often seemed to misunderstand basic human feelings and therefore to act with what appeared to be a lack of tact. True, Juliette was to be the 'Virgin of Spring', the physical representation of the raw and unaffected Earth. But did the Doctor really attach that much importance to that aspect of the ritual? Would it really doom the whole process if one little detail was wrong?

Besides, the Doctor had other things to worry about. He fretted about the wedding invites, some of which still hadn't been delivered and most of which hadn't been answered. He constantly asked Scarlette where she'd obtained the two silver rings, which everybody was assuming would be used in the wedding ceremony itself. Undeniably, the Doctor had been *slightly* tactless in harping on about Sabbath so much in Scarlette's presence, and some noticed Scarlette becoming a little... *frosty* with him. Indeed, at one point Anji took the Doctor to one side and tried to warn him that she didn't trust Scarlette at all.

'Just look what's happening to Juliette,' Anji's supposed to have said. 'Where do you think she's getting all these ideas from?'

Anji seems to have been implying that Scarlette was initiating Juliette in mysteries of her own, and what's remarkable is that the Doctor doesn't seem to have been bothered by the thought. It's possible that his determination on finding the TARDIS was becoming an obsession.

True to what he'd said at the Royal Academy, by this time the Doctor had taken up painting. In the last days of August he sat in his cellar for hours on end, brush in his hand, brow furrowed, staring intently at a wet canvas. Business had dropped away so badly that the House was almost like a haunted mansion, with the Doctor as its subterranean mad-artist-in-residence, and on some nights the sound of his brush was the only sound to be heard. Only once did Scarlette, along with Fitz, interrupt the Doctor while he was working. They were surprised to find him painting rather than toying with scientific equipment, but by then most of his experiments had been moved to the *Jonah*.

It was Fitz who was first to risk looking over the Doctor's shoulder at his work. It was a portrait, of 'an old man serious in appearance with a great red beard', according to Scarlette's journal. When Fitz asked who it was supposed to be, the Doctor replied: 'My grandfather.'

'Really?' responded Fitz, with some surprise.

'No,' announced the Doctor.

It transpired that the Doctor was anxious about his family, anxious that none of them would be able to attend his wedding on the grounds that 'none of them had ever existed'. He'd therefore decided to paint himself a family instead. Fitz asked no more questions after that, for fear of awakening the past.

'A family of elementals,' Scarlette notes in her journals. 'Such a thing hardly bears consideration.'

So it was that the Doctor occupied himself. In retrospect, though, Anji's warning had been right. Juliette was indeed picking up new ideas from somewhere, and they were only adding to the intensity of her dreams.

The best indicator of this is a letter, one of the very few documents (the dream diary being another) in Juliette's own hand. The letter was written to an individual whom Juliette had come to think of as her closest friend, and although it doesn't directly relate to any of the dream-visions it's clear from the text that certain images were preying on her mind. If the language of the letter seems mature for one of Juliette's age, it has to be remembered that this wasn't unusual for a young woman of the era, especially not for an acolyte of Scarlette.

> I told you that _____ [the same symbol as in the dream about the grave] is with me all the time. He is and I do not think I can escape him or would want to. More and more I sense that the things around me in the House are part of *the very same process that gave me life and blood and body*... I am *placed* [i.e. connected?] on this Earth now and I sense that he also wishes to be placed here. He knows it is his true place and perhaps by coming together we will both come to understand what parts we will play in the fate of this world.
>
> I love him. It seems strange to me to have to write down such a thing as it is as natural as being alive on the Earth. I do not love him in the way that _____ [another symbol, probably meaning Rebecca] has told me a romance should be conducted. I love him as you would love the experience of waking up and taking a breath if you had not forgotten how important it is by doing it so much. I have tried to speak to _____ [another symbol, possibly Fitz] and he is very sweet but cannot help me in this. I have heard that priests also love God and that soldiers love their country... it must feel very much the same.
>
> There is no greater love than this. Yet I know that I have been wielded [manipulated?] into this position and despite all I have been told I am in love with the consequences as much as with the act itself.

The 'friend' to whom this letter was addressed was none other than Emily, the same young, enthusiastic sixteen-year-old who'd first suggested that Juliette should keep a dream diary.

But all this took place at the end of August. When Juliette's strange and troubling dreams began, the Doctor was still in the West Indies.

THE CROSS

The rebels of Saint-Domingue, the western portion of Hispaniola, knew little of European politics and cared even less. It's not easy to take an interest in global concerns when you're struggling to survive in a dark, sodden jungle interior, knowing that your relatives are being held hostage to casual torture in the nearest settlements. However, even the most hardened disciples of the late Mackandal must have noticed that the French authorities were somewhat *distracted* in the early 1780s.

It was the war, of course. The war between Britain and America, into which both the French and the Spanish had been dragged. France had neither the resources nor the patience to concentrate on a little thing like a mercilessly bloody slave uprising. As a result, the Maroons – those most organised, most disciplined and most religious of rebels – took the opportunity to do everything they could to weaken the slavemasters' resolve. When they weren't trying to poison the wells, they were using weapons of a more psychological kind. Skulls would be planted at strategic points around the French settlements. Mutilated cadavers would be lashed to trees. The original settlers of Hispaniola had been pirates, and the rebels took up the old standards with relish, planting the skull-and-crossbones on the verges of the territory they felt to be theirs. If Hispaniola had a truly national flag, it was the Jolly Roger.

On August 15, the slaves held a crucifixion, every bit as symbolic as the one dreamed of by Rebecca. It was only a matter of time: the Maroons, before they'd escaped slavery, had been drilled in Roman Catholicism. Mackandal himself was a black Christ in the eyes of many, and to those who'd grown up under the sadism of the Church the image of the nail in the flesh was irresistible.

It was close to midnight when the wooden cross was hoisted into position in the jungle, close enough to a French settlement to make a point, far enough away that the victim wouldn't be found until after his death. Fires were set on either side, the only beacons of light in the wet darkness. Those responsible for the execution retreated as soon as the victim, still dazed from the drugs he'd been given after his capture, had been nailed into position. The victim himself was nobody of consequence, a young man in the employ of the French administration, thought to be an adjutant to a local bureaucrat. He'd only left France four months earlier, so he'd probably never even set foot in the jungle before he'd been bludgeoned and half-poisoned by the Maroons.

The rebels were still nearby, and the fires were still burning, when the foreign man in the velvet suit casually walked into the clearing.

The witness to this event was a seventeen-year-old Maroon recruit called Lucien Malpertuis. He'd later fight alongside both L'Ouverture and Dessalines in the Napoleonic wars, when the French Emperor would take up tactics even more brutal than those of the slavemasters in order to quash the rebellion. After L'Ouverture's death in a French prison cell, Lucien would travel to Scotland, where he'd write his memoirs (in uncertain English) and provide the west with many important accounts of the struggle in Hispaniola. Lucien was one of several Maroons lurking close enough to the crucifixion site to notice the white stranger arrive, and to watch him with caution from the cover of the trees.

They must have been surprised when the stranger arrived. They must have been somewhat more than surprised when he looked up at the semi-conscious figure on the cross, shook his head, and began looking around the clearing for the largest fallen branches available. Within minutes he'd made himself a makeshift step-ladder from foliage and fragments of trunk, which he promptly used to climb up towards the condemned man.

It was at this point that the Maroons decided to make their presence felt. At the lead was Émondeur, an ageing, stick-thin, but particularly hard-headed 'priest' of the unit whose left eye had been taken out by a French bullet and who proudly wore a glass ball in his socket like a trophy. The Maroons employed their usual tactics of intimidation by forming a semicircle around the cross, and therefore around the stranger. To their chagrin, the stranger barely seemed to notice. He proceeded to remove the nails from the crucified man, taking great care to support the victim's weight and prevent any suffocation, then to hoist the man over his shoulder and carry him down the tree-ladder.

Next the stranger spread the still-breathing victim out on the ground, and examined him at length. He'd unquestionably noticed the hostile figures around him, but didn't appear at all concerned. It was only then that Émondeur decided his authority had been challenged enough, and demanded to know who the stranger was.

Ostensibly, the stranger explained that he was a doctor from England who was working for the French administration. (This is dubious. Lucien possibly misheard '*the* Doctor' as '*a* doctor', and probably just *assumed* that the man, as most Europeans did, worked for the administration.) At this Émondeur became angry, and began cursing this Doctor, insisting that this was Mackandal's place and that enemies of Mackandal's kin deserved their fate.

Then the Doctor calmly reached into his jacket and removed an envelope… an envelope which, with Lucien's usual flair for macabre mis-remembrance, is described as 'deepest red and dripping with blood'. The Doctor handed the envelope to Émondeur, who stared at it with his one good eye and clearly had no idea how to react.

With the wedding four months and an ocean away, the Doctor was making sure all the invitations were delivered correctly. It's easy to believe that the Doctor, born traveller that he was, would have relished the chance to deliver the last few messages personally. And is it really co-incidence that he should spend so much time away from the House, almost tactfully, so soon after finding out that Juliette was quite capable of having a life (and secrets) of her own without him?

It's got to be said again, there is *no evidence at all* to prove that Lisa-Beth knew Juliette well before the arrival at the House. The link between Juliette and 'Little Rose' is purely speculation. The truth is, almost nothing is known about Juliette's life. From her own recollections, shared with her friends, all that can be deduced is that she never knew her own parents: she had a sister, possibly a twin, although Juliette believed her to be dead. Juliette's early years seem to have been spent abroad, it's true, in the custody of an organisation whose name she never told. (This sounds unduly sinister. 'Organisation' doesn't necessarily mean some arcane secret society. The eighteenth century was the early corporate age, when interests such as the East India Company would constantly ship what might be called 'human resources' between Europe and the east. There may have been laws against white slavery, but there were notoriously few laws regarding the rights of children, so corporate ownership wasn't unknown.)

The question of what Juliette's owners might have *used* her for remains unanswered. If she had indeed been present at the House of Dutt in India, then she may have been sold into service there. What's more interesting is the question of how she came to England. Scarlette on more than one occasion claimed that she'd 'summoned' Juliette. This isn't literally true, as Juliette was known to have arrived in England on a tea-ship, but Scarlette nonetheless felt she was responsible for Juliette's arrival in Covent Garden. Perhaps Scarlette puts it best when she writes:

One must be so spectacular than none can resist one's pull…

> remarkable people draw other remarkable people to them, by
> accident or will. Two years ago [1780] I opened up my arms and
> bid the world come to me, knowing what lay ahead and what
> companions I would need to complete the purpose. I called, and
> they came.

Grand words indeed. And is there the suggestion here that Scarlette believed she'd called the Doctor as well? It seems odd, after all, that Scarlette should be the first person he met after 'walking to Earth'.

If this was how Scarlette treated Juliette, then it's little wonder Juliette felt so dedicated to her duty. But Juliette was too intelligent and self-aware to be a mere pawn. Her own, illicit, experiments in alchemy prove that. So does her dream diary, in which the figure of _____ is sometimes depicted as a lover, and sometimes as a monster (albeit an *exciting* monster). Consciously or otherwise, she must have wanted to find an alternative to her destiny. And Scarlette? Scarlette and Juliette had the greatest respect and love for each other, there's no doubt about that, but at the same time... at the same time, the Mistress was too strong of purpose to consider all the consequences.

In the last week of August, it became clear exactly how true this was when somebody threw a brick through the downstairs window of the House on Henrietta Street.

The women were in the salon at the time, idling the evening away, waiting for business that hardly ever came. Nobody ever found out who'd thrown the brick, although guesses ranged from rival prostitutes bearing grudges to hot-headed members of the watch who'd decided that nobody was going to come to Scarlette's aid. The women panicked, not because they thought there was a real threat but because this was such a breach of decorum. The message was clear. This House was no longer protected.

When Scarlette came down from her boudoir, she waved the incident aside and said it was a simple matter to have the window mended. At this, Katya finally snapped. Katya, who'd stuck with the House despite her reservations, who'd somehow felt compelled to help the Doctor's cause even though the Russian spy-network must have been able to find her better work elsewhere. She began screaming at Scarlette, claiming that the House was dying, that they were all going to starve to death if the *babewyns* didn't tear them apart first. Scarlette was said to have reached for the shard of glass around her neck, only to remember that it was no longer there.

Finally, Katya started shrieking about the dress. That was probably the turning point.

The previous day, Scarlette had taken Juliette to a reputed couturier's in Charing Cross. The dressmaker was well-thought-of in society circles, certainly rather expensive. However, Scarlette had insisted that this wasn't an *ordinary* wedding dress and that only an extraordinary dressmaker was up to the task. The man in the shop was apparently quite taken aback when Scarlette gave him the details, no doubt being of the belief that wedding dresses should be somewhat sombre in tone. To fashion one in red... and one so elaborate, with Scarlette specifying so many details about its exact dimensions and the materials to be used...

Nonetheless, the couturier obediently had one of his women take Juliette's measurements while Scarlette watched with a zealous eye. On their return to the House, Scarlette refused to discuss the bill with anyone but Lisa-Beth. The women must have started itching right away.

So it was that Katya screamed at Scarlette, while Scarlette stood, unmoving, and took the abuse. And Juliette too said nothing, Lisa-Beth noting that 'she simply watched and could find no way of ending the dispute... though it embarrassed her greatly'.

Of course it did. Juliette still had the sneaking, guilty suspicion that all of this was her fault. Possibly it was at this moment that she decided on a course of action which would change the nature of the wedding completely.

THE SENSIBILITY OF MISTRESS JULIETTE

Émondeur was not by any means one of the great resistance leaders in Saint-Domingue. Unlike Mackandal (the Black Jesus), L'Ouverture (the great military martyr) or Dessalines (the doomed Napoleon of Slaves), he was no great commander or visionary. He was merely the head of one Maroon unit, one of many that kept the struggle going before the grand campaigns of the 1790s. But the encampment overseen by Émondeur was notable for one thing: the savage, carnivorous ape which the Maroons kept there.

The animal was held in chains. The encampment was small, formed out of low makeshift structures which had been assembled out of the debris of the jungle and hidden in the shadows of the undergrowth. At night there was nothing to see at all, except for the occasional fire in the damp darkness. The ape had a hut of its own, a construction not more than four feet from floor to ceiling with its walls stinking from filth. The Maroons had initially hoped to train the creature, perhaps as a weapon against the

139

French, but despite their best attempts to feed it and drug it the ape would tug at its chain and try to scratch the skin from anyone who came within a yard of its enclosure. The Maroons kept it alive, feeding it on any animal carcasses they came across in the jungle, in the hope that one day they'd have a chance to set it loose on the enemy.

When Émondeur showed the beast to the Doctor and Sabbath, on the night of the failed crucifixion, the 'priest' seemed proud of the ape. He claimed that he'd summoned it himself, out of the Circles of Hell, and that his Maroons were so well drilled that they'd managed to capture it alive without suffering more than the odd flesh wound. According to Lucien Malpertuis, whom we can presume was hovering nearby like so many of the rebels, the Doctor looked troubled by this. Sabbath simply looked pensive.

The Doctor warned Émondeur that such creatures couldn't be trained, which made Sabbath smile wryly although he said nothing. But the Doctor was much more interested in knowing exactly *how* the old man had called the beast into the world. Not surprisingly for a man whose religion was such a mixture of Catholic fury and terrorist zeal, Émondeur claimed he'd performed the summoning with nothing more than a prayer. Even Sabbath had to raise an eyebrow at that.

Émondeur went on to say that it had happened on a Sunday, when the men in his charge would regularly hold a form of Church at the camp, during which they'd commune with the Saints and consume a charming delicacy called the 'wafer of *chair du Français*'. On this particular night Émondeur had conducted the service, and while his men had bowed their heads he'd felt particularly inspired. He'd told them that if enough French blood were shed, then the Mackandal-Christ himself might be brought forth to walk the dark places of the island and tear the heads of the slavemasters from their shoulders. Then, in a moment of clarity, he'd gone further. He'd said that indeed, it might be this bloodshed which *removed Mackandal from the stake at the moment of his death and brought him into the present*.

This was a remarkable statement for Émondeur to have made. That kind of complex thought, implying a kind of *structure* inside time itself, was virtually unknown even to the great scientific minds of Europe. But it was at this point that the ape had suddenly come screaming out of the forest. The men had panicked at first, as the ape had leaped over the backs of those kneeling to pray under the night sky, scratching at anyone in its path. Only under Émondeur's leadership (said Émondeur) had the Maroons recovered their wits and brought down the beast.

One imagines the Doctor and Sabbath exchanging glances. While it's true that the 'horizon' on their chart had now extended as far as the islands of the western Atlantic, the notion that even one of the apes could be called by mere casual *words* rather than the complex ritual of the *tantra* was disturbing.

However, it was this one piece of information which allowed the Doctor, in the days that followed, to finally piece together the mystery of the *babewyns*, to finally establish where the creatures had come from, and how he himself was partly responsible for their existence. Sabbath had always blamed the Doctor's kind for the attacks, not because he was a reactionary (not, that is, because he believed 'there are things man was meant to leave alone') but because he felt the investigation of such areas wasn't the province of whores and faded elementals. Now, with the apes seeming closer than ever to the surface of the world, both men would have to adjust the way they saw things.

It's important to remember that Sabbath wasn't a reactionary, because if anything he was quite the reverse. He was a progressive: so progressive that he didn't even consider normal human concerns to be worth bothering with. His ship was a testament to the new industrialism, decades ahead of its time. On the other hand, in most of Europe there was a fashion for the philosophy known as 'sensibility'. Thanks to writers like the late Rousseau, there was an increasing desire to return to a golden, mythical age of Eden. Sabbath would have been contemptuous of such trends, but a copy of Rousseau's memoirs found its way into his library nonetheless. Sabbath must have been amused by the descriptions of the 'morally pure' author's interest in masochism, his involvement in a scandalous society menage-a-trois, his massive paranoid streak and his tendency to call all his lovers 'mother'. Such was the way of the morally pure.

But there was a definite edge of Rousseau-style 'sensibility' in the beliefs of Scarlette. Perhaps it's not surprising, given her Hellfire upbringing, that she tended to look back to a golden age when courtesans were glamorous and the world rang with rumours of the Monks of Medmenham. It was a tendency that, intentionally or not, ended up being passed on to Juliette, the 'Virgin of Spring'. Although back in London, Juliette was just starting to take steps which almost seemed deliberately planned to change that fate, or at least subvert it.

On August 21, Juliette climbed out of bed in the early hours of the morning and once again walked down into the salon. This time she was wide awake, and left her room by her own volition. This time she dressed, though only in her simplest clothes (no red or black), and quietly slipped out of the House.

She'd decided that she had business elsewhere. What she didn't realise was that she'd been seen.

Anji had been distrustful of Juliette ever since May. Her suspicions, later recorded by Lisa-Beth, were further aroused after Katya's argument with Scarlette. Anji noticed that following the argument, Juliette began to spend more and more time with Fitz: not simply talking, but communicating in a way that bordered on the flirtatious. This didn't seem at all in character for Juliette, and Anji was apparently reminded of the way in which the women of the House would banter with their clients before discussing money.

Had Juliette been trying to seduce Fitz? It's not impossible. However, it's more likely that Juliette was testing out her social skills, seeing whether she could deal with men the way her elders in the House did. Fitz seems to have been quite uncomfortable with this new, laughing, tactile version of Juliette. It's easy to get the impression that he liked the attention, but didn't know what to do with it. Anji grew resentful, so it's at least feasible she was jealous.

So Anji was awake and alert when Juliette had her 'waking dream', and followed the girl, at a discreet distance, as she left the House. And Anji later made one final significant observation about Juliette's preparations. She noted that once Juliette had slipped on her shift in the moonlit bedroom, she took Scarlette's glass charm from the dressing table to hang around her neck. Then she paused, took it off again, and put it back in its place.

The suggestion is that Juliette felt it was time for her to use her own weapons.

Anji was still following her, at half a street's length, when Juliette arrived at Cranbourn Street. This was a street to the west of Covent Garden, which had no real reputation but was often haunted by drunks and other 'gentlemen' in the small hours of the morning. Anji watched as Juliette made her way down the cobbled streets, in the yellow light that must have filled the pavements from the few lamps still lit. There may have been prostitutes working on the street, though it was common in Covent Garden for women of the night to hunt in packs rather than alone, so they would have passed through the street wave by wave instead of loitering in the doorways. Anji later recalled that Juliette looked 'uncertain, but not scared'.

Australian Aboriginals in puberty perform the ritual called 'walkabout', in which they're left to wander the desert outback with nothing but their wits to help them survive, an initiation designed to put the adolescent 'in tune' with his world through painful experience. Here on the streets of London, Juliette was undergoing her own, very English, kind of walkabout. Little wonder that Anji believed this was part of some secret witchery, which the Doctor didn't – couldn't – know about.

Halfway along Cranbourn Street, Juliette was stopped by a man whom Anji describes as looking 'shifty'. He seems to have been of the professional classes, though not overly rich. Anji ducked into the doorway of what she took to be a closed shop, and was too far away to hear the conversation: a pity, because it might have revealed much about Juliette's intentions. All Anji could report was that they talked for a few moments, apparently in a civil manner. There didn't seem to be any argument between them, but after a while the man simply walked away. Juliette, Anji claimed, spent some time staring after the man once he'd left her. As if considering a lost opportunity.

As far as Anji knew, Juliette was supposed to be a model of pure and unsullied virtue... and as far as Anji was concerned, the girl was obviously trying to make extra money by putting herself on the streets, proof that something funny was going on. If she'd been more forgiving, Anji might have considered that this impulse could have come from Juliette herself rather than being part of somebody's secret training. The subtext of Katya's rant at Scarlette had been, *why are you spending money on clothes for that girl when she doesn't even earn her keep?* For followers of Rousseau's cult of sensibility, there was no greater sin than failure to live up to the 'natural' work ethic.

It's also worth noting that after her meeting with the gentleman on the street, Juliette returned home, Anji running ahead of her on the way back. But there would be other nights.

Anji couldn't report all this directly to the Doctor, because the Doctor still hadn't returned to London. Throughout August he took full advantage of his access to Sabbath's ship, which meant that he didn't take the direct route either to or from Hispaniola. At one point he and Sabbath even ended up in Vienna, at the Doctor's insistence, where they attended the premiere of (appropriately) Mozart's *The Abduction from the Seraglio*. The Doctor reportedly paid rapt attention throughout, while Sabbath declared that although he saw 'potential' in the work the narrative structure was diabolical. Both of them were nonetheless irritated by the hissing that was heard from several quarters during the performance. The Doctor attempted to get backstage after the premiere, and into the company of Emperor Joseph II himself, but this time even the Doctor's famous charm failed him. He later admitted he was sorry to have missed the after-opera soiree, as he wanted to know whether the Emperor really *did* bluntly tell Mozart that the work had 'too many notes' as later rumours claimed... although it's not known whether the Doctor said this *before* or *after* the rumours began to spread.

So, back in London, Anji had nothing to do but keep watching. And watch she did. On another four occasions, Juliette stole out of the House and into the cold, drizzle-scented streets of London. As Anji's surveillance is only *mentioned* by Lisa-Beth's journals, it's never stated whether any of these later excursions resulted in Juliette being, as it were, better appreciated by the gentlemen of the city. The only one of Juliette's walkabouts that's properly described is the fourth and final one, the reappearance of the Woman in Black.

On the night of August 29 – the day the *Royal George* was lost, possibly an omen – Juliette took her usual route through the half-light of Covent Garden. She passed Charing Cross Road and headed into Cranbourn Street, Anji by now knowing the darkest and gloomiest parts of the area off by heart. At least one man apparently noticed Juliette, but despite making eye-contact failed to approach her. So it was that Juliette came to the corner of Leicester Place.

This was where she suddenly stopped, much to Anji's surprise. Anji saw no place to take cover, and so just stood still in the middle of the cobbled thoroughfare and waited. She realised that Juliette had stopped because something had caught her eye, and moments later the girl was moving again, heading for an unlit building on the far side of the street which Anji took to be a 'dressmaker's shop' (although no such shop is known to have stood on the site at that point).

The shop was closed, naturally, but the darkness in the windows wasn't just caused by the lack of light. They were covered on the inside by black, black satin and black cord, the frame strung with black paper blossoms. Though Anji knew nothing of the dream diary, the similarity to the decorations of the 'black room' is striking.

More striking still, something had been placed in the doorway of the shop as if to deliberately catch Juliette's attention. At first, Anji took it to be a human figure, dressed all in black. Only as Juliette grew closer did Anji realise that it was a mannequin. A faceless dressmaker's doll, and on it hung what was obviously intended to be a wedding dress. But the dress was all in black as well, from its veil to its train.

It was clearly designed to fit Juliette. Anji knew, of course, that Scarlette had ordered a dress for Juliette. But that had been a *red* dress. Just as the accounts are littered with references to the contrasting White Hart of alchemy and the Black Hart sought by Sabbath, the dress comes across as a counterpoint to the one Juliette was scheduled to wear on her wedding day. Anji reached the obvious conclusion, that this was something to do with the secret teachings of the *tantrists*, a dark underbelly of which the Doctor knew nothing. The Black House had clearly been put here for the sake of Juliette, by someone who already knew her night-time habits.

The truth of this became evident when, moments later, the door of the shop opened behind the dressmaker's doll. Juliette stood frozen on the spot, while Anji did her best to shuffle back into the shadows. But the figure on the threshold wasn't what either of them might have expected. Because standing there, surrounded by the black of the drapes, was a bright-eyed and auburn-haired individual whom Anji already knew by sight. Her name was Emily.

7
The World

America. In just two short years, the word had come to mean so much.

As has already been mentioned, the Marquis de Sade was the first to describe America as some great amoral colossus, with its guns booming out to the world like thunder. But after 1780 the whole of the western hemisphere was beginning to feel uneasy. To the ritualists and the witch-courtesans of England, America was a gigantic black stain on the world map, a no-go area that might as well have had 'here be tygers' scrawled across its landmass. The very name made them think of the purges of Matthew Crane; of the witch-hunts of Salem, still influencing the country after all these years; of Paul Revere riding his famous horse (metaphorically, of course) over the bodies of marked Englishwomen; of blackened and bloodied trees, hung with the corpses of those sacrificed to the new world of Washington, Jefferson and Adams.

Yet anyone visiting Virginia in 1782, as summer turned to autumn, would have found quite a different scene. By this point the War of the Revolution was over in all but name. The skies over Virginia were as blue as they had been in the days of Columbus, and the only thing disturbing the earth was the rhythm of the slaves in the tobacco fields. The houses had been repainted, in purest Protestant white, as if each one were a prototype of the big pale house which would one day stand in Washington. The wind would blow through the white oaks, and the gentlemen of the state, with their backs as upright as their reputations, were still old-fashioned enough to greet every passer-by as they strolled about their business. Yes, the word for Virginia was *straightforward*.

But when news of world events reached America, when sailors brought tales of the horrors in Saint-Domingue and London, it was in Virginia that most notice was taken. Because it was in Virginia that Matthew Crane himself had set up his chambers, after the end of the struggle with the British there. General Washington himself had set Crane the task of ensuring that the *Shaktyanda* of America was defended, just as Washington himself intended to defend the country's physical borders: as Jefferson once said, the Americans had no wish to see themselves

146

'going to eat each other, as they do in Europe', thus beginning an absolute rejection of foreign culture which would become the central policy of American society in the years to come. When the American lodges took notice of the rumours from abroad, they must have discussed things over scotch in their drawing rooms as if it were any other business matter. It was in such a drawing room that the red envelope from England would have eventually arrived.

It seems likely that the Americans began taking an interest in the Doctor after his visit to Hispaniola. After all, anyone connected with a negro revolt had to be considered a threat. According to Lucien Malpertuis's later memoirs, the 'ship with no sails' was last seen at dock in Hispaniola on the first day of September, its captain/s having delivered a red envelope to the children of Mackandal. Yet Scarlette's journal makes it clear that the ship had returned to England by the second. Even given the inaccuracy of dating in this period, any ship that could cover such a distance in under a day must have been remarkable indeed. But although it was rumoured in the House that the *Jonah* could simply vanish from the world at will, even Sabbath seems to have had his limits. In a rare letter to one of his own agents, he notes:

> There remains no place on the Earth that is out of bounds to me. But I have to admit that the more freedom I have over the globe, the less the globe interests me… my purpose is to *protect*, and knowing the things I have to protect this territory from I am aware that the globe is not enough. The *Jonah* must be able to explore the further realms, in much the same way as the vehicles of the extinct elementals. Only the corrupted realm of the apes is currently open to me. Yet to go further without loss of my own integrity will require great work…

Interesting to note that he openly describes his mission as one of *protection*, and by 'this territory' he presumably means the world itself.

On September 2 the *Jonah* arrived back in England, coming to a halt a short distance off the coast of Brighthelmstone, a spa town which – under the more convenient name 'Brighton' – was rapidly becoming fashionable as a place of health and healing: so fashionable, in fact, that in the following years the Prince of Wales would allegedly be getting women pregnant there on a regular basis. Despite the late season, the grey skies, the drizzle and the painfully hard pebbles on Brighton beach, when Scarlette arrived in the town it was full of bathers. The bathers had come to follow the advice of the famous Dr Russell, who'd recommended the site just as keenly as he'd recommended blood-letting and the ingestion of viper's flesh. Some of those paddling in the waters on that rocky shore must surely have noticed the woman in red who often stood on the beach, staring out to sea with an unreadable expression... not to mention her young Indian companion.

Scarlette and Sabbath still had yet to meet face-to-face. It was for her sake that the Doctor had asked Sabbath not to harbour his ship, and Sabbath had complied. In that time at Brighton, once Anji had reported the latest news from London, the two men would stand on the rain-spattered deck and talk. The Doctor would watch the beach from a position sixty yards out to sea, perhaps seeing Scarlette staring back at him, a red speck in the distance. The Doctor wished to head back to London, but by now they'd pieced together the truth about the apes and had begun to devise a method of recovering the TARDIS. There were still certain tests to be performed in the bowels of the *Jonah*, though there's no way of even guessing what they might have been.

It was later said that the Doctor once asked Sabbath, in a quiet moment on that deck, how he felt about Scarlette. Meaning, perhaps, whether Sabbath had any regrets about his attempted 'seduction' of 1780. The story goes that a grave look appeared on Sabbath's face before he replied: 'I did what was necessary.'

If all this is true, then it can hardly have made the Doctor feel comfortable. It mirrored his own philosophy so well. Anji had only volunteered to meet the Doctor in Brighton because she wanted to tell him the *real* news about events at the House, involving Juliette and Emily, and the dressmaker's shop off Leicester Place.

Anji was reportedly 'distressed' that the Doctor had greeted this news so calmly. She later told Lisa-Beth that she felt 'he was so obsessed with the hunt for his TARDIS that he failed to focus on the matter at hand'. When Lisa-Beth suggested that Anji's concern about Juliette may have been fuelled by jealousy, Anji snapped back at her with such force that Lisa-Beth immediately concluded she'd been right.

More questions present themselves. Anji believed that Juliette was being taught things the Doctor knew nothing about, that Scarlette was trying to initiate the Doctor's bride-to-be in 'black magic' as well as 'red magic', possibly using Emily as a cat's-paw. This is undoubtedly what she told the Doctor. Did the Doctor confront Scarlette, then? They spent at least one afternoon together, visiting the markets in the narrow, wind-blown streets of Brighton. Or did they understand each other so well by now, the fallen demigod and the courtesan, that he thought no words were necessary?

Perhaps the Doctor believed that Juliette was capable of making her own decisions. Scarlette and Anji left Brighton a day before the Doctor and Sabbath, but when Anji departed for London the Doctor gave her a letter. The letter was addressed to Juliette, sealed with a wax emblem of a bee, and the Doctor made Anji promise not to open it herself.

It's not known whether Juliette ever read the letter. Given later events, it's possible Anji never found the right time to hand it over. The contents prove that the Doctor was not only distracted by the thought of his TARDIS, he was also having 'second thoughts' about the wedding itself. The English is decidedly modern:

> ...I know it's never easy, making a decision that might affect the rest of your life. Especially not when you feel the whole world's waiting to see what's going to happen. And I know I might not have told you everything at once… [but] you can never be sure whether people are going to understand you properly (I'm sure you know that by now).
>
> I'm telling you this because I think it's only fair for us all to have a choice. I know you understand what I'm trying to tell you. My only worry is that you might understand me *too well*.

A last chance to back out of the wedding? A final, thinly-disguised, request for Juliette to share any doubts she might have? If so, then it was hardly necessary. As her dream diary records, by the time the letter was written she already felt she'd reached the point of no return.

Anji was right in thinking that the Doctor was becoming distracted. He wanted to recover his TARDIS because it was his 'lodestone', and perhaps because he felt it was the only possible cure to the sickness which had increasingly been affecting him. But Sabbath knew, and would constantly remind him, that the TARDIS was a weapon. By September they'd worked out how its summoning might be performed, but they still needed a venue where they could feel safe from the attentions of the enemy.

Fortunately, as the Doctor had already learned from Scarlette, there was one man in London who could help them. And he went by the truly unlikely name of Dr Who.

No Return

The last entry in Juliette's dream diary was made on September 4, 1782. Aside from some of the more lurid sexual dreams of late August, it's the most intense of the entries, partly because the reader gets the impression that Juliette isn't describing a dream at all.

In this final dream, she returns to the House on Henrietta Street after visiting 'the home of a friend' (Emily?) to find the House empty. It's evening, but there are no other women in the salon. Most of the salon's furnishings have also vanished: there are spaces where the pianoforte and the chaise-longues used to be, pale squares on the walls where many of Scarlette's paintings have been taken down. The House feels empty, a hollow shell. But there's the ever-present smell of smoke, light from both the burning candles and the oil lamps. Juliette thinks nothing of the emptiness. She simply heads up the stairs towards her room.

It's while she's in her room that things start to change. The chamber makes her feel uneasy, and at first Juliette isn't sure why. None of her own effects are missing, though the room's in half-darkness. Scarlette's glass totem rests on a chair. A single lamp burns above the looking glass. In fact, Juliette feels as though there are *too many* effects in the room. The furnishings are so familiar to her, though, that she has difficulty noticing what's supposed to be there and what isn't.

It's then – with amazingly little surprise – that she realises. The room is full of apes. What she took to be furnishings are living creatures, but the apes seem so familiar to her that she simply didn't spot them until now. They were just *part* of the room, a part which she never normally notices and which seems to hover at the edge of her vision. The apes tell her, though not with language, that she willed them here simply by her understanding. As a result, they're now part of that understanding.

It's the description of the apes that makes the entry so intense. She doesn't describe them as horrors here, but as ordinary elements of her life, and in the later paragraphs there's a sense of almost shocking intimacy as she goes about her daily routine (brushing her hair, undressing, examining herself in the looking glass) while the apes surround her. She's come to accept them, as if her experiences in the Black House have inured her to their presence.

There are certain noteworthy features to this story. For one thing, the description of the 'empty House' may be literally true. The pianoforte had been taken by debt collectors by September, and when some of the House's women left Scarlette's employ they took with them a number of small furnishings which may or may not have actually belonged to them. Business was so lacking by this time that many of the women weren't even bothering to stay there in the evenings. In many ways Juliette's account could be factual, although the suggestion of the apes being in her room without harming her…

Perhaps more importantly, the suggestion of the apes being at the threshold of her consciousness, of them being as much a *psychological* phenomenon as a biological one, was very much in line with the Doctor's own discoveries. Had Juliette really understood the truth?

The Doctor and Scarlette were still absent at this time, so nobody would have been present at the House to oversee the other women. The consequences of this became clear on the afternoon of September 5, when those women who'd remained behind – six of them, the journals record, although only Rebecca, Lisa-Beth and Katya are named – all met in the sparse, half-stripped salon to make a final decision on the future of the seraglio. It was a meeting they probably wouldn't have dared to hold if Scarlette had been in London.

The question posed at the meeting was simply this: *should the House continue to do business?* It was no good carrying on this way, some of the women argued, if Scarlette was going to spend all her time helping the Doctor with his experiments. The House should make a decision as a whole. They could give up now, and seek work in the other seraglios while they still had at least *some* reputation left. Or, they could stick with Scarlette and risk starving to death.

Unusually for the age, it was decided to settle the matter democratically. There might have been some stigma attached to being 'disloyal' to the House, so a secret ballot was to be held. At Lisa-Beth's suggestion, each of the women was given two feathers (taken, one has to assume, from Scarlette's wardrobe), one red and one black. Each woman in turn was to put one of the feathers inside a black oriental vase which was one of the few decorations remaining in the salon. If at the end of the process there were more black feathers than red, then all the women would agree to close the House and (if necessary) depart. If the vote said red, all would agree to stay. Not being a 'working woman' of the House, Juliette had no vote – in fact, she was in her room at the time and didn't even know what was happening – but Lisa-Beth suggested that if the vote were a tie then Juliette should have the deciding voice, something which made a few of the women uneasy as it seemed to favour the Doctor.

It was at this point that things became somewhat complicated.

All the votes had been taken, and Lisa-Beth was preparing to tip out the contents of the vase, when the door of the House opened. The women hadn't been expecting Scarlette to return, and so Lisa-Beth describes them as looking like 'thieves discovered'. But it was Anji, on her own, who walked into the salon.

It transpired that although she and Scarlette had returned to London,

Scarlette had immediately headed towards Soho on an errand she refused to discuss. As a result, Anji was thoroughly peeved by the time she arrived back at Henrietta Street. She'd gone all the way to Brighton to warn the Doctor about Juliette; the Doctor had failed to take any notice; Scarlette was, as ever, keeping her in the dark; and to make matters worse, when Anji asked where Fitz had got to she was told that he was out, and that he'd recently been spending time with a certain tobacconist of St James's who was also notorious for doing a sideline in laudanum.

It was all too much for Anji, who stormed upstairs to Juliette's room, determined to have it out with the girl. As the women watched her go, none of them had the nerve to call out to her and tell her about the vote. An angry, exotic elemental was the last thing they needed.

Anji's confrontation with Juliette was recorded, and one look at the text reveals who recorded it. The witness was in Juliette's room at the time.

My friend was telling me how the aipes had come to her the previus evening. I listened for her story was most thrilling tho it made me feel a shudder for the safety of my friend... I did as I was told to do in her company and said what I had been instructed to, which was that if she could axept [accept] the aipes as part of her then she understood much indeed. I asked her if that ment she was in the mode of [i.e. in tune with] the world around her. She open'd her mouth and I think she was about to give the anser but then there was someone at the door...

It was the woman who they call an *elymental* and she was in a grate rage, so that I was afraid of what she mite do. She shouted that my friend had been a *witch* and other things that I scarce like to write down. She said that my friend had been poisoned in the mind by Scarlette, which I did not understand, and that she had begiled her frend Mr. K [Fitz]. Juliette tryed to be most civil but the Indean woman said as soon as the Doctor got back there would be a reckoning. After that she slammed the door and I heard her in a great distemper on the stairs.

My friend looked at me and thought for moments, then she got up from the bed where she sat and went to follow. I did not know wether I should go too.

The story is taken up by Lisa-Beth. The women, distracted by the shouting, still hadn't tallied up the feathers in the vase. Lisa-Beth was among those who watched as Anji stormed downstairs and left the House altogether. Juliette followed her, though Lisa-Beth noted that the girl seemed unusually composed and calm.

What's most striking about Emily's account of the fight, though – apart from the fact that Emily states, for the first time, that she's following *orders* – is the suggestion that Juliette was 'in the mode of' the world around her. Emily's mission seems to have been to complete Juliette's understanding of this strange connection. Perhaps Juliette's vision of herself, surrounded by the apes, was a symbolic representation of the way the creatures were crowding around the edges of the planet's 'consciousness'. Perhaps she believed that she herself was becoming a *place of power*, like the Doctor's legendary TARDIS.

Emily's writings are so chaotic that it's easy to think of her as being ignorant and witless. Nothing could be further from the truth. She was flighty and melodramatic, but then again she was still an adolescent (although she wouldn't change much as she grew older, as the whole world would learn on her ascension to celebrity in 1798). She was charming, charismatic and certainly attractive. Still some years away from being regarded as a great beauty, she already knew enough about the world to avoid being naive. So if she had indeed been 'primed' to lead Juliette in a certain direction, she was undoubtedly up to the job.

It was raining that afternoon, and raining heavily. When it rained in central London, the dirt would froth up on the streets and the smell of mud would be everywhere, unlocked from the cracks between the cobbles. Where Anji was intending to go, she never said – possibly to find Fitz and his new tobacconist friend – but she must have been wet and irritable as she stomped through the grey streets and tried to avoid being splashed by the passing horses. All that can be said, from the story passed down in the folklore of the London *tantrists*, is that she headed down a street alongside the Thames towards the part of London called the Temple (named, incidentally, after the occult temple once constructed there by the Knights Templar).

The tale records that there was no moment of horror, no great flash of light. No indication that anything had changed. Anji simply turned a corner, expecting to find herself in another damp, filthy London street. She probably had her eyes turned to the ground, so she may not even have noticed what was happening at first. At some point, though, she must have looked up. Perhaps it took her a while to notice: to spot the difference between the bleak, grey buildings of the capital and the bleak, grey buildings of somewhere else entirely. Some versions of the story even claim that other passers-by were quite happily wandering up and down the road, not noticing anything strange around them, as if two worlds had quietly been laid on top of each other. Only Anji, say these tales, could see the way the black sun stared down at the city from the shockingly blue sky behind the rainclouds.

What all the stories agree on is that when Anji had taken the scene in, when she'd smelled the way the rain mixed with the ape-dung in the gutters and seen the way the buildings of the Temple were crumbling into the street, she slowly turned to look behind her. What she saw, not twenty paces away, was Juliette. Juliette, soaked to the skin but unbowed, some say wearing the black wedding dress from the Shop. Juliette only stared when Anji noticed her, the two women facing each other in the ruins of London without saying a word.

There are so many stories of this kind in the history, so many accounts of individuals turning a corner and either finding apes in their path or simply dropping out of the world altogether, that it's easy to start thinking of them as either hallucinations or random incidents. In fact, all the stories have something in common. Note:

– The first ape attacks occurred when ritualists/*tantrists*, Lisa-Beth among them, actively *explored the limits of the horizon and therefore went beyond normal human experience*.

– The captured ape in Hispaniola *was 'summoned' by Émondeur when he suggested a conceptual version of time unfamiliar in the period*.

– Anji and Juliette only slipped into the city of the apes *after Juliette had somehow attained a specific level of understanding*, possibly thanks to Emily's coaching.

The pattern is clear. Understanding summons the monsters: and it's interesting to see how this fits in with the cultural climate of the era. After all, the late eighteenth century was when the western world began to put aside supernatural horrors and create its own new, scientific, myths. The years that followed would see the publication of *Frankenstein*, a tale of terror for a new age, in which mankind would be haunted not by ancient demons but by the consequences of its own curiosity. And to the eighteenth-century mind, the ape was a symbol of the unknown. It represented the exotic, the undiscovered, the horror from the heart of the jungle. One (later) commentator even pointed out that although ancient mapmakers marked unknown territories with the words 'here be tygers', it would have been more appropriate for them to have said 'here be gybbons'. Some of the more religious lodges are known to have believed that the ape attacks were a judgement from God, but from the accounts surrounding the Doctor in 1782 it seems more as if the apes were the human race's punishment on itself. Whenever man or woman explored the darkness, the apes would be waiting there.

Juliette, on seeing the realm of the beasts so close to home, must have wondered whether the decisions she'd made had been responsible for summoning the ruined city to the Temple. But at the time, the cause can hardly have mattered much to either her or Anji.

THE HOUSE OF WHO

It was felt all across the world. It would probably be going too far to say that it was either the Doctor or Juliette who'd caused the problem, but nonetheless witch-cults as far apart as Africa and Australia (newly-settled, and therefore still under the 'spiritual protection' of the aboriginal *wirrunen*) must have sensed that something was afoot. Furthermore, any counter-ritual was guaranteed to make the problem worse. It's tempting to imagine the proud, stately, *straightforward* Mr Crane in America, congenially discussing the troubles with his peers while those (white) men who'd resurrected the old Anasazi ways performed cannibalistic rites in their cellars and clubhouses.

It's not wise to overstate the problem. The world wasn't falling apart: the vast majority of the population could hardly have noticed anything happening. There were no reports of carnivorous apes running amok on the streets of the cities, there were no unexplained massacres in urban areas. But those who kept secrets, those who dressed as politicians by day and indulged in the carnality of the *tantra* by night, suddenly found themselves terrified to make any move that might bring down the wrath of the ape-god on their heads.

Curiously, the one major country which recorded no disturbance at all, not even amongst its archons and its conjurers, was China. A critic might say that this was because the ape-elementals only seemed to punish progressive thought, and China had seemed incapable of that during the eighteenth century. But there could be another reason, and to understand it it's best to return to the pursuits of the Doctor and Sabbath.

Since 1762, Soho in London had been home to a certain Chinese 'quack' who practised under the name of Dr Nie Who. The name seems to have been chosen for its dramatic impact, as although 'Who' was his true surname (or at least an anglicisation of it: a more common version might be 'Woo' or 'Wu'), there's no evidence that he was actually a doctor. The obsession of eighteenth-century high society with eastern exotica stretched as far as medicine, and if India was considered *outre* then China was positively enigmatic. The teeth of big cats, the embryos of unspecified creatures from the bamboo fields, roots which would not simply scream on being pulled from the ground but howl out an entire black opera... all of them were found, pickled and preserved and prescribed, on the wooden shelves of Who's emporium. And as the labels were in Chinese, a language virtually nobody in England could read, customers had to take Who's word for the contents of each jar. This was one of the early populist occult shops, which would change very little over the following centuries... indeed, nearly two hundred years later one would occupy the very site of Scarlette's House on Henrietta Street.

But Who was most notable for his *philosophical* services. Contrary to the usual stereotype of the Chinese, he rejected the teachings of – as he put it – 'the cow-dung merchant' Confucius. Though he may have been a charlatan in terms of medicine, he used his curatives simply as props, part of a system of psychological well-being in which his clients would genuinely discover new (or at least *forgotten*) states of consciousness. It's debatable, in today's world, whether this was genuinely helpful or just a parlour-trick. But those who paid and paid well for Who's methods maintained that during their 'sessions', they experienced... well, it wasn't so much that time slowed down, they said. It was that they found themselves in a blissful, serene environment of no-time-at-all.

It's possible, but by no means certain, that marijuana was involved in this practice.

The Doctor believed, from all he'd heard, that Who could help him in his quest to recover the TARDIS. He and Sabbath returned to England on September 5. The next day the Doctor risked the streets of Soho to find Who's emporium, a tall-but-narrow black-brickwork shop tucked away in a sidestreet, with Rebecca at his side once again.

When they arrived at the shop they found Sabbath already there, his bulk taking up much of the space as he perused the shelves in the cramped, smelly, damp-aired spaces of the shop (legend had it that Who would spray the place with tiger's urine every morning, though his reasons were foggy at best). From Rebecca's later accounts to her friends, the Doctor was a little put out that Sabbath and Who had already struck up a professional relationship, with Sabbath inquiring about the properties of some of the concoctions and Who giving him technical descriptions in flawless English. This bothered the Doctor chiefly because when he and Rebecca entered, Who immediately went into character and asked them how their ever-so-humble servant could possibly help them on this fine morning, perhaps by selling them a genuine vial of tears of the dragon, yes?

Sabbath soon explained that the Doctor wasn't to be toyed with, however. The Doctor made quite a lot of notes in early-to-mid September, perhaps intending to write a follow-up to his *Ruminations* at some stage, but (perhaps mercifully) giving up the idea only weeks later. His brief note on meeting Who:

> I imagine the Dr. [Who] likes to be thought of as old, but his wrinkles look like the wrinkles of someone who's spent too many weeks in a cellar with nothing but fumes for company... I sympathise. Don't be put off by his robes, he wears a silk dressing-gown in his shop just to see if anyone will mention the fact. He knows a great deal... I asked him whether he was afraid that his meditations would incur the anger of the 'bloody apes', but he thinks otherwise. 'The beast will attack those who understand the shape of the future,' he told me. 'But my meditations are the meditations of no-time-at-all.' They have little interest in clocks in China, so that might explain his lack of concern.

Rebecca never spoke at length about the discussions made in the shop, or the deal that the Doctor struck. All she seems to have gathered was that Who agreed to make preparations for a certain procedure, the suggestion being that the Chinese quack's 'no-time-at-all' methods could recover the TARDIS without the risk of summoning the beasts.

But Rebecca would have had other things on her mind. The vote of the women in the House being chief amongst them.

When the Doctor had returned to the House the previous day, he'd come alone. Scarlette hadn't been there, and hadn't been seen since her return to England. The women had been getting edgy, especially as they'd had nobody to tell about their decision. When the Doctor had retired to his basement laboratory, he'd hardly noticed the lack of furniture in the salon. After he'd descended the stairs there'd been grim mutterings amongst the women, who'd pointed out that while the debt collectors had taken the pianoforte they hadn't even touched the bizarre (but obviously expensive) equipment in the cellar.

Nonetheless, nobody had wanted to tell the Doctor the news.

It goes without saying that the vote hadn't gone in Scarlette's favour. But what's surprising is the *degree* by which she'd lost. The three 'non-*tantrist*' women had expected both Lisa-Beth and Rebecca to vote with a red feather: the vote really hung on Katya, who'd done her best to remain loyal to the House despite trying circumstances. Yet when the feathers had been tipped out on to the salon's one remaining table, five of the feathers had been black and only one had been red.

Who, then, had stayed loyal? Or rather, who'd been *dis*loyal? It was in the nature of the secret ballot that nobody asked, although uneasy glances were thrown. Had Lisa-Beth voted black? She'd appeared angry when the votes had been revealed, but then, it could have been a bluff (her journal fails to make the matter clear). Had Katya? Had one of those who'd been expected to stick with Scarlette – Lisa-Beth and Rebecca – voted black in the belief that Katya would vote red, hoping to escape the House and let everyone think Katya had been to blame?

There's no way of knowing the truth. But in the days that followed, Rebecca seemed deeply uncomfortable with the events that unfolded. It wasn't that she had any problem with Scarlette, or with the Doctor – she was too much the visionary to think that they were wasting their time in their battle – it was just that Rebecca was a *demi-rep*, and had been all her adult life. She'd been in America right up until the bloody purge. She can hardly have wanted to see it all happen again, here in England. So despite the result of the vote, she stuck around as long as she could, saying nothing but (presumably) wishing it were all over.

The truth about the ballot didn't begin to emerge until the afternoon of September 6. On leaving Sabbath and returning to the House from Dr Who's, the Doctor ordered a meeting of all the House's 'personnel' in the salon. The numbers were thin. Lisa-Beth was there. Katya was there, although Lisa-Beth noted that she looked anxious, as if ready to take flight at a moment's notice. Fitz was also there, looking tired and ill-shaven after having reappeared on Henrietta Street at four o'clock that morning. Nobody bothered asking him what he'd been doing.

And that was it. Nobody had seen Anji or Juliette since the previous day. The same went for Scarlette. The Doctor was concerned by this, but despite some nervous looks the three remaining 'working women' failed to tell him the reasons. Nonetheless, the Doctor began to brief them. The good Chinese doctor, he explained, was preparing a ritual which would ostensibly make everything all right again. They were to gather together at midnight, on the banks of the Thames near St Paul's Cathedral. Once they were there...

It was during this briefing that Scarlette arrived. Although Lisa-Beth maintains that Scarlette *appeared* her usual self, in her costume of red with her boots clacking on the boards, Lisa-Beth also mentions that there was a 'terrible atmosphere' when the Mistress of the House walked in. She's said to have nodded, quite curtly, to the Doctor: to have virtually ignored everyone else. Her face was frozen, without any expression. Lisa-Beth believed this was because she'd heard news of the vote, perhaps from one of the three women who'd already departed.

In fact, it was because Scarlette knew what was going to happen next and knew just what kind of devil the Doctor would have to deal with. Because she'd visited Dr Who in Soho nearly a whole day before the Doctor had, and five minutes after Sabbath had left the shop she'd received a full report from the proprietor. Who was not a *discreet* man.

When the Doctor concluded his briefing, and announced that they were to meet the *Jonah* at the Thames, Scarlette reportedly didn't even flinch. There was an awkward pause once the Doctor had finished, in which 'many glances were stolen', but the silence was ended when the Doctor clapped his hands and announced that it was time they found out what had happened to Anji and Juliette.

Lisa-Beth adds a postscript to the scene. According to her, as those assembled began to disperse she saw Scarlette reach out her hand for the Doctor's, while still keeping her expression neutral. As Lisa-Beth describes it, it sounds like a small act of affection. Perhaps it's true to say, then, that although Scarlette knew they were going to have to walk into the middle of Sabbath's empire – and although she in no way liked the path the Doctor was taking – she was willing to stand by his side when his battle began.

She just wasn't prepared to let it show.

NATURE

It's the preserve of the upper classes, the English upper classes particularly, to turn everything into a sport. The aristocracy was as bored in 1782 as it ever was, and it didn't take the youngbloods of English society long to see the potential in the carnivorous apes.

Ape-hunting as a pastime of the rich was most probably invented by the three brothers and one sister of the Barrymore family, four sociopathic siblings who in later years would cause a scandal by associating with the Prince of Wales in Brighton, and who throughout their 'reign of terror' would turn physical abuse into something of an art form (their victims were almost always of the lower classes, obviously). Reckless, bad-tempered, childish and irredeemably violent, the Barrymores moved in the same circles as such crypto-occultists as the Countess of Jersey, so it's not surprising that they should have heard about the ape attacks. It's not known which of the four might have hatched the scheme of culling the animals for fun, but by August at least one of the four was in London, scouring the streets whenever word would reach him (via the younger, less discreet, Masonic orders) that there might be exotic animals at large in the city. The 'sport' would largely involve the Barrymores' *phaeton* speeding drunkenly through the streets in the early hours of the morning. Passers-by might have been unnerved to see a figure leaning out of the window of the carriage, usually armed with a crossbow, loudly threatening to shoot anyone who didn't tell him where he could find a baboon to kill.

The Masonic archive records that the Lodges had a great disdain for this sort of activity, although many did feel a certain sense of satisfaction when 'Hellgate' Barrymore did actually succeed in slaughtering one of the wild animals. He later boasted that he'd chased the huge, grey-pelted ape through the narrow working-class warrens of the city, eventually cornering it in a dead-end alley and 'as the brute turned to face [Barrymore] with a loud and bloody hiss' piercing its heart with a crossbow bolt. The ape was said to have thrashed wildly on the cobbles for some minutes before dying. 'Hellgate' had the creature skinned, and for weeks afterward carried the pelt around with him as a trophy, until one night he left it in a tavern while inebriated and it disappeared forever. Later commentators claimed that Barrymore had never faced such a beast at all, and certainly there were stories that some months after this first killing the Barrymore clan broke into a private menagerie and stole a terrified barbary ape so that they could pursue it through the streets as a re-enactment of the glorious hunt.

Though the 'official' ritualists of England may have frowned on all this, many factions of the Grand Lodge began to hold their own, somewhat more sombre, ape-hunts. On September 5, for example, both the Countess of Jersey and Lord _____ (a perpetual double-act since Cambridge) were to be found in London, their carriage circling the area of Charing Cross. If they were indeed hunting apes, either out of a sense of duty or out of upper-class boredom, then they'd certainly picked the right area. And at least one of them would soon regret it.

Around ten o'clock the pair reached the region of Aldwych: walking distance from the Temple area. Unlike Anji, they failed to perceive any change in the environment around them, at least at first. But as they headed towards the Embankment, the Lord began to feel 'distressed' and insisted that they were being watched by 'a thousand and one eyes... it was the one, not the thousand, which alarmed him'. The Countess ordered the coachman to stop the vehicle, believing that the Lord was unwell.

It was then that the Countess noticed a subtle change in the surroundings outside their carriage. The coachman may have noticed it too, because he began swearing loudly, insisting that they should drive away. The Countess commanded him to stay where he was, but the man's protests only became more violent. Before he could whip the horse into action, however, something began to rock the coach.

The description, perhaps significantly, is similar to some accounts of the Gordon Riots. In 1780, Lords and Parliamentarians had been attacked in their coaches by the mob, the vehicles rocked and pushed, the occupants torn out of their seats and manhandled by the crowds. The same thing happened here, to the degree that the Countess believed some ambush had been laid by Irish radicals or violent Tory sympathisers. Her first clue that something was very, very wrong appears to have been the sound from outside. A grunting, scratching noise that was unquestionably animal in nature.

Prior to September 5 the apes had only been sighted individually, Juliette's dream diary notwithstanding. But now the stakes were being raised. Which brings up the question of what happened to Anji and Juliette that night, while the Countess and the Lord were themselves under attack.

The answer is… unclear. As neither Juliette nor Anji tended to leave behind first-hand accounts, the only stories are urban legends, and many of them have the smack of pure myth. After Anji turned the corner and found herself staring at the bleached, broken city of the apes, what *all* the tales agree on is that the apes began to crawl out of the debris. They're described as creatures out of a cautionary tale, their eyes burning, their teeth hungry for the blood of those who knew too much. There's something decidedly creepy about the scene: ordinary Londoners going about their nightly business, completely oblivious to the presence of the snuffling, hungry beasts which ignore them completely and head directly for Anji.

The last thing on which all stories agree is the fact that Anji turned, once more, to face Juliette; and that Juliette's face appeared quite calm, perhaps understanding that there was no point keeping secrets any longer. After that, everything is speculation.

This is the way Emily tells the story:

…but tho the elymental lady [Anji] was in peril it ment nothing to my friend [Juliette]. My friend stept foreward without any hesitation or fear, and she stood in front of the elymental so that she was between her person and the aipes. When they saw this the aipes hesitated. They were barborus animals but they could see my friend's resolve and that she would not run. Then my friend began the *incantation* and advanced upon them, so as the elymental lady watched with surprise and amazement the aipes began to retreat [and] my frend did force them back into the night from where they had come...

This isn't what Scarlette records, and presumably Scarlette had heard the story from Anji herself:

The Beast was everywhere, and Mistress Anji did what any one of us would do in such a circumstance. She turned on her heels and ran. She did not see J. run also, but the last she saw of J. was J. stepping towards the broken city. Anji also saw that though the good people of London had failed to notice anything amiss, there was one man who stood in the shelter of the cracked facades who watched Juliette with interest. Anji believed the man to have been on the watch for a woman of the streets, and to have taken an interest in J. without seeing the danger all around. Anji did not even think to warn the gentleman. She simply ran...

I do not believe from this that J. is dead. It does not necesarily follow.

Notice that Scarlette speaks of the apes in the singular, as *the Beast*, as if they were a disease like 'the pox' or a complaint like 'the Prince'. Notice also that she now refers to Juliette as 'J'... as if she's unwilling to acknowledge her former student's full name. The reasons for this will soon become clear.

Whichever version is closest to the mark, the outcome is certain. Over twenty-four hours later, Anji would return to the House, pale and retching, claiming that she'd spent some time 'lost' in a city which she seemed reluctant to describe as being either definitely London or definitely the *other place* (more on this unusual day-long excursion, and its consequences, later). Juliette didn't come back at all.

But by the time Anji re-appeared, everything had already changed. Because September 6 was the night when the Doctor held his ceremony to recall the TARDIS.

The members of the House met at the docklands of the river Thames, just before midnight. There was a fog over the river that night, which is significant: before the great industrial age there were few great smogs in London, so it was almost as if the city were paying tribute to the machines of the future, TARDIS or *Jonah*, being honoured by this ceremony. There was the Doctor, as usual completely oblivious to the world around him, pacing the bank of the river and looking out across the water. There was Scarlette, in her robes of brilliant red, silent and impassive by his side. And there were the other three women, Lisa-Beth, Rebecca and Katya. They too were in red, wearing their 'bee' uniforms. Perhaps they felt that, as they were about to desert the House, they had a duty to wear Scarlette's colours one more time. Only Fitz was dressed in reasonably normal clothing, although with his lack of fashion sense even he must have looked suspicious.

On the stroke of midnight, the fog parted. Lisa-Beth describes the scene as if a warship-shaped hole simply appeared in the thick air. Moments later the *Jonah* was sighted, although whether it had appeared out of nowhere or simply drifted into view along the river is a matter of opinion.

There was a figure standing on the deck of the ship, and according to Lisa-Beth there was a 'palpable tension' in Scarlette. But the Doctor had already assured her that Sabbath would stay out of the way for the occasion, though he admitted that he had no idea where Sabbath would actually *be*. The man on the deck was Who, and he came attired in his best ornamental robes. Lisa-Beth reports being unimpressed by the old quack, saying that his appearance and his manner were both put on for show, but admitting that (as this was a *ritual* event) the show may have been important. Who's robes were in shades of red and black, though those assembled suspected his clothing may have been hastily improvised from some form of dressing gown.

So it was that the people of the House boarded the *Jonah* for the first time, and to her credit Scarlette was the second to board the ship, after the Doctor himself. Who greeted each of the women in turn, kissing every female hand and issuing a stream of compliments in mumbled English. The women, used to this kind of play-acting, were graceful in return and failed to giggle. Somehow, surrounded by the fog as they boarded this grey steel monster, humour seemed out of place. Even Who's levity felt *wrong* here.

Scarlette remained at the Doctor's side as the party descended into the belly of the ship. Lisa-Beth notes that Scarlette seemed to take in every detail around her, but 'never made it plain that she was searching for the captain'. Even Rebecca was muted, although she *had* seen the Jonah before. Lisa-Beth doesn't record her own feelings, save that she was impressed despite herself on seeing Sabbath's map room, with its catalogue of icons. There was an animal-stench in the depths of the *Jonah*, but at no point did any of the crew present themselves.

Only when the Doctor had assembled his party in the map room did he address everyone en masse, Who standing beside him and nodding in short bursts as the Doctor explained what was about to happen... and, perhaps more importantly, as he explained the true nature of the apes for the first time. Lisa-Beth was the most accomplished *tantrist* amongst them – though not necessarily the most accomplished *witch* – and she seems to have understood the Doctor's briefing better than the rest.

Throughout what follows, it's important to remember that the Doctor perceived time as, at least in part, a psychological phenomenon. Time, in the Doctor's view, was inseparable from the observer's *perception* of time. In this he was far ahead of all eighteenth-century thinking, and very much in line with more modern speculative physics. The Doctor's explanation, as recorded by Lisa-Beth, was this.

The Doctor informed us that all time (and, so he claimed, all of space) could be perceived as an aspect of human thought, although I could see this meant nothing to Katya and her kind. Yet the Doctor stated that human thought has limits. In his philosophy, the mind of man is not capable of understanding *any* mystery or solving *any* puzzle. To him the mind of man is an animal thing, which I can well believe having seen so many men lose theirs over the thought of sexual conquest. A man, or woman, can no more understand time as a whole than an ape can be taught the rules of chess. The Doctor maintained, and still maintains, that we are all of us animal in nature and are not the creatures of infinite comprehension which men like Newton would have had us believe... I do not know whether he applies this rule to elementals also.

He further speculated that there was a point of understanding no human mind could pass. At the limits of our consciousness, he informed us, there comes a point at which *time* and *mind* become indistinguishable. He implied an area of grey where it is no longer clear whether the events we might witness are made of flesh or simply aspects of our own thinking. This is the point which we call *the horizon*. Though as even Mother Dutt knew, no human being ever comes close to the horizon. No man or woman yet born has understanding to reach the point where understanding fails…

…but it is from the horizon that the apes come. They are, believes the Doctor, aspects of ourselves. They are our own ignorance given flesh, born of the place where thought and being are twined. Should we reach the horizon, we will find our own ignorance staring back at us in the shape of these bloody, murderous animals. If we search too deeply, we will find the beasts ready to tear us apart for our curiosity. With every new thought and discovery we move closer to that horizon of understanding, yet our comprehension is such that it is still a greater distance from us than we can imagine.

It must have taken some time to explain this complex notion to everyone assembled. But the story seems incomplete. If this were indeed the true nature of the apes, then why had they never been seen before the 1780s? And why had the Doctor, a self-proclaimed expert in matters of time, never encountered them before?

He had an explanation, of course.

No man or woman, he said, should ever have a chance of nearing the horizon or meeting the apes. The horizon should by all the laws of Nature be safe and stable, beyond the reach of us all, but he had through his studies with Sabbath become convinced that this was no longer the case.

The Doctor was loath to speak of the past, but we understood from Mr. K.'s veiled and not so veiled comments that the world [i.e. universe] had undergone a degree of change. Once the Doctor's tribe of elementals had protected the element of time. It had been their place to maintain a certain *aplomb* [in this sense meaning 'stability' or 'balance']. Yet now they had gone, and in their absence there was great suffering to be had. So accustomed had the world [universe] become to the elementals' presence that when they were removed the world found itself to be weak, like a man who has been ill in bed for so long that he can no longer recall how to use his legs. It was to his shame, the Doctor perhaps believed, that the world had been left so dependent on elemental charms…

…his suggestion was that in these times, the element of time was no longer stable. It followed that its limitations were not stable either, and that the very absence of an elemental force in the world had altered the nature of the horizon. The horizon had moved, was still moving, the lines of time around it moving also so that soon no man or woman would be able to think an original thought without the apes tearing them to shreds. The apes were the guardians of that threshold, but never before had their realm been breached by mankind. Now it seems their realm is all around us.

A theory that certainly fits everything known about the apes. The apes which had attacked the Countess and the Lord, on the previous night, had brought back memories of the Gordon Rioters... almost as if the beasts had responded to the aristocrats' anxieties about the mob (the Gordon Riots had themselves been a kind of violent cautionary tale, at least for the English upper classes).

Scarlette had two questions for the Doctor. First she asked why the apes should have appeared here in Europe and now in 1782, when there were so many other aeons to choose from. The Doctor responded by saying he felt it was something to do with the era's perceptions: humanity as a whole was now beginning to think of time in dimensional/scientific terms, and this 'mass understanding' was likely to have caused a great shift in the unstable horizon. He also felt it was significant that only a year earlier, Wessel had more or less invented the concept of time travel in *Anno 7603*. This was typical witch-thinking on the Doctor's part. In witchcraft and in ritualism, words (in the form of incantations) are used to summon and bind the elemental forces, in order to change the human world. Similarly, the Doctor described Wessel's work as a kind of summoning, a collection of words which had inadvertently brought forth the apes and let them loose.

Scarlette's second question was harder for the Doctor to answer. She asked why these bestial guardians of the horizon should look like *apes*. Fair enough, they were symbols of man's ignorance – the animal inside, dragging humanity back into savagery – but why should they resemble apes? Why not dogs, or bears, or tigers, or rats, or any other species?

The Doctor attempted to gloss over this question. If he truly knew the answer, then it's not surprising he didn't reveal it. It would be over seventy years before Charles Darwin would release his theories about mankind's ancestry, seventy years before Scarlette's generation would appreciate the answer.

So that was the Doctor's explanation. Every human action, every human thought, every new experiment and theory now had an effect on the horizon and the world/universe it encircled. That was why the party had assembled here, on Sabbath's ship, to perform a procedure which the Doctor believed could recall his TARDIS without bringing the apes running.

But even so, the ceremony would have its side effects. Of course it would: the Doctor was bringing an object of power, a lodestone of the elementals, into an already unstable world. It would be on this very night that 'Hellgate' Barrymore would catch and butcher his prize grey ape. Rumour would have it that people living near the Strand would hear a monstrous screeching from behind their walls, as if ancient animals had been bricked up in the architecture. Sailors off the coast of Britain and mainland Europe would report a record number of sightings of the 'silver ship', as if this mysterious metal craft were attempting to be in several different places at once. Before the night was out, the Countess of Jersey – still shaken after witnessing the horrifying, violent death of Lord _____ the previous evening, in an attack she herself barely survived – would face the inner circle of the Service itself, and make a decision which would change the whole of western history.

And they would certainly feel it in America. The white oaks of Virginia would feel it in the earth, while their roots fed off the power of the bloody, buried things which had once ruled the American-Indians but which had now struck a deal with General Washington and his new order. It's easy to imagine Matthew Crane listening to what those trees told him, and then considering, not for the first time, the strange red envelope which had been brought to him from Europe.

By the time the dawn arrived, the Doctor would have his TARDIS back, Anji would have returned to Henrietta Street, and Scarlette's cabal would have discovered the shocking truth about the disappearance of Juliette. And through it all, what of Sabbath?

8
The World and Other Places

DEAR JOHN

To Dr. Jack-of-the-Moon:

I would ask you to forgive me the decision I have made but I know you would not wish me to become sentimental. I know also that whatever I can say it cannot change how you will feel though I hope you will understand my reasoning. I can only guess that you will feel disappointment and perhaps sorrow and for this at least I am sorry. I do not think you will wish to dwell on this and so I will not either.

I hold you in the highest regard and with the greatest affection and though you may not wish to hear it I find myself sad at not being close to you. Yet perhaps I have not been close to you for some time.

In the eleventh century AD, Hassan i Sabbah – guru of the original *Assassin* movement, the death-cult which inspired the word – ensured the loyalty of his followers by building an enormous garden of pleasure. When a new member was initiated into his cult, Hassan would allow the man free reign within this paradise, first dosing the subject with large amounts of narcotics so that he'd believe himself to be literally in Heaven. In that garden the man would indulge in every imaginable human pleasure, experiencing in his blissed-out state all the delicacies and concoctions he could ever desire, while at the same time being attended by the *houris* or 'virgins of paradise'. At the end of this short stay in the garden, Hassan would inform the initiate that he could have a *permanent* place in this paradise, if he died for the Assassin cause. Having had a taste of the afterlife, the subject would nearly always agree to Hassan's request, to the point where members of the cult would willingly throw themselves from tall buildings just to prove their loyalty.

This is worth mentioning because it's hard not to think of Hassan, when one reads the accounts of the Doctor and his TARDIS. Members of the House would rarely be admitted within the doors of this impossible haven, yet when they were they would always return with stories of magnificent, alien vistas; of hallways and caverns containing treasures beyond even the *Arabian Nights*; of entire worlds trapped within the passageways. The *Jonah* may have had its impressive map-room, but Scarlette held that the Doctor's transport could have contained maps drawn on a scale of one-to-one. The TARDIS was said to have everything from its own fast-flowing river (probably an exaggeration) to a cloistered complex not unlike a monastery in miniature. On one occasion Fitz even claimed it had its own opera house, although the Doctor quickly added that he'd only picked that up by accident, having intended to deliver it somewhere before forgetting all about it.

(In terms of eighteenth-century occultism, these dialogues between the Doctor and Fitz are much like the performances of European charlatans such as Cagliostro. Cagliostro and his servant would frequently be overheard at society functions, fondly speaking of things that happened hundreds of years earlier in a well-rehearsed 'double act' designed to make the listener believe that Cagliostro was an immortal being who'd been present at the crucifixion. Which isn't to say that the Doctor was a charlatan... but the similarities are remarkable.)

By the middle of October the TARDIS was at Henrietta Street, though how it got there from the *Jonah* is unclear. Sabbath could hardly have helped: nobody in the House would have worked with him, not after what they'd recently discovered. Whatever the truth, by October 15 the device stood in the corner of the salon, a blue wooden box which promised the Earth and which the Doctor believed would restore him to health.

In fact, it was just about the only furnishing left there. In Covent Garden, everybody knew that it was all over for Scarlette. Her women had left her. Lisa-Beth and Rebecca still lived at the House, for the time being, but nobody did business. Even Katya had vanished. When the afternoon sun shone through the salon windows, it would illuminate great empty spaces, blank walls and floorboards stripped of their red-and-black decorations. The windows had no curtains, so curious men-about-town would stare in at the listless women inside with fish-eyed faces.

The Doctor would usually be inside his miraculous TARDIS, and in the void that remained Fitz and Anji would simply sit around the House, bored and restless. Rebecca would often be found sitting in the middle of the salon floor, laying out her cards in great spirals across the boards. She eventually spent several days working on a pattern of prophecy that nobody else understood, constantly changing the individual cards one by one and pushing the spectacles up the bridge of her nose at regular intervals, apparently trying to create a future she liked the look of. Her behaviour was becoming increasingly obsessive: guilt may have been a factor. Juliette's room had been emptied of all effects except for Anji's, and it was rumoured that Scarlette had burned all the girl's old things, but this is almost certainly untrue. Scarlette herself acted, typically, as if nothing were happening – you don't become a successful procuress without learning to stash *some* of the profits away – but the money was running out and…

…and, to be blunt, there was no end in sight. Everyone had expected that when the Doctor recovered his TARDIS, a great adventure would begin which might take their minds off their troubles. It hadn't. It had simply given the Doctor another place in which to withdraw. Lisa-Beth wrote that she believed the TARDIS hadn't helped to heal him at all. Even before the end of September, she'd reached the conclusion that he was *sleeping* inside that box of his, although she was rarely even allowed a glimpse inside. On one occasion she even said that she thought he'd begun talking to the portrait he'd painted of his imaginary grandfather.

It's not fair to be hard on the Doctor. In the weeks before the arrival of the TARDIS he'd seemed tired, even desperate. He'd claimed that soon the apes would destroy all notion of human progress, yet nothing had been heard of them for a month and the Doctor had apparently done nothing to stop them. It seemed as though the people of the House were simply killing time, waiting for the wedding in December, a wedding which they now knew would almost certainly never happen.

Nobody spoke of Juliette. Neither Scarlette nor Lisa-Beth make any mention of her after mid-September, or explain what happened to her. Because Anji had been quite correct: Juliette had been led *astray*, pushed in directions about which the Doctor knew nothing. But Anji had, wrongly, believed Scarlette to be the one responsible. In fact, Scarlette would have been horrified if she'd known. It may have taken the members of the House a while to unravel the facts, but surely the final damning evidence was one small detail in Anji's account of what had happened on 'the night of the apes'. When she'd run from the Temple region, there'd been a man watching from the shadows. Anji had assumed that he'd been a passer-by, perhaps someone on the lookout for a woman of the streets, incapable of seeing the beasts around him. Yet in her journal, Scarlette records Anji's description of the man, although – with the frostiness Scarlette usually applied when dealing with bad memories – she doesn't record the obvious conclusion.

He was a man of some bulk and power, dressed in a coat much like those favoured by the Admirals of Europe. He had very little hair. The Doctor was quick to step in and remind us all that there are many fat and balding men in London.

Of course, Anji had never met Sabbath. At Brighton, the Doctor had been careful to keep her ashore while Sabbath remained on the *Jonah*.

And then there was Emily. Accounts of Emily's life are manifold (most concentrating on her later, more famous, years), but all the official versions contain gaps, and most of the gaps can be filled by her association with Sabbath. A connection between the two is easy to find. Charles Greville, who kept Emily as his mistress from late 1781, enjoyed showing her off to his society contacts… and Sabbath could certainly have been amongst them. Greville regarded Emily as living *vertu*, a piece of classical art and beauty, and with her wild flair for romance Emily would have felt bored and listless shut up in her Oxford Street home for his convenience. It's easy to see how Sabbath would have recruited her to his cause, with his promises of adventure, of magic, of strange and exotic lands. She was intelligent, charming and (above all) attractive. She was, in short, exactly the kind of person Sabbath *liked* to use as an agent. He was ruthless when it came to exploiting the talents of his cat's-paws.

But Emily was no witch and no warrior. Sabbath must have known that she could never be his 'right hand', as Tula Lui had been. Besides which, in early 1782 Tula Lui had been alive and Sabbath hadn't needed a replacement. All that had changed in July.

It's not clear when Sabbath turned his attention to Juliette. As far as Scarlette and Lisa-Beth were aware, the two never even met before Juliette's disappearance in September. Yet Sabbath knew everything that happened in the House, thanks to Emily. He must have considered, at length, the ritual wedding being planned by Scarlette's clique. He must have decided that such a thing was workable, but not within the purview of a 'failed elemental' like the Doctor. And most of all, he must have known that he needed a new right hand. It's tempting to think that he may even have been lonely after Tula Lui's death, but it doesn't pay to sentimentalise, especially not with Sabbath.

The modern reader can only imagine how the Doctor would have responded to the loss of Juliette. And, more importantly, how Scarlette would have felt. The only time Scarlette referred to it in her journals, shortly after the truth was uncovered, was in describing a conversation between herself and the Doctor. It took place one night in Scarlette's own room, as the two of them lay together on the bed – fully clothed, Scarlette adds – in the flickering light of the lamps. Despite the subject matter, Scarlette describes the scene as being quite gentle, full of regret rather than anger. (The text has been simplified here.)

SCARLETTE: I *did* try to tell you.
DOCTOR: Yes. But I needed his help. We didn't have a choice. *I* didn't have a choice.
SCARLETTE: I know. Whatever he touches, he burns. It's his nature.
DOCTOR: Do you really believe that? [Scarlette takes this as concern for Juliette.]
SCARLETTE: I know you worry. Nobody could fault you for that. I think of what he must have done, to make her believe in him.
DOCTOR: You're angry?
SCARLETTE: Oh, God, yes.
DOCTOR: Just because of Juliette?
[Here, Scarlette notes: 'He knows me so well'.]
SCARLETTE: No. I admit it, it's not Juliette. It's because of myself.

Whether this means that Scarlette blamed *herself* for what had happened to Juliette, or that she was angry at what Sabbath had once done to *her*, is unclear.

'What he must have done, to make her believe in him.' Indeed, Juliette's motivations are a matter for some debate. Scarlette's assumption was that Sabbath had brainwashed Juliette, and at first glance Juliette's dream diary supports this. Sabbath poisoned her mind with strange vapours, subjected her to almost hallucinogenic experiences, trained Emily to say just the right thing at just the right time. However, as the dream diary reveals, Juliette already had anxieties about the wedding. She sensed the Doctor's own worries about his right to use someone in this fashion. The great, shadowy, intense presence that haunted her dreams – representing the Doctor, or Sabbath, or both? – reflected those anxieties. Above all, she felt she had some great purpose to her life *but Scarlette and the Doctor had given her no chance to find out what it was*.

Nobody can say for certain what happened inside the 'Black House', where Juliette would go to meet Emily in the early hours of the morning. Maybe Sabbath himself was waiting for her there. But in the Black House Juliette was given a new dress, a black dress, an alternative to the fate which Scarlette's House had imposed on her... an alternative she desperately wanted (no wonder Emily had instructed her to keep a dream diary). After all, Juliette was experiencing puberty on top of everything else. In truth, Sabbath merely continued the process which the Doctor had already begun, but allowed Juliette to experiment at will and observed at a distance rather than keeping her on a short leash as Scarlette had done.

The turning point had been that night in September, when Juliette had stepped in to save Anji from the *babewyns*. It was as if, by that action, Juliette was finally acknowledging that she was ready to face the consequences of the path she'd chosen. She was ready to use *her* kind of craft, the craft of the Black House, against the enemy. Only then did Sabbath step out of the shadows and take her away from the House for good. In the story of Anji and the Temple apes, the beasts seem remarkably quiet and subdued, ignoring most passers-by to concentrate on Anji herself. Almost as if they'd been trained to.

Which only leaves the question of *why* Sabbath wanted Juliette, why she, more than anyone else, struck him as good material to be his new right hand. It's likely that he knew how much she'd already been influenced by the Doctor. Long before the Doctor had known the truth about the apes, he'd instinctively understood the 'elemental' truth, that the Earth required a form of protector: an elemental anchor, so to speak, that would hold time still around the planet. By the symbolic marriage ceremony, the alchemical wedding of the Doctor (representing the elemental) and Juliette (representing the Earth), the Doctor hoped to bring a new security to the troubled world. And also, perhaps, to give *himself* roots in a universe where he no longer truly belonged. In a sense, what he needed was a kind of 'green card' that would give him the right to interfere in the Earth's affairs, a ceremony which would by its very nature have a stabilising effect on the planet. Or at least, that was the theory.

As later events would prove, Sabbath also wanted to become *rooted*. As his notes have shown, he knew that to travel into the deeper realms (other times, or other worlds?) he'd first have to connect himself to the Earth. On the one occasion when he tried to pilot the *Jonah* outside of his normal territories, this is how he wrote of the experience:

> A lack of cohesion, a certain lack of integrity. I was reminded of Knox's maxim that we might cease to exist if ever we were no longer observed by God... though God had little to do with the experience, my sense was that my own world no longer acknowledged me and as a consequence I was ceasing to be. I gave orders to my crew to turn the ship around while I could still speak.

So although there are no stories to explain how the Doctor's legendary people managed to travel between worlds, there's an implication (in many of the tales Fitz told Lisa-Beth) that on the Doctor's homeworld there was indeed a great 'eye' which watched the Doctor and his kind wherever they went, which linked the elementals to the place of their creation and ensured that no harm came to them when they moved from realm to realm. This process, perhaps, was intrinsic to the Doctor's TARDIS… but it was evidently the one secret which Sabbath had yet to incorporate into the *Jonah*. This was Sabbath's holy grail, his philosopher's stone, the 'Black Hart' he sought throughout 1782. (Significantly, when Sabbath first met Emily she used her given surname of 'Lyon'. Only after her recruitment in January did she begin to use the name 'Hart', almost as if it were a codename. Did Sabbath believe that Emily was the agent through which he could perform his hunt?)

It seems likely that Sabbath believed Juliette could help him with this quest, just as the Doctor believed that the very presence of the TARDIS could help him recover his strength. If this was indeed the case, then very soon both men were to be proved mistaken.

IN SICKNESS AND IN HEALTH

Under normal circumstances the vault of the Church of Saint Simone, on the Caribbean island of St Belique, was a black hole. The walls of the vault were caked in dirt that nobody ever bothered to wash off, as the only people who ever visited the site were relatives of the dead who'd been buried under the cement floor, and as the last burial had been in 1710 the relatives were few and far between. The dense heat made the vault smell of damp and sweet fruits, although the cement at least stopped the dead adding anything to the smell.

But that October, the vault was a riot of colour. Or one colour, at least. The dirty walls had been scrubbed, so even if they were still black they were at least *dry* and black. Garlands of red flowers, orchids as well as dried roses, were hung in ornate rings which had been stitched together by women from the town: the island's *only* real town, situated between the sea and the forest interior. The locals knew a thing or two about witchcraft and *obeah*, so they weren't above helping with the ceremony that was to be performed there. Red paper blossoms and streamers lined the walls, some recovered from the cellars of the Henrietta Street House, some supplied by the infinite cupboards of the Doctor's TARDIS. Moreover, the vault was hung with ornamental paper lanterns, in the oriental style. Indeed, there was something of an oriental feel to the place despite its Caribbean location.

This was hardly surprising. The man in charge of the decorations was the Chinese quack, Dr Nie Who. His transition from London to St Belique seems to have been unusually rapid, so either the TARDIS or some other arcane transportation may have been involved.

The evidence suggests that Who knew about the fate of Juliette almost as soon as the Doctor did, but he didn't let it slow him down. The Doctor had asked him to decorate the location where the wedding was to be held, in order not to offend any of the guests, who would after all be representatives of at least thirteen major powers. The wedding legally had to be conducted in Church, but it had been Scarlette's idea to hold it in the vault rather than the main body of the building, in order to give the affair a more 'satanic' feel. And where better than here, among the witch-poisoned roots of St Belique, where Christianity was only a technicality anyway? Dr Who had set about the task with aplomb, for a very reasonable fee. Not only would he arrange the gathering, he'd also handle the various needs of the guests, which meant making sure that groups hostile to each other didn't spend too long in each other's company. In modern terms this might be called 'handling security'.

Back at the House, the Doctor was still holding out hope that Juliette would return. Scarlette wasn't so optimistic. Take this extract from Lisa-Beth's journals, the day after Anji brought the truth home with her:

> When all of us in the House knew the import of what Anji had said, and knew that Sabbath was the one responsible, there was a silence in the salon. Some like Rebecca seemed only to reflect, but some like Fitz did not know what to say or where to look. It was only after some minutes [moments, surely?] that Scarlette made her move. She simply turned around and strode up the stairs... when she was followed she was found standing within Juliette's room, staring at the dressing-table. Juliette had taken with her the glass splinter on a silver chain, the blood-shard of Mary Culver, which Scarlette had lent her as a relic of the Hellfire tradition.

Scarlette had only lent Juliette the glass totem until her wedding day: it was to be the 'borrowed' part of the 'old, new, borrowed, blue' ceremony (itself a tradition with its roots in fire/earth/water/air elementalism). Yet the Doctor saw the theft of the glass as a *positive* sign. As far as he was concerned, Sabbath's aim was to turn Juliette away from the ways of the House. As long as Juliette carried Scarlette's charm, said the Doctor, there was a good chance she'd return home before the planned wedding day. Nobody mentioned the fact that Juliette had failed to take with her the red wedding dress that Scarlette had commissioned.

Before Juliette's disappearance, the Doctor had begun displaying signs of obsessive behaviour. He'd been worried about the slightest details of the wedding, from the decor of the vault to – bizarrely – the question of whether any of his family would turn up on the day to give him away. Now all that had been replaced by a new obsession, the idea, perhaps rooted in self-delusion, that Juliette would return to him.

Lisa-Beth records that Fitz even feared for the Doctor's sanity. The Doctor was so insistent that the TARDIS had helped his mysterious sickness that he seemed almost hyperactive, and periods of heavy, rapid breathing were common... periods which would be followed by extended disappearances into the TARDIS's interior. (Incidentally, it's a matter of record that Fitz and Lisa-Beth slept together at least once during this period, probably more out of boredom than out of passion. Neither was exactly inhibited, and this should surprise nobody.)

So, with the wedding no more than six weeks away, those remaining at the House busied themselves with whatever they could and tried to pretend that they were being constructive. Often they'd talk about Juliette, though never in the presence of Scarlette or the Doctor, wondering exactly where the girl had been taken and what kind of 'initiation' she might be undergoing at the hands of Sabbath. Fitz and Rebecca would sometimes scour the town, from the Shakespeare's Head to the finest of coffee-houses, listening for news on the grapevine. Lord _____ hadn't been seen in a month, and whispers in the Tavern claimed the Countess of Jersey had been there when the Lord had been torn limb from limb by a pack of wild animals. The Lady, the stories went on to say, had experienced something of a revelation after this. Soon afterwards she'd made a report to the surviving members of the Star Chamber of the Service. Tittle-tattle insisted that when the Countess had left the Chamber, it was the Servicemen, and not her, who'd been shaken by the interview. There was even news of Emily. Two months earlier the wife of the British Envoy in Naples had died, and as the Envoy's nephew was Charles Greville it was said that Greville's mistress might be 'passed on' to the grieving uncle. In retrospect it's easy to see Sabbath's hand in events. Given the events of later decades, an agent in the court of Naples would have been a boon to him.

The other thing which had been noticed in the underworld was the unusual activity of witch-lodges around the world. Envoys from each of the great cults were on the move. An agent of the Virginian lodge had apparently left America, to the consternation of many. The followers of

Mackandal had seized a French merchant vessel, and a delegation of negro occultists had allegedly set sail. Even in the Russian embassy, there'd been talk of personal directives from the Empress herself.

It's not hard to see what was happening. All roads were leading to St Belique. In the centre of the vault of the Church of Saint Simone, Who had erected an enormous table, varnished with smooth red lacquer and lavished with delicate, intertwining wreaths of orchid-blossom. The table was huge, so big that it had been specially constructed inside the vault itself, and though it technically had thirteen sides it was generally referred to by Who's native assistants as 'the round table' (interesting, given that they wouldn't have known much about Arthurian legend). Into each place at the table, a name had been inscribed.

The names matched the names on Scarlette's thirteen red envelopes. In spite of everything, the guests were still expected to come. From the four corners of the Earth they'd begun to warily circle the Caribbean, watching what the others did before they set foot on the island and committed themselves to the Doctor's 'party'.

But on October 24, circumstances would change once again. For the last few weeks there'd been more and more talk of the Countess of Jersey, of how this vain, snobbish and generally unpleasant woman seemed to have suddenly altered in nature. Furthermore, she'd witnessed the death of her co-conspirator the Lord on the same night that Juliette had vanished, and Fitz – with his usual adventurer's spirit – had concluded that there might be a connection. That afternoon, he went with Rebecca to visit the Countess, and although the Lady refused to grant him an audience this research trip was indeed useful.

What Fitz discovered will be dealt with in due course: but he and his friends were distracted from this lead by what happened immediately after the non-interview. Fitz and Rebecca returned to the hollow shell of the House, where they found nobody home except for the Doctor. When they entered the salon, the Doctor was standing in the corner beside his TARDIS. He was leaning against the side of the box, one hand spread out across its doors, as Scarlette later put it (with her usual gift for embellishing events she didn't witness) 'as if attempting to draw new strength from its very wood'. In his other hand, the Doctor was holding a piece of paper and the torn envelope in which it had arrived.

There's no indication of how the note was delivered. But the Doctor's eyes were fixed on it when Fitz and Rebecca stepped into the room, darting backwards and forwards over the page, apparently attempting to take in the full weight of its contents. Fitz later commented that he felt the Doctor was continually reading and re-reading the same sentence.

The nature of the letter is no secret. It was from Juliette, her first communication since her disappearance. It began addressing itself to 'Dr Jack-of-the-Moon', but only the top four inches of the page survive: the rest was, at some later point, torn away. So it's hard to say exactly what sentence caught the Doctor's attention. Knowing the Doctor, it was most likely a deeply personal passage rather than some great revelation. The consequences are clearer:

> Then Jack looked up… having absorbed the essentials of the letter. He was a pale man at that moment. It was Mr. K. who caught his eye. There was, I'm told, a pleading look on his face when he addressed his oldest elemental companion. Yet all he said were the simple words: 'She's not coming back.'
>
> …I do not believe these words were the intent of the letter. I believe that in saying this, my friend was only facing the truth which he has for so long put to the back of his mind. No doubt it was something in the tone of this note which allowed him to confront what we all have felt these past days. Mr. K was unable to console him, for he knew it was true.
>
> Jack said one more thing then. Mr. K. could not divulge what the word was, for it was pained and in no recognised tongue. The word was not yet complete when Jack abruptly fell forward, and Mr. K. hurried to keep him from striking the floor.

A single word, spoken by the Doctor. It's almost reminiscent of the 'magic word' said to be held by Sabbath, which (the stories say) he'd inscribed on the rear of every steel plate on board the *Jonah*. One could very nearly believe that the Doctor was saying *Sabbath's* word, in a last desperate attempt to escape the physical plane and remove himself from the situation in which he'd arrived.

It evidently did him little good. The Doctor collapsed, and Fitz only just caught him. Scarlette records that there was 'a black bile' from the Doctor's mouth after he lost consciousness, which may be colourful storytelling or even a metaphor (even as late as the eighteenth century, it wasn't unknown for people to associate the biles and secretions of the human body with the four primal elements). But exaggeration or not, the time of crisis had arrived. The Doctor had been attempting to hide his sickness for some time, and in one Cagliostro-like moment had even confessed to Scarlette that he'd been suffering twinges for over a hundred years. Now, helpless and perhaps bringing up bile, it was clear that he could no longer contain it. It was clear, too, that not even the TARDIS could save him from it.

Finally, the Doctor was beginning to die.

SACRIFICE MEANS GIVING UP

In the whole of ritual, there's no word more misunderstood than 'sacrifice'. In the Old Testament tradition, every sacrifice would involve a spilling of blood – a fatted calf or goat sacrificed on the altar – and as a result the word has become almost synonymous with bloodshed. But 'sacrifice' only means 'a giving-up'. Blood-sacrifices were made because, in the subsistence-farming world of the Old Testament, to kill one of your valuable animals in the name of your God was to show your devotion above material possessions, perhaps even above your own survival. On the other hand, the 'virgin sacrifice' planned for Juliette had nothing to do with death. She was simply intended to give a certain part of herself away. As Scarlette grimly noted, some time after Juliette's disappearance, 'one can only sacrifice what belongs to one… this above all else may have been the Doctor's misunderstanding'.

But although there was no slaughter involved in the ways of Scarlette and her kind, blood was certainly an important factor. Even in London, no young woman would be admitted into any witch-cult until she had begun to menstruate. Some groups, such as the *Mayakai* who'd played such an important part in raising Scarlette, held that a woman was only initiated when she had sex: while the more masculine groups, mostly outside Europe and including the witch-factions of Mackandal's Maroons, held that a man wasn't a man until he'd killed another (preferably French) human being. This wasn't a sacrifice, it was simply an act of faith. The same ancient ritual insisted that when a member of the aristocracy participated in a fox hunt for the first time he would be 'blooded' with the blood of the slain animal.

When the Countess and the Lord had set out in their carriage, that night back in September, had they really just gone searching for apes out of boredom? It's possible, given the Lord's background, that his intention was to blood himself with the carcass of a dead ape. But unlike the foxes of the Lord's youth, *these* animals could fight back. It hardly seems worth relating the Countess's description of the scene, as the carriage was overturned; the coachman was ripped from his seat; the horse, screaming wildly, was brought down by the teeth that were sinking into its flanks; and the Lord was dragged out of the broken transport through one of the windows. It's perhaps surprising that the Countess herself managed to escape, although she had at least some knowledge of protective ritual.

So in the end, it was the Countess who'd been 'blooded' that night. She'd seen the consequence of 'infernal dabbling', and smelt the foul, rotting-meat stench of its breath. She'd run from the scourge, and although eventually she had returned to the city of London she (like Anji?) had spent some time lost in the bestial city. She had, she claimed, even had one peculiar encounter with what she described as the 'King of Beasts' (about which more later). She had realised, then, that the apes were a form of punishment. The King of Beasts, like the King of England, was as far as she was concerned a gibbering idiot whose kingdom was a den of wilful barbarism, an empire of filth falling into neglect. No wonder her audience had left the Star Chamber shaken. They would have expected this kind of treason from Sabbath, not from a Lady.

It's interesting to compare the Countess's 'initiation' to the events which took place on board the *Jonah* the following night, when the Doctor first called his TARDIS to Earth. So far the ceremony hasn't been described, mainly because the only account of it – Lisa-Beth's – is barely comprehensible. But, filling in the gaps from the context, the ceremony seems to have occurred in the following stages:

1. Once the Doctor's party had assembled in Sabbath's map room, the Doctor had explained that Nie Who was necessary to the process, as he had 'an understanding of time not likely to cause offence [to the apes]'. It was therefore Who who would perform the rites of the ceremony. (It might seem odd, at first, that a quack from the eighteenth century might be essential to the recovery of an artefact like the TARDIS. However, consider this in modern terms. If the Doctor existed in the twentieth century and needed to repair his TARDIS, nobody would raise an eyebrow if he were to call on the services of, say, a modern electronics expert. Yet the TARDIS is described as being so far beyond human experience that in context the idea of a mere computer technician working on it is in itself ridiculous. The implication is that Who had a certain *understanding* the Doctor found useful, regardless of the era's technology.)

2. After the explanations, the door of Sabbath's map room had opened and two of the 'crew' had shuffled into the room. This had caused some alarm, but the Doctor had assured everyone that the apes had been well-trained, hence the clothing. With his usual humour, Sabbath had dressed the creatures as footmen in wide jackets and knee-length socks, although he'd stopped short of giving them wigs or shoes. The Doctor had spoken

to the apes in formal tones, and Who had translated his words into a language Lisa-Beth took to be oriental: why the apes should have understood *him* and not the Doctor is unclear. Perhaps Who was being used as a 'buffer'. Whatever the reason, the apes had then turned and snuffled their way out of the chamber, and minutes later there'd been 'a monstrous humming' in the walls. The ship had begun to move.

3. This is where events become cloudy. The ceremony hadn't continued until the ship had reached a certain point, which Lisa-Beth says 'lay on the p[oint] from which the h[orizon?] was visible'. Her notes then degenerate, for the next two paragraphs, into coded shorthand. The suggestion is that the *Jonah* had left the world altogether, to exist somewhere in the mysterious spaces between elemental realms, but as there were no portholes in the map room the group could only have known their location by going up on deck. If they did indeed do this, then it could explain Lisa-Beth's lapse into gibberish. What would she have seen, standing there on the steel of the ship and looking out at another world? And more importantly, how could she possibly have described it in English, when English hadn't yet developed proper words to accurately describe the passage of time? The only fragment of proper English in these two paragraphs begins 'Scarlette stood with her face turned up to the heavens [more evidence that they'd left the map room], and there in her eyes I saw the light of…' before the text becomes foggy once again. Whenever Lisa-Beth describes such an experience, she describes it almost as being a 'magic lantern' show, popular at carnivals and pleasure gardens in the era. Such shows often involved coloured lights, and were appropriately known as 'phantasmagoria'.

4. At some point in this ghostly journey the Doctor had fallen to his knees, and Scarlette had rushed to his side, believing him to be sick. But the Doctor had merely stared upwards, almost in supplication. Who had stood behind him, whispering into his ear, much to Scarlette's concern. What Who might have said is a matter of conjecture. The Doctor had then clasped one hand to his own chest, and begun to recite words of his own. The others could only have watched, as 'all of us felt the motion of the s[hip] quicken and the m[?] around us did seem fit to bleed'.

5. More of Lisa-Beth's shorthand. It seems that more and more of those assembled had begun to join in with the recitation, though there's no record of the Doctor having rehearsed his group, so perhaps they'd all felt compelled to contribute in their own way. Lisa-Beth notes that Scarlette had been the first to find herself muttering, followed by Fitz, then Rebecca. Some of those on board had simply been describing things

they'd seen in the phantasmagoria around them, pinning themselves to the here and now by attaching words to the numerous futures and ideals they'd witnessed.

6. Then Who had stood upright, from his position crouched next to the Doctor, and spoken a single word. Even Lisa-Beth doesn't have the nerve to record it. She simply writes, '_____'. And this is followed by a single English word: *arrival*.

It's from this point on that the TARDIS becomes a physical entity in the accounts, not just some mythical 'White Hart'. It's a massive, haunting presence, which had come tumbling right out of the horizon towards Sabbath's vessel.

What's most notable about Lisa-Beth's notes, given the ongoing themes of blooding and sacrifice, is her description of the Doctor. The Doctor had fallen to his knees *as if in supplication*. And there's one telling phrase that Lisa-Beth uses. She says that when he looked up with his hand on his chest – the right side, so she assumes he hadn't been touching his heart – he 'looked ready *to give himself up to the v[astness, vagaries?] of time around him*'. It was as if the Doctor had been making some deal with the elemental forces, or at least offering himself up. After all, it wasn't simply for his own sake that he wanted his TARDIS back. He believed that the box's presence on the troubled planet would help stabilise the entire world. Often, when the Doctor would suffer attacks of his unknown and unexplained illness, he would be seen clutching his chest in exactly the same fashion.

What, though, was wrong with the Doctor? Even apart from the fact that the wrong side of his chest was affected, simple heart problems seem an unlikely explanation. They'd hardly account for the 'black bile' described by Scarlette. In the latter part of October, as many physicians would attend the Doctor as would later attend George III during his madness, and with similarly vague results. The Doctor, almost humouring the men, would allow himself to be bled, prodded, even half-poisoned in the name of medical science. Nobody would ever produce any answers. Those who liked to mock Scarlette's coven now wondered if the wedding would now go ahead with no bride and no groom either.

TALES FROM THE WHITE ROOM

The first of the wedding guests arrived six weeks early. Since the start of October they'd been circling St Belique, but perhaps not surprisingly it was the American who made the first move.

The man's name was Mr Van Burgh. He was a tall, pale gentleman of

Virginia, with a drawl that people often found hard to place (Van Burgh *wasn't* a typical Virginian name, some noted), who never spoke the name of Matthew Crane but whose connections were never questioned. As stately as they came, in the days that followed he'd often be seen skirting the forestlands of the island with his walking-cane in hand and his black jacket pulled tight around him, pushing aside the poisonous machineel-stalks as if this were no different from a stroll in the fields of home. It was October 20 when he first arrived at the Church and introduced himself to Who. Van Burgh spent a while inspecting the vault, his face not showing either approval or disapproval. Observers noted that he wore a cross around his neck, yet although he often mentioned God those who met him didn't feel he was talking about a truly Protestant deity. The bottom of the cross was sharpened to a wooden point, which later made some of the other guests think of the great spiked crosses that the Virginian cabal had hammered into the earth, designed to cut into the veins (so it was said) of the ancient sleeping things which had once been worshipped by the Indians.

Van Burgh never spoke of any of these matters. He declared himself to be a man of the enlightenment, a man of reason. He was civil in his dealings with Who, politely asking where he might find lodgings on the island before questioning the exact nature of the wedding. Who reassured him, in his best Anglo-Chinese, that everything was in order. Whether Van Burgh knew of the troubles at Henrietta Street is unclear, but, perhaps ominously, he did state that the men of Virginia expected great things of this ceremony. Who just folded his hands together and bowed. (Still, it's got to be said, the definition of 'enlightened' in this era was still a little loose. As has been recorded elsewhere, as late as 1804 Thomas Jefferson – the greatest mind of the age, according to some – genuinely believed that there were giant woolly mammoths living in the American midwest, on one occasion even sending a party to search for them.)

News spread fast. There was an American on the island. Some took this as their cue to be cautious, while others took it as their cue to act, and only days later the delegation from Hispaniola arrived in order to prove that no American presence would cow *them*. Very soon St Belique would be a hive of activity, as the wedding guests would 'accidentally' meet in the heat-sodden streets of the harbour-town. Mr Van Burgh was civil to all parties, although he did seem to have some contempt for the negro rebels.

If the lodges of the world weren't ready to unite, they were at least on speaking terms. With the apes unseen for a month, a few felt that the crisis was over, though most believed the creatures were simply regrouping. In this ominous shadow, alliances were certainly possible. But for the lodges to reach an agreement, for the ceremony to have a focus and a purpose, there would have to be a wedding. And on the very same day that the Hispaniolans arrived on St Belique, the Doctor was unconscious in a room of brilliant white, on a bed with red silken sheets.

The room wasn't in the House. Henrietta Street had been all but forgotten. Though every single record of the era mentions the white room, as all the Doctor's associates came to visit him during his great sickness, nobody explains where the room actually *was*. As even Who came to the Doctor's bedside on one occasion, it can't have been in England. It may have been somewhere on St Belique, kept apart from the wedding guests who still hadn't heard of the groom's decline, but it's more likely that the room was in the magical gardens of the TARDIS. All the descriptions of it are in that hazy, otherwordly style which Scarlette adopted when speaking of the Doctor's place of power.

The walls of the room were white and plain, almost sterile, and there's no mention of the area having any smell (unusual, in an era where medical health went hand in hand with all manner of stinking concoctions). In fact, the walls were so white that often visitors would forget they were there at all and momentarily believe they were in some secret, faraway place with no boundaries. The light – from what source isn't known – would be bright, enough to make objects within the room seem fuzzy at the edges. The bed was the only large piece of furniture, a huge wooden construction in the middle of the endless space. It's said that against the great oak headboard, the Doctor looked tiny and wasted, a pale figure propped up on red satin pillows. He lay there day after day, clammy and stripped to the waist, half his body lying under the red silk sheets and the other half lying without. Though his neck was propped up for most of the time, his eyes, when open, seemed permanently fixed on the ceiling.

It looked, for all the world, like a deathbed. But nobody seems to have spoken of such things. Indeed, the Doctor's associates attempted to act as though this were just a phase. Fitz would often visit the bedside, and give reports of the latest activity both in London and on the island, even though the Doctor was rarely conscious enough to respond. Anji would sometimes stand at the back of the room, looking itchy. The Doctor's malaise affected his companions badly, not just because they were concerned for him but because they evidently felt that this shouldn't be *happening*: that if the Doctor could fall so sick then something was deeply wrong with the world. The room embarrassed them, and for all their concern they tried to avoid being there whenever possible.

So it was Scarlette who took the best care of the Doctor. It was Scarlette who eventually dragged a red leather chair into the room, positioned it by the Doctor's pillow, and sat there with him hour after hour after hour. She would claim it was her duty to do such a thing for him, although it was often commented that the concern she showed went some way beyond duty. Sometimes she'd read to him, as if hoping the Doctor would find inspiration to regain his health and continue his fight. Sometimes she'd be found simply sitting and squeezing his hand, although she'd primly let go whenever anyone else entered. She'd wash the sweat from his torso, or try to wipe the bile from his mouth, or even feed him when it seemed necessary (though it hardly ever did).

Occasionally, he'd regain his senses and speak to her. The short conversations between the Doctor and Scarlette would tend to occur when they were alone together, although on the Doctor's request his painting of his 'grandfather' was hung on the wall, in the middle of a great white expanse, facing the bed. There are stories that he'd mutter to the painting when he thought nobody was around to hear him, but these may be apocryphal. Occasionally Lisa-Beth would visit, 'visit' being the operative word as by late October she was no longer to be found at the House and perhaps no longer considered herself part of Scarlette's coterie. Unusually for her, she didn't seem to blame anyone in the 'coven' for her financial problems. Normally she'd stand at the Doctor's side, alone or with Scarlette, and self-consciously tell him about goings-on at the Shakespeare's Head tavern or the increasingly odd rumours about the Prince of Wales.

But on the afternoon of the last day of October – All Hallow's Eve, though the date had very little significance in the witch-tradition of southern England – the Doctor suddenly awoke from his semiconscious state. He turned his head, and looked into Lisa-Beth's eyes, and Lisa-Beth records that she felt 'almost like leaping backwards'.

'I won't be here for long,' the Doctor told her. 'One way or another.'

Lisa-Beth hardly knew how to respond to this, but the Doctor continued. It was vital, he said, that their work should go on. He'd been aware of what the apes were planning, if indeed they could plan, ever since the recovery of the TARDIS. He was convinced that the House would be vital in the final battle, although he confessed that he had no idea whether he'd be there to witness it. Then he asked Lisa-Beth a question. Scarlette, he said, would be busy with other affairs from now on. Would Lisa-Beth like to take over the running of the House? Would she, with her flair for resource, like to become its guardian and mistress before the great struggle came?

Warily, Lisa-Beth told him that she'd have no objection to such a thing. In her journals she admits to herself that she didn't know whether the Doctor's query had been simple delusion, a belief that the House was still open and continuing its business as usual. Or perhaps it was something in the nature of the House itself that he saw as vital, something in the way the very structure of the building 'bled'. Later that day the Doctor was attended by both Scarlette and Fitz, but by then he'd slipped back into his daze. This is perhaps a shame, as it was on this very day that Fitz decided to finally share the conclusions he'd drawn.

The Countess of Jersey had refused to grant Fitz an audience, but while he'd been following up the lead he'd begun to notice something about the stories he'd heard, the rumours that the Countess had met a 'King of Beasts' in the broken city. Anji had also become lost in that city, of course. Though she rarely agreed to speak of it, Anji ostensibly recalled running through endless bleached, wasted streets, occasionally calling out to blank-faced passers-by who didn't seem able to perceive the danger around them. Time had no meaning in the ape city, and once she'd returned to the House from her 'adventure' she'd admitted that she'd had no idea how long she'd been away.

But, as she told Fitz, something she'd seen there had stuck in her mind. At one stage she'd run down a fractured street that had resembled a bleak parody of one of the roads of Charing Cross, and on turning her head she'd seen an opening that had led to a square of some kind. There in the square, she'd seen an entire *horde* of the apes, forming a grey-pelted mob which stamped and scratched at the pavement but which hadn't paid her any attention at all. At the centre of the crowd there'd been a mound of some kind, a platform raised above the animals' heads, stinking of dung. Though Anji had quickly moved on, she was sure that there'd been *something* mounting that pile as if taking up a position of honour. And now the Countess spoke of an audience with the King of Apes, if such a creature existed: almost a bestial, idiot counterpart to either the Doctor or Sabbath, an Emperor among beast-elementals.

For all his faults, Fitz's conclusion once again suggests a mind ahead of its time. That afternoon in the white room, he told the Doctor that he believed the apes now had a leader, whereas before they'd been creatures of sheer mindless malice. More importantly, he explained *why* he thought they now had a leader.

The apes had no existence without humanity. They were reflections of humankind's own animal limitations. Now there were hundreds, perhaps thousands, and the closer the horizon came the more they bred. Yet they were still mimicking, literally *aping*, the human race. In any large group of humans, the most primitive desire was to form hierarchical packs, with a single alpha-male leader – usually the strongest or most aggressive member of the pack – at the top of the hierarchy.

As the Doctor himself seems to imply in his *Ruminations*, this aggressive hierarchical model enforces conformity and ensures a violent reaction against any form of progress. And the apes were the very embodiment of reactionary values. They mimicked all the tools of human ignorance, and now they numbered in their hundreds they'd begun to mimic the most primitive form of human social structure. They had a leader, a King of Beasts, a vicious, screeching God-Emperor who ruled from his throne of filth and bones. For the last month the apes would have been busy worshipping and cherishing him, but the inevitable consequence of such a leader would be a new wave of attacks. *Directed* attacks this time, massed attacks, led by the lusts and impulses of the new King. It wasn't so much that they were developing... development was, after all, the antithesis of their purpose... but they were taking whatever measures were necessary in order to drag humankind back into the dirt.

Surely the Countess had reached the same conclusion? It would explain the sudden link she made between the King of Beasts and the King of England, because in the final analysis one was just a distorted image of the other. Scarlette offers the following observation:

> The Beast must worship its monarch as it might have worshipped that terrible black Eye which forms the sun of its realm. Should the Beast devise religion, it will no doubt hold that its King acts by the will of the Eye just as our sovereign acts in the name of an Anglican God.

There's one other thing to mention, about that afternoon. Because according to the folklore of Henrietta Street, while Fitz was trying to explain himself to a dazed Doctor there were events afoot back at the forgotten House.

Nobody lived at the House any more, though technically Scarlette was still responsible for it. So it was largely empty that day, the Doctor's equipment moved to the TARDIS, the last of the small furnishings gone.

The only person left to look after it was Rebecca. Why she'd become so distanced from the others is hard to say, but while her associates spent time in the TARDIS she'd spend it in the abandoned salon, still laying and re-laying her cards on the bare boards with no apparent end to the task.

That afternoon, goes the story, she looked up from the floor and caught sight of a figure in the street outside, standing across the cobbled street from the window of the salon. The figure was female, dressed all in black, and although the newcomer was wearing a veil Rebecca knew at a glance who she was.

Rebecca wasn't at all put out, says the tale. She simply stood and went to the door of the House. There on the step, she met the girl in black and greeted her. They talked for a few minutes, the girl seeming surprised at the state of the House, and concerned when Rebecca casually told her what had happened to the Doctor. The girl asked if there was anything she could do, within reason, but Rebecca said that it was unlikely considering the circumstances. At this the girl nodded, and made to move away, although before she left she pressed something into Rebecca's hand. Rebecca's last words to the girl in black were that she probably shouldn't show herself in public again: there were forces gathering, especially on St Belique, and should they discover the truth about her then she might find herself hunted to the end of the Earth. The girl acknowledged that this was the case.

The next day Rebecca met with Scarlette, and gave Scarlette her missing glass totem, the shard which had cut the throat of Mary Culver in 1762. Scarlette must have known there was no point asking where it had come from.

9
The Threshold

It was called 'the Bloody Code', so once again blood was an important symbol. It was a system of justice which, though not *quite* so ruthless as that practised in France, did everything it could to remind the convicted that the British were still under a King and that the King was a representative of total authority. In Britain, *all* crimes of property were still theoretically capital crimes. Prostitutes could find themselves on the end of a rope for pickpocketing their sleeping clients, servants could be executed for shortchanging their masters, and as for counterfeiters... counterfeiters were not only thieves but *making false images of the King himself*, and George III was quite convinced that there should be no mercy for such vermin. By the end of the 1780s the doomed were being shipped to the penal colonies as often as they were being executed, but everybody knew that Australia was just a rationalist version of hell.

On the first day of November – All Saints' Day – a girl was hanged until dead at Tyburn, the most fashionable place of execution in England. The exact charges against the girl on All Saints' Day were unspecified, but she was said to have been a prostitute and so pickpocketing and/or 'coin clipping' were generally thought to have been her crimes.

The hanging was unusual in many respects. First, it wasn't officially entered in the public criminal records. This wasn't unknown, however, and generally meant that there was something potentially embarrassing about the case and that monies had been spent to stop anybody paying attention. Secondly, the condemned was taken to the gallows in a hood, her face covered with a cowl of leather. She appeared quite calm as she was led to the noose, with her skinny wrists bound behind her back and her long red hair braided at her neck at the lip of the hood. A tiny white-armed figure under the gallows-tree, she looked little more than a child, but there was a quiet poise in her manner which must have struck the crowd as odd. When the floor was taken out from under her and the rope snapped her neck, she only jerked once, and her body barely struggled as she died. It was said that the corpse was to be given over for medical dissection, a relatively recent horror created by the Code. All but the hardest rationalists held the sneaking suspicion that if their bodies went under the knife then they'd arrive in Heaven in pieces.

By the day of the execution, Scarlette was on St Belique. With exactly thirty days to the wedding, and the wedding guests growing restless on the island, she felt the stress of things more than anyone. She'd lost her House, she'd lost her powerbase, and funds were running out fast. Everybody said that the Hellfire tradition was a worn-out memory, and it must have irked her to think that 'everybody' was being proved right. Lisa-Beth noted that when she wasn't at the Doctor's bedside, Scarlette would lock herself away in her private rooms (in the TARDIS, or on the island?) and perform angry, impotent rituals. She would 'smash glass, burn bitter roses, often bloodying her hands with shards and thorns'.

It was in the final hours of All Saints' evening when Scarlette realised she simply couldn't go on this way. Ever since the Doctor's collapse, the survivors of the House had just been hoping for the best, trying to convince the wedding guests to stay until December without any real plan. But that night, as she sat by the Doctor's side and listened to his breathing while he slept, Scarlette finally made her big decision.

Yet the other members of the clique were still under the impression that it was all over. On the next morning, the dying Doctor was attended by all his associates for the very last time. By eleven o'clock they were all gathered round his bed. Scarlette sat by his side, where she'd been throughout the night. Fitz and Anji hovered nearby. Arranged around the foot of the bed were the three women, Lisa-Beth, Rebecca (how did she come from the House so quickly?) and – visiting for the first time in weeks – Katya. Dr Nie Who was also present, lurking at the back of the room, head bowed and eyes hidden under his Mandarin-style hat. Somebody, probably Who, had hired a band of the island's local musicians to provide music for the occasion: the visitors were therefore treated to the unusual sight of six followers of *obeah*, assembled in the corner of the white room, instruments at the ready. The locals never seemed put out by anything the strange foreigners did, and they don't seem to have found the Doctor's rooms at all perturbing. The band played *The World Turned Upside Down* as the Doctor's friends entered, a wilfully ironic choice of tune.

It's doubtful the Doctor ever knew they were there. In a later moment of semi-lucidity, the Doctor would ask Scarlette about the 'seven surgeons' who had come to visit him that morning. He was under the impression, even after the event, that these surgeons had come to dissect him following his execution but had arrived early. He believed there was something inside his body they'd wanted for research purposes, and even went as far as saying that they'd started to cut him open. But at the time those present in the room only noticed that the Doctor's eyes were fixed on the painting at the end of the bed, even when the three red-and-black guardians of the House stepped forward, one after the other, to kiss him on the forehead. When the three women had finished, they stood back, at a respectful distance. All fell silent, with only the music softly playing in the background, waiting to see if the Doctor would manage to speak.

He didn't. The party left the room in silence, gazing at their shoes at they went, and as the last of them departed Who quietly informed the band that the performance was over. It was hardly the grand goodbye that some of them might have hoped for.

By now, the island was crawling with representatives of witch-lodges from around the globe. After the Americans and the Maroons had come the British factions, the Masons and the Servicemen. The island's natives reported seeing a 'man with a skirt of colours' around town, unquestionably a member of one of the Scottish Masonic lodges, who claimed descendancy from the Bruce and insisted on the traditional regalia even though it was deeply unfashionable. The Service officially denied sending anyone to the island, but it's known that a *rat-catcher* was present, posing as an innocent bystander safe in the knowledge that everyone would know damn well who he was. An individual with a French accent made a big impact on the locals by walking around the town, loudly proclaiming himself to be a servant of Cagliostro and therefore (logically) immortal. He'd then impress the natives with a wide variety of conjuring-tricks.

Though all the foreigners had lodgings around the harbour-town, the focus of their attention was the Church. The guests had arrived at a mutual agreement, perhaps an unspoken one, that nobody who represented one of the lodges would set foot inside the Church without a mask. As everybody knew who everybody else on the island was, this was a question of decorum rather than secrecy. The vault was closed to them now, but the main body of the Church (a seventeenth-century building, with stained glass windows depicting a local Christ-figure whose skin was *not quite* dark enough for him to be considered a Mulatto) was used as a meeting-point. Often, one of the hooded Masonic guests would be seen standing before the altar alongside a well-dressed man in a masquerade domino, wearing the face of a medieval Satan, discussing lodge politics. Guests tended to wear masks which befitted their own tradition, although it was another unspoken rule that anyone who dared to wear the face of one *particular* animal would be considered to be in bad taste and sent to Coventry.

A month before the mythical wedding day, at least eight of the thirteen factions invited by Scarlette had arrived on St Belique, and it was on November 3 that for the first time a large mass of the guests found themselves in the Church at once. It was hardly a party. Almost everyone present was wary, particularly as Mr Van Burgh of Virginia refused to wear a mask, in breach of all etiquette. The supposedly immortal Frenchman also came unmasked, though this was less surprising as everyone believed he was permanently in character. In the body of the Church, the guests ended up bunching together in small groups and throwing dark glances at those they felt were beneath them. There were grim rumours that the wedding was a sham, that at best this was a waste of time and at worst it was an elaborate trap. Hardly the union of spirits the Doctor had intended.

Yet it happened again the next day, and the next, when a total of *sixteen* masked and muttering individuals found themselves gathered together. Almost certainly, most had come just to get a look at the others, to find out who was talking to whom and what kind of alliances or conspiracies were being forged. But on that third day of the Accidental Conclave, the meeting wouldn't go quite as peacefully. This time, Scarlette was to get involved.

The guests were arranged in their usual groupings when Scarlette entered the Church. Mrs Gallacher, procuress of a London House of Flagellation who believed (like many medieval monks) that whipping could induce altered states of consciousness, had struck up a quiet friendship with the spider-faced man in the kilt: and the only individual who'd spoken to *all* the others was the Frenchman, who was generally considered harmless. Perhaps surprisingly, the only big argument was between the *rat-catcher* and one of the red-hooded European Masons. Having worked alongside each other for so long, tempers were fraying and the Mason's suggestion that Sabbath be offered an *amnesty* was the final straw.

The consequent shouting-match was interrupted when, without warning, the big oak double-doors of the Church were thrown open by the local priest (who had, it seems, been paid a healthy sum for the 'rental' of his House of God). When those assembled saw Scarlette stride into the building – the first time she'd ever set foot in the Church – even the arguing Europeans were cowed into silence. And even the Masonic archive admits that she looked spectacular that day. She strode into the Church 'like a colossus in red', it's said, with her boots hammering on the stone floor, her red tails sweeping all about her and her dark hair flowing from the braid of roses at her neck. She entered like the Queen of Time, and barely seemed to register those around her until she came to a halt before the altar.

So it was that Scarlette made her first address to the Accidental Conclave. Looking around the church, she must have seen all manner of beasts and monsters looking back at her, a masquerade of devils, angels, minotaurs, punchinellos, blank-faced things and even one American. She barely even blinked, though, as she announced to the lodges of the world that the wedding would proceed come hell or high water. Before any questions could be asked, she went on to say that the lodges had to stand firm *now*, as even as she spoke the King of Apes would be making his own plans.

Then came the masterstroke.

> She said that there would be revels, in celebration of the joining that was to come… much like the great games called by Emperors of old to mark any state occasion. Mistress S. left all assembled parties in no doubt that we were all to take part in this pursuit beginning the following week… her intention being that we should make sport with these apes just as they had made sport with ladies of her profession.

Suddenly, then, Scarlette was determined that somehow the marriage should succeed… in spite of the fact that she was still reluctant to even speak Juliette's name. And had the TARDIS brought her the stories from Tyburn, that a young, red-headed girl had been executed for petty crimes associated with prostitution? If so, then she probably wouldn't have believed that Juliette had died on the gallows. She would have interpreted it as a message, perhaps even a perverse warning. In France, for example, it wasn't unknown for a condemned man – if he had money and therefore influence – to be beheaded in effigy rather than in reality, the law's way of saying that the victim was *socially* dead even if he'd bought his way out of a true execution. Was the peculiar death at Tyburn, with its rumours that the body had never been displayed after the hanging, someone's way of letting Scarlette know that the old Juliette no longer existed? Or was there another explanation?

It's unclear whether the Doctor knew about Scarlette's address to the Conclave. The following day he was said to be more at peace than before. He no longer clutched at his chest, or woke himself with bilious coughing-fits. Scarlette says in her journals that he appeared almost serene, something she took as a sign that things would go well from now on. Even so, it's interesting to note that the language she uses to describe him makes him sound as if he were a corpse already. Perhaps this was the point when he knew he was going to die, and no longer cared. Perhaps he had found peace. And, as later events were to suggest, perhaps he felt that Juliette had found a kind of peace also.

No Peace

> To Juliette, my friend, I leave the screwdriver sonique. It doesn't work properly, and in her own time I doubt there's much she could use it for anyway… [but] she might like to think of it as a totem, like the glass of Scarlette's that she used so well. I have so much bric-a-brac to get rid of, but somehow there's so little I can give her.

The document arrived on board the *Jonah* on November 8. Information on the movements of Sabbath is difficult to come by, but there are enough fragments of correspondence from his agents and informers – Emily Hart chief among them – to build up a rough outline.

It was inevitable that the Doctor would make a will. His TARDIS was said to be overflowing with the things he'd collected on his travels, many of them valuable. The will document, which only survives in part, seems more concerned with dividing up those things that were of *symbolic* value as if they were parts of his own flesh. The document contained thirteen articles on thirteen separate pages, dividing the Doctor's estate into thirteen portions: some pages listed reams of items, others single gifts. Once he'd recovered his senses enough to complete the will, the Doctor instructed that his companions should lay out thirteen boxes on the floor around him (these boxes aren't accurately described, but they seem to have come from somewhere in the TARDIS). Then, with the last of his flagging strength, the Doctor ceremonially tore apart the will and asked that each page be put in a different box. The boxes were then to be stored in the catacombs of the TARDIS, never to be opened again.

'If we never open the boxes, we'll never know whether the pages are still there,' he allegedly explained. The same method, perhaps, that he used when he sent the 'family' envelope at Tyburn. Yet the next day, a message did arrive on board the *Jonah*, where it was read by Juliette. Shortly afterwards the Doctor's legacy arrived as well, somewhat prematurely as he was still alive. It's doubtful that Juliette found any use for it, though Sabbath may have found it interesting.

Juliette's circumstances at this point are unclear. She hadn't been executed, that much is clear. When she'd still kept a dream diary she'd often had visions of herself as a body in a grave, or as a specimen to be opened by the dissection-men, like one of the apes in the Doctor's basement laboratory. And all ritual initiation revolves around the symbolic death, or *sacrifice*, of the initiate. Sabbath himself had apparently learned his 'magic word' on the brink of death at the bottom of the Thames, but initiations were usually designed with the individual in mind, so possibly the hanging at Tyburn had been Juliette's own final test (though there's no record of the body vanishing from the end of the rope in front of the audience). If so, then it must almost have been a kind of grim counterpart to the Doctor's wedding ritual. It's not clear whether Sabbath actually seduced Juliette, whether he took her as his sacrificial 'bride' even for a short while. Perhaps for Sabbath, the public hanging was a much quicker way of getting the same result.

One thing is for certain. When she received the message, and understood what it meant, Juliette cried for the only time in recorded history.

(Incidentally, the Doctor's legacy to Juliette was a curious device which he'd created during his early days at Henrietta Street, before the arrival of the TARDIS. The 'screwdriver' was a narrow tube of glass, mounted on a steel handle and run through with a complicated arrangement of wire, which when activated lit up with what Scarlette called 'hoops of lightning' and produced an alarming warbling sound. The construction of the device had kept the Doctor happy for some weeks, although he'd frequently said that it was only a mock-up - metal would have been preferable to glass, he'd claimed, although the correct alloys weren't available even in London - and when it had been completed he'd found very little use for it anyway.)

Back on St Belique, the excitement was building. Though the guests still murmured to themselves that the wedding was doomed, all were curious about Scarlette's promise of revels. They were more curious still when, in the following days, she hired a number of local men to begin moving certain items around the island. Most remarkable was the blue wooden box, which Scarlette had transported to the thick forest not fifty yards from the harbour-town. The 'jungle' skirted the town in every inland direction, and the TARDIS was carefully placed at precisely the point where the settlement seemed to meet the wilderness. Furthermore, the natives were becoming less and less visible. Locals were beginning to steer clear of the foreigners, to shy away from the jungle's edge, to shut themselves securely indoors when it wasn't absolutely necessary for them to be outside. *Obeah*-Christian religious symbols began to appear, hanging from doors by the dozen.

Finally, on November 10, Scarlette called a meeting of the Accidental Conclave. It was the first time such a meeting had actually been *called*. She instructed the guests not to gather at the Church, but at the TARDIS on the edge of the forest, and gather they did. It was a hot day on the island – 'November' meant little there – so by the time the visitors came together they were sticky with sweat under their masks, grunting and complaining in such a way that the differences between the lodges were all but forgotten. Waiting for them at the TARDIS was Scarlette herself, as majestic (some would say 'superior') as ever, in the same red-and-black garb she always wore when addressing the Conclave.

Even by the Conclave's standards, the claims she made that day were thought to be extreme. She indicated the box behind her, and then…

> …she insisted that the box was a lodestone of the highest elemental power, and through it the elemental energies were to be bound to the Earth. Even now the Device's power was of an untold nature. For its weight was such that when activated by correct ritual it would bend and warp the world, in a manner familiar to the Sanskrit-speaking peoples, til every *babewyn* in its realm would scream in fury.

The reference unsettled her audience, but Scarlette was undeterred. Her assistants (the archive doesn't specify who) then moved amongst the guests. Each of the masked men and women was given a spear, a weapon of local manufacture but not used even in that region for some generations. Each spear was tied with a length of red ribbon, which many in the crowd felt had probably been blessed, and Scarlette kept one of the weapons aside for herself. The Virginian began to look distinctly unhappy at this point. As those assembled reluctantly accepted the spears as gifts, Scarlette brought events to a climax.

> She turned around from the Convocation [i.e. Conclave] so as to face the lodestone at her back… it was noticed then that many others of her coven were assembled all around us between the trees, so that we would have feared a trap had not we been armed by her. When she faced the lodestone she brought up her arms in [a grand] gesture, before she spoke the word. *The word was ____.*

A magic word, like Sabbath's? Or just a piece of showmanship? The Conclave was in no doubt that this was a powerful ritual indeed, as the lantern on top of the blue box began to flash and the forest was filled with 'a terrible wailing, like that of beasts'. As the guests exchanged glances and peered anxiously around the forest, they became aware that something was changing. The overall impression was that there was a sense of *movement*, even though neither the guests nor the TARDIS changed their position. There was the feeling of a summoning being performed, of time or space being reeled in. At this juncture Mr Van Burgh spoke out, complaining that this kind of 'trick' would only enrage the *babewyns*, should there be any observing from their own realm. But it soon became clear that this was the point.

The Scots Rite Mason was apparently the first to see it. He let out a great cry, and all assembled turned to see the shape emerging from between the trees. At first it must have seemed like a shadow, detaching itself from the darkness of the jungle's edge. It was plainly confused, turning in circles and hissing at anyone who stared at it. It didn't immediately attack, but when Scarlette took an unflappable step towards the creature it finally made its move out of the shade.

It must have been a slap in the face to most of those assembled, who'd decorously avoided even speaking of the animals openly. To call one wilfully, and in such company… to a ritualist it must have been like publicly discussing one's venereal diseases. Yet the record relates that Scarlette, without even breaking her stride, simply thrust out her arm and speared the animal through the heart.

It seems odd that it should have been so easy to kill one of the creatures, given the fear they generated amongst the ritualists. But then, the ape had been summoned without warning: it would have been bewildered and at a disadvantage. Whatever the truth, it made an impression. As the beast lay twitching in the mulch of the jungle, Scarlette calmly announced to the guests that for too long they'd neglected to seize the initiative. The apes could be summoned; slain; even controlled. As a way of celebrating the Doctor's marriage, she went on, this day would see the beginning of a great hunt – no doubt inspired by the small-scale hunts of London – in which every guest would have the opportunity to slay the beasts and 'blood' themselves in whatever manner they saw fit. Other weapons could be provided, if the spears weren't sufficient. For the next three weeks the forests would be stocked with the creatures, snatched from their world just as they snatched women and *black coffee* practitioners from this one.

It must have taken a while for that to sink in. The lantern of the TARDIS was flashing, and those assembled soon realised that the ape Scarlette had slain wasn't the only one to be called. The lodestone was still attracting the creatures. There was some unease then, as the assorted ritualists began to notice that there were other shapes moving in the deeper regions of the forest. But once again it was the spider-faced Scotsman, a Mason of the warrior tradition even though from his bulk it's unlikely he'd ever seen actual warfare, who took the initiative. With what the archive calls 'a grand cry of the Craft', he leapt forward into the trees and let fly his spear from his hand.

The story has it that the spear sailed through the branches of a nearby tree, then pierced the skull of another ape which had been waiting in ambush in the branches. As the author of the story was also a Mason, however, this is almost certainly just a way of boasting about the hunting prowess of his own tradition. The important thing was, Scarlette had made her point. The apes had suddenly become prey.

Scarlette's strength always lay in the power of ceremony, and there was no better example than the great November hunt. She'd devised this particular 'spell' quite carefully, and it didn't take the guests long to get into the spirit of the thing. Unsurprisingly, those who came from aristocratic traditions set about the hunt immediately. Within hours of the first kill they'd begun to devise rules of conduct for the sport, and within days they were telling their servants to have their hunting pinks brought over from Europe. Other lodges were more reluctant, and spent the first day or two debating the matter in the Church before realising that if the aristocrats were the only ones to slay the apes, then they might gain a kind of advantage. After all, if they bloodied themselves in the entrails of elemental monsters, who knew what strengths they could gain?

Every day, at noon, Scarlette would stand before the TARDIS and speak the same (sadly never-recorded) word. Every day, more apes would come to fill the forest. By November 12, every lodge represented on the island was taking part in the wedding-revels, either actively hunting the apes or simply observing events. In the first four days, there weren't even any casualties on the human side. The apes would generally be confused and off-balance on their arrival in the world, and faced with armed opposition – the first guns were introduced on November 13 – few managed to even get close to the hunters before being slaughtered. (As an incidental detail, it became an immediate custom of the hunt to tie a red ribbon around one's weapon, whether that weapon was a spear or a firearm.) While the hunt was in session the islanders would retreat inside their homes, although no ape was ever seen venturing into the town. By sunset the hunt would have mopped up every surviving animal, leaving the forest clear for the next day's 'celebrations'.

It was a brilliant piece of psychology, but then, Scarlette was an exceptional ritualist. She'd given the guests exactly what they wanted: not just a kind of sport, but a sport which every faction could turn to its own ends. The blood and spoor of the apes was religiously collected by the hunters, for use in their own ritualistic activities. Lodges competed to see who could capture the most grey-furred heads, thus satisfying their constant need to outdo each other. Even guests like Mrs Gallacher could become involved in the festival atmosphere which soon developed. The natives too found the hunt to be to their advantage, as a small but lucrative trade began in suitably exotic hunting apparel and livery. Even when there was finally a fatality – one of the Maroons, cornered by an ape before his associates could come to his aid – the survivors simply became hungry for revenge. In one move, Scarlette had found a common ground between lodges; demonstrated the will to fight back against the King of Apes; and, perhaps above all, distracted the guests from actually thinking about the wedding.

She was aware, however, that the hunt had to be watched closely. More than once, hunters came upon certain *constructions* in the jungle, piles of carefully-arranged rock and marble which didn't appear to have been created by the natives. The significance of these is obvious. Whenever it called more apes, the TARDIS stood at the threshold between the world and the realm of the monsters. Occasionally it would be as if the apes' world were trying to impinge on the island just as it had impinged on London, so that the hunters would glimpse the 'black eye' overhead or see ancient, half-ruined buildings covered by the undergrowth. The piles of rock they found were like those that had been described by Anji, after her experience in the beast-realm. They were monuments to the King of Apes, piles of rubble stuck together with dung in honour of the *babewyns'* new god-ruler. The evidence suggests that the hunters soon realised this, because whenever they encountered such a mound they would destroy it, and those lodges who felt themselves in competition with the others would claim bonus points.

They must have known, even then, that the King of Apes would not take kindly to this kind of sacrilege.

MIXED BLESSINGS
On November 16, just over two weeks before the alleged day of the

wedding ceremony, a new guest arrived in the harbour-town. She was a warrior of the *Mayakai*, the oldest known surviving member of the 'pureblood' *Mayakai* line, who'd been lodged in St James's since the fall of the rest of her kind. It's possible that Scarlette herself had a hand in transporting this elder she-warrior to the island.

In London, the old *Mayakai* was considered something of a curiosity. It was well known that the woman could barely move, her joints having succumbed to a kind of paralysis, her breathing stifled by a growth on her lungs. In London she spent her life laid out in a bed in a spartan room, staring up at the ceiling while her two servants, women who had once been prostitutes in the capital but who had now adopted a puritan lifestyle and wore plain black dresses to match, solemnly attended to her needs. Whenever a visitor would call they'd throw a veil over the *Mayakai*'s body, a silken sheet so fine that more than one visitor described it as 'a spider's web'. It would have been like visiting some kind of living, breathing marble oracle: certainly the visitors never came to watch her *do* anything, as the *Mayakai* rarely even spoke. And when she did, it would be in a croaking, snapping Polynesian language that barely anybody could decipher.

The *Mayakai* was carried into the harbour-town in a form of sedan chair, a framework of wood long enough to allow her to remain horizontal, surrounded by curtains of the same spider-web which covered her body. A cortege of four black-clad, blank-faced Englishmen carried the chair, and flanking them were the two female servants, who threw grey petals ahead of the procession in disturbing silence. The locals, watching from all sides, must have wondered whether it was a *funeral* being conducted on the island rather than a wedding.

Scarlette met the procession in the street that led to the Church of Saint Simone, and in the hush which followed she bowed down on one knee in front of the chair. The crowds could only wonder who this web-shrouded foreigner was, if she had the power even to make the English witch-queen bow. There was a long pause after Scarlette knelt, in which the only sound came from the old woman's sickly, rasping lungs. Everyone who witnessed it must have realised that Scarlette was waiting for something, a sign from the elder sorceress, although the old amazon hardly even seemed to notice Scarlette at all. It was some time before the woman finally managed to speak, a single phrase in her own obscure tongue.

Little is known of the dead language, but Scarlette records the meaning of the exchange. In that moment the *Mayakai*, the only individual on

Earth towards whom Scarlette felt she had any fealty whatsoever, was giving Scarlette her *blessing*. In return, the next day Scarlette arranged to have one of the apes from the forest captured alive and taken to the old woman's lodgings, surrounded by chains and gagged with a metal bit. The female servants pressed a knife into their charge's hand, and there on the island the elder warrior made her first kill (albeit with a great deal of help) in some years. No doubt she appreciated the opportunity.

The *Mayakai* wasn't the only new arrival to make her presence felt that week. For days the other wedding guests had told their spies to keep watch on the coast, making sure that none of their kind arrived unexpectedly. In theory the spies were watching *all* incoming boats, but amongst the British lodges it was silently acknowledged that there was one vessel in particular to look out for. They knew full well that Sabbath had already been invited to the wedding, and as it wasn't common knowledge that he'd stolen the bride there was still some debate about whether the Monster would show himself on December 1.

As it happened, Sabbath's ship was never sighted. But for certain people, the situation became clearer in the third week of November.

At this point, the women from the House were still on the island. Following the closure of the House, Rebecca, Lisa-Beth and Katya had all intended to return to Britain and go their separate ways. They'd been brought to the island to say their last goodbyes to the Doctor, and now they were having difficulty escaping. Not having the money for passage home, the only way they could return to England was via the TARDIS... and that meant asking Scarlette. But either Scarlette refused to send them or, more likely, they were reluctant to ask. There seems to have been an agreement between the women that they'd present Scarlette with an ultimatum on December 1, once the wedding had failed to occur. (Even so, there were efforts to leave before this date. Lisa-Beth records that two days after the *Mayakai*'s arrival, she and Katya attempted to seduce Fitz *simultaneously* in an attempt to get him to spirit them away. Sadly, Lisa-Beth doesn't record the outcome.)

It must have been particularly hard on Rebecca, who clearly felt guilty about abandoning Scarlette anyway. In the period between 13 and 19 November, she would often take walks in the forest, observing the Revels as the masked wedding guests – the British in their full livery, the Maroons in their coats of blood and feathers, the clownish French envoy of the Cardinal de Rohan on his fat grey stallion – slashed their way through the undergrowth in search of their prey. As Rebecca carried no weapons, this must have been a hazardous practice. Fortunately she never stumbled across any of the apes, although on November 18 she was very nearly cut down by one of the hunting-parties who mistook her for another kind of prey altogether.

As with any sport, the hunt had generated a culture of its own, and the culture had sprouted its own legends in mere weeks. One of the Masons had already claimed that he'd come face to face with the King of Beasts himself, sitting hunched and slavering on a throne of human skulls, though this was commonly held to be a 'fish story'. Another popular legend held that there was a far more dangerous animal on the loose. It was like one of the beasts, said the tales, but it could take on the form of a beautiful maiden and entice unwary huntsmen to drop their guard. The myth maintained that one hunting-party (whose, nobody was quite sure) had pursued this succubus into the dark heart of the island, until the creature had cast a spell and vanished into thin air.

It's a matter of debate whether any of this was based on real events. But on November 20, Rebecca was to meet a 'succubus' of her own.

As Rebecca later related the story, it happened near sunset on the eleventh day of the Revels. The hunt would have been winding down for the evening, and Rebecca noted that she could hear the cries of the huntsmen not far away, collecting the remains of the day's apes. Rebecca herself was some way into the forest, further than she usually travelled, at the point where the darkness of the canopy made it unwise to go on without lamplight. Besides, so many hunting-parties had been past that a series of well-defined pathways had been laid in the forest, and this was the place where the pathways ended.

She was just about to turn back when she noticed a single human figure, standing quite still at the end of one of the pathways, a black silhouette against the sunset. It was the same figure Rebecca had seen through the window of the House during her last afternoon at Henrietta Street, and true enough, the stories are remarkably similar.

Neither woman seems to have been surprised by the other. Rebecca asked the woman in black what she was doing there, and the woman replied that it seemed a good place to be, 'amongst the rest of the hunted things'. Then Rebecca asked whether she'd come to see the Doctor, or perhaps Scarlette. The woman hesitated, then said that there was most probably little she could say to Scarlette, although she asked after the health of the Doctor. When Rebecca informed her that he was dying, the woman hesitated again, before asking whether Rebecca thought it would be acceptable for her to see the Doctor once more.

This time, Rebecca said that it probably was. Things had changed since

October: now the Doctor was felt to be not merely *sick* but actually *doomed*. However, Rebecca made one stipulation. If you see the Doctor, she told the woman in black, then *you must make it perfectly clear to him that the connection between the two of you is severed, and that his heart no longer belongs to you*. At this the woman agreed, before turning her back and vanishing into the jungle.

Rebecca may have shared the story of the woman in black with someone that night, and it may have spread throughout the island, because when the Revels began the next morning there was a renewed determination to catch the 'succubus'. Those factions who kept a tally of kills even went as far as to put a bounty of a hundred points on the woman's head. As the idea of a succubus hunt spread, new stories emerged about the mysterious creature's powers. She'd once been human, said one story, but she'd made a pact with the Devil and now had the power to become pure vapour and vanish at will. She was rumoured to be the mate of the King of Beasts, a human consort and accomplished witch. The Maroons even held that she was an aspect of the Black Virgin herself, their answer to the Holy Mother of the Catholic slavemasters. It's doubtful whether many of the guests took these stories seriously, but a bounty of a hundred points was nothing to be sniffed at.

And yes, the hunters were becoming increasingly aggressive. Scarlette had been expecting this. As the wedding day approached and there was *still* no sign that an actual ceremony would be held, the guests took out their frustration on the apes, or indeed on any other animals of the forest which got in their way. It didn't help that the prey was getting thin on the ground. At the beginning of the Revels each use of the TARDIS had called forth a whole host of animals, but now the apes were becoming scarce. The Hispaniolans proudly declared that they'd very nearly wiped the beasts out, although nobody else believed this. It was as though the animals were no longer blindly following the summons. Once or twice those creatures which *did* come failed to attack as usual: they were sighted hiding in the trees, hissing and licking their claws, as if biding their time.

Then, on November 22, the Frenchman – the guest with the closest links to the Catholic Church – received news from the Vatican. There was a certain Cardinal there at the heart of the Holy Roman Empire who, according to the Pope's informers, had interests in Satanism. (This may sound shocking, but at the time occultism was often practised by the high-ranking members of the established Church. Cardinals viewed themselves as arbiters of religious morality, and many felt that to *truly* understand the Devil it was necessary to dabble in the Devil's arts. This doesn't mean the Vatican was literally full of Satanists.) The errant Cardinal had somewhat overstepped the line, said the reports, by attempting to call up Mephistopheles and draw up a pact in the style of *Dr Faustus*. The Cardinal had evidently believed he was so pure that God would forgive him even this.

But one night the Cardinal had turned himself in to the authorities, pale and shaken, pleading for the protection of the Pope himself. The priest had claimed that his summoning of the Devil had been a success... but the Devil hadn't been the suave, intelligent agent of darkness the Church had led him to believe. The Devil had been an idiotic, drooling animal, who sat in court at the centre of a grey, ruinous Hell. The Cardinal had been dragged through the streets of purgatory by Satan's grey-furred minions, and brought before His Majesty's throne. The Devil had been an ape, muscular and matted with blood, reclining on the throne as if he were one of the crown princes of Europe. He'd worn a crown of bloody thorns and human teeth, and held a sharpened femur as his sceptre. As the Cardinal had cowered in fear, Satan had screeched wildly at his demonic minions, which had scraped and bowed in their hundreds around him. Then Satan had pointed at the sky with the bone-wand. When the Cardinal had looked up, he'd seen that instead of a sun the scene was lit by something so horrible he hadn't been able to describe it.

All the images here are familiar. Yet, bizarrely, the Cardinal had *survived* and been returned to his rooms in the Vatican. Though he had no idea what it was, the Cardinal now felt sure that some form of bargain had indeed been made. And this must have come as a shock to the huntsmen. Previously the apes had simply been animals, but now... now it was almost as if they were capable of making plans.

Over the next few days, more of the apes' ceremonial rock-piles would appear in the forest. Worse, there'd be two more fatalities, huntsmen who'd go missing in the jungle and be found, eviscerated, shortly before sunset. On both occasions the bodies would be found pinned to the rock-piles, guts exposed to the sun, like offerings to the great black thing in the sky that the Cardinal hadn't been able to describe.

RE-ENGAGEMENT

In London, there was a curious hush. The House on Henrietta Street was deserted, and nobody in the neighbourhood seemed to know who owned it or what was to be done with it. Somebody broke the windows in mid-November. The prostitutes of London, who'd spat at the backs of Scarlette's women and started rumours that the House had spread the pox of the King himself, found themselves suddenly uneasy now that Scarlette had vanished from the country. There were no apes or nightmares, but it was as if they were holding their breath, scared that one bad wind would reduce London to bleached grey rubble. These were tough times for everyone. Career politicians like Charles Greville still failed to ally themselves with the new government, and as a result Emily Hart found herself reduced to a state of near-poverty. Twice she wrote to her 'good friend' Sabbath for help, but Sabbath was too concerned with other matters to reply.

Yet in his conscious moments, the Doctor didn't seem to understand any of this. He spoke as if the House were still open, as if he had great plans for it. (Sabbath himself once noted that being a creature who depended only on his 'place of power' for food and shelter, the Doctor had no understanding of money even as a concept.) But one morning, the day after the ominous news had arrived from the Vatican, a change seemed to come over the Doctor. He sat bolt upright in bed, apparently understanding where he was and what was going on. Scarlette tried to quieten him, although the Doctor informed her that 'they're all here' and insisted that Scarlette should immediately report to the Church. When she asked why, the Doctor only pointed to the painting of his non-existent 'grandfather' at the end of the bed.

Thirteen envelopes had been sent out, and most of the groups invited had already arrived on St Belique. The one invitation to which there'd been no response was the one marked 'Family'. The painting had been a poor proxy, but now the Doctor was apparently sure that the genuine article had materialised.

Was there indeed another elemental on the island? Scarlette's journal is typically vague on the matter, and although she went straight to the Church it's not clear who she met there. However, a new guest did indeed arrive that day. *Every single account* of the November Revels mentions him, and yet all of them fail to give him a name.

Assembling a picture out of all the accounts, he's described as a clean-shaved, dark-haired man in distinguished middle age, handsome in some respects even though to some of the British witnesses he came across as 'swarthy and difficult to place'. He was slim and well turned out, and he made an impression on the island by always dressing in tight, straightforward clothing of prim black... apart from the rosette of blue and white which he wore on his lapel. He would often be seen simply standing in the vicinity of the other guests, hands folded behind his back, observing intently without becoming involved in any of the visitors' many disputes. Whenever people would ask each other about him, in muted whispers, the dark-haired gentleman would simply bow his head to them. His accent was English, although some said they detected a little Latin in his features.

In the wedding invitations Scarlette had insisted that House colours were to be observed wherever possible, but this newcomer deliberately flew in the face of this tradition by wearing his rosette at every opportunity. Strangely, Scarlette doesn't seem to have cared, and in the first two or three days they were often seem walking together in the town as if they were 'of one lodge'. A remarkable sight indeed.

The wedding guests were allowed into the vault of the Church *en masse* on November 27, the first time there'd been a large assembly there. The atmosphere was excited, even aggressive. There'd been almost no apes to kill over the previous days. As a result, the bored guests had begun speaking of the wedding again, now only four days away. As they arrived in the red-decked vault, Nie Who showed them to their allocated seats around the great thirteen-sided table, one guest from each delegation. They sat there in their masks, giving away as little as possible while hoping that the others would give away everything, from the skull-headed priest of Hispaniola to the Russian visitor who'd chosen a rather rude Venetian-style carnival mask with a suggestively long and erect nose.

Just after eleven o'clock the man with the blue-and-white rosette entered, unmasked, and was watched by all as he slid into his own seat (the one reserved for 'family'?). But there was no introduction. He was closely followed by Scarlette, who immediately moved to the chair allocated to the Hellfire Set. It was clear, even before she spoke, that a great announcement was going to be made. The *rat-catcher* had wagered the Frenchman twenty points from his killing-tally that the wedding would be called off, so Scarlette's announcement must have come as something of a surprise.

Scarlette's speech survives in full, and it's worth repeating.

Gentleman. Ladies. I hope that you have all been entertained for this last fortnight, and I trust that although a few of you have lost colleagues in this sport you will have considered the experience a worthwhile one. I have showed you, I hope, that we have nothing to fear from the *babewyns* except the consequences of our own vision. I have also showed you that no enemy is beyond defeat, not even if that enemy has a King next to which, I fear, even the monarch of all England appears of good temper.

Most of you will have heard of my friend, whom we call Doctor. You will have heard of the miracles he has been known to work, the great feats of alchemy and of learning that he is said to perform; and these stories are not untrue. He is an elemental, as are those he has brought with him. I can tell that none of you are surprised by this. Some of you have even met him, I am aware of that. Then you must have realised that the purpose of these celebrations, of this wedding, is a symbolic one. He has great strength, such that I shall not even attempt to convince you of it. Yet he no longer has the authority to involve himself in the affairs of this world. Not being rooted in this Earth, he does not have the power, either in his body or in his intentions, to stand alone against the Beast.

It was the intention of this ceremony that the Doctor and the Earth be joined. But I refuse to lie to any of you. Things have gone amiss. Please: hear me out. The intended, whose name I shall not even speak, is not here. She may well be dead. If she is not, then she has at least experienced that *little death* with which every one of us here must be familiar. It was her place to *be* the Earth, to which the Doctor would be married, and to this end she was prepared. I can only blame myself for the failure of that preparation.

Gentlemen. Ladies. We have lost nothing. Though there is nobody else who has been prepared in the manner of the intended, this ceremony requires only the consent of one who is a part of this Earth and who has an understanding of what is required. Perhaps the Doctor cannot draw as much strength from such a woman as he might like, but nonetheless he will become once again a protector of this Earth. For without him, I assure you, we can only place our fate in the hands of men you would not wish to trust. [Meaning Sabbath?]

There *will* be a wedding, no matter what. I have already spoken with your mistress [indicating the servant of the *Mayakai*], and received her blessing. It was perhaps my folly that led to the loss of the Doctor's intended, and so it is my responsibility to ensure that not everything is lost along with her. You will notice this ring [indicating her finger]. You will, I am certain, have guessed its significance by now.

Four days from now, on the first day of December, the Doctor and I shall be married in this Church. This was not what was intended, but nor is it a matter of concern. I shall not pretend that I have anything but affection for the Doctor. I shall do my duty to the world: and I expect that the Doctor shall do his duty in turn.

The reaction?

The reaction was mixed. Some were concerned, at the thought of a dangerous, unpredictable (i.e. 'menstrual') sorceress like Scarlette bonding with an elemental; some, such as Mrs Gallacher, were congratulatory but pointed out that it would hardly be a *white* wedding; and some, like Mr Van Burgh, simply observed. The stranger with the blue-and-white rosette didn't appear at all surprised, and calmly helped himself to some of the wine (red, naturally) that had been provided by the hostess.

This, then, was Scarlette's decision. It was a matter of duty, and perhaps a case of desperation. But one question remains unanswered, and the journals are vague about it. The question is: *had Scarlette even bothered to tell the Doctor?* The Doctor, who in his semi-delirious state often didn't even seem to know that Juliette had left him?

Ever since 'family' had arrived on the island, the Doctor had seemed more alert, though less than well. Nonetheless, as if encouraged by the thought of the wedding ceremony, for a while he was at least capable of sitting up in bed and talking for short periods. It was probably because of this that over the following days, Scarlette allowed representatives from each of the lodges to visit the Doctor's bedside, one at a time.

These audiences were all much alike. The guest would be invited into the room, where they would be slightly perturbed by their surroundings, not to mention the cold stares of the Doctor's assistants. The guest would find the Doctor sitting up in the bed, propped up by soft pillows, always wearing a red-and-black nightgown. Though the Doctor would be awake, he'd seem distracted, and often crumbs of buttered toast could be seen clinging to his well-trimmed beard. The guest would formally introduce himself, and the Doctor would brightly apologise for his garb, but explain that he was a bit under the weather at the moment. Small talk would often be exchanged, though whenever the subject of the wedding would be raised Scarlette would step in and hurriedly change the subject. Some would notice that at times like these, Mr Kreiner and Miss Kapoor would exchange worried glances. The Doctor, however, would appear quite unaware of anything strange going on. A few noted that there were four empty chairs arranged by the bedside, and on each one a set of clothes had been folded. Four dresses, almost like uniforms for women, in red and black. There was a certain air of finality in the way they'd been left there.

By the evening of November 29, each of the wedding guests had visited the white room for a formal introduction. That night, once the last of the visitors had left and the Doctor's elemental assistants had retired to their own lodgings, Scarlette found herself alone with the Doctor for the first time in some days. She records that he was sleepy, unable to keep up the pretence of good health any longer, and when she asked him how he was he closed his eyes and mumbled that he needed rest before the ceremony to come. Scarlette agreed with him, kissed him once, and left him in peace.

At least, this is the way she'd have the evening remembered. It's quite possible that it was then, as she lowered the lights in the white room, that she finally told him her plans for the wedding. If so, then it's impossible to say whether he argued with her, or even whether he would have been able to.

The next morning, the last of November, the hunters gathered at the edge of the forest for the final day of the Revels. At noon Scarlette herself addressed the crowd, as they waited impatiently by the TARDIS for the day's apes to be called. She made another of her speeches, with all those present noticing a certain nervousness in her: some later joked that this 'maiden' was beginning to get scared that her consort might make an honest woman of her. Scarlette thanked all those assembled for the 'great works' they'd accomplished during the Revels, before turning to face the TARDIS – somewhat wearily, a few said – and speaking the word that would set its lantern flashing.

It's worth recording that on the final day, no apes at all were caught or even seen in the forest. The hunters were obviously disgruntled, and Scarlette, too, was disturbed that day. It was the day before the planned ceremony, the same day, ominously enough, that the British government finally acknowledged the independence of America. When she attended the white room in the evening, the Doctor was asleep, but she noticed something amiss about the chamber and it took her a while to realise what it was. One of the four empty chairs had been disturbed. The red-and-black uniforms of the House had been left there, neatly folded, perhaps in the hope that the Doctor might see them and realise the truth of what was happening around him. But as her journal records, Scarlette found that one of the four dresses was no longer arranged quite as neatly as it should have been. It was as if somebody had crept into the room during the previous night, worn the clothes for a while, then removed them again. Almost, as Scarlette concluded, as if the intruder had wanted to give the Doctor a chance to see her in the colours of the House one final time before he died.

Scarlette, of course, didn't record *whose* dress had been moved. No doubt she would have claimed that she had more important things to record in her journal. After all, less than twenty-four hours later she'd be standing before the altar.

10
The Kingdom of Beasts

LAST RITES

In the early hours of the morning, on December 1, 1782, Scarlette was to be found perilously close to the edge of the forest where the apes had been set free during the Revels. Witnesses describe her actions as 'erratic', by which they actually mean that she was drunk.

For some time she'd been pacing the forest, with her red uniform-dress stained by the dirt of the wilderness, and those who saw her admitted that they had no idea how she'd managed to navigate the tangled undergrowth without falling flat on her face. By two o'clock she'd made her way back to the TARDIS, on the cusp of the forest and the town. The last guest to pass her by saw her leaning against the faded blue paintwork of the box, caressing it in a way that 'displayed a form of affection'. Scarlette saluted to the onlooker as he walked past, and the guest swore that although he at first assumed that Scarlette was greeting him, she was in fact talking to the Device.

'You'll understand, of course,' she's said to have told the TARDIS. 'You've been through all this with him before.' (The TARDIS, incidentally, had by this point acquired a special significance for just about everybody on the island. Fitz had said that it was a pity there wouldn't be room for it in the vault during the wedding, as it would have qualified as old, new, borrowed *and* blue.)

The accounts make it sound as if Scarlette were losing her mind. But of course, the accounts are biased: most of the lodges still wanted to believe that this entire affair was a colossal joke. Still, it's clear that she was under a great deal of stress. Though Scarlette was no artist, she often liked to 'doodle' in the endpages of her diaries – mostly grotesque, badly-scrawled caricatures of public figures like the King, or Charles Fox, or the multi-headed dragon that was Washington-Crane-Jefferson – and in the back of her journal for this period is a picture that's hard to ignore. Sketched in pencil, it's a scene depicting a decadent, lascivious jungle-scene which wouldn't have been out-of-place in a Victorian penny-dreadful. We see a throne, surrounded by thick foliage, as though we're looking at the Empire of some great African chieftain. We see hastily-drawn stone idols all around, like baboon-faced totem poles. Yet on the throne sits a huge, fat, bloated human figure, pale and with massive jowls, so corpulent that he almost seems to sink into the chair. His eyes are black blotches, making him look drunken and idiotic, and his sweaty bulk is squeezed into the clothes of an English gentleman.

It's clearly supposed to be Sabbath. The size of the figure is massively exaggerated, certainly, and the other features of the drawing tell the viewer exactly what was on Scarlette's mind. Because sitting at the foot of the throne, naked and chained around the throat like a slave-girl, is a slight female figure who must surely be Juliette. She looks up adoringly at her master, while on either side drooling apes hold up enormous fern-leaves, fanning their Emperor and his concubine.

It's notable that Sabbath is shown in exactly the same surroundings that were associated with the King of Beasts, even if Sabbath was quite plainly as keen on destroying the ape empire as the Doctor himself. It's also very tough on Juliette, which wasn't untypical.

On the evening of November 30, Scarlette held what in modern terms might be called her 'hen night', although the celebration was open to men *and* women, with both sexes believing it was largely staged for their benefit. The event was held in a tavern in the harbour-town, where, beginning at eleven o'clock, a Cyprian Auction was held.

'Cyprian' was yet another eighteenth-century word for 'prostitute', one that Scarlette particularly liked as it suggested an ancient tradition, a kind of sisterhood-cum-guild. In London, Auctions were often held in the more notorious taverns, where the greatest of the city's courtesans would parade themselves before the clientele – the *rich* clientele – and the men would engage in a kind of primal contest by bidding against each other for the affections of society's most sought-after celebrity coquettes. Now Scarlette brought the practice to St Belique, for one night only. Tables were set up at the back of the tavern, and along this stage (the modern expression would probably be 'catwalk') would promenade all the working-women who happened to be available.

Mrs Gallacher was one of the first to take the stage, wielding the cat-o'-nine-tails which had made her so popular in England. There were several Caribbean women from the island itself, as the audience consisted of cheering local men as well as the more bawdy wedding guests, who wasted no time in adapting to this curious foreign custom. About halfway through proceedings, Lisa-Beth put herself up for auction. She had a reputation on the island as a 'White Tigress', and she may have been deliberately playing on this image when she took to the stage with a

212

sneer on her face and a complete disdain for the audience. Needless to say, she attracted high bids indeed.

The Cyprian Auction is worth mentioning for two reasons. First, because Juliette was one of those up for grabs. Not that she was in personal attendance, of course: this was another example of Scarlette's bitterness. Towards the end of proceedings, the head of a mannequin was brought before the crowd. The head was dressed in a bright red wig, its face smeared with make-up probably intended to make it resemble a child prostitute. Though no body was attached, it sat on the shredded remains of a red dress (Juliette's old wedding dress?) with its face shrouded by a thin veil of dyed-red muslin. Scarlette, who for the most part acted as Mistress of Ceremonies, announced that this particular Cyprian was 'Mistress Rouge-Vierge, Purest Woman in London, whose integrity will be guaranteed to you for the price of a smoking-pipe'.

Needless to say, there were no takers. Indeed, as soon as Scarlette made her announcement the crowd began to boo and jeer, some even throwing their empty glasses at the stage. As Juliette's 'defection' to Sabbath wasn't public knowledge, one can only assume that Scarlette had primed the audience. It was, in a sense, another ritual. The ritual humiliation of Juliette, Juliette the traitor, even though the girl herself couldn't have been there to see it.

This makes Scarlette sound harsh, perhaps, but Scarlette saw the 'failure' of Juliette as a very personal failure. She'd adopted the girl, as part of her own kin: when she ridiculed Juliette, she must have known that she was ridiculing herself. It's not at all surprising that with Juliette gone, Scarlette might offer herself up as a proxy in the wedding ceremony (although, to be frank, she was closer to the Doctor than Juliette had been). Perhaps there was even a hint of jealousy in Scarlette's vicious parody, Scarlette acknowledging that her wedding was only the result of someone else's absence. There was a distinct air of self-hatred in the events of that night. Whenever a woman would be auctioned above 'a respectable value', Scarlette would down a glass of the local ale, much to the delight of the crowd who were cheering her on as much as they were cheering for the women on stage.

Is it really hard to believe that Scarlette should have had this self-destructive streak? As more than one commentator has pointed out, eighteenth-century courtesans were nothing like twentieth-century prostitutes. If anything, they were more like twentieth-century rock stars and actresses. The 'pimp age' would change all that.

But the second thing that has to be noted about the Auction is that

Scarlette was by no means *completely* dispirited. The last individual up for offer was Scarlette herself, by this time so drunk that even the toughest men in the crowd were astonished she could stand. Bids began high, and rapidly got higher. Scarlette egged the audience on by pointing out that this was her last evening of 'maidenhood' before her wedding, and if anyone wanted a born-again virgin then this was their last chance. When the bidding reached the stage where men were offering *bags of gold doubloons*, it became clear that this was all a game: as she herself announced, 'none of you can afford me and none of you are worthy of me'. The bidders then began making clearly ludicrous bids, including 'the philosopher's stone, given that one day I discover it' and 'all the sunken treasure of Port Royal', until Scarlette announced that anyone wanting to bed her would have to pay at least *two* philosopher's stones and staggered off the stage, to much applause.

Scarlette's auction wasn't the only celebration held that night. Other 'parties' were more low-key, however. Just after midnight, as the day of the wedding officially began, the Doctor left the mysterious 'white room' for the first time in over a month.

Naturally, he still couldn't walk. It was Fitz who helped him out of his sick-bed. From somewhere in the pleasure-gardens of the TARDIS, Fitz recovered a 'contraption' (as Scarlette's journal later calls it), very much suggesting a modern wheelchair. Fitz pushed the Doctor all the way into the town, through the deserted streets and towards the harbour. There, he parked the Doctor on one of the stone fortifications which had originally been built to defend against privateer attacks from the sea. He then found a chair for himself, so that he and the Doctor could face each other while still being able to glance at the ocean below.

They drank together, there in the early hours of the morning. It was a quiet sort of bachelor party, but perhaps one that befitted the Doctor. Fitz produced a bottle of champagne, probably supplied by either Who or Scarlette, and the Doctor at least had the strength to lift the glass to his lips himself. Fitz later told Scarlette that although the Doctor's speech was slurred and (at times) confused, he was nonetheless able to continue a conversation.

'He understands, you know,' the Doctor allegedly said at some point. Fitz asked exactly what he meant by that.

'Oh, the nature of things,' the Doctor went on. 'A universe without elementals. I know more than he does, but he belongs here far more than I do. No wonder she left.' (Note that 'elementals' is the word Scarlette records, and it may not be the term the Doctor actually used.)

214

Was this all senseless, delirium-inspired babble? Or was the Doctor talking about Sabbath? Fitz obviously didn't want to discuss the matter further. Between them they finished the bottle of champagne, and spent some time looking out across the darkened harbour below. There was a strong wind blowing that night, so it must have brought the smell of salt and timber up to the stone wall. It's easy to imagine the Doctor staring out to sea, just as Scarlette had done at Brighton, searching for any sign of a metal ship somewhere off the shore.

It would have been at around this time that Scarlette was seen on the edge of the forest, worse for wear after her experiences with the local ale. She and Lisa-Beth certainly left the tavern together. Scarlette was talking loudly, insisting that *he* wouldn't allow the wedding to take place, that thanks to *him* the jungle was closing in around them and the enemy was drawing closer... though Lisa-Beth admits that she didn't know whether Scarlette meant Sabbath, or the King of Beasts. However, she knew an opportunity when she saw one. It was now, while Scarlette was inebriated, that she finally said something she'd been meaning to say for some time. She told Scarlette, in no uncertain terms, that it was *definitely* over. The House was gone, and Lisa-Beth's job description didn't generally involve the destruction of monsters. She announced that although she intended to stay for the wedding, neither she nor 'either of the other women' could be expected to carry on in this fashion. Indeed, Lisa-Beth went even further than that. She implied she was sick of the *tantra* altogether, sick of the responsibilities it had brought her. She had, after all, only started out in this profession for the money. Significantly, it had been some months since she'd last painted her trademark red diamond on her forehead.

Scarlette didn't even stop walking as Lisa-Beth said her piece. She kept on towards the edge of the forest, taking staggering but nonetheless majestic steps, not even looking back at her companion. And all she said was: 'Well, I know *that*.'

Shortly thereafter, Lisa-Beth left Scarlette to head back to the TARDIS alone. She had business to attend to at the tavern.

Much later that morning, Lisa-Beth was awoken from her sleep at the stroke of eleven. She'd imbibed some quantity of alcohol herself, so in the end it was only the throbbing of the Church's bells that roused her. She woke to find that 'I had been reimbursed for my night's labours', but for once the money wasn't the first thing on her mind.

Outside the boarding-house, in the rapidly-emptying streets of the harbour-town, the bell was still chiming. It was the day of the wedding, and the guests were being called to the ceremony.

* * *

215

If the meetings in the Church had been masquerades, then this was the carnival.

There were ten horses, all of which had presumably been acquired from the islanders, and all of which made their way through the town's streets towards the Church as the bell tolled. If the onlookers hadn't been scurrying for cover, they might have once again wondered how this could possibly have been a *celebration*. It looked more like a scene from the Revelation, ten monstrous horsemen and horsewomen making their way to the place of final judgement. The horses were big, muscular, powerful: most of the guests had tried to make sure that their own mounts were more impressive than the others. Each one was ridden by a single figure, the majority of the attendees hidden by their chosen masks, although on this day they'd gone out of their way to make an impression. They came in robes of a hundred different colours, they came in clothes embroidered with silver and gold, they came as if they were the three magi following the star. Their faces were the faces of animals, of characters from the Commedia del Arte, or in some cases of creatures which didn't have faces at all. A skeleton; a medieval Devil; a white-faced harlot with red-painted cheeks; a snouted beast with the tusks of a boar and the red eyes of a Russian bear. Even Mr Van Burgh came masked this time, although nobody could quite understand what his mask was supposed to *be*, and the only one present who ignored the masquerade was the elder *Mayakai*. Unable to ride unaided, her servants had provided for her something akin to a small version of an Indian pagoda, which had been mounted on the back of an enormous workhorse. The servants walked at her side, as most servants did.

One way or another, all thirteen of the parties who'd been invited had come, although for one reason or another three of them didn't arrive on horseback. In the procession through the town, a hurriedly-dressed Lisa-Beth stood in (ironically) as representative of the Hellfire Set on Scarlette's behalf, while Katya walked by the side of the Russian delegate, on the orders of the Empress herself. As the horses headed up the slope of the hill towards the Church, only one guest was truly absent. There was no sign of the show-offish Frenchman, who'd claimed to be a representative of Cardinal de Rohan and friend of Cagliostro. He'd sent an apology ahead of him, saying that he was having some troubles with his costume but that he'd be at the Church in time for the ceremony. Many of the other guests had been quietly glad of his absence.

Those assembled represented every great lodge on Earth, including those which rejected the very ideas of witchcraft or masonry. The guests included Catholics and Protestants, rationalists and freethinkers. It went beyond mere politics or methodology. The *babewyns* threatened all of them, and this was what had ultimately brought them together: the Beast which seemed to be the very embodiment of human ignorance.

(To the modern mind this may seem odd, as in later years the kind of 'witchcraft' practised by Scarlette would be viewed as 'superstition' and therefore as a form of ignorance. In fact, the magical thinking employed by the eighteenth-century lodges was a *cultural* process rather than a literal attempt to explain the world. As with Wessel's *Anno 7603*, the skills of the *tantra* were a method of understanding the human psyche's relationship to time, space, and the environment of mankind. Throughout his *Ruminations*, the Doctor seems to imply that there's no difference between 'magic' and 'fiction': both are collections of words designed to alter the state of the human mind. Anyone who believes there was really a conflict between 'science' and 'superstition' during the Age of Reason may be missing the point. 1782 was the year in which Watt invented his new rotary steam engine, and really it's surprising that there's no record of the apes attacking *him*.)

The preparations for the wedding ceremony had begun early that morning. At around nine o'clock, Scarlette had been found asleep on the edge of the forest, curled up next to the reassuring mass of the TARDIS. From dawn onwards, witnesses had seen her lying slumped against the device, according to one source 'with her hands spread across its surface as she slept... as if drawing power from its presence'. But at nine she'd awoken, to find the man with the blue-and-white rosette standing over her. The man had helped her to her feet, so the journal says, and had led her off to one of the boarding-houses in the town.

At around eleven the bells had started to chime, and that was when the people of St Belique had begun to withdraw into their own homes. Something of importance was about to happen here, and nobody within a hundred miles could have failed to notice it. The two main participants in the wedding must have felt as if the world were ending. Scarlette was still in an upstairs room at the boarding house as the procession headed for the Church, watching from the window, by this point fully dressed. It was Anji who'd helped Scarlette with her gown, insisting that in her condition Scarlette *needed* help... although Scarlette grumpily insisted that she was quite capable of fixing a corset, whatever the hangover. Anji's role, as the closest thing Scarlette had to a bridesmaid, is ironic given that she still didn't trust Scarlette and thought this whole wedding was a bad idea ('the Doctor doesn't even know where he is, let alone what he's doing,' she reportedly said at one point).

But it was Anji who helped Scarlette with her final preparations, in that old, damp room of rotting timber. It was Anji who reassured Scarlette that she looked fine, and Anji who ran through the checklist of ritual items which Scarlette had to take to the altar. Something old: Scarlette's glass totem, the one link to the glory days of 1762. Something new: the dress, by definition. Scarlette had already ordered the servants at the boarding-house to take away Juliette's red dress and have it burned, and some days previously Dr Who had somehow managed to produce a new dress at short notice. Something borrowed: the key to the TARDIS. Anji and Fitz had become joint guardians of this most powerful totem, and Scarlette had admired this ritual of safekeeping. There in the room overlooking the street, Anji took the key from around her own neck and after some struggling hung it on the same chain as the glass totem.

Which just left something blue. The island's most mysterious visitor had thoughtfully left behind a gift, when he'd escorted Scarlette to the guesthouse. It was a flower, but a fake one, an intricate rose of blue and white satin. The petals were in a curious pattern, so that it resembled no known genus on Earth, and Scarlette balked at first as it so closely resembled the man's own Whig rosette. But the guest had explained that this was the whole point of the marriage. Traditions would be mixed: new bindings would be made. Scarlette had accepted this with a nod (she must have known it anyway), and allowed the man to pin the bloom to her dress even though it clashed horribly with the red velvet. It was, the man had insisted, what the Doctor would have wanted.

Thus armed, and meeting Anji's approval, Scarlette left the room and made her way downstairs. When she walked out into the street and headed up the slope to the Church, those who saw her noted that despite her dress she walked like a warrior on the way to a duel. Typically, for Scarlette even her own wedding was a great battle.

And then there was the Doctor. Since his illness had begun he'd become thin and frail-looking, and on that morning both Fitz and Nie Who – sharing the role of best man, at this late hour – must have known that to act as if this were his 'big day' would be, as it were, a little *tasteless*. The Doctor had spent the entire morning on the island's fortifications, looking out to sea, eyes open for once. But shortly before noon, Fitz had cleared his throat and asked whether the Doctor wanted to get ready now. Somehow, the idea of him wearing anything other than his 'usual' clothes at the altar had seemed... ridiculous. The Doctor had nodded, and asked to be taken somewhere private so that he could change out of his nightgown and into the green jacket and ruffled shirt he'd worn when he'd first arrived in London.

As far as can be established, the Doctor dressed himself that morning. Reading the notes that survive, it's easy to get the impression that he simply didn't want to disappoint Scarlette by turning up to his own wedding as a vegetable. But he never rose from the wheelchair as he pulled on his clothing. He only seemed determined to show his strength when Fitz moved behind the chair, to push him to the Church.

At this point, the Doctor refused point-blank. As Fitz and Who looked on, he began to squirm in his chair, trying to pull himself up on to his feet. It must have seemed an impossible task. Even apart from the sickness, the Doctor hadn't supported himself in over a month. Fitz stayed close at his side, ready to catch him if he fell, but the Doctor was persistent. Thirty seconds later he stood, limbs shaking yet fully upright, finding his balance again.

Many of the accounts of the day tell stories of the Doctor's long walk to the Church. By that time the guests were assembled inside the building, so they can only have seen him through the doorway: a figure of tragedy, supported by his two friends, but nonetheless insistent on keeping his dignity. They saw him not as a dying man, but as the last survivor of a tradition they could scarcely imagine. As he made his way up the slope, step by painful step, they must have felt as if the universe itself were rejecting his presence and trying to stop him reaching the chapel.

More than once, he had to stop. On one occasion Fitz believed that he was about to collapse, and it seemed as if he were trying to avoid retching. But after a while the Doctor looked up at his companion, and smiled, and carried on as if nothing had happened.

'This has gone on long enough,' he's said to have muttered, as he began the last stretch before the Church. 'Juliette will be waiting.'

Fitz corrected the Doctor's error, something which must surely have made him uncomfortable.

'Yes,' the Doctor replied. 'Scarlette will be waiting too.'

When the Doctor reached the grand stone arch of the Church, those assembled inside apparently stepped back, as one man, to allow him entry. He stood on the threshold, unsupported, Fitz and Who standing anxiously behind him in case he should pass out. The Doctor looked puzzled, at first. He took in the Conclave, the myriad of masked, unearthly faces around him, as if he couldn't understand why he'd suddenly found himself surrounded by so many monsters.

'So,' he's said to have mumbled. 'You've all come for me, at last.'

Then his eyes fell on the figure at the back of the crowd, dressed in red from her neck to her train. The moment when the Doctor faced Scarlette in the Church is another scene which appears in most of the accounts, but the best is probably the record of Lucien Malpertuis. It may be the stuff of legend, but it makes the point well.

The Mistress [Scarlette] moved on to meet her groom... the Doctor's eyes lit up in flames when he saw her. I heard somebody say later that her countenance had reminded him of why he was here and who he himself had to be. Mistress Scarlette with much ceremony lifted her arm, and there was no expression on her face. All eyes were on the Doctor to see what he would do. There was some relief among his companions when he slowly raised his own arm, allowing Mistress Scarlette to join with him [i.e. link arm-in-arm]. After this had been done the Mistress turned, towards the main body of that House of God...

There were those who considered the ceremony to be a great performance and nothing more, but I know there [was] not a single man or woman who did not feel relief when the bride and groom walked towards that stairway which led down into the depths. On their passage there was especial satisfaction on the face of the gentleman with the Whig rose[tte] upon his collar, who had kept his head bowed until the Doctor had passed him by.

As has already been mentioned, there was already a sense of something great and fundamental unfolding, a feeling across the island that the thunderhead was about to break. And even the most sober, serious records maintain that the second both the Doctor and Scarlette were inside the Church, something did indeed happen to the world outside. There was a sensation of *closeness* reported in the homes of the townspeople, not so much because of the heat but because everyone became aware of a lurking, sweating presence which pressed against their lungs and made their skins prickle.

These reports are at least feasible. The Doctor – the old elemental order – was about to be bound to Scarlette, and thus to the Earth itself. It's not surprising that the Earth should have noticed, and, indeed, that those forces waiting just beyond the Earth should have noticed too. When the screaming started from the poisonous machineel trees, even those on the island who had no connection to the lodges must have suspected that it was the messengers of the King of Beasts, declaring absolute war.

Before events reached their conclusion, the battle proper would have begun and many of those now inside the Church would be dead.

UPSIDE-DOWN

It was as the Wrath of God Himself.

That was how the 'storm' over St Belique was recorded, by those assembled from the Masonic tradition. A curious choice of words, as by the 1780s 'God' was no longer the Big Man of the establishment. British government had broken the back of the Church in the early 1700s, and although it made something of a comeback in the late eighteenth century it did so only as an arm of the state. It was now the Church's task to lend moral authority to the gentlemen of Westminster and, where necessary, to reinforce the belief that everything was a matter of *property*. (This included women, incidentally. Perhaps this is where the 'pimp age' truly began.)

So it's hard to know how the Englishmen at the wedding would have reacted to the priest who'd been chosen to conduct the ceremony. Robert Ashton Kemp had been an Anglican priest in Birmingham before he'd been spirited out of Britain by Scarlette and her coterie. He was a Man of God with something of a reputation, even apart from the fact that he was notorious for turning up at services as drunk as a lord. Tolerated within the Church simply because it would have been too much trouble to shift him, he once gave a sermon, probably while intoxicated, in which he claimed that God was almost certainly a woman or at least a man with certain *womanly features*, in order to have birthed the universe. (If this claim makes him sound progressive, it should be pointed out that he'd also gone on record as saying that the Garden of Eden had probably been located in the South of France and that Pitt the Younger was actually a mechanical homunculus constructed by Pitt the Elder... Kemp had a flair for making trouble rather than for original thought.)

When the wedding guests filed down the stone steps into the underground chambers of Saint Simone, with the Doctor and Scarlette moving solemnly forward at their head, this alarming priest was already waiting for them. The guests therefore found themselves being led into the undoubtedly cramped vault, where Kemp was standing on the great wooden thirteen-sided table, which Who had transformed into a stage just for this occasion. A series of wooden steps had even been erected, leading up to this new altarstone. As the guests looked on, Scarlette and the Doctor – the former keeping her head held high, witnesses said, the latter stumbling slightly and obviously relying on his partner for support – moved with agonising slowness to the foot of the steps. Some accounts claim that Kemp was as drunk as ever that day, although they may have been unfairly influenced by his reputation.

There was, of course, something of a hubbub in the air when the guests shuffled into their positions (loosely, it's got to be said) around the table. Awed silence wasn't their style. Kemp quietened them all by slowly turning to face the entire congregation, then shouting: '*If you buggers will give me a moment's peace, I can get this over with.*'

An unconventional start to an unconventional ceremony. In the vault, though, Scarlette's red gown seemed nowhere near as odd as it might have done anywhere else. In the corner the local musicians had gathered, once again playing *The World Turned Upside Down* instead of a more traditional wedding march. It was a bitter-sweet choice of tune: the song had been the 'theme' of the American Revolution, the anthem of order overturned. Perhaps the Doctor himself had chosen it, reminding those assembled that a new order was being forged here, but at the same time reminding them of past failures (i.e. America). Mr Van Burgh can't have complained. While the guests shuffled their feet and waited for the priest to begin his litany, the women of Henrietta Street stood at the rear of the vault and watched their feet, either too respectful or too nervous to look up. They were in House colours, but only because the invitations had requested it: they didn't wear their uniforms. The clean-shaven man with the Whig rosette, at his space by the table, also kept his eyes low. Fitz and Anji are described as 'waiting' near the doorway, which suggests that they were reluctant to get any nearer to the table. One almost gets the impression of people who don't want to be too close to an explosion.

As the priest Kemp cleared his throat and began to speak (one record insists that he spat out phlegm, but there's no reason to take this seriously), the Doctor and Scarlette are said to have turned to each other and smiled. It was a genuine smile, say the observers, if a weak one. For the Doctor it was an acknowledgement that things were about to change, that despite everything the two of them could achieve what they'd set out to achieve. He was weak, he was pale, he was staggering, but he was still the Doctor. And for Scarlette it was a smile of true affection, even if it wasn't the most *heartfelt* kind of love that bound them together.

There was no alchemy here, no peculiar witchcraft. It was an ordinary, straightforward ceremony. The Doctor and Scarlette tore their glances away from each other and obediently looked up at Kemp, waiting for the moment when they'd have to make their vows. The words 'I do' were spoken twice, without irony or drama or anxiety or pretension. They were simply spoken, as they had to be. And the guests watched in silence, at least until the priest asked the question which was always likely to cause embarrassment: whether any man *or any woman* knew any reason why these two should not be bound in lawful matrimony.

It was always going to be a sticking-point. There were so many present who might want to intervene, who could point out that the wedding wasn't being performed *quite* in accordance to tradition or that the Doctor didn't even exist according to the records of the British government. But Scarlette kept her eyes fixed firmly on the priest. There were no threats, no warning glances, not even any awkward throat-clearing. Nobody in the vault made any comment.

At least, not until the sound of opening doors drifted down from the Church above. The eyes of the guests, and the eyes of the red-and-black bridesmaids, must surely have focused on the stairs as the footsteps were heard. Moments later, a new figure entered the vault. The very sight of him elicited a nervous mumble from the crowd.

It was, everybody immediately guessed, the Frenchman: the servant of Cagliostro who'd failed to materialise in time for the procession. But now his tubby body was hidden, by the most ornate costume in the vault. His frame was concealed under numerous silks, overlapping robes of glittering gold and green, neutral colours in this war between red-and-black and blue-and-white. He looked like one of the stage magicians of Vienna, in oversized sleeves and with an oversized train at his heels. But what really seized the attention was the mask. This stout, clownish man had never worn a mask before, and yet now he wore one which could hardly have failed to make an impression. It was the mask of an ape. It was grotesque and exaggerated, its jaws wide open, presenting the assembly with a gaping black maw where a human face should be. The mask was fashioned out of genuine grey fur, the eyes gleaming red spheres, like polished billiard balls.

At first it seemed like the height of bad taste. But then this ape-faced newcomer moved towards the table-altar, with a determination that convinced those assembled to make way for him. By now even the Doctor and Scarlette were watching, blank-faced and slightly thrown. The ape-guest stepped right up to the stairs, at the feet of the bewildered priest, and there he made what can only be described as 'eye contact' with Scarlette. For some moments he looked her dead in the face, like a staring contest with only one genuine pair of eyes.

When the *ape* eventually lost the staring contest, by taking a deep and respectful bow to this bride who wore red, the guests must have breathed a collective sigh of relief. Once he'd finished bowing to Scarlette, the ape bowed to the Doctor; then to the disgruntled Kemp; then to the assembled guests. Finally, with a dramatic sweep of the cloak, he turned away from the table and made his way to the back of the vault. There he stayed for what remained of the ceremony, arms folded with his hands inside his big silk sleeves, simply watching. After a few moments the guests realised he'd finished his party-piece and turned their attention back to the ceremony, although the bridesmaids looked nervous at having him stand so close.

At first it might look like a childish stunt. However, the wedding was a symbolic one, and this was the most symbolic act of all. The ape, the enemy, had simply bowed as if to say: *See! Even the ape-lords can't stop you now.*

The man behind the mask had played things perfectly. It's written that Scarlette, on realising that the newcomer meant no disrespect, only nodded seriously as acknowledgement that this was all part of the ritual. And though the Doctor had furrowed his eyebrows in puzzlement – it's fair to say that he was used to somewhat less symbolism, in his attempts to save the world – he raised no objection.

So it was that Kemp reached the part of the ceremony in which he instructed the Doctor to place the ring upon the finger of his intended. At that the Doctor turned to his right, where Dr Nie Who was waiting, and with a little bow that one suspects might have owed *something* to the Chinese quack's showmanship Who passed the silver ring into the Doctor's hands. The Doctor nodded and mumbled something, nobody knows exactly what, as he accepted it.

One final glance passed between the Doctor and Scarlette before he slipped the ring on to her finger. He already wore the *other* silver ring himself, and had done for several days. The Doctor himself had suggested that he should only put his ring on as part of the ceremony, but Scarlette had refused, saying that 'his heart sealed the pact on his side'. The Doctor had ostensibly looked alarmed at this, as if he were meant to take it as a literal threat. As for the glance at the altar, however, there are many interpretations as to what it might have meant. One of the Servicemen present describes it as 'a look of the greatest apprehension... they were guilty about what they had done'. Mrs Gallacher, on the other hand, says that 'they were unsure, it's true... but I saw the little nod they gave each other at the last'. The uncertainty was felt outside the Church, as well. Some held that the screeching from the forest grew worse than ever, and that there was the sound of scratching and scraping, as something prepared to make its way out of the tree-line for the first time.

Whatever the truth, the ring was on Scarlette's finger, and Scarlette was seen to smile again as it slipped over her knuckle. Fitz and Anji were seen grasping each other's hands, while the courtesan-bridesmaids clenched their teeth. Maybe they, too, could feel the approaching threat. There wasn't even a break in the tension when the priest said, with great ceremony: 'I now pronounce you... man and wife.'

In the calm that followed, the Doctor and Scarlette paused to look at each other. They stared into the details of each other's faces, their feelings unknown, their certainty clear to all. Hardly anybody even noticed the priest informing the Doctor that he could now kiss the bride. It was all just a formality. But everybody heard the Doctor, quite distinctly, as he whispered the words:

'Are you ready?'

And everybody heard Scarlette, as she nodded and told him:

'As always.'

The Doctor and Scarlette kissed, there before the thirteen-sided table. The passion and exact nature of the kiss aren't known, though. When they came to write their memoirs, all the surviving witnesses would focus instead on what happened next, the very instant after that kiss sealed the pact and the great scream swept in from the forest. By all accounts, this was the point at which the world disintegrated.

'LOOK ON MY WORKS, YE MIGHTY...'

It seems unfeasible, in retrospect, that nobody on the island of St Belique saw *anything*. In later years, when asked about the events of December 1, the locals would tell stories of the great apes which came vaulting out of the forest. They would say that the animals poured through the harbour-town in their dozens, perhaps in their hundreds. They would say that the creatures began a kind of stampede, which thankfully ignored the houses to either side of the dirt road and instead headed straight up the hill-path towards the Church. And yet if anybody asked these locals who'd *seen* this sight, or asked how one could be sure it wasn't simply another legend of the *obeah*-people, the locals would just shrug and claim that they'd heard it somewhere. Actual witnesses, there were none.

In fact, according to native lore, nobody on the island even ventured out on to the street until the noise of the howling, clawing cavalcade had faded completely. The first few locals to come out into the light of day found that the storm had passed, that there was no sign of any apes, or of thunder, or of western sorcerers. It might have been a perfectly normal, peaceful day in the Caribbean if it hadn't been for the women who left the Church, some minutes later.

Of all those who'd attended the wedding ceremony, only two stepped out of the Church. These 'survivors' were Lisa-Beth and Rebecca. The women were somewhat dazed as they left the Church and stepped out into the blazing light of day. They quietly walked down the dirt road into the heart of the town, where the natives greeted them with some caution. Sadly, nobody asked them straight out how the Church could be so quiet after so many wild animals had poured through its doors. One native man did tentatively ask what had happened to the other visitors, to which Lisa-Beth replied: 'They won't be back today.'

Later on a few of the natives ventured into the Church, hunting-spears at the ready. The weapons were all tied with red ribbon, naturally. They found the building empty, the wooden table in the vault overturned, the decorations slashed to pieces. There were no people to be found, alive or dead. The only thing of interest they discovered was a wreath of flowers, red blossoms from Europe, which had been trampled underfoot by persons unknown. It was taken by a local woman and for some months afterwards hung on her door, as a charm against whatever horrors the island might still present.

Apparently, nobody had caught the bouquet.

So where had those inside the Church, the guests, the priest, the bride and the groom, gone? And why had Lisa-Beth and Rebecca been spared? The latter question might at least have a simple answer. Whatever had happened during the wedding ceremony, it had removed all the assembled members of the world's lodges. Lisa-Beth and Rebecca had both expressed a desire to leave Scarlette's employ, for their own reasons. They, and they alone, were no longer part of any tradition. Then again, that still begs the question of why Katya was taken along with the others. Perhaps it was because Katya was a representative of the Russian *Ereticy*. Alternatively, it could have had something to do with the secret ballot taken by the House's women in September… it's hard to even guess.

But all those who vanished that day, and who survived their later experiences, had a story to tell. All the stories seem unbelievable, and yet all of them are in accord. It was as if this one great ritual, this bonding of the Earth and the elemental, had pushed all those assembled over the edge and into the Kingdom of Beasts.

In his own memoirs, Lucien Malpertuis treated the whole thing as a poison-induced hallucination of the kind which was once common in Saint-Domingue (whose ritualists, to this day, use potent fish-venom in their work). He claims that when the Doctor and Scarlette came together, 'the world itself did open': his English was always a bit on the pompous side. He goes on to say that he and the other Maroons from the vault, led by Émondeur, spent several days wandering through a jungle much like that of Hispaniola. But the wilderness, he said, was bleached grey. The trees seemed calcified, the colours worn out of the leaves and buds, and though they resolved to treat this environment as no different from the Frenchman-hunting-grounds of home it soon became clear that the *Maroons* were the hunted ones here.

The story becomes clearer in combination with the testimony of the Masons. Far from arriving in any wilderness, the Masonic parties present insist that they discovered themselves to be in a 'vast library'. Though it's never explicitly stated, it's described in the Archive as being almost exactly like the Archive itself, the hidden repository of all Masonic wisdom in Musselburgh. The chamber was large, its ceiling vaulted and a good thirty feet high, with bookshelves lining every wall and piles of ancient, heavy volumes surrounding the bemused guests. Everywhere there was the smell of rotting paper, while through the tall, stately, Georgian windows those present could see

> …the very bluest of skies without… though the light which fell
> upon the Earth, and which illuminated the magnificent volumes
> within the library, was tainted with the black of ignorance.

Predictably, the library was overrun by apes. The animals paid the travellers little attention, but squatted on the reading-tables and hunched themselves on top of the stepladders. They were fondling the books 'in a most improper manner', suggesting something almost obscene. The apes clumsily pulled ancient tomes from the high shelves, thumbed through them with claws covered in blood and bile, browsed without understanding anything they saw. They ripped pages out at will, stuffed the paper into saliva-rich mouths, or even (horror of horrors) wiped their backsides on the knowledge of generations. One of the witnesses even claimed he saw an original *Key of Soloman*, that most valuable and mythical of occult texts, being carelessly thrown back and forth by the beasts: beasts which would occasionally stop to open the book and sharpen their claws on its pages. Many of the Masons fled the scene through the library doors, while the apes smashed the windows and threw age-old codices from the higher shelves.

Then there were the other stories. The Servicemen found themselves in a place much like Westminster itself, where idiotic animals filled the benches of Parliament, picking fleas from each others' pelts while the 'leader of the House' threw dung at the creatures in Opposition. Mrs Gallacher, flagellator and procuress, later told her friends that she'd found herself in a boudoir much like that of any semi-reputable English bordello. She'd seen a woman laid out on a bed, she'd claimed, but perching on that woman's stomach (in a manner not unlike Fuseli's *Nightmare*) had been a bloody-snouted ape which had already torn open the poor woman's chest 'in a moment of casual cruelty'. The ape had turned to glance at Mrs Gallacher as she backed away towards the door, but seemed too concerned with picking over its meat to follow her.

Easy to recall what the Doctor had already learned about the realm of the apes. *Whenever the traveller visited the place, he or she took a piece of him or herself too.* It was as if every one of those present at the wedding had seen his or her own territory, defiled by the enemy, like a vision of his or her tradition's own future. No account survives of what Mr Van Burgh, the Virginian, saw. The white-fronted houses of the new America, perhaps, stained with filth and claw-marks. Maybe even apes wearing the polite hats of American slave-drivers, whipping the white men who laboured in the tobacco fields.

The most detailed, though not necessarily the most reliable, story comes from Scarlette herself. Though she hadn't known *exactly* what to expect at the moment in which she bound herself to the Doctor (and vice versa), by her own admission she expected to be transported alongside him. Not so. When she vanished from the Church, she was to find herself among ancient ruins, old even by the standards of the Kingdom.

There were grand pillars, but the pillars had cracked and fallen. There were idols, graven images of enormous elephantine heads, with huge circular eyes and grill-like mouths, snapped tusks protruding from their faces. But the statues had sunk into the dirt, and been overgrown with grey, dull foliage. There were things which might have been pyramids (Scarlette's description is vague), or at least stepped ziggurats like those of the forgotten South American civilisations. Every surface, she says, was inscribed with the symbolic languages of dead races. All this under a blue sky, all this under a black sun.

Her accounts of oversized, animalistic structures are more than a little suggestive of Polynesian ruins, of the buildings which might have been left by the *Mayakai* if the *Mayakai* hadn't been so thorough in destroying their own culture before their extinction. There were no apes to greet her in this desolation. Her only company, she claims, was a single female figure who stood among the fallen totems and bleached creepers. It took her a while to recognise her companion, as it turned out to be none other than the elder *Mayakai* warrior, the woman commonly believed to be the last surviving member of her race.

It's unlikely, of course. The elder *Mayakai* was confined to bed, after all... and the Kingdom of Beasts isn't described, even in the most fanciful of texts, as some astral dream-realm of unlikely encounters. It was a harsh, brutal place, where the real world overlapped the horizon and bloodshed was always the result. Yet here, Scarlette claims she met the woman who'd helped tutor and initiate her, an aged amazon-cum-sorceress who couldn't possibly have stood on her own two feet. Perhaps it was another metaphor. Scarlette's next recollections are almost reminiscent of the later writings of Shelley:

> I looked about this fallen grandeur, and did despair... and I asked the Mistress, to whose word I had always held, why it should have come to this. She could only croak in her own tongue... [that] this was the nature of things, as even the *Moak* [giants] had commanded it. This struggle, she wished to remind me, was intended to firm the future of all our kind. To this favour, as Shakespeare might have said, the present had to come...
>
> The Mistress was never one for delicacy of thought. It was a harsh lesson, to which I did not altogether subscribe.

And what of the Doctor himself? Barely able to even walk on his own, it's easy to think of him as an invalid, as helpless in all this chaos. This doesn't seem to have been the case. Weak as he may have been, his presence was still strong enough to influence the writings of all those connected to these events. The story of the Doctor is recorded in *four separate accounts* of his wedding day... even though not one of the wedding guests witnessed what happened to him. It's as though all those at the Church realised that he was the important one, that they had to be aware of his actions even if he were a million miles away.

The Doctor, say the stories, emerged from the transition on the slope of a hill much like that on which the Church of Saint Simone had been built. He was weak, at first, and finding nobody around him he was forced to sit down on the dead and blackening grass. Looking down into the valleys below, he saw the whole of the Kingdom of Apes laid out before him. He saw the English roads collapse into the architectures of Vienna and Rome, as dark-pelted animals lazily ripped apart the frescoes and cloisters. Beyond that he saw the coast, an ocean of slurry with a harbour created out of the presence of Sabbath and his ship. He even saw the Square – alarmingly described as being much like the Place du Carrousel in Paris, site of the guillotine in years to come – where an enormous throne of bone and dirt had been erected, and where the Doctor could ostensibly see the bloated King of Beasts himself, howling out orders to his minions.

It was while the Doctor sat and observed these things that he found somebody approaching him. A man was walking towards him across the grass of the hill, a man with a blue-and-white rosette on his lapel. The four versions of the story differ wildly as to what the man had to say, one claiming that he simply congratulated the Doctor on his wedding, the next maintaining that he'd come to announce the beginning of the final, apocalyptic battle. The third version, its provenance unknown and its text found only in the 'Sabbath Book', is stranger still. It records the conversation in detail, incomprehensible as much of it is.

DOCTOR: Have we met? I'm sorry, my memory isn't what it was. I shed most of it a long time ago.

THE MAN: Met? Oh, I'd say so. Believe it or not, we used to know each other quite well.

DOCTOR [with recognition?]: Good grief.

THE MAN: Ah. Spoken like the man I used to know.

DOCTOR: You've lost that terrible beard, then.

THE MAN: But of course. I have whatever it is you lack. And vice versa. Have you forgotten? Oh, I'm so sorry. You've forgotten *everything*, haven't you? [Irony?]

DOCTOR: You're behind all this? No, of course you're not. Not your style at all.

THE MAN: Here, Doctor, I'm simply a guest. Thank you for the invitation, by the way. Most touching. Admittedly, I would have preferred something more personal…

DOCTOR: And would you mind telling me what that rosette's meant to be?

THE MAN: A sign of my allegiance to the great Whig cause. I've become an exponent of democracy.

DOCTOR: Why does that not sound convincing?

THE MAN: My dear Doctor, I'm telling you the truth. I told you. I have to offer the universe whatever you can't. If you've decided to take on the colours of your new sweetheart, then it's up to me to side with the Opposition. Perhaps one day you'll consider destroying the universe. Then I'll be in the awkward position of saving it.

DOCTOR: You don't expect me to believe that, surely?

THE MAN: Your friend in red came closest to the truth. What does she call you, again? Her 'elemental champion'? Very perceptive of her. There are only four of us left now, you know. Four of us in all of the universe. We have certain standards to uphold.

DOCTOR: Then I suppose you're going to say that you don't want to kill me.

THE MAN: It's hardly the time for that any more, wouldn't you agree? While our kind still walked tall, we had the whole of space and time as our battlefield. These days, I'm afraid our little duels would be utterly meaningless. You've met Sabbath, of course.

DOCTOR: Yes. He reminds me of you. I think.

THE MAN: How interesting. He reminds *me* of *you*. Our replacement, Doctor. The new breed. All our kind in one, and a mere human being, too. We can hardly return to our old routines, with his kind in charge. Can we?

DOCTOR: I'm sick. I'm helpless. You must know that.

THE MAN: I rather think that's my point. Do your duty, Doctor. However tedious it may be. Save the universe. Become King of Time. Go after that irritating black object in the sky. Whatever you think is necessary. Once you've done that… well, perhaps the universe will be ready for us again, who can say? Then we can set about destroying each other properly. Otherwise, I'm afraid this is hardly our arena any more.

Or, as in the fourth version of the story, the man might have simply pointed to the harbour below him. According to the story there was a ship in that harbour, shining like metal in the black sunlight. It's written that when the Doctor saw the vessel, and the tiny, red-haired figure who hung from a noose on the deck, he immediately leapt to his feet (despite the obvious disability, one notes) and hurtled down the hill towards the dock.

In the world more familiar to mankind, however, one more thing should be added. Some hours after the bizarre wedding ceremony,

Rebecca Macardle investigated the lodgings of *all* the visitors to the island in the hope of finding some trace of them. All the rooms were empty, except for one, that of the exuberant Frenchman with the fat grey horse. She found the Frenchman himself there, half-naked on his bed, both bound and gagged. Once she released him, he informed her that he'd been there since dawn, when person or persons unseen had entered his room and struck him a blow from behind.

So it couldn't have been him, who'd dressed in the mask of an ape and given his wordless consent to the marriage of Scarlette and the Doctor. It must have been some other stout, some would say overweight, gentleman with a flair for drama. By the time night drew in on December 1, however, the guest list was hardly the issue.

11
The Universe

Christmas came and went, with no comment other than the usual English complaint about the cold. New Year came and went as well, leaving things much as they were before. At the beginning of 1782, Parliament had been in a state of uproar, the government on shaky ground and the Whigs manoeuvring for position. At the end of the year, the situations were much the same, with Shelburne's government looking as unstable as North's and the world waiting to see whether the King would be able to weather the storm. So the time the Doctor spent at Henrietta Street was the period of transition, when nobody knew what the future held or where tomorrow's battle-lines would be drawn. Whether the war against the apes was a reflection of that, or a consequence of it, is up to the individual to decide.

1782 had also been a good year for the 'new science'. In London, Dr Graham's infamous Temple of Health and Hymen had finally been closed after a campaign by the *Morning Herald*, the doctor having spent several years laying 'infertile' women out on his miraculous electrical bed and expecting them to suddenly conceive amidst a cradle of bizarre electrical devices. The gulf between the new science and the practices of the old alchemists was evidently closing, and 1783 was to see much more of the same. Later in the year, Casanova would slip his notorious letter into the diplomatic bag of the Venetian Ambassador, claiming that Venice would be razed to the ground by an earthquake on May 25. Casanova wrote the message out of spite, having already been exiled from Venice, but it says much about the nature of the times that the 'prophecy' would be taken seriously by many and lead to mass evacuations of the city.

By January 1783, Lisa-Beth and Rebecca were back in London. They presumably arrived back in England by ship, as the TARDIS was still standing on the edge of the forest of St Belique. The price of hiring a merchant captain to make passenger space for a journey all the way to England would have been high indeed, so one can only guess at the services the women must have performed for the crew. Lisa-Beth had moved back to the rooms off the Strand by late January, while Rebecca...

well, history fails to record what happened to Rebecca. All anybody can say for certain was that for most of January, nobody was asking any awkward questions about what had happened to Scarlette and her kin. The cream of underworld society had vanished in December, and nobody wanted to get too close to the mystery. It was, everyone felt sure, the final end of the Hellfire era.

Occasionally one of the professional women of London would dare to ask what had happened on December 1, or at least dance around the subject. It had been over six weeks since the mysterious vanishing on the far-off island: surely, there'd be no survivors. But Lisa-Beth, while feigning indifference, would at least *try* to hint that time wasn't the same kind of animal in the Kingdom of Beasts. For every day that passed in England, she'd say, either a mere second or an entire century might pass in the other realm. It's a belief reminiscent of folklore, of old legends that those who visited the faerie worlds would return young while their families and friends had grown old... but it's also an idea typical of *tantrists* like Lisa-Beth.

Besides, it might have been true. When Anji had vanished into the ruined city in September, she'd disappeared for a whole day but had later admitted that she'd had no sense of the passage of time. And whatever Lisa-Beth said, nobody was likely to contradict her. Society was more than happy to draw a veil over the whole subject. There'd been numerous ape-like visions on December 1 itself, but apart from that nobody had sighted or smelled the creatures in a long time. Even the usually-cautious Servicemen and Masons were ready to believe that the threat had gone, that the apes had threatened them only during the troubled in-between year of 1782, and that the New Year had brought a new start.

And this was undoubtedly the whole rationale between the wedding ceremony itself. When the Doctor and Scarlette had kissed, the Doctor had bound himself to the Earth and 'officially' declared himself to be the planet's champion. By his very existence, he distracted the apes away from the Earth itself. *I bear the power of elementals,* he might have said. *I carry the heritage of those who once kept things like you in check. You will only fight me, and those who carry fragments of my legacy.* Almost certainly, he felt that even if he died (and in the days before the wedding, his death was considered inevitable) he'd die drawing the apes away from his new home. So in a sense, the ritualists of Britain were right. The gateway between the Earth and the Kingdom of Beasts had been closed simply by the person of the Doctor himself. It's interesting to wonder whether any of those gentlemen had paused to think what might happen if (and when) the Doctor died.

But perhaps it's not true to say that the gateway had been *completely* closed, because one route to the other Kingdom still existed. As ever, accounts of Sabbath's activities in this period are sketchy, but thanks to the correspondence with Emily his location can at least be deduced. The *Jonah* was moored in the harbour of Port Royal, a noteworthy fact as Port Royal hadn't actually existed since the late 1600s.

Back in the seventeenth century, Port Royal had been a city almost exclusively run by pirates, a harbour on the coast of Jamaica known for its ale-houses, its prostitutes and its fights, and for very little else. Not that the settlement was lawless: it was simply run according to the laws which governed life on board the pirate ships, so both homosexuality and female emancipation were championed in the Port alongside the kind of brutal throat-slitting which left many tavern-goers dead in the gutters. In modern terms it's tempting to compare Port Royal to Las Vegas, a self-controlled community both built and run by organised crime, except that in the seventeenth century it was debatable whether piracy was actually a *crime*, as such. Piracy was a political act, the greatest pirates having been sponsored by the British government to loot and destroy the fleets of Catholic nations like Spain. It was only when the pirates had begun attacking British ships *as well* as Spanish that the pirate had been reclassified as a terrorist.

Yet Port Royal had ultimately fallen. Appropriately enough, this Sodom of the modern world, this town built on plunder and excess, had been buried by an earthquake; drowned by the sea; hastily forgotten by the Europeans. Even so, Sabbath was using it as his base of operations at the beginning of 1783. How can anyone explain this? It's possible that part of Port Royal had somehow been claimed by the Kingdom of Beasts, that the old ways of the pirate-prostitutes had attracted the apes' attention and that the harbours of the town had become attached to the edge of the grey city. Easy to imagine Sabbath's metal Leviathan waiting just off the shore, watching the struggle on the mainland. Or it could even be that Sabbath had equipped his vessel to travel underwater – unlikely, technologically speaking, but who can say for sure? – and that he chose to lurk in the sunken ruins of the drowned town. It's not hard to see how Port Royal would have appealed to him. Sabbath was, in a way, the ultimate pirate. A man prepared to strip down the techniques and devices of both establishment and elementals, taking whatever he needed whenever it was necessary... and of course, the skull and crossbones of the pirate ships had influenced so many occult rituals in the decades since the days of the buccaneers (it was pirates who'd originally settled Hispaniola, and who'd caused the followers of Mackandal to dress their rituals up in the bones of the dead). The capital of the pirates: the home of sponsored terrorists who'd turned their backs on their home nation. Such a fitting locale.

It can be said for sure that by the middle of January, both Sabbath and Juliette could be found on board the *Jonah* at the ghostly or drowned docks of Port Royal, halfway between one world and another. A letter from Sabbath, dated January 16/17, makes this obvious. In the letter, Sabbath explains to the unfortunate Emily that he can't directly help her with her financial troubles in London, and he subtly makes it clear that he's got bigger fish to fry. Noticeably, he goes to great lengths to tell Emily that Juliette is perfectly safe and well.

Emily had reason for concern. Because six weeks earlier, on the day of the wedding – if the word 'day' could be applied to the time of the Kingdom – Juliette had been hanged in a noose, near to the point of death, off the side of the ship.

It all comes down to folklore, of course. After his conversation with the man on the hill, the Doctor supposedly spotted Juliette dangling from the rope down at the dock, swinging limply against the side of the *Jonah*. As he neared the harbour, with his body tearing itself apart from the effort, he saw that Juliette wasn't alone. There were shapes on the vessel, stinking apes who peered down over the deck and watched Juliette hang, and not those who'd been trained by Sabbath. The Doctor let out a 'great cry', by all accounts, waving his arms wildly on his way down the slope to the sea. But the apes just looked up at him lazily, hardly reacting and then turning their attention back down to the dying woman below them.

Juliette, say the tales, wasn't struggling as she hung from the rope. It can't have been a proper lynching, seeing as her neck hadn't been snapped. The suggestion seems to be that the apes had boarded the ship – where was Sabbath? – and found the rope lying around on the metal deck. Discovering Juliette, they'd tied the noose around her neck and lowered her over the railings as a kind of game, watching with bored faces while they let her slowly asphyxiate.

At least, that's *one* interpretation.

Evidently Juliette was hanging right next to the hard stone of the dock, because the Doctor could reach her dangling body from dry land. His body must have been suffering, pushed to his limits, when he reached out and dragged Juliette's limp form towards him. By the time the Doctor reached her Juliette's face was bleached and contorted, her eyes shut, her lips as dry as bone. The Doctor went into a flurry of activity, his (shaky) hands desperately untying the rope, cradling her close to his body as he worked. The apes only looked down, letting him go about his work as if it were the most unimportant thing in the world.

At least one version attests that once the rope had been loosened, the Doctor engaged her in 'the deepest of kisses', although in retrospect this was probably just an attempt to get air back into her lungs. Many hold that there were great red welts on Juliette's neck for some time afterwards, where the rope had cut into her skin. The kiss of life may well have been the last thing the Doctor did, before he lost consciousness after his sudden burst of activity. Did Juliette recover, even as he slipped away? Did she awake to find herself in his arms, and if so, then how must she have felt?

However, that's perhaps not the real question. The legends as they're told imply that Juliette was lynched by the apes… but this particular Beast was hardly civilised. Claws were its usual method of attack, not the noose. Even given that the apes tended to parody human activity, even given that the hanging seems to reflect the 'symbolic' execution at Tyburn, it seems odd that the creatures should adopt this elaborate method and be so unconcerned about its outcome.

Maybe it's best to look at things from Juliette's point of view. She was a girl who'd had nothing, when she'd arrived in England. She'd been adopted by Scarlette, and introduced to a lifestyle in which she'd had no control over her own fate at all. She'd been betrothed, then forced to confront the fact that her husband-to-be was part of a plan no native of Earth could have fully understood and who (arguably) wasn't even a human being. She'd been taken away from this questionable destiny, but her new 'keeper' had made it clear that in order to go on she had to go through a symbolic death-rite designed to demonstrate that whatever identity she'd had in the past, it was now well and truly gone. She was young, she was vulnerable, she was juggling several different identities, and everything she'd been told in the last year had led her to the conclusion that death was no big thing.

It's fair to say that Sabbath wasn't on board the *Jonah*, when the apes crawled on to its decks that day. So nobody had been around to watch what Juliette did. It might be wise to dwell a little longer, then, on the question of who'd tied the knot in that noose.

CANNIBALISM IN ALL ITS GLORY

In Westminster the politicians of the two major parties were biting into each other's flanks, factions and counter-factions greedily consuming each other's flesh, storing up the energy they needed for the Corporation Age to come and the Industrial Revolution that was to follow. In Saint-Domingue the French did their best to suppress the uprisings of the Maroons, while simultaneously holding their breaths to see how the American War would be resolved. But even these events seem like nothing next to the grand, mythic stories of the Kingdom of Beasts.

The Masonic version is typically lurid, typically Old Testament in its vision of death and apocalypse.

> The Emperor of Beasts did sit on his throne, wrought from the bones and skulls of victims. The other animals did dance around his seat, in a procession as grandiose as it was repulsive... standing, the Emperor did raise the crown of thorns from above his head as to display the sign of his strength to those about him. With that he did turn his back on them and look to the sky, where his blasphemous Godhead stared down upon his triumph... and when the apes did bring him news in their senseless tongue of the men [and women] who had come to the Empire to oppose them. Thus did the Emperor give his devotions to his God, and thus did they all prepare war against the men who had fought them and eaten of their flesh.

The 'men' were the guests at the wedding. To refer to them as guests somehow weakens them, though. These were representatives of some of the most powerful witch-lodges of the world, and in the weeks before their abduction into this realm they'd been trained to hunt the apes by Scarlette's Revels. Transported to the Kingdom, left to fight or die, they weren't likely to let the apes overwhelm them without a struggle.

It's impossible to establish a proper timeline for these events, but it evidently started with the Maroons. Finding themselves in the jungles of the Kingdom, Émondeur and his men immediately fell back on their usual sneak-tactics. They stalked the apes in those wilderness areas, just as the apes stalked them, destroying the monuments of the King exactly as they had on St Belique. And they weren't alone. The Masonic guests, seeing the apes destroy (at least in shadow-play) their sacred library, at once began devising traps for the animals. The Servicemen did much the same, as did the few Russians. Soon these groups began to mix, coming together in the labyrinthine streets of the crumbling city and fighting a protracted guerrilla war against the apes. The apes may have formed themselves into a hierarchy, but with their hatred of all things *knowledgeable* they can hardly have had tactics to match those of the humans.

The above Masonic account mentions humans 'eating of the flesh' of the apes, and this is certainly true. The Maroons were probably the first to think of the more practical aspects of survival here. With harsh determination, they began to slaughter the animals for food. The beasts were skinned, their pelts taken as trophies; their bones were removed, to be used in rituals of thanksgiving to the black spirits who protected the Maroons in their struggle; and, most importantly, their flesh was eaten. The Maroons believed the creatures would taste of pork, and so, it seems, they did. The broken carcasses of the animals would smoulder over campfires under the bright blue sky (there's no record of night ever falling in the Kingdom), filling the forests with the scent of bubbling fat.

Fitz and Anji, the twin elementals, were survivors just like the others. To begin with the two of them seem to have stumbled blindly through the backstreets of the city, avoiding rather than confronting the animals. Some time later, though, they found an encampment of other humans on the edge of the Hispaniola-style forest. The humans were mostly Maroons, Malpertuis among them, but some errant Englishmen had joined them. Mrs Gallacher was there as well, keeping order by jovially threatening to whip anyone who stepped out of line.

It was here that both Fitz and Anji realised what had truly happened, when the Doctor and Scarlette had bonded. The guests had been transferred into the Kingdom of Beasts, certainly, but more importantly they'd become a genuine *army*. Here at the camp, even the softest and fattest of English gentlemen was forced to consider how he might use his own particular ritual skills to bring down the enemy. This was the frontline, where those who believed it was their duty to protect the planet were compelled to put their money where their mouths were.

Fitz wasted no time in establishing himself as the leader of this assembly. Much to the disdain of Anji, Fitz frequently gave speeches to the assembled ritualists which may have been cribbed from the great military addresses of the past. None of the others, Maroon or Mason, negro or Virginian, argued with him. They must have respected his status as an elemental, even though Fitz was quite cheerful in admitting that if they were to survive this then they'd have to locate the Doctor.

Or, muttered some, to locate Scarlette. She at least might still be alive.

The location of the Doctor. Something that was on everyone's mind, and a question that can easily be answered thanks to a most unlikely source: Katya. Disciple of the Empress Catherine, most unexpected of soldiers, it was she who oversaw the survival of the Doctor in those fierce non-days of the Kingdom.

Though most of those transported to the city found themselves in bleak reflections of their own homelands, Katya's story, as she later related it to her colleagues, was quite different. She arrived at the entrance to a vast grey palace, which at first she took to be like the palace of Catherine herself. It was a truly enormous building, surrounded on all sides by the broken city streets, as if the whole construction had been dropped into the landscape from a great height. Indeed, there were certainly enough huge, jagged cracks in the cobbles. The gateway to the palace was wide, like a mouth into the underworld, although there were no sentries to guard it: and the other buildings in the vicinity seemed to collapse towards the site, as if their walls were falling before it, bowing in reverence. The palace had a tower constructed at each corner, spires which later witnesses felt sure were supposed to be silver, but which (like everything else in the realm) had come to blank greyness. Against the blue sky the towers looked as black as soot, and the most central part of the building had fallen into such disrepair that the elaborate carvings had been scraped away so that none of the faces could be seen. There were no apes when Katya arrived there, no sounds of hooting from the streets. This was a part of the Kingdom which the animals had yet to deface.

As it's described in Scarlette's journal, it was almost like one of the ruined temples of the *Mayakai*. But Katya herself maintained that as alien as it was, the building somehow reminded her of the House on Henrietta Street… or at least, the House as it had been after the arrival of the Doctor. Not in its appearance, perhaps, yet she felt they somehow 'shared the same blood'.

Katya seems to have spent some time at the gateway of the palace, reluctant to enter but equally reluctant to explore the rest of the fetid city. It was some time after her arrival, though nobody can say exactly how long, that she became aware of a noise from one of the ruined streets nearby. At first Katya panicked, concealing herself behind one of the palace's massive stone towers, before she realised that the figure approaching her was quite human.

Juliette had arrived at the palace. Juliette, with the red hangman's-marks around her neck, dressed in the same ceremonial black gown in which her failed execution had taken place. Surely, though, Katya must have been as alarmed by the girl as by any ape. She came dragging a body over the broken cobbles, a prone form 'nearly twice her size and weight'. Katya soon realised that it was the body of the Doctor.

Finally, with her face covered in sweat and her black dress clinging to her body, Juliette looked up and noticed that she wasn't alone. The tension in the air must have been appalling, as Juliette and Katya faced each other across the ruins. They had never really seen eye to eye, but now... Katya must have eyed up the body of the Doctor, and wondered what Juliette had done to him.

Juliette uttered a single sentence, to break the silence which followed. She said: *'This is where he belongs, I'm sure.'*

Katya said nothing, according to her later testimony. If Juliette was unnerved by this then she had no opportunity to say so, because at that point the Doctor attempted to speak. Flat on his back in the middle of the palace's 'courtyard', he said something Katya couldn't identify. Both Katya and Juliette moved in closer to him as his lips moved again.

The Doctor slowly opened his eyes, though he looked straight through the two women who anxiously hovered above him. He looked up at the looming, darkened mass of the curious palace, at its black towers set against the bright sky. The only word he managed to say, as he looked up at the haunted palace, was:

'Home.'

During his time at Henrietta Street, the Doctor had often spoken of other worlds and other elemental realms. There was a definite similarity between this palace and the otherworldly spires he described in some of his more distracted, absent-minded moments. It was always Scarlette's belief that the home of the elementals had long since been destroyed, but perhaps this was the one part of that realm he'd carried with him into the Kingdom... or perhaps the apes themselves had brought it here, making it clear that they were bound to no world and no time, that they could infest all of history if such a thing pleased them. Whatever the nature of the palace, both Juliette and Katya seemed to understand that it was significant. This is why they lifted his body between them, and helped him to stagger through the gigantic entrance to the palace. There must have been a feeling, too, that they were escorting him into his final resting place: his deathbed, rather than his salvation.

The palace isn't a mere incidental detail. Everyone on the island, once they'd learned of its existence, would somehow realise that all roads led there. In the days (or hours, or weeks?) that followed, the lodges which had been transported to this Kingdom would find themselves converging on the building. And so, too, would the apes.

Some time after Katya's arrival, the King of Beasts conducted the 'ceremony' described in the Masonic stories. The King was declaring war on the humans, in his own grunting language, letting his followers know that the humans and their protectors would be torn limb from limb. This animal rite was witnessed by none other than Lucien Malpertuis, who acted as a spy for the Maroon-Mason army by concealing himself in the wreckage of a great Venetian cathedral overlooking the King's square. But no square in Europe could have been so caked with dung, so full of creatures so repulsive, so thick-skinned, so eager to tear into each other's skins to achieve the approval of their leader. Lucien reported that several apes in robes, tattered and torn pieces of leather which looked as though they'd been flayed from the backs of men, came forward then to 'anoint' the King in the blood and dung of his followers. If everything the apes did was a reflection of humanity, then this unpleasant ritual was like nothing so much as a parody of the formal blessings of the Church.

It was only after this that the apes began to pour out of the square, swarming in a horde that numbered hundreds, climbing over each other with razor-sharp nails as they headed through the narrow, disintegrating streets. Lucien mentions their great cry of war, of sheer animal malice. They would rend all intruders. They would slay the elemental and his cohorts. Lucien ran ahead of them, in the hope of joining up with the other humans before the wave of flesh and hair could reach them.

At around the same time the Maroon-Mason-elemental alliance arrived at the 'courtyard' of the grand palace, having finally found their way from the forest. Fitz and Anji were there, and when he saw the shape of the palace it's said that Fitz 'recognised the place for what it was... as he'd seen this world before'. There was no sign of Katya, or the Doctor, or Juliette: by that point Katya and the Doctor were deep inside the building, while Juliette (who, despite bringing the Doctor to this place, had *not* been made to feel welcome by Katya) had once again disappeared. Fitz announced that he felt this was a site of great import, and when asked why he simply said it was an 'elemental kind of feeling'. Most of his new followers nodded sagely. Anji just clacked her tongue.

It was only after this that Lucien arrived, with his Paul Revere-style warning. Within moments the assembled humans, no more than two-dozen in number, could hear the sounds of the ape-horde tearing its way through the city towards them.

Fitz ordered the humans to stand their ground and prepared to fight. Though all of them were dressed in their wedding-clothes, they were at least unmasked and prepared for war. The Maroons had fashioned spears from the raw material of the forest, while several of the Masons and Servicemen carried firearms, though nobody was tactless enough to ask why they'd brought weapons like that to the wedding ceremony. All weapons were now welcome, and all of them were drawn, trained on the streets around the palace as the humans lined themselves up inside the gaping maw of the building's gateway.

While they waited for the first wave of animals to arrive, none of them could have guessed that help was on its way in three very different forms. For one thing, there was Sabbath. Juliette seems to have made her report to him as soon as she'd returned to the *Jonah*. She must have described the condition of the Doctor, the utter helplessness of him when he'd been carried into the palace. Famously, Sabbath made one observation on hearing this. He noted that the siege had begun, and that his own private quest was nearly at an end. With that, he readied himself to join the battle.

There was other, more familiar, aid for Fitz and his comrades. Mere seconds before the first of the apes arrived at the alien palace, a single figure was seen striding towards the fortress along one of the crumbling streets. The ritualists were expecting to see a wave of apes tumbling along that road, so Anji had to tell them not to open fire when she saw the stately, red-clad silhouette which approached. Rumour has it that when he realised who it was, the Virginian seriously considered firing anyway.

So it came to pass that Scarlette arrived, even as the apes – their claws scraping on the nearby cobblestones, and their stink clogging up the atmosphere even if they weren't yet visible – drew closer. Standing before the crowd of men and (few) women, Scarlette casually drew two muskets from her belt, never explaining where the weapons had come from or even where she'd been. At that moment, it was clear that Fitz would no longer be giving the orders.

Scarlette calmly but firmly told her army that it was their duty to hold off the apes for as long as possible. This palace was the last stronghold of the elementals, she said, and its defence was the duty of all those who held the elementals' legacy. With that she joined the other armed ritualists, turning to face the surrounding streets, ready for the *babewyns* as they came into view.

Nobody even considered arguing with her, not even the Virginian, as the opening shots were fired.

EARTHBOUND

The third source of help was, literally, a world away.

In late January, both Lisa-Beth and Rebecca arrived back at Henrietta Street. *Arrived* makes the process sound like a conscious decision, but apparently things were somewhat more coincidental. Lisa-Beth passed the old House, or so she claims in her journal, simply because she happened to be in the Covent Garden region. But when she arrived at the building which had been her home for much of the past year, she found Rebecca there.

The women hadn't met since their return to London, when they'd gone their separate ways. Yet here was Rebecca, back turned to the narrow, bustling street on a Tuesday afternoon, staring through the windows into the stripped salon. Several of the panes had been shattered, and it was clear that nobody had set foot inside the place in nearly two months.

Rebecca merely nodded to her, and Lisa-Beth nodded back. She confessed to Rebecca that the Doctor, while he'd been delirious in the white room, had asked her to take over the running of the House. He'd been hopeful, even to the end, that the building would keep its doors open in spite of the storm. Rebecca 'only shrugged' on hearing this. Did Lisa-Beth hope that Rebecca would give her some kind of reassurance, and say it couldn't be helped? If so, it was too much to hope for.

For some time after that they stood in silence, while people bustled past them in the street. Then, after a while, Lisa-Beth became aware that somebody else was standing before the front of the building. She saw him first as a reflection, a shadow in the broken glass at the front of the House. When she and Rebecca turned, they saw the man standing just behind them on the pavement, a man they'd both seen before but never been introduced to. He was dark-haired and clean-shaven, and on his smart black shirt he still wore a rosette of blue and white. His hands were folded nonchalantly behind his back, as if he too were contemplating the sad fall of the House.

Lisa-Beth was eager to confront him, perhaps frustrated at her own lack of action, and demanded to know what he was doing here. The man hardly reacted. He simply informed her that he was preparing to leave. His little visit was over, he said. He went on to speculate that he might well just go back to sleep, if he couldn't find something to alleviate the terrible boredom, and only wake up when the universe was once more in a fit state for somebody of his calibre... even if it took a million years.

A cryptic message, indeed. And with that the man turned his back on them, to walk away from the House. Lisa-Beth shouted after him as he went, demanding to know who he thought he was, but without turning to face her the man simply said that he'd be *most disappointed* if the women failed in their task at this stage.

Rebecca stepped forward then, and held Lisa-Beth's arm, though it was hardly necessary. Lisa-Beth admits that the man had stung something in

244

her, perhaps reminding her of the duty she still felt she owed the Doctor. So the two of them watched the gentleman vanish into the crowd, before turning their attention back to the front of the House.

It was, says Lisa-Beth, Rebecca who forced the lock and allowed them both to enter.

Can a word like 'meanwhile' be used, to bridge the gap between the Earth and the Kingdom of Beasts? If it can, then *meanwhile* the battle for the palace was already under way. Of all the bloodthirsty images of the other realm, none are worse than this. Scarlette, both pistols drawn, letting loose the first shots as the apes come into view along a road which 'seemed to have been torn from the architecture of Vienna itself' (Masonic archive). The armed members of the Conclave following suit, pistols at the ready, blowing bloody chunks out of the animals' bodies. The remaining beasts barely even noticing, ripping their colleagues to shreds as they vault over the corpses. The apes would keep pouring through the streets from the King's Square, and really it's a miracle that the humans held them off for as long as they did. As Scarlette herself describes it, it was like one of the *bull-runs* of Spain, hundreds upon hundreds of sweating, hairy, shrieking bodies crowding the streets and pushing each other aside. The humans stood firm in the gateway of the palace, those with firearms at the front, those without – like Fitz, or Anji, or the by now hysterical Mrs Gallacher – standing at the rear, clutching whatever makeshift weapons they could gather.

In less than a minute, the first humans had fallen. Unsurprisingly, it was the Maroons who suffered: they were always better prepared to lay their lives on the line than the others. Scarlette gave the order, in bellowing tones which must have surprised all those present, to fall back *slowly*. As far as she was concerned, they were buying time for those concealed deeper in the palace. She must have been prepared to see herself and all her comrades die, if it would give the Doctor more time. Inch by inch, yard by yard, the apes made their way into the palace.

Some fell back faster than others. Fitz and Anji realised early on that they were virtually useless in close combat, and that they'd do more good attending to the Doctor. At this stage, of course, nobody knew *for certain* that the Doctor was inside the palace... but somehow everyone assumed he'd be there. Fitz was certainly convinced that the Doctor would be found at the heart of the stonework, even if Anji was more cynical. So it was that the two of them left the frontline, and made their way through the crumbling vaults of the fortress, heading for what they estimated to be its centre.

Descriptions of the palace interior are manifold, but all of them describe something approaching one of the ancient, Sultan-ruled palaces of the *Arabian Nights* (it may or may not be coincidental that a new English version of the *Nights* was to be published in 1783, to much public interest). There was a labyrinth of great hallways beyond the huge gate, and all of them displayed an angular, hard-edged architecture which reminded many of the unusual buildings of the Far East. But the décor within the halls had all the pomposity of Westminster. There were statues, enormous figures in stained black stone, of Presidents or Prime Ministers forty feet from head to toe. Though the apes hadn't infested the palace, a few had evidently visited it, as the statues' faces had been torn away while their hands had been cleanly snapped off. Then again, that could have been simple entropy. The statues were dressed in colourless stone robes, their empty necks hung with huge chains of office, wide collars at their necks and books of law in their hands. There were massive inscriptions at the base of each idol, written in an archaic alien language which even the Doctor's confidantes couldn't decipher. Nonetheless, Fitz claimed to recognise the style. As he and Anji made their way through the citadel, their footsteps must have echoed through the halls like the pounding of hammers.

It's not known what they expected to find in the central chamber. It's possible that they were hoping for some machine of elemental manufacture, which could solve their problems once and for all. If so, then they were to be disappointed. The chamber was as bleak as the rest of the building. The area was immense, by all accounts, like an amphitheatre rather than a hall. There were five walls, the floor a perfect pentagon (or at least it *would* have been perfect, if the flagstones hadn't been dislodged and stained by age and dirt). Surrounding the vast floor were five stone barriers, behind which an uncertain number of calcified grey seats had been positioned. The rows of seats seemed to go on forever – the hall 'was so high that no ceiling were visible, save for a blackness o'erhead which might as well have been the night sky' – but the general feeling was that this was some form of debating chamber, a forgotten Parliament of a fallen civilisation.

A senatorial arena to defy even that of ancient Rome. A single symbol painted in faded colours on the black floor of the huge chamber, a closed eye, suggesting the eye of Shiva (one of the favourite gods of the *tantrists*) which, Indian legend held, would destroy the world if ever it opened. And in the dead centre of the chamber, in the dead centre of the eye, lay the Doctor.

Lore claims that it took Fitz and Anji a whole minute to reach him from the hallway, which might indicate the size of the area. The Doctor lay flat out on the stone slabs, and crouching at his head was Katya. Even before they were anywhere near him, it was clear to Fitz and Anji that the Doctor's condition had worsened. He was still, apart from his chest, which rose and fell so rapidly that his lungs seemed fit to burst. Still dressed in her gown of red and black, breast heaving under the silk, Katya's face was set in steel and yet quite pale while she attended the fallen Doctor.

What state must he have been in, by this point? It had gone beyond simply coughing up bile. Breathing was now the only thing he could do. Indeed, one version of the story claims that 'his eyes clouded over with the bile… making them orbs of black set into his countenance'. When Fitz and Anji arrived at his side, panting and out of breath, he wasn't even able to gaze up at them. Anji barely knew where to look, having understood that death was coming and that there was surely no escape, while Fitz could only murmur something about his mother. And Katya? Katya looked up at them, and shrugged. Fitz tried to give her a reassuring look. She'd done everything she could.

Then, quite unexpectedly, the Doctor raised his hand. His eyes were still fixed on the ceiling, or possibly so full of jet black that they couldn't see at all. But with unerring accuracy, his fist clamped itself around Anji's arm, something which made not only her but all those assembled jump out of their skins.

'I'm sorry,' he said. 'You should never have come this far.' It sounded like nothing so much as his final statement.

And this from someone with an illness that nobody could identify, let alone cure. It had been widely believed in the House that it would be cured upon the arrival of the TARDIS, and when *that* had failed everyone had immediately assumed that the wedding ceremony would do the job instead. The feeling was that the Doctor was sick due to the absence of a 'place of power', as was the way of the elemental. Yet he'd now been officially, even legally, bound to the Earth… and it had done no good. Something in his body continued to poison him.

This deathbed of the Doctor, in the old and echoing debating chamber of the palace, is described as being one of the great tableaux of the age. It's reminiscent of West's *Death of General Wolfe*, or the later *Death of Nelson*, even though there was nothing heroic about the Doctor's stance as he wasted away on his back. But the battle was still being fought outside, a fitting backdrop to such an event. No doubt the Doctor would have approved of a death in the middle of such a noble stand, as befitted a champion of Earth. As his very existence hung by a thread, perhaps he clung on to his life just to give his associates time to fight the enemy and prevent the Earth being overrun.

Perhaps it's the way he would have wanted it.

BLACK

It's so easy to see Sabbath as one thing or another, to perceive him as *just* a fanatic or *just* a freethinker or *just* a pirate or *just* the villain of the piece. He was so adept at playing roles that it's sometimes hard to see where the character ends and his mission begins. He was a dangerous man, that much is unarguable. Yet although he may have seemed zealous, or arrogant, or even on occasion psychotic (c.f. his determination, some time after 1783, to have the Doctor killed at all costs), he was also both intelligent and driven. The infamous 'Sabbath Book' is often too oblique to render any clues, but in this collection of papers, documents and letters, Sabbath himself sets out his goals.

> The Service trained me to protect 'the interests of the State'. Very well. I shall do exactly as they say. Though how could I, one who has been declared a criminal by his own nation and certified a danger to all mankind, believe that by 'my State' I mean the Kingdom of Britain? I have become a citizen of the world, for better or worse. The world is my estate. It is part of my given duty to protect that estate, however hostile its tenants are to that purpose… as only I, and Leviathan, have understood what is to become of it. I am a servant of the territory, then. It is not to be left in the hand of amateurs, certainly not to be left to the discretion of failed elementals. This is, as my associates in their Whig circles have told me, a new era. Then so be it. It is for humanity to protect its 'state'. I offer myself, as humbly as might be necessary, as the spokesman for humanity in this matter.

For the modern reader, this eloquent speech can be summed up in one simple phrase. *I do what creatures like the Doctor used to do, because his kind have proved themselves inadequate.*

A harsh judgement, perhaps, but while the Doctor lay dying in the wrecked palace Sabbath had not been idle. He had for some time been researching the known texts on elementals and their kind. He'd been receiving messages from his contacts, following up the most obscure leads, obtaining the most unlikely tracts from as far afield as the Americas and the Vatican. While the lodges fought the beasts on the enemy's own home ground, Sabbath had been reaching his own conclusions as to how things would, how things *must*, proceed.

So, on the 'day' that appeared to be the Doctor's last, Sabbath set out from the *Jonah* in its harbour and headed for the heart of the Kingdom. Juliette was at his side, dressed in her usual black and bearing the red marks around her neck, but no longer a cowed and obsequious young girl. She walked as though she were Sabbath's *aide de camp*, rather than an apprentice.

At the palace itself, things were not proceeding well for Scarlette and her army. It might have been a folly which drove her anyway, the belief that if she held the apes off for long enough then the Doctor would find some miracle solution. By the time Fitz and Anji reached the central chamber, the humans had been driven back into the grand hallways of the palace. They continued to fire on the horde, although ammunition was obviously scarce, and despite thinning the enemy out there was no end in sight. An increasingly large number of human bodies was starting to litter the black stone floors.

Ultimately, Scarlette gave one final order to her 'followers'. She told the remaining Masons, Servicemen and Maroons to fend off the apes for as long as they had ammunition. When their weapons were exhausted, they were to scatter in different directions and attempt to find *some* way back home to Earth. They'd done all they could, and only the Doctor could possibly help them now. With that, Scarlette re-holstered her own empty guns and began the march through the echoing hallways of the palace, perhaps in the hope that she could assist whatever ritual the Doctor had devised to end this nightmare.

So it was that Scarlette, too, arrived in the central chamber and saw the Doctor dying in the centre of the Great Eye. So it was that she joined Fitz, and Anji, and Katya, and Mrs Gallacher, and a handful of the other ritualists who'd retreated to this place, all of them hovering at the Doctor's side. Those assembled cleared the way when they saw her hurrying across the great floor of the chamber in her riding-boots, and made space for her at his head. The Doctor was still staring up at the ceiling, eyes dark, ribcage rising and falling far more slowly now. Anyone could see that his death was mere minutes away.

Then Scarlette, under the gaze of Fitz and Anji, put her hand under his neck and slowly lifted his head. He didn't respond, and there wasn't even any change to the rate of his breathing. All present watched as Scarlette lowered her face to his ear, and began to whisper.

The *myth* claims that she spoke of all the worlds she'd seen, while she'd been here in the Kingdom of Beasts. She allegedly told him that she'd seen untold alien cities, like 'dwellings on the Moon' (the notion of life on Mars hadn't occurred to anyone of importance other than Voltaire). She told him that if he should die then it wasn't just Earth which would be in peril. Hadn't the apes taken this place, this once-magnificent palace, from the Doctor's own world? Weren't they prepared to ravage *any* world, in the form of apes or reptiles or bats or whatever else? Wasn't the universe itself at stake here?

How anyone else heard her words remains untold. The effect of them, however, is clear. The effect was absolutely nil. Once she'd finished her speech, Scarlette

…looked into his eyes, and saw that nothing was there.

Finally, she had to concede defeat. Slowly, very slowly, she lowered his head again. She looked up at Fitz then, and Fitz could only shake his head, though Anji glanced at him as if to say: 'so, what do we do now?'

There was a noise from outside the chamber, at that point. The humans in the halls of the palace were falling back, crying out, some of them screaming as if the animals had already fallen on them. Those gathered around the Doctor became more anxious still, as news reached the chamber that the apes had ceased their random assaults on the human defenders. Instead, the animals seemed to have adopted *fire* as their weapon of choice. The front of the building, said the cries, had been set aflame. The robed apes, the 'shamans' of the ape-race who'd given their blessing to the King himself, had approached the palace bearing lighted sticks and branches. The hall beyond the gateway had been torched, and now the blaze was spreading inwards, helped by the dry breeze from outside. The floor may have been stone, but there were untold 'pipes and conduits' - possibly rubber - beneath those flagstones, which were all too ready to burn. The humans had fallen back, and some of the apes had advanced, too mindless to understand the threat of fire to their own persons. Even now it was burning the apes as well, a handful of the creatures already rolling over and over in the hallways in an attempt to put out their pelts.

When she heard this, Scarlette is said to have glanced once more at the fallen Doctor. Once more, and for the last time, she seems to have been looking to him for guidance. Hoping against hope that he'd supply an escape route, even now.

Of course, the Doctor said nothing. So Scarlette stood, taking a deep breath, and turned to face those warriors who'd assembled here in the chamber. She opened her mouth, ready to deliver what she must have intended to be her last and most impressive speech. It *had* to be. It could only have been a mass for the dead and dying.

It's impossible to guess what Scarlette might have told her audience. Because as things turned out, her jaw froze as soon as it had opened, and her attention strayed to one of the many great archways which ringed this most magnificent (if broken) of chambers. The attention of the others soon followed.

It's not known how Sabbath entered the palace. The memoirs suggest that he didn't enter the chamber by the same route as the others, so possibly he'd worked out some path into the heart of the palace which circumvented the gateway, the apes and the flames. He stood there in the high archway, his greatcoat flapping around him in the hot breeze from the entrance, his shaven head lowered so that he faced the chamber like a bull about to charge. Juliette stood at his shoulder, attentive and alert, so neatly turned out in her black dress (and with her long hair scraped back across her head, a tidiness unknown during her stay at the House) that she might have been mistaken for a soldier.

It was the first time Scarlette and Sabbath had come face to face since the horrors of 1780. They regarded each other for a while, it's said, Scarlette with her head held high and her jaw set firm. According to one source, she actually *hissed* when she saw him, like a feral animal protecting its territory. It's possible that the territory in question was the Doctor. As for Juliette… Scarlette refused to even acknowledge her.

Without a word, Sabbath stepped forward. Even the most hardened warriors in the chamber, even elementals like Fitz and Anji, couldn't help but take a step back. Only Scarlette stood her ground, especially when it became clear that Sabbath was walking towards the Doctor. Yet all he said, when he was a mere three yards away from the prone body, was:

'I know what's wrong.'

If he'd said anything else, if he'd greeted her or called her by her name or made any attempt to talk himself into her favour, then things might have been different. But when he spoke those words, Scarlette paused for only 'the briefest of moments' before she stood aside. Surely Fitz and Anji must have tensed their muscles, or felt like crying out, when Sabbath moved to stand over the Doctor's body?

In the silence which followed, Scarlette glanced at Juliette – still standing in the archway – just the once. If anything passed between them, then it isn't recorded.

And what Sabbath did next isn't recorded either, at least not accurately.

It's unthinkable that those present might have left the room at this point, with the fire and the apes bearing down on them. So there's no real explanation for the fact that nobody, not even Scarlette herself, ever wrote of Sabbath's actions in full. The only account which can be *called* an account came from Lucien Malpertuis, who'd been one of the last Maroons to enter the chamber.

Lucien had a penchant for exaggeration and metaphysical imagery. What follows is his testimony, but it must *not* be taken literally. Though it's unquestionably based on real events, it's a fairy-tale version of the story, drenched in symbolism. That Sabbath performed some form of operation is clear, but even Sabbath himself wouldn't have claimed the supernatural powers invested in him by this account. The reader should make his or her own mind up about the true nature of the procedure.

> The Man Sabbath stepped to the fore so that his shadow fell across the body of this Doctor... the Doctor was so sick by this time [that] his eyes were black as pitch, and all knew that soon he would be dead. The Man Sabbath had no feeling or sentiment on this. He knelt to one side of the Doctor's body, without hesitating, and he lifted his arm which we saw was sheathed in a glove of black [rubber?] up to his elbow...
>
> What I saw next was an act of which the spirits themselves would be proud. He had no charm to protect him, but the Man Sabbath plunged his arm into the chest of the Doctor until his hand had all but gone. Whether he cut the flesh first I cannot say, although the women there [not Scarlette, we can assume] were struck by horror. While he worked in the unfortunate's chest he spoke, and I was put in mind of those lessons taught here [in Scotland, where Lucien wrote this account] when a doctor will instruct his students as he cuts into a body. The matters he spoke of were matters of the Doctor, his patient, and also the ways of the Doctor's lodge.

Lucien's account is garbled here, full of West Indian mysticism, so it's best to *precis* it. Sabbath explained to all those present that each elemental, when it left its own world to visit places such as the Earth, had to be *rooted* in its native soil (the Doctor's *Ruminations* suggest as much, and the implication is that this 'rooting' was in some way related to the processes of the TARDIS). Yet this faculty was so taken for granted by the Doctor's kind that they never even considered its exact workings. Buried deep in the body of each elemental, said Sabbath, was a link – a blood-tie, the women of Henrietta Street might have called it – which anchored the elemental to his own realm, which ensured his survival and 'integrity' when he left his world of origin. Sabbath, perhaps inspired by his Serviceman's training, called this link 'the Great Eye'.

But in the Doctor's case, there was a problem. Legend had it that the Doctor's home had been lost many years previously. As a result:

> That part of this Doctor which rooted him to his home had become poison to him... the organ through which he was watched by the Great Eye, by which the powers of the elemental world were passed to him, had grown sick and corrupt. It tried to grant him the privileges of a world long since dead... and so had pumped into his body all the disease and darkness of a kingdom reduced to black nothingness.

Nobody could seriously be asked to believe that Sabbath literally opened up the right-hand side of Doctor's chest, at least not without some instruments of cutting. Yet when they allude to the event at all, the other witnesses acknowledge that *some* operation was performed, even if it was far more complex than Lucien suggests.

But at the end of it all, his hand removed from the Doctor's chest, Sabbath turned around to face all those gathered in the chamber. There must have been looks of horror on the faces of everyone there, from Juliette to Fitz, from Scarlette to Anji, from the Maroons to the Masons, if Lucien's tale is in the least bit true. If Sabbath really did face them, with his gloved hand held out before him, a still-beating heart in its palm. A heart which was as cancerous and as sick as the Doctor himself had been, a heart as black as pitch and pulsing with the same bile which had, apparently, often been seen flecking the Doctor's beard. Or, as Emily put it in a letter to one of her acquaintances:

> Mr. S had at last acqired that devise which he believ'd rooted the elemental to his home and allowed him safe passage between worlds... finally he had found the Black Hart.

It was then, notes Lucien, that the Doctor's eyes cleared of their black vapour. It was then that he opened his mouth and began the longest of all screams.

12
The House

THE DOCTOR, AS HIMSELF

February 1783. A whole year, to the week, since Scarlette had returned home from an afternoon in Marylebone alongside a curious man in a velvet coat who'd claimed to have something of a heritage.

On February 8, anyone who visited the House on Henrietta Street might have been forgiven for thinking that nothing had changed in those twelve months. The Doctor was there once again, as was Scarlette. So, too, were Lisa-Beth Lachlan and Rebecca Macardle, both of whom were in some way responsible for the Doctor's return. But it was hardly a happy homecoming. On the evening of February 8 the Doctor lay on one of the old beds in an upstairs room, his friends once again surrounding him, a large patch of blood staining the right-hand side of his shirt.

He wasn't the only one recovering from a shock. Society, the society of the underground, was already adjusting itself to the fact that several of its lost members had returned overnight. In Westminster as in Hispaniola, in Paris as in Covent Garden, those who'd attended the wedding suddenly reappeared with tales that even the elders of the Star Chamber would have found hard to match. They were like prophets, returning from a revelation, and the fact that many of them *hadn't* come back only put those who *had* in an even better light.

To understand how the Doctor had found his way home, it's best to delve into the legends of the Kingdom of Beasts one last time. Because while Sabbath was doing *something* to the Doctor within the central chamber of the palace, a group of British ritualists closer to the entrance (including the over-enthusiastic Scotsman, who'd become a *true* warrior of his clan since he'd arrived there) was engaged in one of the most desperate struggles of the entire war. Before the human contingent had retreated into the great palace hallways, they'd spotted a procession of the ape-shamans approaching the building with an enormous wooden cross hoisted between them: the trunks of two machineel-trees, crudely lashed together. It wasn't so much an affront to Christianity as it was a particularly painful form of death, because mounted on that cross was a figure, a human being, and both he and the crucifix had already been set

254

on fire. The man was still alive as the procession reached the palace, and the shamans hauled his blazing carcass towards the gateway, the unfortunate victim screaming profanities with every step they took. His face was already unrecognisable, but those who heard him cry out claimed he'd sounded like the missing priest, Robert Kemp.

Mercifully, those humans on the frontline hadn't had time to listen to the screaming as the apes had advanced. But now, trapped in the hallways of the palace with the flames closing in on all sides, the survivors must have wondered whether the same fate lay in store for them. Beyond the wall of fire that swept in from the entrance they could see the silhouettes of the apes, long-limbed shadows cavorting in the ruined halls. Some reported seeing ape-shamans move in to 'officiate', while others said there was an even greater presence lurking near the gateway, the King himself waiting for the slaughter to be concluded.

Then the unexpected happened. The most striking account comes from those who'd been trapped *outside* the building, who'd been engaging the apes in close combat at the gateway when the shamans had set the fires at the walls. This small group of men, among them several Masons and the *houngan* Émondeur, had started to retreat into the streets of the city after they'd been cut off from their colleagues. Now the ranks of the men were being slowly reduced, by frenzied, suicidal apes who would occasionally leap forward and tear one of the Masons limb from limb before his comrades could cut the creature down.

The group had been reduced to half a dozen men, maybe less, when things started to change. The first they knew of it was when the beasts suddenly stopped their attack, and turned, with puzzled and irritated grunts, towards the palace gateway. By this time the gate was in flames, so it hardly seemed likely that *anybody* other than a dumb animal would risk stepping through it, but as the men followed the gaze of the apes they realised they could see several human outlines simply walking through the fire. The shapes were moving quite calmly, several of them holding hands, as if (writes one source) 'the elements themselves bowed to their wishes'.

The silhouette at the front of this bizarre procession was the Doctor himself, and even the apes looked astonished as he stepped through the fire and into view... as much as apes could. All the descriptions of him agree on his determination, the demeanour of 'a force of nature' as the fire licked his coat-tails. He had one hand clutched against the right side of his chest, it's said, and observers could see the red stain beneath his jacket. After him came Scarlette, as stone-faced and as unbowed as the

Doctor himself, following her 'paramour' without hesitation. Then came Fitz and Anji, and after them Katya, and after them a host of Maroons (including Lucien?) who'd been courageous enough to walk through the wall of fire in the footsteps of this man-spirit.

There's no mention of Sabbath, or of Juliette. As later events were to show, they both felt their work in the Kingdom to be done.

The Doctor, that most alien of elements, had become something quite new. All those who saw him step out of the palace, into a blackened courtyard surrounded by apes, said that he was 'as one who had the aspect of a *man*'. A man: one born of the Earth, or at least bound to it. His (mythical?) link to his homeworld gone, replaced by his bond to Scarlette and the Earth, he could now finally present himself as the champion of his adoptive world.

If he'd walked through the fire alone, the apes might have ripped him to pieces there and then. They were animals, though, and thought in purely animal terms. This was the figurehead of a new tribe, almost a new race. It's said that when the creatures cast their eyes across the entrance, at the black figures lined up against the dancing flames, they backed away just a little... because although they may have outnumbered the humans, no beast in the universe would have failed to recognise a territory challenge like this one.

The humans stopped moving, once they were clear of the fire. Only the Doctor carried on. He walked forward, hand still on his chest, into the centre of the cobbled space around the palace. On his feet once again, the elemental figurehead he was always intended to be, the still dark-eyed Doctor regarded the animals around him as if they were no threat at all.

Then he issued the challenge itself. Nobody records whether he made the declaration in English, or just in the body language which he must have known *all* ape-creatures would understand. He stood there as the leader of his tribe, and challenged the leader of his enemies to come here and face him personally.

As the archives suggest, the leader was already close at hand. The grunting apes looked to their shamans for help – unable to think for themselves, as in any primitive hierarchy – and the shamans, in their robes of skin and fat, could only look to a higher authority. The creatures carrying the burning man, now reduced to nothing more than a skeleton, stood aside. They cleared a path at the top of one of the many streets of the grey city, and from that street marched a retinue like no other.

It was the King of Beasts himself. He didn't walk, of course, because pack-leaders never do. His massive grey bulk was supported by a framework of canvas, or according to one source 'a bed of human skin', like one of the sedan chairs which were so out of style in London. The skin/canvas was supported by poles of wood; the poles were held by other, lesser, apes; the apes were led by two of the shamanic 'priesthood', burning wooden staves in their forepaws. The apes not only parted when the procession approached, they positively grovelled, bowing their baboon-like faces until their snouts almost touched the ground.

The King is described, in all the texts, as the greatest possible monstrosity. A massive, powerful creature, strongest and most brutal of his kind, his pelt was a lighter grey than most of the others despite the streak of sheer black that was said to run down his spine (dried blood, possibly). He was bulky and bloated, muscular and bloody-eyed, his long, heavy arms dangling over the edge of his transport and idly scratching at the flesh of the servants beneath him. When he opened his mouth, it's said that the stench of rotting flesh from his jaws could be smelled fifty yards away. Worst of all, there was the crown of teeth and briar-stems, which seemed to have been designed to offend every human being who witnessed the obscene spectacle… a reminder of the Kings and Princes of Europe, of all the bloody and miserable mistakes they'd ever made. The King of Beasts' belly was fat, covered in rolls of loose flesh, but as he must have been seven feet from claws to crown this couldn't have made him look any less intimidating.

Even so, the Doctor was undaunted. The procession stopped no more than four or five yards from the spot where the Doctor stood, unblinking, waiting for his audience with the cannibal-god. When the servants came to a halt, the King gave an almighty yawn, which threatened to suffocate all those present. He flexed his enormous arms, and then, as the red-shot eyes of all his subjects fell on him, he let out a huge scream of triumph. In a sketch of the scene, part of a painting commissioned (but never completed) from the artist Benjamin West at the behest of the Grand Lodge, the black eye sun can be seen surrounding the King's head as he sits on his makeshift throne. It's like a halo, granting the ape its power while simultaneously watching every move he made. No written record mentions the great eye, however.

So what did the Doctor do, when faced with this behemoth of an animal? He simply took another step forward. He let every creature present, every human and every *babewyn*, see that the King filled him with no fear at all.

And then, presumably in the same language he'd used to call the King in the first place, he challenged the monarch to single combat.

In retrospect, it was a stroke of genius. The only real logic the apes understood was the logic of animals, the law of tooth and claw, of strongest-leads-the-tribe. Had the Doctor remained a man of his own people, he would have had no power to make this challenge. But thanks to the wedding he was the King of Time, the King of *Earth* Time, and thanks to the presence of the other lodges he was the undisputed leader of the humans: even Scarlette, prone as she was to dominate *any* situation, was happy to defer to him. No ape could have misunderstood this. The leader of the humans was challenging the leader of the apes, the most primal form of ritual in existence.

Did the King of Beasts look around him, searching for help from his followers? It's tempting to think so. But for most primates, a challenge to authority is a matter of personal combat rather than pack democracy. So the King of Beasts stood from his majestic slouch, raising himself up on his fat but powerful hind legs. He stretched his arms again, and he bellowed, a howl of sheer animal fury which left those assembled in no doubt that he was ready for a fight. Scarlette stepped forward then, perhaps to give the Doctor support as the Doctor looked up at his huge opponent. She didn't have time to reach him, though. As she moved towards him he spoke one phrase, this time in a human language that all his compatriots could understand.

'You want the territory that's under my protection,' he told the King of Beasts. 'All right. Then we'll fight on that territory.'

All the stories of the Kingdom, all the rumours and legends, end here. It's as though the battlefield of the Kingdom ceased to be important, after the palace had burned and the last fragment of the Doctor's old homeworld had been taken away. The final stages of this fight would take place on Earth.

Thus it was that on February 8, the Doctor was found back at Henrietta Street. How he got there is a matter of debate, although Lisa-Beth holds that the TARDIS returned at the same time, to sit in its old position in the corner of the salon. Picture this scene: the Doctor in his bed, bloodied but unbowed, regaining consciousness as his colleagues gathered around him. It almost suggests that the events of the Kingdom had all been a dream, from which he was now awakening just in time to deal with the threat in the real world.

As for Sabbath, the Doctor's unlikely saviour... he was to play no further part in the battle against the King himself, and nor was Juliette. They weren't idle, though. Those who knew the truth about the events of 1782 noted that throughout February the 'rum ship of silver' was

258

sighted in sites as diverse as Virginia and Sicily. Those apes which were rumoured to still haunt the world, such as the one held captive by Émondeur, vanished from the face of the Earth one by one. Sometimes, when the errant apes would be found butchered and flayed in the backstreets and wildernesses, rumour would hint that there was something of a woman's touch to the killings: a certain aesthetic in the state of the animals' skins, which almost smacked of London fashion. Some of the apes just vanished, their carcasses never found.

Evidently, Sabbath was quite happy to acknowledge that it was the Doctor's role to deal with the King himself. Almost certainly, though, he considered this to be the *last* great stand of the elementals rather than the beginning of a new era for the Doctor. Besides, from February onwards he and Juliette had other matters on which to concentrate.

THE SIEGE OF HENRIETTA STREET

The events that took place at the House on February 8 are often known as 'the Siege', but as the battle lasted almost no time at all it was hardly a 'Siege' in the normal sense. Unless, of course, those who gave it that name acknowledged what all those who'd fought in the Kingdom of Beasts had suspected. The palace and the House were in accord, bound together by blood. The Siege had begun a world away, and only the final moves were made in Covent Garden.

It's not hard to see why so much importance should be attached to this 'last stand' at the House. For one thing it was well recorded, catalogued in the journals of those who survived not as one of the myth-battles of the Kingdom of Beasts, but as a real, and vital, historical event. It also set in motion the events which would end in Scarlette's funeral, a week later, although this is hardly noted in the establishment's accounts.

What would the Doctor have seen, when he regained consciousness in the House on that day? He would have found himself in Scarlette's bedroom, and in Scarlette's bed. The House had changed somewhat since he and his friends had left it. In Scarlette's room the walls were adorned with works of (counterfeit) art, the four-poster returned to its space in the corner. If it wasn't *opulent*, it was at least *respectable*. The rest of the House followed suit. The pianoforte once again stood in the salon, while the walls of the hall and the bedrooms were hung with tapestries and paintings, including one of the earliest prints of Fuseli's *Nightmare*. New rugs had been laid on the floors, new paint applied to the walls. Those broken windows at the front of the House which hadn't yet been replaced had at least been boarded over, and while fuel had been scarce

259

at the end of the previous year, on that particular evening the oil was burning all through the building. The House was once again filled with lamplight and body-heat, even if there were few women to seat themselves provocatively on the chaise-longues.

The rebirth of the House had been down to Lisa-Beth and Rebecca, of course. Unable to discover who actually *owned* the House, even though they knew that Scarlette had once paid the rent, they'd simply broken into the building and begun to redecorate. It's impossible to say where the money had come from. Successful prostitutes in Covent Garden often hoarded money for their later years, it's true, but even the combined savings of the two women couldn't have accounted for all the new furnishings. To be romantic about it, it may even have been Sabbath who'd had a hand in things, reversing his earlier decision (for once) and encouraging his contacts to pump money back into the old bordello. If he did, then it was probably to keep the Doctor and company out of his hair, such as it was, rather than out of sheer compassion.

Alternatively, the women might just have sold off all the equipment in the cellar. No debt-collector had ever dared touch it.

Nonetheless, it was in this rebuilt seraglio that the Doctor found himself when he sat bolt upright in bed, shortly after nightfall on February 8. It's not clear how long he'd been lying there, underneath the red sheets of Scarlette's boudoir. It's only recorded that he had an enormous smile on his face, even if everyone could still see the huge red mark under his shirt. When he took in the décor of the room around him, he just looked delighted. And all his friends were there to greet him, Fitz and Anji, Lisa-Beth and Rebecca, Katya and Scarlette. Only Who was missing, having vanished into the aether on the wedding-day (later rumour claimed he'd gone back to Soho as if nothing had happened).

Both reliable accounts say that shortly after the Doctor's recovery, there was a knock on the door. Given the happily-ever-after feel of the occasion, all those gathered must have expected a hundred other old friends to be standing on the doorstep. Rebecca went to answer it – it had always been her duty to greet new clients at the door – while Fitz and Anji tentatively asked the Doctor how he was feeling.

The Doctor brightly replied that he was well, although he added, somewhat cryptically, that he was 'only one and fifteen-sixteenths the man he used to be'. He absent-mindedly scratched at his chest while he said it. Scarlette smiled at this, and reached out for his hand, squeezing it affectionately. The two of them regarded each other for some moments there in the boudoir. Fitz and Anji didn't interrupt this little reunion, although for once they weren't embarrassed by it either. It was, as they must have realised, the first time since the wedding that the two of them had been able to speak to each other.

The conversation didn't last long. Scarlette had barely asked whether the battle was over, and the Doctor had barely replied that the final steps were yet to be taken, when the cry came from downstairs.

Both Scarlette and Lisa-Beth believed that *they* were the first to the door of the bedroom. Whatever the truth, most of those gathered around the bed jumped to their feet and scrambled to the entrance of the room. Scarlette's chamber was on the first floor up, and the door led straight on to a wooden-railed balcony, which oversaw the salon below and therefore the front door of the House. So as Scarlette, Lisa-Beth and the others crowded on to that balcony, they would have seen Rebecca down below, pushing the whole of her weight against the door. It was dark outside, the only light being from the lamps, so nobody would have seen anything of the creatures on the doorstep: except, that is, for their claws. There were hands pushing at the door, grey-black fingers forcing themselves between the wood and the frame. Rebecca was doing her best to hold them back, but she was hardly built for the job.

Scarlette immediately called out to her, telling her to move away. The final part of the Siege had begun, the apes converging on the House at last. The Doctor had challenged the King of Beasts to combat, and the House was the venue. It had, as the Doctor had always intended, become the bridgehead to all the Earth.

Did the people of the outside world see it? It seems insane to think that the apes could enter the House from Henrietta Street itself without being noticed. There's no record of any passers-by seeing animals in such a busy London thoroughfare, beating and scratching at the black-lacquered door (it's worth noting that the animals only came through the *door*, not the windows, perhaps suggesting that the door was their only possible entrance into the bridgehead). Then again, Lisa-Beth's version of events claims that there was a very *human* screaming from outside, and the very fact that the battle became known as the Siege of Henrietta Street implies that the outside world noticed something. Either way, Rebecca did as Scarlette told her and moved from the door, bolting up the staircase without hesitation. The door flew open at once, and the hairy, scrabbling bodies of the apes tumbled through into the hall. There were too many of them to count, but all of them were shamans, wrapped up in their blubbery robes. They were evidently the ones who'd stayed loyal to the King, when the other, lesser, creatures had backed down in deference to the Doctor.

Fitz immediately began to make suggestions of his own, but if he was trying to issue orders then his words were barely comprehensible. Anji tried to drag him back into Scarlette's bedroom. The others all looked to Scarlette, even Lisa-Beth, although Scarlette's first move was to reach for those parts of her belt where she'd once kept her pistols. And her guns had been emptied of ammunition in the Kingdom of Beasts.

Nonetheless, she insisted that they should all stand their ground, even as the first of the apes looked up from the hall of the floor and began to screech at those assembled on the balcony. While the first of the animals were digging their claws into soft wood at the bottom of the staircase, the Doctor himself was stepping out of Scarlette's room. All eyes turned to him as the apes began to scramble up the stairs.

The Doctor only nodded, and Lisa-Beth claims that Scarlette curtly nodded back. Both may have known what they had to do. After that the Doctor turned his back on all of them, and headed for the *next* stairway, which led up from the balcony on to the higher floor of the building… the floor where Juliette had made her home, before her fall from grace. Fitz and Anji started to bicker, but soon decided to follow him.

This left Scarlette at the top of the first flight of stairs, facing the sunken, burning eyes of the *babewyns*. It also left the women of the House once more looking to her for instructions. Scarlette wasn't thrown, however. Mounted on the wall behind the balcony, not far from the top of the stairway, was the same fighting-sabre which Lisa-Beth had seen Scarlette use so well against the Doctor on her first visit to the House (although it's a miracle that she and Rebecca had managed to recover it after the debt-collection crisis of the previous year). Scarlette wasted no time at all in arming herself, tearing the sword from the wall.

If it seems romantic, it also seems hopeless. The apes flooded into the House one after another, and only Scarlette stood between them and the upper floors. One woman with a sword could hardly have been expected to keep them all back.

As for the Doctor… he was the first to reach Juliette's room, on the third level of the House, so nobody else was there to record what exactly he found. From those who followed him, though, the basics are obvious. Because waiting for the Doctor in that room, his massive bulk squatting over Juliette's old boudoir, was the King of Beasts himself.

The way the King had arrived here is, at least symbolically, easy to understand. While the other animals poured through the veil of *Shaktyanda* to reach Henrietta Street, the King had been summoned directly to the heart of the House by the ritual of the challenge, ready to face the Doctor in single combat. The description of him later told by Fitz, in Fitz's last days at the House, is reminiscent of Juliette's dream diary. In the cramped space of the upstairs bedroom, perhaps even surrounded by the thin smoke which accompanied most hallucinatory experiences, the King was as at home as any piece of furniture. Scarlette's account, excitable as it was, says it all.

> The Beast itself was among us then. I am reliably informed that as the Doctor stepped into that room the Beast pushed out its arms, so as to shatter the window and punch a hole the size of its fist through the ceiling. Its jaws were frightening in aspect... it had none of its foul worshippers to defend it, or to keep up its great belly, though it showed no fear when it looked into the eyes of the Doctor [Scarlette ceases to call him 'Jack' at around the time of the wedding, oddly]. It must be said also that the Doctor showed no fear as he looked back into the gaze of the Beast.
>
> My friends Mr. K. and Mistress K. told me that they heard the cry of the Beast, plunging into its assault... [as] they clambered the stairs towards that room. It was followed by a most distinct tearing of flesh and bone from above.

Back downstairs, the tearing of flesh was also in the air. At least the shamans here hadn't used fire as a weapon, possibly fearing that they might hurt their pack-leader. Yet still they came, one after another after another, bounding up the stairway. Scarlette 'dispatched' several of the creatures as they tried to mount the balcony, at least a dozen of the animals falling to her sabre. The floor of the salon, Lisa-Beth goes on to say, was 'wet and bloody with the carcasses of those that had fallen from on high'. In fairness, none of the three other women were exactly helpless. When one of the apes leapt from the stairway and gripped on to the railings of the balcony, Lisa-Beth managed to kick at its fingers until it lost its grip and tumbled to the floor below. For the first minute or two, then, it seemed that things were going well.

Then Scarlette lost her sword. It was hardly a surprise: the enemy had weight of numbers on its side. Several of the apes pushed forward at once, their 'fetid breath and rank hides' overwhelming her and forcing the blade out of her hands. She slipped back, away from the stairs, as the apes climbed on top of her. Somehow, by some fluke, she managed to survive this. She succeeded in forcing the first of the animals away from her, and sent it rolling down the staircase. It fell among a group of its comrades, still only halfway up the steps, those creatures falling back in turn. Down in the salon, the rest of the horde tossed around the furniture, overturning the chaise-longues and shredding some of the paintings in frustration. The legs of chairs were quickly turned into clubs.

The second of the apes on top of Scarlette was wrenched away by the other three women, and ended up falling over the railing, breaking its back on the floor below. This victory, however, had gained them seconds rather than minutes.

Once again, and for the last time in the war of 1782-83, Scarlette decided that only in symbols could she find the power to end this madness. Lisa-Beth – implacable, mythology-proof Lisa-Beth – writes that while Katya and Rebecca could only panic, Scarlette

took in a deep breath… seeing that Beast of hers gathering below her, unwilling to give up. The Mistress [the only time Lisa-Beth ever calls her that] must have known what she was required to do. At the top of the steps she reared up to her full height like some true mare of the night, her red wedding-gown blazing around her still. Her sword was lost, fallen somewhere in the hair and blood below us. She reached instead for that fragment of glass which hung on a silver chain at her neck…

Once more the apes pushed at us, jumping and leaping on each other's backs to be first at the head of the stairs. Hand on her glass totem, Scarlette did not even turn away when she told us to retreat upwards to the sanctuary of the Doctor. She said she knew how this battle would have to end, so that the Doctor might play his part.

I know that we all three of us hesitated before we turned. In that hesitation I for one saw that she released the chain from around her neck. When the nearest of the demons bolted at her unarmed person she was awaiting it, with the totem of glass held out towards it. It was then that I turned away. I saw that K. and R. had already turned, the better not to see what followed.

I recall fast movement up the next flight of stairs. The ape could not have immediately torn into Scarlette, for even when I was halfway up the flight I could still hear her speaking behind me. R. insisted after this that Scarlette had in the heat of battle given a last message to be told to the Doctor, though I believe it may have been the curious mind of R. which devised this version of the history. Myself, I believe her final words to this enemy to have been: 'All right, you hairy bastards. I'm ready for you.'

The 'sanctuary of the Doctor' was anything but a sanctuary, however. What's most noticeable is that neither Fitz nor Anji seem to have said anything, or done anything, to interfere with the battle taking place inside the room. They were still standing on the threshold, frozen, when the three women arrived. They must have realised that for the struggle to be concluded, this fight had to be between two combatants and two combatants alone. The Doctor and the King, rival elementals.

But the sight which greeted Lisa-Beth as she entered the room was unexpected. The boudoir had been wrecked, the weight of the ape-god having torn at the walls and all but smashed the remaining furnishings (Juliette's room, unlike the others, had been left largely bare). The King of Beasts lay sprawled across the boards, his massive body taking up much of the space in the middle of the floor. His enormous legs were kicking in the air, occasionally making huge dents in the wall by his side. The ape's arms extended from his body on either side, and although Lisa-Beth says that 'the fingers were twitching' they did nothing to protect the rest of his body from attack.

Straddling the big barrel torso of the animal, perched on his ribcage with one leg on either side, was the thin and pale-faced form of the Doctor. He had something in his hand, and was repeatedly bringing it down on the gigantic beast's head. At least, that was Lisa-Beth's first impression. When she moved a little further into the room, past the staring, unmoving figures of Fitz and Anji, she saw that he was actually assaulting the ape's thick neck. Whatever he was holding in his hand, it was sharp. He was hammering the object into the animal's throat, and even Lisa-Beth admitted to finding the sight alarming, as if there were something bestial about the Doctor himself. He'd chiselled his way through the front of the neck, half-severing the King's head from the body. As was the way with the creatures, there was no blood or matter from the wound other than 'that which one might expect'.

The King was dead. It was obvious that the King was dead, yet the Doctor still hammered into the neck, as if determined to thoroughly decapitate him. Even when the head was finally severed, the Doctor kept banging his weapon against the floor. In the end, it was Rebecca who stepped forward to stand at the Doctor's side: Rebecca, who perhaps had a greater understanding of the *symbols* that were needed than anyone other than Scarlette herself.

The next time the Doctor brought up his arm to strike a blow, Rebecca put her hand on it. The Doctor stopped at once, his head turning sharply, to look her dead in the eye. Even Fitz and Anji were stunned into silence by the utterly blank look on the Doctor's face.

Rebecca simply shook her head, and at that point the Doctor seemed to realise that this battle was over. He lowered his arm, and let go of his cutting-tool, letting it roll on to the floor. That done, Rebecca herself bent over, to grasp the head of the dead King by the hair of its scalp – the mouth still frozen open, blood coating the snout, eyes sunken into darkness in the skull – and to lift it away from the body.

This was the final iconic image of the Siege of Henrietta Street. The others could only watch, in silence, as Rebecca lifted the big severed head in one hand and calmly walked towards the door. For a moment longer the sound of the horror outside, the scratching of the apes and the death they brought with them, drifted into the room. Then Rebecca shut the door behind her.

There could hardly have been multiple witnesses, then, to the final end of the battle. Almost nobody could have seen the horror on the stairway, or of the ultimate statement to the *babewyns*, when Rebecca lifted the severed head of the King high into the air and every ape in the salon looked up to see the dead, dark eyes of their pack-leader on the balcony. The best description of the scene is a purely aural one, the screeching which Lisa-Beth heard from the safety of the upstairs room, the scream of rage and disappointment when the apes saw that their primate hierarchy had fallen apart. When they knew, as much as animals ever could know, that in this primitive contest of strength the elemental had proved his own blood to be older, wiser, and more powerful: that it was his kind who'd always held sway over time and space, not demons with the faces of baboons.

Did they vanish into the night, swarming out of the door and into the darkness, leaving only bloodstains and bodies behind them? Did they disappear in a puff of opium-smoke, or did the 'horizon' take them all? It hardly matters. All Lisa-Beth records is that there was screaming, and then there was silence. They hadn't been destroyed, of course, and the universe wasn't – *couldn't* be – as stable as it had apparently been in its prime. But the apes had retreated, at least for now, sent away from Earth in a symbolic rite which had taken a year to perform and which had left the Doctor permanently bound to the planet.

One can only guess what results might have been achieved if the Doctor had married Juliette, his intended Virgin of Spring.

When the silence reached the upstairs room, the Doctor's associates spent some moments staring at the door, probably waiting to see whether Rebecca would re-enter. She didn't, so for the first minute or so the others might have believed her to be dead. It was in that brief moment of peace that Lisa-Beth saw the weapon, which the Doctor had used to overcome a creature of hair and muscle that had been at least twice his size. Perhaps she expected it to be some elemental device of wonder, but to her it only seemed to be a broken scientific instrument of some kind. It looked like a narrow glass cylinder, although the glass had been shattered so that all that remained were a few sharp and bloody shards protruding from the steel handle. Even as it lay there on the floor, the broken end of the device was crackling with what Lisa-Beth calls 'blue fire'. Even though she admits that the sparks looked 'as sharp as razors', she was unclear as to how such a small instrument could have cut through the beast's neck so quickly. She also found it hard to say whether it had been the glass edge or the blue fire which had done most of the damage.

As Lisa-Beth hadn't read the Doctor's will, she would have had no reason to recognise the legacy he'd left to Juliette. It certainly wouldn't have crossed her mind to wonder how the Doctor's miraculous 'screwdriver' had come to be there, so long after it had been sent to the *Jonah*. Lisa-Beth and Rebecca may have redecorated the House, but unless Rebecca had been making her own adjustments in secret then somebody had been moving the props around without any of the Doctor's coterie noticing.

What's beyond question is that on February 8, the device became as great a totem of power as Scarlette's own shard of glass. It was an object of *meaning*. The King of Beasts might have been a powerful, vicious monster, but could it have even understood the importance of that one small length of glass and metal? Could it have begun to appreciate, as it had died, all the horror, the affection, the heartbreak, the trust, the mistrust and the *importance* that it represented?

The apes knew all about savagery. Even the strongest of their shamans, however, had no grasp of the strength which was represented by the Doctor or by Scarlette.

The Doctor may have realised this very fact at the time, because once his friends had taken in the scene he turned to them with a look on his face that was more a look of puzzlement than anything else. The previous days, or weeks, or months, had been hard on him. Rebecca had stopped him making an ape of himself, preventing what might have been a nasty slide into savagery. Now he barely seemed to understand what had just happened, or even the fact that the struggle was over. When he looked around the room, taking in the shocked and expectant faces of his peer group, his only question was a simple one:

'What happened to Scarlette?'

Lisa-Beth records that she and Katya looked at each other, then. Neither of them knew whether they should answer him, or tell their elemental the truth about the fate of the woman he'd married.

THE RIVER

British folklore maintains that in the early 1800s, during the Napoleonic wars, a certain French warship – the *Chasse Maree* – was shipwrecked off the coast of England near the town of Hartlepool. All human hands were lost on the Longscar Rocks, says the story, but the one survivor of the wreck was an ape. A living souvenir, presumably, from one of the far-distant lands the ship had visited.

The ape was washed ashore, where it was found by the people of Hartlepool: people who, in this parochial age, had never even seen a picture of such a beast before. As the locals gathered around the stunned animal, they reached the obvious conclusion. The creature was a Frenchman. After all, hadn't they heard that the French were human and yet *less* than human? Hadn't they been taught that the men of the continent looked *something* like the men of the British isles, but with more hair and far less civilised charm?

So the ape was hanged, states the legend, executed by the locals as a French spy. The story's told even to this day, so much so that the people of Hartlepool are sometimes (with good – if insulting – humour) known as 'monkey-danglers'.

Like so many of the tales of the era, the legend's almost certainly untrue. Apart from anything else, there's no record of any ship called the *Chasse Maree* in that era, let alone one lost off the coast of England. Besides, illustrations of apes were common in the early nineteenth century even if very few people had seen one of the animals in the flesh. It's a piece of folklore most probably devised by one of Hartlepool's rival fishing-towns, to make the competition sound like buffoons.

Nonetheless, it's telling. It tells posterity that even in the 1800s, the ape was the symbol of something *exotic*, of something bloody and dangerous from far away. It was the most buried, most primal part of mankind, ready to threaten humanity again at any opportunity. As the eighteenth century drew to a close, the *Frankenstein* age began and the message to the world was clear. All change gave birth to monsters... except, of course, that most of those monsters were borne of the past rather than the future. As later generations were to discover, the more humanity tried to avoid the monstrosities of progress, the more apelike and savage humanity itself became. Perhaps a ritualist would have speculated that the apes weren't simply the price of progress. They were the initiation, the trial by fire, that made progress worthwhile.

On February 24, 1783, the British government fell once again. The chaos had lasted the best part of a year, and only now was the *true* new order of the age about to manifest itself. The new money was ready to begin its grand struggle against the old blood, and the Countess of Jersey was part of that process. In 1783 she began to associate with all manner of Whig politicians and arch-manipulators, seducing her way into the heart of the new society. The new Britain, *corporate* Britain, would spawn the Industrial Revolution itself. It would create a world of new ideas and new machineries, of unprecedented corporate corruption but at the same time unprecedented scientific knowledge. In the years to come there'd be blood and fire; war and renewal; the burning of coal and the burning of peace-treaties; human workers redefined as machine parts while freethinkers made the most glorious of discoveries. Perhaps, then, the Countess really *had* learned something from her experience with the apes.

Everything revolves around symbols, in the history of 1782-83. So Scarlette's funeral, held on February 9, might well be interpreted as the greatest symbol of all. The old order, some might have argued, had ended with the Siege of Henrietta Street. That was why there *had* to be a funeral, one way or another.

It was snowing that day in February: February, like March, was a colder month then. The procession left Covent Garden at six o'clock in the morning, when the sun was still only half-risen and most of London hadn't woken up for the day. Those who carried the coffin crossed the open ground around Oxford Street, heading in the direction of Mayfair, leaving grey footprints behind them as they waked across the snow. They didn't make much noise as they went, and there weren't many in the *cortege*. It would have been unseemly to give Scarlette a traditional Christian funeral, and unless one counted Dr Nie Who – or indeed, the Doctor himself – there was no priest in attendance.

The coffin was carried by the women, by Lisa-Beth, Rebecca, Katya and Anji. The two doctor-men dragged behind, heads bowed, though in the Doctor's case it was probably more than just a mark of respect. Fitz Kreiner walked at the very rear of the group, alongside a man referred to in Lisa-Beth's journals only as 'Mr. Small-Bear'. The man was a representative of the Service, the only one of the other lodges which had sent a member to the funeral. Though 'Small-Bear' himself may have been a minor player in events, the Doctor welcomed his presence. The rest of the lodges were basking in their victory, no doubt, gloating at the defeat of the apes and turning their attention back to their own ambitions. Only this one man had acknowledged the importance of Scarlette, this adventuress and sorceress, this woman who'd stood astride the underworld and made the victory possible in the first place.

It was Rebecca and Lisa-Beth who'd arranged the last rites. Lisa-Beth had insisted that Scarlette had left instructions as to how the ceremony should be conducted, though she neglected to say exactly when or where Scarlette had done this. The Doctor hadn't argued. When it had come to planning the funeral ceremony itself, Rebecca had drawn a card from her augur's deck, to determine whether the funeral would be conducted by earth, fire, air or water. The result had been *The Queen of Cups* or *Queen of Hearts*, the suit of water, which was why the procession was making its way to the Tyburn river.

In twelve months there'd been four rituals, one for each of the elements that Scarlette had held so dear. The March Ball of 1782; the summoning of the TARDIS; the wedding ceremony itself; and now there was her own funeral. How could it have ended any other way?

The Tyburn river was a stretch of water at the very heart of London. It ran from Haverstock Hill right into the Thames, but since the seventeenth century onwards it had officially been used as a sewer and by the 1780s it had already been covered over. It was (and still is) one of London's 'secret rivers', one of those streams which runs quietly beneath the feet of the city's inhabitants, black and invisible. Perhaps because it shared its name with such a prominent place of execution, in Scarlette's time those who knew about the hidden paths of London often referred to it as the Black River.

There was an entrance to the river's sewer-passage just north of Mayfair, and that was the destination of the funeral procession. The entrance to the tunnel was subterranean, a heavy but largely unused wooden door at the bottom of a damp, moss-covered stone stairwell. There was silence when the Henrietta Street coven arrived at the door, apart from the occasional echo of horse's hooves from the nearby streets. It was the Doctor who moved down those big stone steps to open the door, forcing it open despite the mould which had grown around the frame. The four pallbearers stood looking down at their shoes, coffin supported between them. There'd been mutterings on the way here, but to the eighteenth-century mind it would have been tasteless to speak at the gateway to the underworld itself.

The sewer was a circular passage, wrought out of stained yellow brick. The river itself ran down the centre of the shaft, a great wide stream of black in the half-light of the passage, but even those who stood on the narrow 'platforms' on either side of the water found themselves knee-deep as the river ran towards its ultimate destination. Fitz was carrying a lamp, as was the Serviceman. It wouldn't have been much light, to brighten the gloomy, cavernous interior of the sewer. According to Rebecca, Scarlette herself had expressed a preference for the site, in the event of a funeral by water. Perhaps Scarlette had intended it as a final grim joke, a 'burial at sea' conducted not only in the bowels of the city but in the cloying darkness of the sewers. She can hardly have expected there to have been such a reverent atmosphere, when the pallbearers quietly mumbled to each other but nevertheless managed to carry the coffin into the main part of the passageway.

But perhaps there was another reason for Scarlette to have chosen this place. A far more telling one.

The pallbearer-women stood 'up to their ankles' in the water, lowering the box so that it touched the surface but keeping it steady. 'Box' seems as good a word as any, as the coffin was hardly elaborate. If the House had any interest in the expensive funeral rites practised by London's morticians, then they had little money to spare now. The coffin was a simple box, in lightweight wood, and there was no inscription on the lid. The ceremony was an epitaph in itself.

Standing over the box, the Doctor began to speak, whispering his own interpretation of the last rites. It was then that the four pallbearers let go of the coffin, Katya giving it a small nudge when it looked as though it might not join the flow of the river. Slowly it slipped away from the curved floor of the passage, entering the black waters in the middle of the stream. It didn't exactly float, but it didn't sink to the bottom either. The flow was fast enough to draw the box along, the plain casket picking up speed as it drifted down the passage. Those among the mourners who'd been taught the old myths might have seen the river as a tributary of the Styx, while those familiar with the legends of London would have known the other stories that were told about the Tyburn. Further along its path, the Tyburn forked in two before reaching the Thames, and ancient pre-sewer folklore held that a kind of augury could be performed by dropping an object of value (a 'sacrifice' in itself) into the water, divining the future by seeing which of the two paths the object took. Yet there were other, more arcane, legends. It was said in some circles that certain things dropped into the buried river *never* reached the Thames, that somewhere after Mayfair an object of a precise nature would find itself swept along a *third* route which even the old Roman geographers hadn't recorded.

Nobody could say for sure where that third branch of the black river might lead, but if Scarlette had indeed expressed a preference for the site then it's easy to see why. The *third path* would take the coffin to places unseen and unknown. As with the old stories about sleeping Kings, about age-old warriors who lay beneath England until the day when they'd be needed again, a burial in that part of the Tyburn was no burial at all. It was an unknown quantity, much like Scarlette herself.

Was that what they felt, the pallbearers and the mourners, the Doctor and the doctor, the elementals and the *tantrists*? When they saw the coffin slowly drift away from them, to be carried out of reach down the yellow-brick tunnel, did they reflect that nobody had really died at all?

The Doctor himself is described as standing there in the shallow part of the water, with his shoes flooded and his head held low. His beard was as well-trimmed as always, his ruffled shirt as unruffled as ever, but those who knew him well had seen the bandages on his chest and understood what had happened to his heart… figuratively or otherwise. And Lisa-Beth records one more telling detail about the scene, as the Doctor stood in the dankness of the passage. She notes that the Doctor silently touched the ring on his finger, the ring of silver which exactly matched the one he'd slipped on to the hand of Scarlette in December. It was clear to all, says Lisa-Beth, 'that his intent was to draw off the ring and toss it into the black waters after his friend'.

It was, again, Rebecca who stopped him. It was she who placed a hand over the Doctor's hand, making sure the ring stayed exactly where it was. Perhaps it was her way of making sure he knew that this wasn't over, that this was *never* over. Dead or alive, Scarlette was the element which bound him to this Earth and justified his existence as the creature he was. He may not have *loved* Scarlette, as human beings understood the term – could a creature such as himself even appreciate such an idea? – but she was a symbol to him, just as he himself was a symbol to all the Earth. Whether the Earth knew it or not.

Lisa-Beth fails to record how long the party stood there in the half-dark of the Tyburn passage, listening to the rushing of the water and wondering where it would take the casket. Eventually, though, they turned away one by one and headed back into the light of day.

* * *

And on February 13, the Doctor finally departed.

He was well again by this point, so well that for some days he seems to have been darting in and out of his TARDIS on a variety of obscure errands. Those who were allowed into the mystical pleasure-gardens of the box claimed that he'd spent some time 'setting and re-setting the machineries of the device', but there's some confusion here. Though the TARDIS was described as returning to the salon on its arrival from St Belique, by February 13 it was apparently standing out in the open on Henrietta Street, on the frost-bitten cobblestones in public view. Passers-by must have given it a wide berth, perhaps linking it with the stories of mysterious objects which had always accompanied Scarlette and her tribe. If the stories are to be believed, then the TARDIS had moved further than the short distance from the salon. It's suggested that the Doctor had taken the machine 'all across the globe' (Lisa-Beth), searching for any remnants of the ape army which might not have followed the shamans into retreat. If this is so, then he might have been surprised to find that the matter was already in hand. He also expressed an interest in discovering the nature of the black-eyed sun which had inspired the creatures, admitting that he had no idea whether the object had been controlling them or simply driving them into a rage. Indeed, this was a quest that was to eventually obsess him.

The night before his departure, Lisa-Beth had found the Doctor standing in Scarlette's old room, staring at his reflection in the looking glass. He had, once again, been contemplating his beard. Lisa-Beth hadn't said a word, but the Doctor had told her that he thought it'd be best to keep it, at least for a while. Just to remind him that his form and function *weren't* set in stone... not any more.

A short conversation had then occurred, during which the Doctor had asked Lisa-Beth about the future of the House. With some shrugging, Lisa-Beth had told him that the House would remain open. However, its direction would have to change a little. Lisa-Beth had herself sworn to give up the ways of the ritualist and the *tantrist*. The *tantra* might have taught her certain lessons about the nature of time and history, it was true, but tomorrow's world wasn't the world of the Hellfire Clubs. As on many other occasions, the Doctor only nodded. Sagely.

The last goodbyes were said in the salon of the House, the Doctor, Fitz and Anji on one side, Rebecca, Lisa-Beth and Katya on the other. There was a lot of embracing at the last minute. The Doctor held on to Rebecca for far longer than expected, while Katya made such a fuss of Fitz that

Lisa-Beth feared 'he might suffocate'. Anji was the first to leave the House after the farewells, followed by a reluctant Fitz, followed by an even more reluctant Doctor. He, far more than his companions, had his roots in this place now. Nonetheless, he eventually turned away from the waving women of Henrietta Street and walked across the cobbled, frosty road towards the TARDIS. There was a slight hail in the air, Lisa-Beth tells, but all three of the travellers did their best to ignore it as they headed towards the blue box that was tucked away between the buildings on the other side of the road.

The three women, once more dressed in their everyday clothes, didn't follow the Doctor and friends out into the cold. They peered through the glass panes of the salon as the Doctor stopped on the threshold of his machine. They expected him to turn back and give them one final wave, or at least to smile over his shoulder.

He did neither of these things. He simply froze. It was then, says Lisa-Beth,

> ...that I knew he had felt what was in the air; I knew he suspected,
> at last, what had been kept out of sight.

The next thing Lisa-Beth knew, he was running. He'd turned away from his magical box and headed along the length of Henrietta Street, tails flapping in the cold wind, bounding out of sight away from the House. There was silence in the salon, the women knowing what was going to happen even as Fitz was poking his head out of the TARDIS.

Lisa-Beth's account of the day ends there. But there's another source, another journal, just as detailed. Because on February 13, while his companions could only look on, the Doctor rushed through the streets of Covent Garden towards Cranbourn Street, towards the same area where Juliette had met her woman-in-black. What impulse guided him is impossible to say. All that can be said, from the journal which survives, is that when he reached Leicester Place he found somebody waiting there. A woman, clothed in red from head to tails, her black-booted feet planted firmly on the cobbles and her hands folded behind her back. Possibly she'd felt him approaching, even as he'd sensed her waiting there... waiting for him to leave, so that she could return to the House.

Their conversation, as it's recorded in her diaries, was long and convoluted. What follows is a summary, a simplification, stripped of all its symbolism and romance except where it's absolutely necessary. It's enough to say that they would have stood there for some while, facing each other in the London cold, before the Doctor finally spoke.

DOCTOR: I knew. I knew you were there. I could *tell*.

SCARLETTE: Then it's true. Something still joins us. For richer or poorer, in sickness or in health.

DOCTOR: They told me you –

SCARLETTE: I can only tell you that I'm sorry. It was… only right.

DOCTOR: Right?

SCARLETTE: Did you think the two of us could go through what we did, without my knowing you well enough to understand you? Do you really believe I could hold you to this world and no other?

DOCTOR: I'm sorry?

SCARLETTE: You required a world of your own. You have no heart, now. No heart that protects you.

DOCTOR: The TARDIS will protect me. It always has done.

SCARLETTE: Nevertheless. The Earth is your home now. But only your home, not the limit of your domain. Your purpose is to protect far more than one single world.

DOCTOR: You pretended to be –

SCARLETTE: I had to. So that you could leave this place. This Earth.

DOCTOR: I'm sorry…?

SCARLETTE: How could you ever fulfil your purpose, knowing that the two of us were bound together? How could you ever leave?

DOCTOR: We *are* bound together.

SCARLETTE: I know. And you have more to consider than *my* world.

DOCTOR: But –

SCARLETTE: Go to your business, Doctor. Please. Just as I'll go to mine.

DOCTOR: You did all this? This… *lie*? Just so I'd want to leave?

SCARLETTE: Just so you could. It's in your nature that you should go. It's not the place of anyone to stand in the way of that. Not myself, and not even you.

DOCTOR: But I don't *have* to leave you.

SCARLETTE: I dearly wish you didn't even have to think of such things. As long as we have each other's favour, this will be your home. You can be assured of that much, I'm certain.

DOCTOR: We held a funeral, you know. You would have liked it.

SCARLETTE: I'm told it was a little too sombre, thank you.

Nobody chose to record how the conversation ended, how the two of them left each other. Nobody could even say whether they kissed, or at least, whether the Doctor kissed Scarlette's forehead (as was his custom). So it's not possible to say whether it was harder for him or for her, when he turned back towards the shelter of his TARDIS. Nor is it possible to say what Scarlette felt as he vanished into the crowds and the thoroughfares of Covent Garden.

These stories have a tendency to be unreliable, or incomplete at least.

FICTION

'The object of the obscene ceremonies was to invest the king with the necessary magical powers to combat the demoniacal forces threatening the kingdom: internal division and external attack.'

Collier's Encyclopaedia, on the subject of *tantra*.

Chapter 13

This is true:

On August 18, 1783, the largest meteor ever seen by the British Isles blazed an uneasy trail across the sky from the urban heart of Scotland, over the south-western edge of London itself and out towards the sea. At least, 'meteor' seems a good enough word: those who knew that science had proved such things to be impossible referred to it as a 'fireball', and the observatory in Greenwich later reported it to be a cluster of vivid, multicoloured lights, travelling in formation before finally exploding into a rain of fire somewhere in the vicinity of Ostend. Indeed, this being an age of such poor communications, it wasn't until the *Gentleman's Magazine* pieced together all the eye-witness reports that anyone even acknowledged it as a single phenomenon. Robert Blake painted a picture inspired by it, *Approach of Doom*, which seemed so pertinent to the times that his brother William (himself a visionary artist, in contact with angels and monsters of various descriptions) insisted on making an engraving of it.

On the night of the Great Fireball, Juliette was standing on the iron deck of the *Jonah* and considering what it might mean to be *part* of such an event rather than just a *witness* to it.

She'd positioned herself at the prow of the ship, with her pale hands on the black railings, and if it had been a ship of the navy then the spray would have been splashing against her face by now. She'd lost track of the time she'd spent here, with the lights of the world turning into greasy streaks of fire around her, with the air rushing past so fast that she could hardly even breathe out. It was, she knew, all part of the process. The ship was pushing towards the horizon, forcing itself against currents far more fundamental than those of the English Channel.

In fact, she only began to recover from this peculiar *Shaktyanda* state when Sabbath joined her on the deck. Obviously, she had no need to actually *see* him emerge from his studies at the heart of the *Jonah*. This was his vessel now: it was an extension of his will, a part of his purpose, his body rooted into its metal walls just as he himself was rooted into the Earth. He only had to set foot on one of the decks and Juliette would feel him there. And not just because of his weight.

He seemed remarkably unaffected by it all, though. Juliette liked that.

'Well now,' he said. 'Where should we go first?'

Juliette forced the air out of her lungs, then sucked in more, letting the salt of the sea – wherever the sea might have been located, in this morass of space and time and God-alone-knew what else – fill up her nose. She was sure she felt London flash past her, although whether the city was beneath her, or around her, or even inside her, she couldn't accurately tell.

'Hardly the question that comes to mind,' she said, politely but firmly. 'I'd rather know whether we'll be coming back.'

There was a half-smile on Sabbath's face when he spoke, she could hear it in his voice.

'Ah,' he said. 'Longings for home.'

'Please, don't mock me. We have unfinished histories here.'

Sabbath nodded, she was sure of it even though he was behind her and she'd by now closed her eyes to take her mind off the colours. 'We have unfinished histories,' he agreed. 'Not necessarily here.'

'We're rooted here, surely?'

'We have a certain attachment to the Earth. Not to our own time.'

'Here,' Juliette insisted.

He didn't answer her, but she was sure he was still smiling, even if she couldn't actually feel it in the humming of the decks. Eventually her curiosity got the better of her, and she turned, opening her eyes to him.

Sabbath stood close to the centre of the deck, next to one of the openings which led down into the vessel's stomach. He looked exactly as she'd imaged him. Greatcoat thrown loosely over his shoulders, head down but bright eyes raised, watching her carefully. There was, as she'd guessed, a smile on his face. If the storms of light and colour around the *Jonah* made any impression on him, then he didn't show it. One hand was planted nonchalantly in a pocket of the coat, while the other was idly scratching his chest: it had vanished under the coat and into his shirt, which reminded Juliette of something although she couldn't say what. From here she could just see the off-white bandages beneath the cloth, the big red stain where the scar on his chest had leaked a little.

The smell of salt probably came from the ocean, if indeed there was an ocean anywhere around them. It made Juliette think of blood anyway.

'What was wrong with the Doctor's heart?' she'd asked Sabbath, when they'd left the grand palace of the ape-world and headed back to the *Jonah*. Six months ago, now. Six months of watching the trained apes hunt down the wild apes, of listening to Sabbath while he taught his animals to perform the surgery and, later, while he recovered in the dim black-walled rooms below decks.

'*Nothing,*' Sabbath had told her. '*The heart was in perfect working order. It was only serving its purpose. Rooting him to his home territory, the same thing it'd do for anyone. The problem was, his territory no longer existed. That was the cause of the poison.*'

'History seems to have been playing on your mind recently,' Sabbath said, suddenly. It took Juliette a moment or two to follow his drift.

'I worry,' she told him.

'I see. You believe you've still got business to attend to here.'

It wasn't even disguised as a question. Juliette raised her head to him, a sign that she was ready to acknowledge her past even if she wasn't quite prepared to confront it. 'Can you blame me?' she asked.

'No,' said Sabbath. 'Do you worry what he'll think of you, now you're gone?'

'Of course.'

She didn't explain what she was really thinking. She didn't have to. When Sabbath had shown her how far the ship could travel, how far he'd expanded the borders of his 'territory', she'd known full well that such a journey would make her more than a simple human being. She'd be able to step outside her own time of residence, to look at the whole of her lifetime from the outside, to see the consequences of every action she'd ever taken. Soon the *Jonah* would go further, into the deeper realms, into parts of time even the *tantrists* could barely imagine. One could barely see such things and still consider oneself to be a *person*, as such. One could hardly go that far and not dwell on thoughts of history.

She often lay in the bunks in the depths of the *Jonah*, alone or otherwise, thinking of all the things she'd said in the presence of her colleagues at Henrietta Street. She wondered, sometimes, if she'd concealed too much and given too little of herself away. She tried to see herself as *they* might see her, from the inside of time. As an innocent? As the guilty party? Would they look back on the things that had happened in her room, the secrets and the experiments, as the actions of a stupid little girl or of a female Iscariot?

'It's probably a good thing you've started thinking that way,' mused Sabbath. 'I think we can safely say that history's our profession now. Our employment, if you like.'

'We have our duty,' Juliette responded, and she was a little surprised to discover that she actually meant it. It sounded so much like the kind of thing that Sabbath would say... but then again, she'd set foot on this ship of her own free will, so she really shouldn't have been surprised that she'd become a part of it.

280

Sabbath nodded, and it took Juliette a while to realise that he was nodding *at* something. She turned back, towards the prow, and the blaze of light that was fast approaching the front of the ship. Not just the streaks of brilliant colour, as the world flashed past below them or around them or inside them. A point of intensity, towards which the ship was being navigated by its unseen crew.

'It's happening?' she asked.

'Yes,' said Sabbath.

Yes. They were moving fast enough, they'd been travelling for long enough, they'd seen enough of the Earth pass them by. Standing there on the deck, Juliette felt her own heart pumping in time with the deck, in time with the great double-rhythm which she felt sure was being dictated by Sabbath himself. She knew, without question, that Sabbath had already decided on their destination. The apes had threatened to tear the Earth apart, and although the Doctor had pushed them away it was only a part of a larger problem.

You had to see things on the grandest possible scale. Just as she intended to see her own lifetime, stretched out before her, as soon as the ship finally took them away from the world.

She became aware that Sabbath was behind her. Not close enough to touch her, but close enough that she could feel his breath on the side of her face, close enough that he could have put his arms around her if he'd wanted to do such a thing. They stood there together, watching the sky beyond the prow, the air around them full of the smell of salt and the light of elementals and the beating of three hearts.

'_____,' said Sabbath.

And in the very last moment that could be said to have been spent *on Earth*, Juliette thought of the Doctor.

Addendum
The Future

THE DOCTOR: It's impossible to give a definitive account of the Doctor's travels after 1783, mainly because he himself *refused* to let it be possible. He was, according to his admirers, a nigh-immortal being who could walk through time and even (occasionally) change his appearance: therefore, anybody could impersonate him with impunity. People claiming to be eighteenth-century occult 'charlatans' like Cagliostro or the Comte de Germain were crawling out of the woodwork as late as the twentieth century, so it's hard to know what to make of the numerous individuals who've claimed to be the Doctor since the Siege of Henrietta Street. Perhaps it's best just to say that he remains one of modern man's truly mythic figures, and leave it at that.

EMILY HART: After Sabbath's apparent departure from Earth, Emily (who later returned to her given name of Emma) settled down in Naples with the British Envoy Extraordinary. She eventually became the talk of her native country in 1798, as the mistress of one of Britain's most noted Admirals, one of the new breed of naval heroes produced by the Napoleonic wars. It was exactly the lifestyle she might have hoped for, in her youth. Appropriately, one English newspaper satirised this scandalous affair in a cartoon called *The Nightmare of the Nile* – another parody of Fuseli's *Nightmare*, its title inspired by the fact that Emma's lover had recently won a victory at Aboukir Bay – in which the Admiral was depicted as the little nightmare-goblin, sitting on Emma's chest and peeking under her nightdress.

THE COUNTESS OF JERSEY, 'THE INFERNAL': History doesn't remember her as a great ritualist, but as a great manipulator and seductress. She campaigned for the Whig party in the great London elections of 1784, became the mistress of the Prince of Wales (later King George IV), and may have been party to any number of diabolical Whig schemes throughout the 1780s and 1790s. As expected.

FITZ KREINER AND ANJI KAPOOR: Neither of them reappear in historical archives… at least, not in the eighteenth century. There *is* a record of one of them dying in the twenty-first century, but as records are notoriously bad at keeping track of elementals it may have been a different individual altogether.

JULIETTE: Unlike Sabbath she *did* return to her own place and time, though as something of a changed woman. She's known to have spent some time on Hispaniola, perhaps consulting with Émondeur and his brood. The last known record of her activities places her at Charenton Asylum in 1805, where she visited one of the inmates and witnessed one of the bizarre plays often staged by the lunatics for the benefit of society guests. She vanishes from history altogether after that date.

LISA-BETH LACHLAN AND REBECCA MACARDLE: Lisa-Beth did indeed go on to handle the practical matters of the House. When Scarlette turned her mind to other interests in late 1783, Lisa-Beth ran the business almost single-handed. No record of Lisa-Beth exists after 1789, so perhaps she joined Scarlette on the barricades during the French Revolution… unlikely as it may seem. Rebecca's known history is longer, but vague. Like Lisa-Beth she worked in the House until at least 1789, and after that she seems to have found employment in central Europe as an agent of a government agency which saw a certain potential in her unusual talents. There's no reliable record of her death. The House eventually closed down in the women's absence, having served its purpose admirably.

THE MAN WITH THE ROSETTE: Nothing more is known about him, although at least one of those individuals *claiming* to be the Doctor in later years stated that the strange black-clad man had returned 'in a most unexpected capacity'. There's room for plenty of speculation here.

KATCHKA ('KATYA') NAKHOVA: Tragically, Katya died in September 1783. She was evidently the victim of a homicidal client, although the details were kept from the city watch on the orders of Scarlette. Scarlette's journal, in one of its last entries before the departure from Britain, records that the killer was 'dealt with in a reasonable fashion'.

DR NIE WHO: His shop in Soho was open until at least 1796. No explanation has ever been given as to what happened to him between the wedding ceremony of 1782 and the funeral in 1783: there's no record of oriental pagodas being part of the Kingdom of Beasts, so possibly his

Chinese sense of 'no-time' protected him from the attentions of the King and the apes. Though Who doesn't appear to have been an important figure in eighteenth- and nineteenth-century occultism, the stereotype of the 'oriental wise-man' would live on long after his own era. It's interesting to note that the name 'Dr Who' later entered twentieth-century culture in a suitably exotic context: it was the name given to the mad scientist in the 1967 Japanese movie, *King Kong Escapes*.

SABBATH: The best guess is that he was seen on Earth only once more after 1783, at least during his own lifetime... but as with the Doctor, sightings in the nineteenth and twentieth centuries were common. Understandably, legends that *someone* is looking out for the safety of history itself are still popular today. Perhaps the most telling myth comes from the early twentieth century, when Sabbath was rumoured to have arrived in Europe in the years leading up to the Second World War. Typically, he was described as being utterly indifferent to the massive conflict which was to come.

SCARLETTE, THE ADVENTURESS OF HENRIETTA STREET: What can be said about Scarlette, most legendary of all the *presences* of London, except perhaps for the Doctor himself? Stories are often told in ritualistic circles about the original 'woman in scarlet', most of them horribly distorted by time. She's said to have visited America after the Siege, despite the obvious risks, and to have confronted General Washington himself; to have been in Paris during the uprising of 1789, presenting herself as a Mistress of the Revolution; to have visited Egypt during the occupation of Napoleon; even to have witnessed the Battle of Trafalgar. All that can be said for sure, from the records which survive, is that she spent the months after the Doctor's departure finding herself a new 'apprentice' who had more than a little of Juliette's blood in her veins. Apart from that, it wouldn't be going too far to say that the stories are too numerous to recount here.